Look for
by S

Angel of Destruction

"Space opera of the first caliber . . . fast-paced, with plenty of action and adventure. . . . Susan R. Matthews is a fine storyteller." —*Midwest Book Review*

"A chilling and engaging novel of false accusation and the power of personal responsibility." —*Booklist*

An Exchange of Hostages

"A riveting character study of a conflicted young man . . . the book [has] a dark energy that, coupled with Matthews's intelligent prose, her genius for the unexpected, and her keen sense of atmosphere, produces an extremely compelling read."
—*New York Review of Science Fiction*

"Powerful, insidious, and insightful—a singular accomplishment for a tenth novel, let alone a first."
—Melanie Rawn

continued . . .

THE DEVIL
AND
DEEP SPACE

Susan R. Matthews

A ROC BOOK

ROC
Published by New American Library, a division of
Penguin Putnam Inc., 375 Hudson Street,
New York, New York 10014, U.S.A.
Penguin Books Ltd, 80 Strand,
London WC2R 0RL, England
Penguin Books Australia Ltd, Ringwood,
Victoria, Australia
Penguin Books Canada Ltd, 10 Alcorn Avenue,
Toronto, Ontario, Canada M4V 3B2
Penguin Books (N.Z.) Ltd, 182–190 Wairau Road,
Auckland 10, New Zealand

Penguin Books Ltd, Registered Offices:
Harmondsworth, Middlesex, England

First published by Roc, an imprint of New American Library,
a division of Penguin Putnam Inc.

First Printing, November 2002
10   9   8   7   6   5   4   3   2   1

Copyright © Susan Matthews, 2002
All rights reserved

Cover art by Ray Lundgren

 REGISTERED TRADEMARK—MARCA REGISTRADA

Printed in the United States of America

PUBLISHER'S NOTE
This is a work of fiction. Names, characters, places, and incidents either
are the product of the author's imagination or are used fictitiously,
and any resemblance to actual persons, living or dead, business
establishments, events, or locales is entirely coincidental.

About the Author

Susan R. Matthews was born in a barrack in Fort Benning and raised in Kentucky, Germany, Idaho, North Carolina, India, and Washington State. The first woman commissioned out of the Army ROTC detachment at the University of Washington, she spent the next few years as the operations officer of a Combat Support Hospital in Virginia. Now employed as an internal audit function by an aerospace manufacturing firm, Susan lives in Seattle.

Dedicated to the Intemperate Muse
according to his Excellency's good pleasure

Chapter One

An Unfortunate Combination of Circumstances

"I have your report from Burkhayden, Specialist Ivers," the First Secretary said, looking out the great clearwall window over the tops of the fanleaf trees in the park below. "I apologize for taking so long to get to it. I find it rather strongly worded in places."

Rather strongly felt, Jils told herself, wryly. But Burkhayden and everything that had happened there were months behind her now; except one thing. "Yes."

The First Secretary looked tired, even from behind. Jils didn't think she'd ever seen him lean against anything in all of her years of working with him. She could understand his fatigue, though; with the recent and unexpected death of the First Judge, Sindha Verlaine was at the defining moment of his entire career.

If the Second Judge at Chilleau—Verlaine's Judge—became First Judge, Verlaine would become the most powerful civil servant under Jurisdiction; Chambers here at Chilleau, with their beautiful gardens and their tall whitewashed walls, would become the center of known Space, since whatever might be in Gonebeyond was not worth consideration.

If the Second Judge failed to negotiate the Judicial support that she needed in order for her claim to prevail, however, it would be all over. Second Judge Sem Porr Har would remain one among eight equally powerful Judges for the rest of her life, and First Secretary Verlaine would still be nothing more than the senior administrative officer at Chilleau Judiciary.

Good enough for most men.

Not good enough for Sindha Verlaine, who had been working toward this moment for his entire adult life—twenty-plus years by the Jurisdiction standard, in service to the Judicial order.

Verlaine turned from the window, his expression open and candid. In the bright morning light his normally pale complexion was an unflattering claylike color, and it was clear from the drawn contours of his face that he had not been getting enough rest for some time. "Please. Sit down, if you will, Bench specialist. I mean to be very frank with you."

He almost always had been. The relationship between a Bench intelligence specialist and the administrative staff of any given Judiciary could become adversarial, because men like Verlaine weren't accustomed to being told *no*—and only Bench specialists and Judges could do it. Bench intelligence specialists answered to no single Judge, but to the Bench itself.

Some Secretaries that Jils had coordinated with had tried to wheedle, threaten, influence. Verlaine had never stooped to subterfuge; she respected that in him. So she sat down in one of the several chairs that were arrayed to one side of the window, in front of his desk.

Verlaine nodded his thanks for her cooperation and picked up a flatform docket from his active file, backing up against the forward edge of the brilliantly polished wooden desktop until he was sitting on it, file in hand.

"Chilleau Judiciary got off on the wrong foot with Andrej Koscuisko from the very start," the First Secretary observed, mildly. "It's past time I faced up to my responsibility for what's gone wrong there, Specialist."

There were reasons Verlaine might have for taking time out of what had to be a hellishly grueling schedule of political coordination to talk about a single individual.

Koscuisko was the Ship's Surgeon assigned to the Jurisdiction Fleet Ship *Ragnarok*—Ship's Inquisitor. Several months ago Verlaine had sent her to Burkhayden to obtain Koscuisko's services for Chilleau by fiat, and

Koscuisko had reacted by doing the one thing no one could have anticipated—reenlisting in Fleet, when no other offered inducement had moved him from an apparently single-minded determination to be done with the practice of Judicial torture and go home.

Koscuisko was just one man, though his public profile was higher than most due to the personal notoriety he had won at the Domitt Prison: but Koscuisko also had family, and his family was very influential within the Combine.

When the Dolgorukij Combine spoke Sant-Dasidar Judiciary and its Sixth Judge were obliged to listen, or risk expensive and awkward civil challenges. The support of the Koscuisko familial corporation could be the key to the Combine's endorsement of a chosen candidate, and the Sixth Judge had to defer to the Combine's wishes if she meant to keep the peace. That meant that the Sixth Judge's support for Chilleau's bid lay with the Dolgorukij Combine to grant or to withhold.

Nor was Koscuisko simply one among a powerful family, but the inheriting son of the Koscuisko prince, and would be master of the entire familial corporation in time. That made him the man with whom Sant-Dasidar Judiciary would expect to have to deal during much of the tenure of the new First Judge. It was in the Sixth Judge's best interest to cultivate Koscuisko's goodwill accordingly, and pay careful attention to his feelings.

"I have read your report, Specialist Ivers, and I have decided. Chilleau Judiciary has wronged Koscuisko, and it is my responsibility because it was my doing. But the timing is awkward."

Funneled special assignments in Koscuisko's direction to keep the pressure on, assigned him to the *Ragnarok* even knowing that three out of three of the *Ragnarok*'s previous Inquisitors had been unable to tolerate the work to which Fleet Captain Lowden had put them. Verlaine was right; he had wronged Koscuisko.

Clearly Verlaine meant to send her to Koscuisko now with concessions. Jils didn't see where timing could really affect Koscuisko's reception of whatever Verlaine had to say one way or the other; she knew Koscuisko's feelings about Chilleau Judiciary. And Bench Specialists didn't run personal errands with political motivations behind them. "What would you like to tell me, First Secretary?"

"It goes deeper than just Koscuisko. Though he must be admitted to be the most visible symbol of the entire system."

Of what? Of Inquisition?

Verlaine set down his flatform docket and cast off from the desk, starting to pace. He was a very thin man, not tall, but very quick in his movements; he frequently gave Jils the impression that the energy of his mind could not be contained within his body. "The Second Judge has agreed to issue a statement of intent. Her proposed agenda."

It would be the formal announcement of her desire to step into the First Judge's position. No one had issued such a statement to date; it had only been twenty days since the death of the First Judge had been reported. It had been a surprise. People were scrambling.

"When she does she will challenge the rules of Evidence as in the best interest of the rule of Law and the Judicial order. It will be controversial. I must have Koscuisko on her side."

Jils was startled into a question. "Rules of Evidence, First Secretary? Does she really mean to question the Protocols?" Because the Second Judge was a brave woman if she did mean to do that.

The Bench had come to rely more and more on Inquisition as its instrument of state over recent years; that was why there were Ship's Inquisitors, Judicial torturers. And still civil unrest continued to increase, regardless of—or even possibly as a result of—the increasingly savage methods to which the Bench resorted to contain it.

"It costs too much," Verlaine said, simply. "In more than just money. But more than that, it's just not working, Specialist Ivers. The more the Bench leans on confession extracted under torture for validation, the less credibility the rule of Law can hope to retain. She will need all of the help in this she can get. She will need Koscuisko's support."

For a Judge to question the usefulness of her own Inquisition was a genuinely stunning development. If the Second Judge spoke out against the Protocols, she challenged the most useful weapon in her own inventory. There would seem to be little political capital to be made with such a slap in the face of the status quo; was it possible Verlaine meant exactly what he said, that torture did not help keep order in the long term, and cost too much besides?

"I know better than to accuse you of trying to deploy me on a partisan political mission." It wasn't done. "So where do I fit into all this, First Secretary?"

Pivoting in mid-pace Verlaine turned back to his desk and the flatform docket, which he picked up and held out to her. "Except that that's just what I'd like you to do, Specialist Ivers. Complete a personal errand, in a sense." The note in Verlaine's deep voice was ambiguous; nerves—or self-deprecating humor? "I can't deny my partisan interest in the potential payoff, here. I can only ask that you believe me when I assure you that at least part of my motive is genuine and disinterested."

There was something odd in the First Secretary's demeanor; he seemed almost embarrassed. Jils opened the docket and reached out to leaf through its stacked pages; then stopped where she was, page one, paragraph one, *In the circumstance of the recently renewed engagement of service, Andrej Ulexeievitch Koscuisko, Ship's Surgeon and Inquisitor, it is the judgment of this Court* . . .

Verlaine meant to cancel Koscuisko's Writ.

Without prejudice. Having been extended under and as a result of inappropriate duress contrary to the rule of Law and the Bench's responsibility to protect its citizens from unreasonable and unlawful imposition.

There was more. There was an advance copy of the Second Judge's proposed statement of intent, and Jils could pick out the pertinent titles with ease. *Regrettable vulnerability of the system to abuse. Multiple instances of failure, not excepting Chilleau Judiciary's own shameful failure to protect the rights of displaced Nurail souls at the Domitt Prison. Immediate moratorium on imposition of the Bond and granting of any new Writs to Inquire.*

There it was, in plain text; and that meant that this was not a flatform docket but an incendiary device capable of destroying Chilleau Judiciary at one blow in the wrong hands.

"Are you sure about this, First Secretary?" She had to ask; she had to hear it from him. If Koscuisko was minded to be vengeful he could create a very great deal of trouble for the Second Judge by leaking this to her anticipated opponents before she had a chance to make her case. The Fifth Judge at Cintaro in particular would pay a very great deal of money for the document in Jils's hands.

"It's the only way I have any hope of convincing Koscuisko that I'm serious. I was wrong; he's suffered for it. I need his help. But I mean to try to make things right whether or not he's willing to support the Second Judge, Specialist Ivers."

Because the Bench judgment was to be executed at Koscuisko's will and pleasure. It was already fully endorsed. All it needed was his seal to make it official. All he had to do was sign, and he was clear of Fleet and Inquiry forever.

No quid pro quo for Chilleau Judiciary; no *if then, else.* Jils thought about it. As Verlaine had warned her, the errand he proposed had clear political overtones; and yet she was a Bench intelligence specialist, she was expected to make up her own mind about whether to accept or reject any given assignment. That included taking her own counsel about whether the immediate partisan impact of her mission was outweighed by the greater good of the Judicial order.

"Where is the *Ragnarok,* First Secretary?"

All right. She'd go. She'd carry this liberating document to Andrej Koscuisko, and find out whether he would even see her, after what his last interview with her had cost him. But she'd wait to see whether she would trust Koscuisko with the full power Verlaine offered to put in his hands.

"In maneuvers at the Pesadie Training Grounds, Bench specialist. But Koscuisko's due home on leave. If you're willing to perform the errand, agents of the Malcontent will see to the necessary arrangements, on Azanry."

On Azanry, where Koscuisko's family was?

Verlaine certainly had the political angles tabled out as acutely as he could. A Bench intelligence specialist taking relief of Writ to the inheriting son of the Koscuisko familial corporation in the very heart of the Dolgorukij Combine . . . where every move a man like Andrej Koscuisko made would be seen, analyzed, interpreted, then acted on by an immense and arcane machinery of tradition and ethnic solidarity. Working toward the will of the Koscuisko prince . . . or of the man who would be the Koscuisko prince, and perhaps there was not even so very much difference at this point.

"I'll take your Brief to Azanry." What was owed Koscuisko was fairly owed. She'd been there when he had been forced to gnaw off his own leg to escape the trap that Chilleau Judiciary had set for him, the trap that she herself had sprung on him. She had a right to be there when Chilleau prised open the jaws of the trap and apologized and begged him to accept a replacement leg with the sincere compliments of First Secretary Verlaine. For the rest of it—

"Thank you, Specialist Ivers." Verlaine knew that he was asking her to intervene in a more-or-less personal relationship between Chilleau and Andrej Koscuisko, but that was all right. He'd read her report. He knew what she'd had to say about his attempt to co-opt Koscuisko in the first place. "I appreciate your cooperation. We'll alert the Malcontent to your expected arrival."

For the rest of it she'd review the docket, and if its contents conformed with the rule of Law she'd do what she could to enlist Koscuisko's cooperation in turn. And while she was there, on Azanry, maybe she'd ask the Malcontent for something on her own behalf.

Garol Vogel had dropped out of sight on an exit trajectory from Port Burkhayden months ago, and had not been heard from since. Maybe the Malcontent knew what might have happened to him. No other source of information Jils had consulted had been able to offer any help.

Bench specialists were supposed to be difficult to seek, locate, identify. But not by other Bench specialists. "Very good, First Secretary. I'll keep you informed." She couldn't shake the feeling that more had gone on in Port Burkhayden between Andrej Koscuisko and Garol Vogel than she'd realized.

If the key was on Azanry somewhere, Jils meant to find it.

The little Wolnadi—one of the *Ragnarok*'s complement of four-soul fighters—careened past its target on a high oblique trajectory to plane; weaponer Smath screamed, from her post on the aft cannon, and Lek Kerenko grinned with pure delight to hear her curse. "Damn you, Lek, slow down!"

He would not slow down. It was just a training exercise; but Security 5.1 had the best kill-time on board the Jurisdiction Fleet Ship *Ragnarok,* and Lek did not mean to yield the honors to anyone.

"On target, Smish!" He didn't have to yell—he had the innership. She wouldn't let the team down. She was eight for eight out of the gate, perfect record, confirmed target kill on all vectors.

"Trajectory shift on proximal target," Murat warned. Lek frowned in deep focus on the new data Murat sent through and made a quick rephase calculation in his mind.

Fleet didn't mean for 5.1 to finish this target run with a perfect score. Pesadie Training Command wanted evidence of substandard performance on the *Ragnarok*'s part, to support cancellation of the First Judge's research program; they weren't going to get it.

"Lateral eight point from directional?" Lek asked Taller on power flux, coding his approaches. Taller's post was right next to the navigation comps. The Wolnadi fighter was a small craft. Lek could see Taller shake his head, scowling.

"If we have to. If you're sure."

Yes, they'd pushed the propulsion systems hard from the moment they'd cleared the *Ragnarok*'s maintenance atmosphere. But that was what the ship's engines were there for. Motive power. Maneuverability. Lek knew his ship. The Wolnadi would do it.

"If I take a sub on target minus-two, can you pick off target minus-three on the way?" Lek asked Smish, just to let the weaponer know what he was doing. Because he already knew that she could do it. If she couldn't do it, he wouldn't be asking.

"We're already good on time, Lek, why push it? Yes."

She was frustrated with him, because he was pushing her hard, as well. It was an unusual position to be in, a bond-involuntary telling unbonded troops what to do; but the *Ragnarok* didn't have enough bond-involuntaries assigned to make up a second full team after 5.3, so there they were.

Security 5.1, Lek's team, did have an unbonded navigator assigned; but Eady was on fifthweek rotation this cycle. And Lek was better than Eady was. "On target. Fire through."

If she couldn't make the target minus-two kill before they hit target minus-three, they'd lose points on execution. The flight sphere was set up to maximize the challenge, and the targets were to be taken in order. The targets—the little remote decoys—were moving; Lek just had to move faster. That was all.

"Confirmed," Murat said approvingly, from his post on observation scan. Lek didn't have time to congratulate Smish on her marksmanship, though, because she had mere fractions of an eighth to refocus her considerable prey instinct on the next target.

"Minus-two on monitor. Please confirm target acquisition."

Lek shoved the linear propulsion feeds to the maximum, firing his laterals as he went to spin the ship and finesse its trajectory. The next target was well below the arena's theoretical floor axis, and fast approaching the boundary, but he could fly through the center of the arena, and that saved time. Nothing to go around.

"Target minus-one within six degrees of escape," Murat warned. Lek checked his stats. Fleet really did want them to fail the exercise. There was no way to get from one target to the other in time. Was there?

He could do a fly-through, maybe, if Taller could give him a pulse to shield their forward path, and clear the debris from the target so that he could take a direct line on the next without fear of hulling out on some piece of scrap metal—

"I confirm target minus-two. Targeting. Firing."

Smish was too busy concentrating on her own task to yell at him. Lek was just as glad. He knew what he was doing, and they knew that he knew what he was doing, but his governor would not let him take chances with the ship if he made the mistake of letting himself become nervous about his margins. So he had to avoid getting nervous; or else his governor would conclude that he had destruction of Jurisdiction property in mind, and shut him down.

The sensor screen lit up with the impact report from the target's remains. The kill was good. "Blow me a hole, Taller," Lek suggested. "We can still catch the last one."

Taller sent a plasma burst out ahead of the fighter's path, shaking his head as he did so. "Whatever you say. But we're already ahead, Lek, you don't have to prove anything."

Lek threaded the Wolnadi through the narrow passageway that the plasma bolt cleared through the debris of target minus-two. "Ahead isn't good enough. We're maximizing. Smish. Target acquisition?"

Nobody flattened the line. Nobody had hit all the targets in sequence and on time in the weeks they'd been here. He had a chance. With Smish's eye for her targets and his feel for his navs, they could do it.

The last target was on-screen. Lek could see it; they were heading straight on, and the subtle blue sheen of the flight sphere's containment field glowed dimly against the backdrop of black Space and distant star-fields. It was going to be close; their quarry was doing everything it could to escape.

"Targeting," Smish said.

Lek eased the propulsion up just a hair, one eye to his return trajectory. He needed power in reserve to return to base. "Firing. Confirm kill on three. Two. One."

The forward display screens blossomed, then blanked as ship's on-board display recalibrated itself. Explosion; good. That was it for the last of the targets, then.

Lek heeled the ship into its return arc and brought its speed up as quickly as he dared. All he had to do now was get back to the *Ragnarok* on time, and they would have beaten Pesadie for good and all. After years of being mocked by their Fleet counterparts as idle vacationers on an experimental test bed—if not worse—the crew of the *Ragnarok* had shown Fleet that they could obtain and execute with the best of them.

Pesadie Training Command had done everything it could to discredit the technical and fighting abilities of the Jurisdiction Fleet Ship *Ragnarok,* under cover of capability evaluation. But the *Ragnarok* had accomplished every task, exceeded every benchmark Pesadie had set against them; and defended its honor, to the last.

Jennet ap Rhiannon stood on the observation deck of the Engineering bridge with her arms braced stiff against the waist-high railing, looking down through the soundproof clearwall into the well of Engineering's command and control center, where the *Ragnarok*'s last battle exercise was displayed on ship's primary screens.

It was a pleasure to watch the Wolnadi fight. None of the crews had embarrassed the ship, but this one seemed to be particularly aggressive, and Jennet sent a question back over her shoulder to Ralph Mendez while she watched. "Security 5.1, First Officer?"

The Wolnadi took its target on a high hard oblique roll, clearly planning on blasting through its own debris field on its way to the end of the set. She could see the final target start to move toward the perimeter; someone in Pesadie Training Command had noticed the Wolnadi's successful attack as well, and was taking measures to challenge their final approach—to make it as difficult as possible to get the final kill.

"That's them, Lieutenant," Mendez replied, Santone dialect still flavoring his syntax even after all of his years in Fleet. "Look at him go. Would you have thought a bond-involuntary could show so much ginger, and get away with it?"

No, she wouldn't. Bond-involuntaries were much more likely to be characterized by an aggressively—or defensively—conservative approach to life, for their own protection.

"Kerenko, I think," Lieutenant Seascape said, from the shadows behind Jennet. "I thought Koscuisko was taking his Bonds home?"

"Andrej's taking Security 5.3, Lieutenant," Mendez corrected. "Kerenko's on 5.1. He wanted to take all six

of them home, but he can't take St. Clare anyway, no
new governor yet. And Fleet would only authorize one
Security team."

That was right. There were only six bond-involuntary
troops assigned to the *Ragnarok* right now, well short of
the hypothetical full complement of twenty-five. Nor
were bond-involuntaries the only troops the *Ragnarok*
was shorted; there were only three Command Branch
officers left on board, since murder in Burkhayden had
removed both Captain Lowden and Lieutenant Wyrlann
from the chain of command several months ago. Acting
Captain Brem, acting First Lieutenant ap Rhiannon, acting Second Lieutenant Seascape, and that was it.

"That ship sure doesn't move like a failed technology,"
Jennet said, though she knew there was no sense in being
bitter about it. The *Ragnarok* was shorted Command
Branch and bond-involuntaries alike because everybody
expected the ship to be scrapped as soon as the new
First Judge was seated. Such was the future that awaited
the pet research projects of dead First Judges. "Whoever
gets that team will get quality."

"Son of a bitch," Wheatfields growled from his post
in the pit of the Engineering bridge below, his voice
projected into the observation deck from the station's
pickups. "Be careful with those vectors, damn it, that's
an expensive piece of machinery."

The Wolnadi's weaponer hit the target solid and true,
and the starburst blossom on-screen was familiar and
beautiful in its way. A pulse from the Wolnadi's forward
jets cored the debris field and the Wolnadi dove through
close behind it, only just trailing the newly emptied space.
Jennet could appreciate Wheatfields's nervousness: if the
navigator misjudged his speed, he could hull the fighter.
But it was all part of the age-old conflict between Engineers and pilots, after all.

"He'll be careful, Serge," Mendez assured Wheatfields.
Wheatfields looked up toward them resentfully—so he was
on return feed, listening as well as sending. "Or you can
take it out of his hide. If there's any hide left." After
Mendez himself was finished with Kerenko, should Kerenko make a mistake. Wheatfields did not seem to be

impressed, turning back to watch the screens without comment.

The last target was running for the perimeter of the exercise field as fast as it could; if the target escaped from the containment field, the kill wouldn't count. Pesadie didn't expect them to perform well. Pesadie had made that perfectly clear, and it wasn't supposed to be easy—but Pesadie's aggressive tests had gone well past fair challenge.

Jennet knew that Pesadie had expected them to play along, and queer their own performance. She wanted the kill all the more badly for that. The fighter gained on the target moment by moment; there was the shot, but was the kill good?

Explosion. Dead target. Jennet tightened her grip on the railing with satisfaction, tracking the fighter's progress on-screen. Beautiful.

It had been close, though, so close that the containment field itself showed signs of reaction to the impact. The faintly glowing blue sphere that delineated the flight sphere was distorted, wavering, pulsing from dim to bright and back to dim again as it absorbed the kinetic energy from the particles of debris that the explosion had sent right up against its borders.

The containment field's boundary belled outward for a moment or two, just touching the tiny blip of an observation station hung clear of the flight sphere to track the execution of the exercise. Jennet shook her head.

"Anybody on that watchball's going to get vertigo." Because the containment field's energy had set the station into a perturbation wobble. In her student days it'd been a standard prank—getting as close to the containment field as she could, in order to destabilize the containment barrier and rattle any rank that was observing in the backwash.

There was another explosion. Jennet stared. The observation station? But how? The fighter was well on its way back to base, there had been no round fired . . . and if she was right—she hoped she was wrong—

Jennet turned her back on the Engineering bridge to face Ship's Intelligence Officer, who was hanging from the ceiling at the back of the dimly lit observation deck with her great leathery wings folded demurely around her. "Two?"

First Officer was staring at the screen as well. So he had the same concern. "Yes, your Excellency," Two said, her mechanically translated voice calm and cheerful, as it was programmed to be.

Jennet sank back against the railing, stunned. She wasn't an Excellency. The only Command Branch officer who rated "Excellency" was the senior officer assigned, and that was the acting Captain, Cowil Brem. So Brem had been on that observation station. And he was dead. What had gone wrong?

"They're going to want to interrogate the crew." Mendez had straightened up to his full height, folding his arms across his chest. He didn't sound happy; she didn't blame him, because he was right. Fleet would want to talk to the crew of the Wolnadi to explain their role in the explosion.

The Wolnadi's crew had no possible role in the explosion that she'd seen—they'd been heading back to the *Ragnarok* before it had happened—but they'd been closest, and it was the obvious explanation, wasn't it? Training exercise, live fire, death of the commanding officer. Worse than that, this was the third Command Branch officer assigned to the Jurisdiction Fleet Ship *Ragnarok* to die by violence within the past few months.

Someone was sure to see conspiracy at work. There were two problems that faced them, then, and the fact that no one deserved to be threatened with the penalty for killing a Command Branch officer when it had been an accident was only the first. The second problem was that once Fleet started asking questions, it almost never stopped with only three or four confessions.

"Seascape. Go and get Koscuisko. Tell him he's leaving now, right now, Captain's orders." She knew what she had to do. Fleet would want to test for Free Government plots, or maybe even mutiny. They'd start with the crew of the Wolnadi and go on from there.

Mendez was looking at her, somewhat skeptically, and Seascape hadn't moved yet, waiting for a cue. Jennet didn't blame her. But she didn't have time to stop and give a speech about how unsuited she was for Command, unexpected responsibility, the help she'd need from more experienced officers if she was to hope to avoid discrediting her Command. Brem was dead; she was the senior Command Branch officer on site, and that made her the acting Captain of the *Ragnarok*.

"First Officer, please go and get that crew to the courier as soon as they dock. I'll meet you there. I'll explain to 5.3. I want those people out of here."

Fleet couldn't ask them questions if Fleet couldn't lay hands on them. Let Koscuisko take 5.1 home with him on leave, not 5.3. By the time Koscuisko was back Fleet would have straightened everything out, so long as she could ensure that they didn't just take the path of least resistance at the expense of the crew of the *Ragnarok*.

"Vector transit is logged, Lieutenant," Wheatfields said, his voice calm and matter-of-fact over the station pickup. Turning around, Jennet gave the Engineer a crisp nod that was equal portions of acknowledgment and thanks.

"Never mind explaining to 5.3," Mendez said. "Explaining to Andrej. That'll be the test, Lieutenant. I'll be waiting to see you do that. Coming, Seascape?" He would go along with it. He agreed with her. So he knew she was right about Fleet.

"I'll talk to Pesadie once Koscuisko is on vector," Jennet said to Two, who was just hanging there, taking it all in. "Did we even know where the observers were? I know the fighter didn't." Most observation stations were unmanned. But it wasn't because they were dangerous, in any way. What had caused that explosion?

"We had no idea." Two's translator was permanently set on "chipper," no matter the seriousness of the situation. "Were it not for the deviousness of your Intelligence Officer you still would not know. Please be careful, Captain. We have had very bad luck with our Command Branch lately."

Yes, Two was brilliant; but the joke was still in poor taste. If it had been a joke. Did Desmodontae joke? Was there a concept of humor in the Desmodontae worldview? Who knew? Two was a bat. Hominids were her natural prey. A much less intellectually sophisticated hominid species, perhaps, but Jennet knew quite well that on a certain level she looked like lunch to Ship's Intelligence.

"I'll keep it in mind. Keep Fleet off if you can, please."

She had to get out to the courier bay in the maintenance atmosphere, where Security 5.3 was only waiting for their officer of assignment to leave his going-away party before departing on home leave for Azanry in Koscuisko's system of origin, the Dolgorukij Combine. They had probably been looking forward to the vacation. And she was going to deny them the treat at the last possible moment.

It was ugly, but it had to be done. She had to get that fighter crew out of the way before Fleet could start talking about Protocols.

Surveying the scene in his office with satisfaction Andrej Koscuisko—Ship's Surgeon, Chief Medical Officer, Ship's Inquisitor—drained his cup and lofted it high over the heads of three intervening revelers to where his chief of dermatology sat tending the dispenser of punch. "How does this happen?" he called, with challenge and confusion in his voice. "There is a cup, and it is empty."

And only then did it occur to him to hope that Barille would not try to toss it back to him, once refilled. There was already enough of a mess on the floor: snack wrappers escaped from the waste container, bits of paper garlands.

Barille bowed cheerfully from his post. "The situation shall be speedily amended. Sir."

Andrej Koscuisko was not exactly drunk. But he was unquestionably in such a very good mood that not even the unexpected appearance of the Ship's Second Lieutenant—Renata Seascape—could perturb his genial humor. He was on holiday. He was going home. He was taking his people with him, or at least some of his people.

"Lieutenant. A surprise." She stood in the doorway to his office, which was full of people and decorated for the occasion with colorful garlands of fish tails and fins and cheerful smiling fish-faces. Andrej had at first tried to believe that they could have no idea how rude it all was; but there was no real use trying to pretend that Infirmary had not in all this time learned that Dolgorukij men customarily thought of their genitals in piscine terms, so it was a mark of affection, really. "Come in, sit down, have a drink. Have several. There's plenty."

And it all had to be gone before the next shift came on, because one really did not party in Infirmary, not even in the Ship's Surgeon's private office. Which Mahaffie would be sharing with Colloy and Hoff during his absence, and Andrej wished them all joy of the documentation, with a full heart.

Seascape smiled and bowed. "Thank you, your Excellency, no thank you." She had to raise her voice to make herself heard; Volens had started to sing. Something about a river, Andrej thought. "Sir. Your presence very urgently requested in courier bay. Time to go, sir. Please come with me."

Time to go? Rising from his desk Andrej squinted at his timepiece. Surely not. Someone threw a fish-fin at Seascape and it stuck in her hair, but she was otherwise unmoved. Well. Perhaps it was time. Because he was tipsy, and could have mistaken the schedule.

"If you say so, Lieutenant." It was a tricky business, making his way to the door; it meant getting past Aachil, and Aachil always got a little over-affectionate when he was drunk. Not like Haber. Andrej wouldn't have minded kissing Haber, but he rather drew the line at Aachil. "Gentles. Thank you for your good wishes, good-bye, I'll be back in three months. Please do not save any documentation for me. I grant it all to you, with all my heart."

The party was in full spate. It would do very well without him. Barille was in pursuit, with a full cup of punch; Andrej couldn't very well have Barille coming out into section with uncontained liquor, could he? "Yes. Thank you." Almost to the door. Andrej drank off half the cup before handing it back. "But really, I must go. The Lieutenant says so."

She was getting impatient, too. "If you please, your Excellency, we've got to get to courier bay."

That was odd. What urgency was there, really? Everything was ready to go, his kit packed, his people cleared. But not understanding what was happening was something that a man grew to accept when he was drunk, or even when he was merely not exactly drunk. So rather than argue with her Andrej put his arm around her shoulders—for support and stabilization only, of course, he was a little unsteady on his feet. "Yes, yes, Lieutenant, coming immediately. Tell me. Have you ever to Azanry been?"

He was going home. It had been nearly nine years. He was not going home to stay, to try to rebuild a life of some sort after eight years dedicated to the practice of atrocity as a professional torturer; no, that fantasy had died months ago, when Bench intelligence specialist Jils Ivers had brought him word from Chilleau Judiciary that had forced him to re-engage with Fleet, to save himself from the administration that had been responsible for the Domitt Prison.

But he was going home.

Bench intelligence specialist Garol Vogel had shown him a Bench warrant with his name on it, in Port Burkhayden. Someone wanted him dead. If someone with the power to obtain a Bench warrant truly meant that he should die, the odds were good that he did not have long to live. So he had to take care of some personal business before he could be free to concentrate on who and why and how he was to protect himself. He had to ensure that Marana would be all right if he was killed; Marana, and his young son Anton.

"Never had the pleasure, your Excellency, though I understand it's very beautiful," Seascape said. "Here's the lift, sir. It'll be this way."

What? Oh. That was right. He'd asked her a question.

"I suppose one's home is always beautiful." The half-cup of punch he'd downed on his way out of his office had fuddled him, but the walk did him some good. His head was just clear enough for him to realize what an inane thing that had been to say. Stildyne's home had never been beautiful to Stildyne, for instance, as far as Andrej had ever heard him talk about it.

Or perhaps Stildyne's had simply never been home at all in the sense that Azanry was Andrej's. That could be. Stildyne's childhood and upbringing had apparently been as ugly as Stildyne himself was, also through no fault of Stildyne's own.

The lift doors sealed behind them; they were alone. Andrej leaned up against the back wall of the nexus lift, waiting for the fog to clear from the forefront of his mind.

"Your Excellency, there's been a change of plan," Seascape said.

Andrej stared at her, wondering what she was talking about. "How do you mean, Lieutenant?"

Seascape seemed uncomfortable, but resolute. "Necessary to make a last-minute substitution, sir, Security 5.1 for 5.3. We're to be met by the First Lieutenant. She'll explain, but you should at least be forewarned."

Substitution? What nonsense. And yet it didn't seem to be a joke; Seascape seemed quite serious. Any number of things to say occurred to Andrej, but she was the most junior officer on board—so whatever was going on was not likely to be her fault. A man had to take care how quickly he took offense, when liquor might be interfering with his perception.

The nexus lift stopped; it wasn't far to the courier bay from here. One turning, three turnings, straight on; First Officer stood in the corridor waiting for them, pointing them toward the ready-room with a gesture of the arm and hand before he followed them into the room to close the door behind them.

Through the observation window in the connecting door, Andrej could see his Security 5.3, drawn up in the muster room adjacent. What were they doing there? They were supposed to be waiting at the courier itself, not on standby.

The ship's acting First Lieutenant ap Rhiannon stood between Andrej and the door to the next room. She waited until Mendez had sealed the door, and then she spoke. That was a little forward of her; perhaps the impertinence could be excused on a formality, as her superior officer was not on board.

"Your Excellency. I regret that I must make an alteration to your travel plans, sir. It will be necessary for you to take Security 5.1 rather than your previously selected

Security 5.3 home with you on leave. And it is critically important that you leave immediately."

Said who? Jennet ap Rhiannon? Andrej folded his arms across his chest and raised his eyebrows at her skeptically. She was shorter than he was. And he out-ranked her. Who did she think she was, to tell him what to do?

"I'm not inclined to make any such substitution, Lieutenant." He'd been through a great deal with 5.3, or rather they had been through a great deal with him. Because of him. On his behalf, for his sake. "I have clearance for 5.3. I'm taking them with me. What possible interest could you have in interfering with my holiday?"

And yet the First Officer was here, and he was not jumping down her throat for overreaching her position. First Officer rarely tolerated breaches of rank-protocol; Andrej therefore asked the question in a curious, rather than an overtly hostile, tone of voice. Oh. Perhaps a little hostile. Perhaps. He didn't like Command Branch interfering with his life. Captain Lowden had had altogether too much to do with Andrej's life, until someone had killed him at Port Burkhayden.

"In the recently completed exercise from which Security 5.1 has just returned, a target was destroyed near the containment perimeter." All right, she clearly seemed to feel that she was making an explanation. He would wait. "Shortly afterward, an observation station proximal to the final kill exploded. I don't know if 5.1 knows about the explosion. I'm quite sure they don't know where our own remote observation team was when the explosion occurred."

Andrej began to see where the argument was headed. He didn't like it. "Lieutenant, I have promised these people, and long anticipated this. Is it truly necessary?"

Even through the liquor and the partying, however, Andrej's mind could track the logic. Command Branch officer dead. Explosion proximate to fighter manned by Security 5.1. *Interrogate the crew for any potential evidence of conspiracy to commit a mutinous act. Aggressively investigate all implied or explicit disaffection among the crew.*

"Your Excellency, through the death of acting Captain Cowil Brem I have assumed command of the *Ragnarok*. In the legal capacity of your commanding officer, I direct you to take Security 5.1 and clear this ship with all expedient speed."

How dare she use such language with him? She had the technical authority, but it was just that, a mere technicality. And yet she was right. She was the senior Command Branch officer, and that made her acting Captain.

That didn't mean he had to like any of this a bit. "First Officer. What have they been told?" It was capitulation on his part, and she would recognize it as such. But he dared not leave without understanding exactly what Lek Kerenko knew, and what supposed; Lek was bond-involuntary, and vulnerable.

"I told 'em that Fleet would try to pick the team apart, to cover for the embarrassment of being blown out of the water by an experimental ship. So they were going on assignment. Captain's direct and explicit orders."

Well, it would do, and it was all he had. Very well. "I will say good-bye to my Security," Andrej said firmly, and not very respectfully either. "And then I will leave straightaway. By your leave, of course, Lieutenant."

He didn't wait for leave. He went through the intervening door into the muster room, where Security 5.3 stood in formal array, waiting for him. There was to be no chance to explain; what the Lieutenant proposed was to willfully evade normal Judicial procedure by removing persons potentially of interest from their immediate environment, and that might create trouble in the hearts and minds of bond-involuntary troops.

Bond-involuntaries had been carefully schooled in the performance of their duty. Emotional conflict was the signal for the governor that each had implanted in their brains to punish what was clearly either a transgression or intent to transgress. So he could say nothing to his people except that he was sorry, that he would miss them, that they would be sure to come with him next time.

She was overreacting. Surely. Yet he had seen too much during his term of duty to be able to believe that there was no chance of her worst fears becoming reality.

*   *   *

Stildyne could see Koscuisko in the next room, talking
to 5.3. He wished Koscuisko would hurry up. The sooner
they got clear of this the easier it was going to be to
manage; and starting this exercise with Koscuisko already in a filthy mood was not what he had anticipated—
but a man could only deal with what he had to work
with. Not what he wished he had.

Koscuisko stepped through the door into the courier
bay, and Security 5.1 came to attention smartly, lined
up beneath the belly of the craft and waiting only for
Koscuisko's word to be away. It was a nice courier; a
Combine national, the property of the Koscuisko familial
corporation in fact. One of the things that still amazed
Stildyne after four years and more with Andrej Koscuisko was how inconceivably rich the man was—at least
so far as disposition of material goods was concerned.

"Thank you, gentles, and we must leave very soon, but
I want a moment. Stand down. Stildyne. Kits on board?"

Stildyne knew what urgency First Officer had concealed behind his calm demeanor and his careful drawl.
If First Officer was worried Stildyne was near frantic;
but Koscuisko would not be hurried.

"Cleared and ready for departure, your Excellency,
immediately. As the officer please."

Koscuisko frowned at him a little over that. He didn't
usually resort to formal language with Koscuisko; it was
almost a form of bullying. It was the only way Stildyne
could come up with to express the urgency he felt. First
Officer wanted 5.1 clear of the *Ragnarok*. Stildyne didn't
know why—exactly—but that didn't concern him. First
Officer knew what he was about.

"These people have just come off exercise, Chief."
There was a touch of admonition in Koscuisko's voice,
a hint of reproach. "And in particular the navigator has
been worked hard. Not that the entire crew has been less
fully challenged, but do we demand that Lek perform a
vector transit now? This moment? Lek. Should truly we
be asking such effort, from you?"

All right, maybe Koscuisko was not simply being difficult because he was angry and frustrated. It was possible that Koscuisko was checking to be sure that Lek was

centered, clear, and well within the tolerances imposed by his governor. "It's just a vector transit, your Excellency." Lek didn't quite shrug, but the idea was there. "Not a problem, sir. And Godsalt has already done the calculations."

There was no halt or hesitation in Lek's voice. If Lek had any apprehension, he would let them know by using more formal and submissive language—"as it please the officer." For Lek to use "your Excellency" and "sir" in direct address meant that there were no issues with his governor for Koscuisko to confront. Koscuisko nodded, and made an effort to clear the trouble from his face. "Well, then, let us be off, there is no time like the present. Chief."

Stildyne didn't need to say anything. Koscuisko went up the ramp into the courier. Stildyne nodded, and 5.1 broke out to man the stations—finalize the checks, close the ports and portals, seal the courier for launch.

Stildyne himself followed Koscuisko up the ramp, slowly. Thinking. Wondering. Why was First Officer in such an apparent hurry to get these people away from the ship? What did Koscuisko know? And what would Koscuisko tell him?

It was an unfortunate complication to the start of a man's holiday. But maybe once they'd passed this rocky bit the track would be smooth and level for the duration of Koscuisko's home leave.

Chapter Two

Damage Control

Admiral Sandri Brecinn sat at her ease in her war room watching the course of the exercise on the massive screens that filled the whole half of the room: top, bottom, sides. "What do they think they're doing?" she demanded, watching, as the Wolnadi made an audacious move on its next-to-last target. "Eppie, I'm going to want a blood test on that navigator. He's got to be on something."

An appreciative chuckle ran through the room, passing from sycophant to toady to sidekick. Brecinn stretched comfortably. She was in her element, surrounded by her people, and they all knew that nothing the *Ragnarok* accomplished during this exercise would make any difference in the end. The *Ragnarok* was history. History, and a very significant addition to her asset account.

"You might have to hold the crew here for a while." Eppie, her aide, picked the line up and stretched it out ably. "Once you start looking into such things. Who knows how far it goes?"

Brecinn liked Eppie. Eppie was a reasonable person. They were all of them reasonable people, people one could deal with, people with whom one could do business. Well, almost all of them. Some of the observers were unknown quantities. The armaments man, Rukota, for one; Brecinn didn't know too much about him except that he was very solidly protected—his wife had an intimate understanding of long duration with somebody's First Secretary.

The Clerk of Court that Chilleau Judiciary had sent to take legal note of the proceedings, however, was a woman with a very interesting past about whom Brecinn's sources wished to say surprisingly little; that piqued Brecinn's interest. Noycannir was just a Clerk of Court, one who didn't seem to be very well placed. Her apparent status was inconsistent with what little Brecinn had been able to find out about her contacts. So was she a different sort of an observer? And why exactly was she here, under cover as an exercise observer?

If Noycannir was here on a secret mission she had yet to approach Brecinn about it, which showed a lack of respect on Chilleau's part. Chilleau was getting too self-confident by half. The Selection was far from certain, and—favorite or no favorite—Chilleau's victory would not be guaranteed until the last Judge had logged the consensus opinion of the last Judiciary. That was weeks away.

"No sense of propriety." Brecinn vented some of her frustration with Chilleau Judiciary at the expense of the Wolnadi crew on-screen. The *Ragnarok*'s fighter had taken its next-to-last target; it had only one left. "Anybody with a feather's-weight of sensitivity would settle for a solid showing. Instead of this—shameless display—"

That crew knew as well as anyone that the program was as good as cancelled. If they had any sense at all, they'd be doing what they could to facilitate the cancellation, and hoping for a few crumbs of the spoils to drop their way. If they were reasonable people, they'd play along. Nobody was going to be looking closely at anybody's personal kit once the ship was decommissioned, after all.

The Wolnadi closed on its last target. Brecinn frowned.

There was an observation station right there, just there, to the other side of the containment field. The *Ragnarok*'s observation party was on that station. The Wolnadi wouldn't know that, or at least they weren't supposed to know. *What was she worrying about, anyway?* Brecinn asked herself, and took a deep breath, willing herself to relax. The odds of the fighter missing the target, breaching the containment field, and hitting the observation station were low indeed.

Maris had sworn that the stock he had stowed there was stable. Fresh stuff. New loads. Rocket propellant didn't start to degrade until it got old, unless it had been contaminated. Maris knew better than to have sold her inferior goods. He knew she needed them to satisfy the debt she owed to reasonable people.

And the fighter didn't miss the target. Admiral Brecinn sat back in her chair, satisfied and annoyed at the same time—satisfied, that she'd been concerned over nothing; annoyed at the fighter's arrogance in pushing for a perfect run.

The fighter heeled into its trajectory, starting back toward its base ship while the debris from the target blossomed in the familiar dust-rose of a solid kill. The target had been very close to the boundary; the plasma membrane of the containment field belled out, fighting to absorb the energy of the blast, and kissed the observation station, sending it tumbling.

There was a murmur of amusement from the observers assembled, nine in all, seated in ranks arrayed before the great monitoring wall—getting a lick from energy wash was a harmless mishap, a pratfall, more amusing than anything else unless it was your bean tea that got spilt. Still Brecinn frowned, despite herself.

Armaments were intrinsically unstable to a certain degree, but it was a moderate degree, a very moderate degree, and it wasn't as though she could have redirected the *Ragnarok* party. They'd made the selection at random from the available platforms as part of the exercise protocol.

She hadn't thought about excluding that one station until it had been too late, not as though she really could have without drawing attention to herself, and not as if that was the only station she was using for storage. The storage spaces were all inerted anyway. Why should she worry? Nobody paid any attention to what might be stored out on unmanned observation stations. Nobody cared about miscellaneous stores.

There was a sudden flare on-screen, and the room fell silent. Brecinn stood up, staring.

"What was that?"

It couldn't be. It would be such disgustingly stupid luck.

"Observation station, Admiral," the technician on duty said, disbelief clear in her voice. "Seems to have exploded. No coherent structure on scan."

No trace of a lifeboat, then. They hadn't had time. They hadn't had warning. There was plenty of debris; that was all too depressingly obvious, and somewhere in that debris floated the probably fractionalized bodies of the people who had been watching the exercise from remote location. The *Ragnarok*'s acting Captain. A Command Branch officer. That meant a full-fledged accident investigation. She couldn't afford one.

Some of the debris in that cluster would bear unmistakable chemical signatures of controlled merchandise— armaments, bombs—that could be traced back to specific points of origin, failures in inventory control, even the occasional warehouse theft. It would be difficult to explain, almost impossible to overlook. Unimaginably expensive to deny.

"Poll all stations," Brecinn ordered. "Let's be sure of our facts before we send any formal notices. We'll take a short recess while we confirm whether the station was manned. Two eights, gentles, and reconvene here."

Taking a recess was risky. They were her staff, true enough, but they would be watching for the first hint of uncertainty on her part to gut her carcass and throw her to the scavengers while they hurried to harvest everything they could salvage ahead of a forensic accounting team. She had to have time to think.

One by one, her people stood and left the room. The Clerk of Court from Chilleau Judiciary excused herself; the armaments evaluator from Second Fleet put his feet up on the back of the chair in front of him, with every apparent intention of having a nap in place. Fine.

Eppie and one or two of the others would have gone directly to her office. They'd be waiting for her. *Damn the* Ragnarok *and its crew anyway,* Admiral Brecinn told herself crossly; and went to join her aides and advisors for private conference.

Strolling thoughtfully through the halls beneath the Admiral's management suite Mergau Noycannir switched on her snooper with a casual gesture that mimicked rubbing behind one ear; and was immediately rewarded.

". . . damage assessment, as soon as possible. We needed those rounds to fulfill a contract coming due. We'll have to make up the difference in cash, if this gets out."

Eppie, Mergau thought. It was a daring act of espionage to have planted a snoop on the Admiral. As it was, she could only afford one of the timed sneakers. One quarter of an eight, and then it would disintegrate into anonymous and untraceable dust. With luck, no one would even have discovered that there had been a transmission.

"That means an inventory of all the stations. Not just to discover what went up. To be sure we know what's where." Admiral Brecinn's voice, annoyed and anxious. From the way the others' voices rose and fell in volume, Mergau guessed that the Admiral was pacing.

"We'll have to cover for it somehow, Admiral. After all. Command Branch. Bad luck all around."

She'd suspected Brecinn's command of black marketeering from the moment she'd arrived. She recognized some of the names and faces from the secured files at Chilleau Judiciary. Here was evidence; but more than evidence, perhaps.

"Our counterparts are counting on us to be well placed for the new regime. We lose their confidence, we lose everything. We've got to contain this somehow." The Admiral again, and she sounded just a little—frightened. Mergau Noycannir knew what frightened people sounded like. She recognized the subtle quavering behind the fine false front.

"Admiral, it was an accident. It could have happened to anyone." Mergau knew better. Brecinn apparently did, too.

"People who conduct business with professionals don't

have accidents, Eppie. No. We can't afford to let it be an accident. We need a cover, and we need it fast."

Mergau knew her time was running out; the snooper would stop transmitting at any moment. She could extrapolate well enough from what she had heard, however, and with that she could build the perfect solution to the Admiral's problem. Her problem as well.

Admiral Brecinn needed to cover the fact that the explosion that had just killed the *Ragnarok*'s acting Captain had resulted from the illegal stockpiling of stolen armaments for sale on the black market; Mergau needed all the protection she could get.

Admiral Brecinn only knew that Mergau was a Clerk of Court at Chilleau Judiciary. She didn't know how low on the First Secretary's table of assignments her placement had become. Mergau naturally had not hastened to explain how sadly reduced her position was from the days when she had brought the Writ to Inquire back from Fleet Orientation Station Medical at the First Secretary's desire; and she did have contacts, even yet.

That was how she had arranged for the forged entry of Andrej Koscuisko's name on an unauthorized Bench warrant.

Had the Bench warrant been exercised, it would not have mattered, in the end, whether it had been forged or not. Once the thing had been done, the Bench would have been forced to stand behind it, or admit to the falsification. The Bench couldn't afford to do that. They'd have had to defend the warrant as true, if anyone ever found out about it—not that there'd been any reason to fear that anybody ever would.

But the Bench specialist to whom it had fallen to execute the warrant had recorded it as written against somebody else entirely, and that raised all kinds of difficulties.

Someone had said something that Mergau hadn't quite caught, handicapped as she was by the directional nature of the snooper. Admiral Brecinn's response made the nature of the question clear, however. "Ap Rhiannon. Priggish little self-important bitch. Crèche-bred. Of all the luck."

A tiny spark of heat against the skin at the back of

her ear, too brief to be painful; the snooper died, and destroyed the evidence of its existence. Where she'd tagged Brecinn, the Admiral would not even notice the snooper's disintegration.

Mergau continued in her thoughtful meditative stroll, heading for the water-garden outside the canteen. There was a great deal to think about here. Admiral Brecinn needed help. Mergau needed protection. Mergau didn't know quite how it was going to play out, not just yet. But she was confident.

Somewhere in this morning's events she was going to find the key to her salvation, and defense against the chance that some Bench specialist would turn up some day to confront her with her failed attempt to satisfy her vengeance against Andrej Koscuisko with a Judicial murder.

The observation deck cleared out. The Admiral had left the room; her staff had melted away into the figurative woodwork. The Clerk of Court that Chilleau Judiciary had sent to observe the exercise had similarly excused herself. That meant that the room was as clean as any on station just now, and General Dierryk Rukota had no particular desire to go anywhere.

The technicians were still here, of course, working the boards: status checks, population reconciliation, traffic analysis. All to try to determine for a fact whether the *Ragnarok*'s Command had been on that observation station when it had exploded.

Someone brought him a cup of bean tea, and Rukota accepted it with a nod of grateful thanks. Good stuff, too. He had no grievance with technicians. He just didn't think he liked Fleet Admiral Brecinn, or her pack of scavengers.

Everybody knew that the *Ragnarok*'s research program was due for cancellation with the selection of a new First Judge. It was traditional. New First Judges needed all the leverage with Fleet that they could get, especially during the early formative years of their administration—leverage a new research program, with a generous provision of funding from tax revenues, could provide. That didn't mean they had to be so obvious about it.

The *Ragnarok*'s black hull technology was the culmination of twenty-four years of technical research, hundreds upon thousands upon millions of eights of markers Standard, untold hours of labor, and the product of the focused intellect of some of the finest mechanical minds under Jurisdiction.

It was bad enough that the program had to be at least suspended while the new First Judge, whoever she was, decided exactly what to do with it. Rukota wanted to see Fleet concentrating on doing what it could to harvest the lessons learned to date, rather than blowing it all off as yesterday's news. The ship had performed well in test and maneuvers. There were solid innovations there in its design.

Flying on the order of that last fighter's run spoke for esprit as well; people who didn't care about where they were and what they were doing couldn't be bothered to shave their fuses like that. So the ship had more than just its experimental technology going for it. And Fleet would throw that away, too, dispersing the crew in every which direction when the time came to decommission the hull.

It was a very great shame to put so much into a battlewagon and never let it meet the enemy. And yet the enemy—the Free Government—was not one that could be met with at all, by even the greatest of battleships. They were small and only loosely organized, poorly armed, ill provisioned.

Fighting the Free Government with great ships like the *Ragnarok* was a little like deploying a field gun against the small annoying birds that were forever mocking one from the trees downrange. They were always long gone before a round could impact. All a person ended up with was wasted ammunition, and an overabundant supply of surplus toothpicks.

Rukota sipped his bean tea and stared into the great sweep of the observation screens, brooding. Jurisdiction Fleet Ship *Ragnarok*. He knew an officer on board that ship; he'd been young ap Rhiannon's commander not too long ago, when he'd had a stubborn pocket of resurgent civil resistance to deal with and she'd been sent to command his advance scout ships. It hadn't been a pleasant experience, at least not for him.

Ap Rhiannon was crèche-bred, inflexible, intolerant, and all but unteachable. When she'd seen that elements within Fleet's own supply lines had been aiding and abetting the insurrectionaries—for a nice profit—she'd redirected her assigned ships to intercept an arms shipment, and shut the pipeline down.

There had been a very great deal of embarrassment in upper Fleet echelons. He'd been blamed for not keeping a closer rein on her, when it hadn't been any of his doing one way or the other. She hadn't even told him. That had given him deniability, and saved his career; but it had bothered him at the same time, and bothered him still.

Had she not told him in order to reserve the blame for herself, when blame came—as it was almost certain to? Or had she not been able to decide whether he was in on it?

She'd made her point about black-market traffic in armaments. And been assigned to the *Ragnarok* for her pains, a dead-end assignment on a dead-headed research vessel headed for decommission with a crew that Fleet had notoriously been packing with malcontents and malingerers for years. And here he was, for his own part, pulled off-line to provide administrative support on training exercises. As close to drydock as an officer could get.

He knew where the *Ragnarok* was on-screen; its position was marked, and with its maintenance atmosphere fully expanded the lights were easy to pick out against the black backdrop of space. So when something disengaged from the *Ragnarok* and started moving out and away from the ship it caught Rukota's attention. Small blip. Picking up speed quickly enough to indicate a courier of some sort.

Rukota leaned his head back against the low headrest of the chair in which he sprawled, and caught a technician's eye. "What's that?" Ap Rhiannon coming to see Admiral Brecinn, perhaps, though what her purpose might be was not something Rukota felt he could easily guess.

The technician squinted at the light-track, and then

consulted a log. "Oh. Ship's Surgeon, General. Home leave."

Right. The blip wasn't tracking for the station. It was angling out toward the Pesadie exit vector, leaving the system. Ship's Surgeons were ranking officers; they were also Ship's Inquisitors, and Ship's Inquisitors never, ever, ever traveled without Security.

There was a thought at the back of his mind, a vague and unformed suspicion that there could be something interesting about that courier. If he thought about it—

If he thought about it, he might discover something that he'd have to call to somebody's attention. It wasn't any of his business. Pesadie was jealous of its rights and prerogatives; they didn't need any help from him. He had as much as been told so, and by Admiral Brecinn herself.

Shifting his feet from the back of the chair in front of him to the floor, General Rukota put it all out of his mind. Pesadie Station was responsible for its own Security. Let them deal with it.

"Thanks," he called over to the technician, still hard at work on the assessment task. "Good bean tea. Best of luck with damage control."

So long as he left the area he didn't have to worry about keeping his own suspicious mind in check. A quick nap before Admiral Brecinn reconvened, and any miscellaneous thoughts he might have would be safely put to rest.

Andrej Koscuisko was very close to sober and not entirely happy about it. Standing behind the navigation console in the wheelhouse, he watched the forward scans, listening to the traffic in braid over the intership channels.

Lek—their navigator—was tired. Combat evaluations were intense enough to be exhausting even with dummy ammunition, and these had been live-fire exercises. If Lek was given a chance to start to wonder about all of this . . .

"Courier ship *Magdalenja,* Dolgorukij Combine, Aznir registry. Koscuisko familial corporation ship. Requesting release of precleared passage."

Lek sounded steady enough. And once they were on vector Andrej could have a quiet talk with him. There were drugs on board. He never traveled without drugs strong enough to overrule even a governor, and after what had happened to St. Clare—whose governor had gone critical at Port Burkhayden, and nearly killed him—Andrej had stocked his kit for triple redundancy. He was taking no chances with his Bonds. He was responsible for them. They trusted him to take good care of them.

The courier was approaching the perimeter of Pesadie Training Command's administrative space, ready to clear the station. From here it was only a matter of three hours' time before they reached the exit vector. The vector was patrolled, of course; exit from Fleet stations was controlled as strictly as authorized entry. But the transit plan had been precleared. There was no reason for anyone to challenge his departure; Andrej concentrated on that. No reason.

"We confirm, *Magdalenja*." Pesadie Station's port authority sounded bored. Almost casual. "For the record, confirm souls in transit, please."

Lek looked around and up, back over his shoulder, seeking guidance from Andrej. Or perhaps from his Chief, Stildyne, who stood to Andrej's left; but this was Andrej's arena. He knew what to do. Ap Rhiannon surely had not intended her ruse to go on record so soon after its initiation.

"Voice confirm," Andrej said, and if he sounded a little irritated it was because he was unhappy. "I am Andrej Ulexeievitch Koscuisko, Chief Medical Officer assigned to the Jurisdiction Fleet Ship *Ragnarok*. Traveling home on leave with my Security also duly assigned, and I have not been home in nearly nine years, so I would appreciate your cooperation in expediting clearance."

Meaning, *if you dare insult a ranking officer by insisting on a voice-count just because it is the letter of the procedure, said ranking officer is entirely capable of taking it personally, with subsequent negative consequences to your very own personal career. Which will be ending.* Andrej didn't usually resort to bullying, but if a man was going to pull rank there was no sense in being the least bit subtle about it.

It took several moments for the voice confirm to clear; to claim to be Andrej Koscuisko was not something that could be lightly ventured. He held the Writ to Inquire, and could lawfully deploy the entire fearful inventory of torture in the Bench's Protocols on his own authority. Making a false claim to the authority of a Judicial officer was a capital offense; and an abomination beneath the canopy of Heaven to take pleasure from the suffering of prisoners in chains—

But that was an old guilt. Old, if ever present, sin. No less deep and damnable now than the day Andrej had first begun to realize that he was a monster, but it had been nine years, Creation had not risen up to swallow him and take him to his punishment, and Andrej needed his wits about him to get past this procedural check and to the exit vector. He could not abate his sin by brooding on it. There would be time enough for that in Hell.

"Thank you, your Excellency." The Port Authority sounded much less casual now. "No offense intended, your Excellency. Cleared to vector. If I might presume to offer personal good wishes for a pleasant holiday, sir." *No, you insolent groom's boy, you may not.* It was presumptuous. But Andrej had already made himself unpleasant. He wanted the Port Authority to be too grateful to be out from under his displeasure to think about placing any additional administrative requirements in his path.

"You are very kind, Control, thank you. *Magdalenja* away here, I think? Yes?"

This was Lek's signal to pick up the thread, and he did so smoothly, with no hint of tension in his voice. "*Magdalenja* away here, Pesadie. Going off comm to prepare for vector transit."

Clear.

The corvettes standing by at the entry vector could still cause a fuss, but it was much less likely that they would do so now that Andrej had snarled at Pesadie, and they had been unlikely enough to interfere with him in the first place.

It was just his nerves. And his nerves weren't the

nerves he should be worrying about. "Mister Stildyne, may I see you for a moment?"

There was a private lounge just off the back of the wheelhouse, and it had all the privacy screens on it that a man could wish. Stildyne followed him into the lounge and pulled the barrier to, sealing the room.

Andrej went to the drinks cabinet at the far end of the lounge and considered the available options. Wodac. Cortac brandy. The proprietary liquor of the nuns over whom his elder sister was abbess, widely renowned for its healthful botanicals. Alcoholic beverages from one end of the Combine to the other, and all Andrej really wanted was a cup of hot rhyti, and something for a headache.

"How are we to hope to manage, Chief?"

Stildyne was up to something, behind Andrej. Andrej could hear the little chime of metal against fine Berrick ceramic ware, the seething of liquid coming to a boil. *Trust Stildyne to have found rhyti*, Andrej thought, gratefully.

"Well, you're not helping, your Excellency. It's not a problem so far. But if you're paying too much attention to Lek he'll start to wonder."

Stildyne was right. Of course. Andrej smelled the rising fragrance of top-quality leaf, and smiled almost in spite of himself. He was going home. It was only for a visit, and he had a very great deal that would have to be accomplished; but he was going home. He had not been home in more than nine years. He was going to meet his son at last.

"I can explain, Chief. Lek is Sarvaw. I will have a quiet talk with him. You may not appreciate quite what it is to be a Sarvaw, and be borne deep into the heart of enemy territory." It wasn't that Stildyne hadn't heard about the peculiar relationship between Sarvaw and other Dolgorukij, over the years. Yet how could any outlander really understand?

Stildyne had come to stand behind Andrej now, holding out a cup of rhyti. Beautiful stuff. Very hot, and milky, and smelling every bit as sweet as Andrej liked it. Stildyne was good to him. "We may need to lean on that, your Excellency, but first things first. We'll clear the vector. Then you should probably go talk to people. I'll leave you to your rhyti."

And sober up. Stildyne didn't have to say it. After more than four years together they understood each other better than that. It wasn't the norm for relationships between officers of assignment and Chief Warrant Officers, no, but had it not been for Stildyne's willingness to exceed the normal parameters of his assigned duties Andrej was very sure that he would not have survived Captain Lowden.

"Very good, Mister Stildyne. Thank you."

Andrej had enough to get through at home, if he was to hope to leave Azanry prepared to seek the unknown enemy who wanted him dead—someone with the Judicial influence to have obtained a Bench warrant for his assassination, one that Garol Vogel had declined to execute almost as an afterthought, months ago, at Port Burkhayden.

He didn't know when he would find the time and strength and courage to address the thing that had gone wrong from the beginning between himself and Security Chief Stildyne.

Jennet ap Rhiannon sat in the Captain's office with Ship's Primes around her, watching the monitors.

She wasn't sitting behind the Captain's desk; the kill was not confirmed. It would be premature. This office had the access they all needed to be sure they were on top of what Pesadie might be up to, however, so there was no choice but to gather here, whether or not the issue of the captaincy was unresolved.

Wheatfields didn't fit very comfortably into the chair in the conference area. But Wheatfields was oversized. There was no way around it. The Chigan ship's engineer was a full head taller than the late, and by and large unlamented, Captain Lowden had been; and Lowden himself had been toward the upper limit of the Jurisdiction standard.

"There's no room for misinterpretation in the ship's comps. Not as though that ever stopped Fleet," Wheatfields was saying, his eyes fixed on a monitor. "We were firing training rounds, even though they were live, so the explosive payload was reduced. That last target was destroyed well in advance of the explosion on the observation station. Whatever set the remote station off, it wasn't one of our rounds."

They were tracking the courier ship on its way to the vector. Three hours had elapsed since its launch; the exit vector security had yet to go on alert. Another half an hour and the courier would be on vector, functionally out of reach for days, at minimum. Out of Pesadie's reach forever, if she had anything to say about it.

First Officer took a drink of bean tea and grimaced. "This stuff gets nastier every day. We ought to press for resupply while we're here, now that we're going to have to wait an investigation out. What's the Admiral up to, Two?"

Jennet shared Mendez's sentiments about the bean tea. The *Ragnarok* had always had a certain degree of difficulty breaking stores away from Fleet depots—as an experimental ship it had always taken second best. Things had begun to deteriorate at a discouraging rate after Lowden's death, though. Lowden had been as corrupt as imaginable in some ways, his personal misuse of interrogation records among them. But he had at least had the political influence required to keep the *Ragnarok* well stocked.

"No official communication." Two had to stand in her chair; she didn't sit at all in any conventional sense. Since she was fully two-thirds of Jennet's own height she was unnaturally tall amongst the assembled officers as they sat, but the Captain's office had no provision for Two's preferred mode—which was hanging upside down from the ceiling. "Traffic suggests a full-scale inventory on all observation stations and several warehouses besides. We have some eights in which to decide what to do. Perhaps as much as two days."

Two's voice was mostly out of range of Jennet's hearing. The translator that Two wore gave her an oddly accented dialect, but at least it was female, like Two herself.

The translator always took longer to process than it took Two to speak. Two sat there solemnly with her black eyes seemingly fixed on Jennet's face, waiting for the translator to catch up. It was an illusion, that fixed regard. Two didn't actually see any farther than the first flange of her wings' extent—an arm's-length, more or less.

"I'm still not sure what it is, exactly, that you mean to accomplish, your Excellency."

Ship's First Officer had always been very straight with her. There was no disrespect in his tone of voice; there was no particular change in his demeanor. Jennet could understand that. These people were all senior. She was the third person to be acting Captain of the *Ragnarok* in a year. And Mendez had never paid as much attention to rank and protocol as others in his grade class: that was the only reason he hadn't been drafted into Command Branch himself, long since.

"I'm making it up as I go along." There wasn't any sense in pretending to be smarter than Ship's Primes. She needed their agreement to do anything, rank or no rank. When it came down to it rank only existed so long as everybody agreed that it was there. "The best way I could think of to keep these crew out of Fleet's hands was to get them out of the area. If Pesadie can't get started on them, they can't begin to touch the rest of the crew. They'll have to try something else. A real investigation, maybe."

"All they have to do is wait till the crew comes back." Wheatfields was calm, dispassionate—uncaring. She'd learned that about Wheatfields. There was very little that aroused his interest, and practically nothing outside of Engineering. "What does this give us? Apart from irritating Pesadie, and I don't care, it's your neck anyway, Lieutenant."

In the months she had been assigned to the *Ragnarok,* the number of times Wheatfields had spoken to her could be reckoned up on the fingers on her hands. Or even on the fingers of Wheatfields's hands, and he had only the four fingers and the thumb to her five, since he was Chigan and not Versanjer.

To Jennet's surprise it was Two who answered for her. "Pesadie must provide some suitable answers to questions from Fleet while they wait for the crew. Or even while they send for the crew. Pesadie maybe cannot wait. They'll have to start some alternate investigation. It will only show that the *Ragnarok*'s fighter could not have fired on the observer."

Well, not that that particular issue would be a problem in and of itself. There were too many copies of the record, surely. At least three copies of training records were maintained by Fleet protocols; one of these was on the *Ragnarok*, and not under Pesadie's direct control accordingly. If Pesadie wanted to tamper with that, Pesadie would have to get past Wheatfields to do it.

But the easy answer was that the round that the Wolnadi fighter was to have deployed had been exchanged for a more lethal weapon intended to destabilize the containment barrier, communicating sufficient disruptive energy to cause the station to explode—killing the *Ragnarok*'s Captain by design.

It would be easy to prove out by confession once Pesadie got their hands on the Wolnadi's crew. Not every Inquisitor with custody of a Writ to Inquire had Koscuisko's delicacy of feeling where truth and confession were concerned.

People could be made to say anything, under sufficient duress—unless they were fortunate enough to die before they could compromise themselves. Their crewmates, other Security, Engineering, the entire crew of the Jurisdiction Fleet Ship *Ragnarok*, up to and including—she realized with a start—its acting Captain, ap Rhiannon, already unpopular in some Fleet circles for having taken an uncompromising approach to black-market weapons dealing in the recent past.

Mendez was watching the monitor, drinking his bean tea absentmindedly. The on-screen track that represented Koscuisko's courier had closed on the entry vector, and was gone. "Well, that's put one of however many parts behind us," Mendez said. "Koscuisko's away. So now we'll all find out. Not that I'm arguing the abstract point, Lieutenant, your Excellency. If you can make this work, we'll all be just as happy about it. With respect."

"We'll get formal notification from Pesadie Training Command about Cowil Brem." There were things they needed to see to in the time they had left before an audit team came on board. "We'll take it from there.

Wheatfields will sanitize the Wolnadi line. Let them try to figure out how we're supposed to have done it. Two will be listening to Pesadie while they think about it."

She stood up. And, somewhat surprisingly, Wheatfields and Mendez stood up as well, while Two hopped down out of her chair, bracing herself against the floor with the second joints of her great folded wings. Respect of rank. It was an encouraging sign.

She didn't really care if they gave her the formal signs of subordinate rank relationship or not, though. All that mattered was that they came together to protect the *Ragnarok* and its crew. Somebody at Pesadie had been storing something on that observer that they oughtn't have; it was the only explanation she could see for the explosion.

And it was her duty to the *Ragnarok* to ensure that nobody made a scapegoat out of its crew to cover an administrative irregularity: not with lives at stake.

"We have the Pesadie vector, your Excellency." Turning away from the station as he spoke, Lek stood up and bowed to his officer of assignment. Koscuisko could see perfectly well for himself. The publication of the fact was a mere formula, but ritual was important, especially in the lives of bond-involuntaries. "Three days, Standard, to the Dasidar exit vector, Azanry space."

Koscuisko nodded briskly in appreciation. "Thank you, Lek, ably piloted. Now. Let us all to the main cabin repair, so that I may put you on notice, the ordeal which you face when we are at home on my native world."

Koscuisko was considerably relaxed, from a few hours ago; but not for the otherwise obvious reason, because Koscuisko didn't look or sound as though he'd been drinking. Recovered a bit from his going-away party, then. Lek followed his fellows, taking advantage of his position to linger for just a moment in the wheelhouse.

It was a pretty little courier, and it spoke his language. Or at least it spoke a language he had learned as a small child, before his trouble with the Bench, before his Bond. He'd understood why Koscuisko had selected Security 5.3 to take home with him on holiday, given that Koscuisko could take only one team; Koscuisko had tried to get as many of his Bonds in one basket as he could, and there was nothing personal about Lek's situational exclusion from the privileged party.

But none of the others were Combine folk. It made Lek so homesick to be talking to Koscuisko's courier that he wished he was back on the *Ragnarok,* rather than going with Koscuisko to Azanry. So close to home. So far away from his own people.

Distracted for a moment by the strangely painful familiarity of the courier's accent, Lek lingered a bit longer than he had intended. Someone stood in the doorway between the wheelhouse and the rest of the ship; someone big and solid and silent, patiently waiting. Stildyne.

"Sorry, Chief." It wasn't Stildyne's fault that Lek was Sarvaw, after all. "Daydreaming. Coming directly."

Stildyne could easily have made a point about it, but he simply turned and left the room. Stildyne had mellowed since Koscuisko had come on board; he'd been considerably rougher to deal with when Lek had first met him—though he'd never been abusive. He'd taken some of the customary advantages from time to time, true enough, but he'd always been a reasonable man, and fair. Koscuisko was too hard on Stildyne. Koscuisko didn't understand how much worse than Stildyne warrant officers could be, when you put some of them in charge of bond-involuntaries.

Glancing around quickly to make sure that everything was in order Lek followed his Chief out of the wheelhouse and into the main cabin, where the officer of assignment was sitting on a table at the far end of the cabin, swinging his feet. He'd changed his dress boots for padding-socks, Lek noticed.

The rest of the crew were seated in array in front of Koscuisko, except for Stildyne standing in the doorway. Lek found a place at Smish's left; Koscuisko nodded at Lek and began to speak.

"We have not had a chance to talk, gentles, because we were in such a hurry to be gone before someone could change their minds again, and send me away with people of Wheatfields, from whom all Saints preserve me."

That was by way of a joke. Ship's Engineer was a moody and difficult man with very particular reasons to detest Ship's Inquisitors; Koscuisko was a proud and self-assured officer who was accustomed to having his own way. The personalities had not blended well on board the *Ragnarok*. Over the years a species of truce had gradually evolved between them, but it was still a fragile sort of détente.

"We are to be on holiday, gentles, and yet the environment into which I bring you is not one in which we can all equally be comfortable." Koscuisko didn't look at Lek when he said it. Koscuisko didn't need to. They both knew who Koscuisko's thrice-great-grandfather had been. Koscuisko didn't need to know the details of Lek's family background to understand that he led Lek into the presence of his enemies.

On the other hand, though Koscuisko was the living descendant of Chuvishka Kospodar, he was not Lek's enemy. Koscuisko had earned Lek's trust over the years they'd been together on the *Ragnarok,* and in so doing had made Lek more free, even under Bond, than Lek had ever hoped to be until the Day when it expired at last—if he lived that long.

"We go first to a place that is called the Matredonat. It is my place. My mother's family made of it the present when my father cut my cheek, what would that be, when I was held up to the world as his inheriting son."

The details of Aznir blood-rites were arcane and not widely published, but Koscuisko's general meaning was clear enough. "Living at this place you will meet my friend Marana, and my son. I also will be meeting my son, for the first time, as you are. He is eight years old. His name is Anton Andreievitch, because I am Andrej his father."

Lek knew by the eager tension in Smish's body beside him how interested she was in this news. They were all interested. There had been guarded talk among them, but Robert St. Clare—who knew more about Koscuisko than anyone on board, including Stildyne—had either been unclear on the details or too reticent to gossip about them. Koscuisko's friend Marana, Koscuisko had said. It seemed an odd way to describe the mother of his son, even given that Koscuisko was Aznir and Aznir were peculiar.

"This place of mine, the Matredonat, is in the farmland, but there are hills behind. There is riding. One may swim in the river if one does not mind the fish. They are very large fish. And that brings to mind a point."

If Koscuisko's estate was in the grainlands Koscuisko would be talking about the old ones, the huge, old, wise, green-and-gold fish with their solemn expressions and their faces that were like the private member of a man. His fish. The old ones were as long and sometimes longer than a man was tall, and the roe that the females carried was worth its weight in hallucinogenic drugs. Lek wondered if the others knew that when a man like Koscuisko spoke of his place, he meant an estate the size of a respectable city, or larger.

"Lek and I have blood in common, in a way. He will be able to explain much when I am not with you." Koscuisko's reference startled Lek out of his meditation; Koscuisko was being very frank indeed, to admit to genetic ties between Aznir and Sarvaw. "Among these things about which it may be necessary to explain are requirements of hospitality. You are to be lodged each of you apart in guest quarters, because you are my Security. The household will wish to ensure that you lack for nothing that will increase your comfort under the roof of the Matredonat."

This was going to be awkward. Stildyne did have women, from time to time, but women were not his preference. Maybe Koscuisko's people would make allowances for the fact that Stildyne was an outlander, Lek decided. Maybe they'd call for a Malcontent. If they did that, Stildyne was in for an interesting experience. . . .

"The difficulty here is this, Miss Smath." Why Smish? She tensed beside Lek, when Koscuisko said her name. "There is no tradition in my house of a woman warrior. To Security is to be offered the hospitality of the house."

Suddenly Lek realized how long he had been away from home. How thoroughly he'd learned to think in Standard. He had not even thought about it. Koscuisko was right.

"It will be a little unusual. But you need not feel the

least bit reluctant to decline, should your interest not tend in that direction. I assure you that you will not give offense."

Warriors were greeted with soft words and warm embraces, granted the privilege of taking comfort with the women of the household. The fact that Smish was a woman herself would be considered secondary to her role as a warrior, a Security troop. Someone was probably going to offer sexual hospitality to her and so far as Lek knew Smish had as much interest in having sex with women as Stildyne did—or even less.

"Thank you, sir." Smish sounded a little confused overall. She wasn't Dolgorukij. She wouldn't know. "I'll keep it in mind."

Koscuisko nodded. Then Koscuisko turned his attention to Lek himself, looking directly at him while speaking in general to the team. "There will be much that is strange. I can only guess, remembering how it was when first I left Azanry for the school at Mayon. I could not warn you about everything if I talked for three days, and I would rather have something to eat."

Home food, Lek thought suddenly, and smelled remembered fragrances in his imagination. Thin little cakes made with soured grain mash and cream. Thick soups of stewed root vegetables, and when times were good meat to go with cabbage and watergrass.

"Therefore I will only say this, though I repeat myself. I request you all pay particular attention to what Lek does and says while we are home. In this way you can be sure of keeping your dignity in the land of the outlander."

It was a sensible suggestion, yes. But it was much more than that, though none of the other people here might realize it. Koscuisko told them all to point on him, Lek Kerenko, Sarvaw. That would be a sign to the Dolgorukij into whose territory Koscuisko was carrying them all, and Lek was grateful to Koscuisko for having thought of such a natural way to give him face in an unfriendly environment.

"And now I mean to go and lie down. Perhaps Lek will consent to discuss with ship's computers on your behalf and find out where the liquor has been stored.

There are three days from here to Azanry, and we are on holiday."

Lek didn't want liquor. He wanted root stew and cabbage-stuffed sausages; but this was an executive courier, and there was no hope of finding such homely food as that. He'd just have to make do with pearl-gray roe and cured fish wrapped in flour skins, he supposed. It was a hard task.

But someone had to do it.

Chapter Three

Reasonable People

Admiral Brecinn stepped down into the observer's pit at her headquarters at Pesadie Training Command with some inventory reports in hand. It had been a day since the anomalous incident had occurred; it was time to put the *Ragnarok* on notice. The inventories had put her on notice as well. She was going to need a strong bargaining position to hold her own against the reasonable people, when they demanded their merchandise. She didn't know where she was going to find the leverage.

"Contact the *Ragnarok,* if you please," she said, nodding to the technician at the comm station. The full complement of observers were here, just for the sake of the formalities. The inventory had had to be done twice, which had complicated things. Once for the official record, and once for the other record, the real record, the one that showed her where she stood in the profit and loss registers in her dealings with undocumented trade.

All right, illegal trade, but it was only illegal because people elected a too-narrow interpretation of the laws. Reasonable people knew how to conduct business without undue administrative procedure getting in the way.

The signal cleared from the *Ragnarok,* its position in the training area highlighted by a pinpoint halo on the star map even as the interface screen opened across much of the forward display area. Projected in this way Jennet ap Rhiannon was about twice life-size, seated at the desk in the Captain's office, her First Officer standing behind her, looking bored.

Admiral Brecinn didn't know much about the *Ragnarok*'s junior lieutenant and she didn't really care. Reasonable people had hinted that ap Rhiannon was not the sort of intelligent and responsive officer Fleet needed, which was a shame. Fleet needed good officers, especially in the lower ranks.

As the links all fell into place along authenticated lines of communication, ap Rhiannon stood up. Not a moment too soon, Brecinn thought, with contemptuous amusement. Junior officers rose to their feet in the presence of superior officers. Ap Rhiannon was being close to insubordinate.

"Pesadie Training Command presents its heartfelt sympathies to the *Ragnarok* on the loss of its Captain." Brecinn opened the engagement on the offensive, without waiting for whatever ap Rhiannon might have wanted to say by way of ingratiating herself. From what Brecinn had seen and heard of ap Rhiannon, she didn't have the sense to know when she ought to be doing her best to curry favor . . . like now, for example. "And expresses its concerns over the cause of this distressing incident."

Brecinn chose the word carefully, and employed it for full effect. *Incident*, not *accident*. Whether or not ap Rhiannon had the political sense of the average bulkhead was none of Brecinn's concern. The word would put ap Rhiannon's people on notice that Pesadie thought there was quite possibly sabotage afoot: ap Rhiannon's people, and Brecinn's observers, as well.

"Thank you, Admiral Brecinn." On-screen, ap Rhiannon had seated herself once more. She was clearly intent on pushing the rank privileges associated with her status as acting Captain of the *Ragnarok* to their fullest. "We are also deeply distressed by the unfortunate accident that has deprived Fleet of not only one Captain, but several other valuable resources as well."

Ap Rhiannon's choice of words in turn was lost on no one in the room. Brecinn had said *incident*. Ap Rhiannon said *accident*. It was just short of calling the Admiral a fool in public.

Ap Rhiannon only dug herself deeper into her own trap as she continued. "In my capacity as the senior Command Branch officer on board of the Jurisdiction Fleet Ship *Ragnarok* I respectfully request the immediate assignment of a duly detailed Fleet Incident Investigation team to determine the exact cause of the accident."

A what?

Brecinn was all too fully aware of the attention of the observers in the room fixed on her, wondering how she would react to this. She couldn't allow it.

"You are doubtless aware that there are no such teams assigned to this Command," Brecinn noted, coldly. This was an intolerable imposition on ap Rhiannon's part. "In the absence of a duly selected First Judge Presiding, no such teams can even be chartered."

Ap Rhiannon was counting on just that, though, Brecinn realized suddenly. Ap Rhiannon was technically well within her rights as acting Captain to demand a Fleet Incident Investigation team. In fact, now that she had made her claim in official transmission—and in front of all of these witnesses—Brecinn was left with no choice but to accede.

"Understood, Admiral Brecinn." Ap Rhiannon was clearly trying hard to keep the note of gloating out of her voice. Brecinn was sure of it. The ghost of a jeer crept into her language, nonetheless. "With all due respect, I cannot insult the memory of my former commanding officer by accepting anything less than the most careful investigation of the accident that took his life."

It would take weeks, at minimum, to locate a Fleet Incident Investigation team that could be assigned. Then it would take weeks more to wait for the new First Judge to be seated so that an administrative investigation order could be issued. Fleet Incident Investigation teams were not ordinary, everyday affairs. The Bench liked to keep an eye on them.

"As you wish, ap Rhiannon. I will forward your stipulation to Chilleau Judiciary on priority transmit." She'd confused the people who were watching her. She could tell. Even that Clerk of Court from Chilleau Judiciary was staring at her, while the expressions on the faces of her staff smoothed quickly from surprise into undisguised admiration. They'd guessed her strategy. She'd just reminded them all of why she was Admiral.

"In the interim period, however, evidence must be carefully placed on record by a neutral observation party. I will send a preliminary assessment team as soon as possible to begin this important preparatory work."

She didn't have a strategy, not yet, but nobody else needed to know that. She'd think of something. Ap Rhiannon couldn't bar a properly constituted preliminary assessment team, not with her request for a Fleet Incident Investigation team going forward.

Ap Rhiannon apparently realized that she was outmaneuvered; she was churlish about it. That was all right with Admiral Brecinn. The Lieutenant shouldn't have tried to get clever with her. "As you say, Admiral Brecinn. We will await your preliminary assessment team. Will that be all, Admiral?"

Ap Rhiannon underestimated her opponent if she thought she could seal off her boundaries so easily. "We'll let you know when the team is on its way. Pesadie away, here." She terminated the communication link with a forceful nod of her head to the technician on the board, and smiled. *Take that, you pathetic amateur.*

It was half for show and half pure honest spite, and Brecinn could see by the expressions exchanged among the reasonable people on her staff that it served the purpose. They believed she had a master plan. So she would, in time.

Brecinn rose to her feet to signal that the morning's work was winding down. "Thank you, gentles, and goodgreeting to you all."

She had one day before she'd have to talk to anyone about it. There was no time like the present to be started. Forcing a confident stride, carefully keeping a serene smile on her face, Brecinn fled with all deliberate speed to go to ground in her office, and make plans.

Mergau Noycannir had not been idle since the snoop she'd planted on the Admiral yesterday had shown her a possible line of approach.

Despised and discarded at Chilleau Judiciary she

might be, but she had contacts that had yet to fail her, developed over the years with favors and information and the general exchange of mutually profitable courtesies that characterized the conduct of business from one end of Jurisdiction to the other. She hadn't needed more than a few quiet inquiries to get her all the information she could wish with which to build a strategy.

Following Admiral Brecinn out of the observation hall Mergau kept close enough behind her to make it clear to the others that she meant to talk to their superior officer, in order to forestall any such actions on their own part. She waited to speak until the Admiral had passed through her administrative complex and stood in front of her office door, however, because what she had to say was to be between the two of them alone. "Excuse me, Admiral. I have a concern. May I have a moment?"

Brecinn was a tall woman. Mergau could not see her face, standing as the Admiral was with her back to the administrative area, caught in mid-movement as she set her palm to the secure on her private office. Mergau could see the fabric shift across the back of the Admiral's shoulders, though, and it was as good as a scan-reading.

"Dame Noycannir. You surprised me." Yes. Mergau already knew that. She waited. "By all means, then. Come in. What can I do for you?" Her presence was not welcome, Mergau could tell that easily enough. But unless she missed her guess, she was about to make herself Admiral Brecinn's very close friend and intimate acquaintance.

The door opened. Brecinn stepped through into her private office. Mergau followed. The lights came up as the Admiral crossed the room. Mergau looked around her appreciatively. Large office. Very nicely done, lots of plants—conspicuous consumption of water; at a headquarters located on an asteroid platform that was as good a rank-signal as anything.

The Admiral had a taste for architectural forms in furniture, it seemed, very expensive stuff. The two Per-and chairs in front of the desk alone were worth three or four times Mergau's annual salary on the casual market. "Please," Brecinn urged. "Sit down." She was playing it well; Mergau could appreciate that. There was little indication in her tone of voice of the impatience that she had to be feeling.

Mergau settled herself in one of those very severe, very expensive Perands. "Now that I have your attention I'm not quite sure where to start, Admiral. Can I be sure that our conversation can be privileged?"

Meaning, *Are your privacies in place?* And, by extension, *I want to talk business, and it's not precisely open-air business.* Admiral Brecinn toggled the remote, looking past Mergau as her door sealed itself shut.

"Privacy is in effect, Dame, at your request. What is this all about?"

Mergau frowned, to present the appearance of concentrating. "Well. Yesterday's unplanned and unfortunate event. Very awkward. One anticipates a good deal of interest from Fleet—too much interest for any reasonable person to be asked to tolerate, if you ask me."

She used the phrase with deliberate intent. She herself had always been careful to minimize her exposure to reasonable people as a class: because benefit bred obligation. But everybody knew about the existence of reasonable people. And Clerks of Court had more opportunity than most to place themselves in a position to be of use, and to gain insight.

Admiral Brecinn did not react to the phrase in itself. She was clearly testing Mergau out, unsure of Mergau's position. "Well, it is very unfortunate, Dame. Yes. And it will be an annoyance to have a stream of investigators through here. But what can we do? Cowil Brem is dead."

Very deliberately, Mergau shrugged. "Accidents happen. Why should they be allowed to upset the normal course of operations? Fleet has enough upset on its hands just now. The Bench is not well served by diverting police resources to investigate miscellaneous training accidents when they're needed to keep the peace during the selection process."

Civil unrest was a fact of life. It was only to be expected that it would increase during the period of uncertainty between the death of one First Judge and the selection of the next.

"You state the obvious, Dame, but what can be done?

And you'll excuse me, but I have a lot of work to do. So if . . ."

Mergau held up her hand to stop the Admiral, interrupting politely but firmly. "That is my issue exactly, Admiral Brecinn. What is to be done? I think I may be able to offer some assistance."

On the face of it, it was an impertinent thing to say. Mergau put full weight on the words, enough to give the Admiral pause, and was rewarded with Brecinn's raised eyebrow, encouragement to continue.

Mergau leaned forward. It put her at an odd angle because of the peculiar slope characteristic of the chair; hominids of Perand's class were by and large longer in the torso than the Jurisdiction standard.

"Admiral Brecinn. Let me be utterly blunt with you. There's been an accident. There will be an investigation. It will cost money, and investigations almost always get out of control. Unimportant and unrelated issues are turned up by auditors anxious to justify the expense of their investigation. It's all so unnecessary."

She had Brecinn's full attention now. The Admiral wasn't giving her many cues; Brecinn was corrupt, but not stupid. Mergau liked dealing with corrupt people. Stupid people were just boring, and frequently endangered one's own goals.

"All we need is a suitably logged confession set, Admiral, and we can close this unfortunate incident with minimal expense and exposure. I can help. If you are interested."

Picking up a decorative stone from her desk Brecinn turned the smoothly polished thing over and over in her fingers, thoughtfully. "It's my fiduciary duty to the Bench to weigh the costs and benefits of all planned approaches, Dame." Brecinn still revealed nothing—unless her use of the loaded word *fiduciary* was intended to hint at the underlying rewards that Mergau might expect to share if she came up with a good approach. "But surely it's premature to speculate about mutiny. Assassination."

Mergau shook her head. "Not at all, Admiral. I am completely confident of my information. The Second Judge does not like to publish the fact, but I hold the Writ to Inquire for Chilleau Judiciary, Admiral Brecinn.

And I say that the crew of that Wolnadi will confess their Free Government connections and treasonable intent for the Record in due form, before they die. All you need to do is provide me with the crew."

It wasn't exactly true to say that she held the Writ to Inquire for Chilleau Judiciary. Her Writ had never been revoked or rescinded, to spare the First Secretary the embarrassment of putting the failure of his experiment on record. But he hadn't used her Writ for years, not since she'd failed to get results from those Langsarik prisoners that the Bench specialist had brought to Chilleau Judiciary. Not since the Domitt Prison. More than four years.

Admiral Brecinn didn't need to know that.

Mergau had failed to get the information out of Vogel's Langsarik prisoners, and Vogel had taken the surviving Langsariks and turned them over to another Inquisitor. She'd been operating under a handicap— she'd been on Record, her actions had been recorded for the purposes of Judicial review. She had not dared subvert the Protocols. This would be different. All she needed were confessions on Record. Nobody would be there to observe how she had gotten them.

"You're very sure, Dame Noycannir," Brecinn said. She didn't sound perturbed by Mergau's suggestion; nor did she sound convinced. "It could all come down to some harmless accident. How will we know?"

Mergau relaxed into the deep curve of the back of the Perand chair. "You're right, of course, Admiral. It could all be a silly misunderstanding. Nobody's fault. An accident."

Exactly as it had been, in a sense. It was just bad luck that the senseless accident had taken several lives, and would expose some awkward, off-the-record financial arrangements and material transactions.

"We should evaluate the situation up front with clear and unbiased minds, that's all. The incident will take investigation. The crew will be interrogated." At least, in Preliminaries. So long as charges had not been preferred, that was a fairly innocuous process. But charges would almost certainly be preferred sooner or later against somebody. All Brecinn had to decide was whether she was willing to risk those charges against herself and members of her staff rather than some Security crew from a test-bed ship due to be offlined soon anyway.

What was it to be? Minimizing the damage, the exposure, the risk at the cost of a few crew from the *Ragnarok,* or letting delicacy of feeling overwhelm common sense, and the greater good of the majority?

"There will necessarily be a series of collaterals," Brecinn noted. Mergau knew by the fact that Brecinn was thinking about it that she was halfway there. "We're not just talking about four people here. And there's bound to be Judicial review. Command Branch requires it."

"The Bench has other things to worry about right now, and among them is its sacred duty to maintain public confidence in the rule of Law. If anybody wants to ask any questions when it's all over it's only going to raise unnecessary issues, and the Bench is going to have its hands full with political stabilization for the next few years."

Brecinn wasn't looking at Mergau any more. She was staring past Mergau's left shoulder at the far end of the room, her face all but expressionless. "We do need to be here for Chilleau Judiciary when the new First Judge is seated," Brecinn agreed thoughtfully. "And that means with our credibility intact. If we risked a scandal now it could cost Chilleau support she'll need. We can only provide it if we've put this behind us by the time the Selection is made."

Just so. Mergau sat quietly, content to let the Admiral do the job of convincing herself to sacrifice lives on the *Ragnarok* to political expediency. The personal benefits—escape from exposure as a black-market trafficker, negotiating leverage with reasonable people—were strictly subordinate to the greater good of the Judicial order. Of course.

Brecinn took a deep breath and focused her eyes on Mergau's face. "What's your interest in all of this, Dame?"

Almost there. Mergau smiled. "You mean apart from my keen awareness of how much the First Secretary values the support of Pesadie Training Command?"

Verlaine cared no more for Pesadie's political support

than for any other such Fleet partisans. Brecinn didn't
need to know that. Brecinn was more than willing to
believe herself to be an important key to Verlaine's
long-term strategy.

Mergau let her head sway on her shoulders, ever so
slightly, in a gesture of complicity and conspiracy. "And
apart from my personal interest in doing the best for the
next First Judge, I'd like to do business with you, Admiral. We could consider my assistance in this little matter
services on account, for the future. On deposit, if you
will. I know there's interest to be had, if I can demonstrate to you that you can rely on my discretion."

As far as that went. It didn't have to go very far. The
plan, in fact, didn't go any further than what Mergau
had proposed just now; she was still thinking things
through. But if she pulled this off, she could earn invalu-
able protection . . . and blackmail opportunities, if it
came to that.

Admiral Brecinn leaned forward over her desk and
offered Mergau her hand, in the quaint, old-fashioned
manner that some people had of doing business in good
faith. "I begin to see the long-term requirements of the
situation," Brecinn said. "Thank you, Dame. It's never
easy to believe treason of any Fleet resources, but our
duty to the Judicial order clearly requires us to investigate. The more quickly we can resolve things the better
it will be for everyone."

This transparent rationalization required a solemn response from her, and not a hearty chuckle. "Quite right,
Admiral. I will tell the First Secretary that I have offered
my services, and extended my stay. If you could detail
an aide to show me what facilities you have available.
And I'll need access to the Record on site."

No time like the present to be started. The Admiral
would have work for her very soon, of that Mergau
could be confident. "Of course, Dame Noycannir. I'll
send someone to you in quarters directly."

She would gain armor here that would protect her
even from the chance that Garol Vogel would return
from wherever he had gone, and uncover the forgery
of the Bench warrant that should have ended Andrej

Koscuisko's life. Somehow, Mergau knew that she would be coming out of this more powerful, more influential, more secure than she had ever dreamed of being.

When General Dierryk Rukota reported to Admiral Brecinn's office he was surprised to find Dame Mergau Noycannir in company, and a clearing signal on the communicator screen at the far end of the office. The signs were not good. But what was Noycannir doing here?

"You sent for me, Admiral." Rukota had been detailed here to observe as a representative from the Second Fleet; Admiral Brecinn was not in his chain of command. He didn't worry about observing all the formalities. He'd be polite, but he was an artilleryman, not an administrator.

At least he'd used to be an artilleryman before he'd attracted the wrong sort of attention from the reasonable people that seemed to fill Fleet's administration these days. His tour of duty with ap Rhiannon had been the last straw, apparently, because he'd been on one detail or another ever since, and there was no hint from anybody about a return to an active line posting yet.

"Yes, thank you, General. I'm just putting a call in to Second Fleet." Brecinn in turn barely acknowledged his rank, though she could hardly avoid acknowledging his presence. Maybe she wasn't entirely to blame for that. Second Fleet wasn't particularly on Brecinn's side, and exercise observers were frequently called into play as double agents to collect information on mismanagement to be used, if necessary, to offset any criticisms that Pesadie might level at the Fleet resources undergoing evaluation.

Noycannir hadn't stood when he'd come in; so she felt she was on an equal rank footing with him—a change since yesterday. The implications were intriguing. He'd heard gossip about Noycannir from his wife, during their infrequent rendezvous.

There were disadvantages to being married to one of the great beauties of the age; one of them was not having her all to himself. Another was having to put up with the jokes that people made about children that looked like almost anybody other than their mother's husband, but Rukota knew better than to care. They were all his children. She was his wife. He was their father, no matter who the sperm donor might have been.

Since nobody was standing on ceremony he guessed he would just seat himself and say the first thing that came into his head. Brecinn was barely paying attention to him anyway. "Why are we waiting to talk to Second Fleet, if I may ask?"

"We're going to ask Second Fleet to extend your detail, in order to accomplish a very sensitive task for us," Brecinn said. "I know it's an imposition on your time, General, but you're really the very best person we have at hand for this mission."

It was the preliminary response team. He just knew it. Admiral Brecinn had only two choices for a commander to field such a team: someone from Pesadie; and someone not. If they sent a team comprised entirely of people from Pesadie, there would be protests and accusations of partisanship from the beginning of the investigation. And of all the other people here to observe the *Ragnarok*'s training exercise—numbering two in total— he was the only person who could credibly be detailed to command an audit team, howsoever ad hoc and informal.

Second Fleet was on the line—Brecinn's counterpart, Command General Chehdral herself. Rukota suppressed a sigh. Chehdral was not part of the network of corruption as far as Rukota knew, but she had no particular use for him—not because of any personal animus, but because she was fully staffed for officers in his grade. Chehdral would be just as glad of something that would occupy Rukota's time for a while longer. It would be the assessment team for him for certain, then.

"Admiral Brecinn. What can we do for you?" It wasn't really a question, just a polite sort of a greeting. Not much of a greeting, either, come to that.

"General Chehdral, I've been privileged to enjoy the support of one of your command in recent weeks. You sent General Rukota to participate in evaluating the training exercises we have been conducting with the JFS *Ragnarok*. We'd like to keep him on for a few months.

We need the line commander's insight on some issues that have come up."

Well, it wasn't as if she was likely to come out and say "The *Ragnarok*'s Captain has been blown up and we need someone to help us control the damage." Was that what they wanted him to do? Manage the fallout? Or just pin it on the *Ragnarok* and get on with life?

"General Rukota is with you?" Chehdral asked. "Yes. General. What do you hear from your family?"

His wife was in retreat, helping the First Secretary at a Judiciary not to be named manage his not inconsiderable stress. His children were with their mother, with his parents, or in school. Nobody particularly needed Rukota himself. His was a relatively small role in the life of his family.

"They are well, General Chehdral, thank you for asking. There is nothing at home that requires my personal attention." He couldn't pretend to be needed at home, though he appreciated the offered escape hatch. It was clearly of no particular interest one way or the other whether Rukota stayed or not, for Command General Chehdral. She shrugged.

"You are seconded at Admiral Brecinn's request, General Rukota, to serve as needed or until further notice. Orders to follow. Are we done, Brecinn? This is Command General Chehdral, Second Fleet. Away, here."

She always had been a woman of few words. That Rukota was inconvenienced by the words she had shared with him was not her issue.

It was quiet in Brecinn's office, so Rukota took the initiative. "What do you expect to accomplish with the fielding of an immediate response team, Admiral?" His question came out sounding perhaps a little more confrontational than it really needed to be. Brecinn did not seem to notice.

"Dame Noycannir has prepared a brief." A flatform docket, which Brecinn held out for him to take. He had to stand up and lean forward to take it. He'd never liked Perand chairs; they compressed the spine and gave him muscle cramps. "Due to the extended period of time likely to elapse between now and the arrival of an accredited Fleet audit team, it's imperative to capture what physical evidence there may be. It would be too easy for vital information to be lost."

Or discarded. Or destroyed. "Physical evidence of what, Dame, exactly?" Rukota asked, looking at Noycannir. If this was about an honest attempt to protect the truth he was a Chigan's bed-boy. "It seems a little unusual to send an investigative party to the *Ragnarok* to seek evidence pertinent to something that occurred on an observation station."

Noycannir dropped her eyes, almost coyly. "You'll forgive me if I protect privileged sources." As though she had some. Perhaps she did. He had no reason to suspect that she was making it all up. Did he? "There are disquieting indications. We need to establish a baseline as soon as possible."

Either she was truly in a position to know something, or she and the Admiral meant to blame the accident on the *Ragnarok* somehow. She was a Clerk of Court at Chilleau Judiciary, true; she could be operating on a level much different than that about which Rukota's wife had told him.

Or she could be dirty, as Brecinn was dirty, as Pesadie Training Command was dirty, as increasing numbers of Fleet administrative staff appeared to be. Reasonable people. So why select him?

He'd worked with ap Rhiannon before, and lived to tell of it. Did they assume that he resented the trouble that ap Rhiannon had caused him, and would turn a blind eye to plots on the part of Pesadie—or even actively forward them? Or did they mistakenly believe that his presence on Brecinn's hunting party would put ap Rhiannon off her guard, convince her that she had a friend in him who would protect her interests?

"When do we leave, Admiral?" He would read Noycannir's brief. And he would keep his own counsel. Who knew? Perhaps by the time the accredited team ap Rhiannon had demanded arrived to take charge, he would have some interesting things to say to them. About Admiral Brecinn. And about Mergau Noycannir.

Anything was possible, in this age of wonder.

*　　*　　*

Bench intelligence specialist Jils Ivers sat beneath a canopy on a crossing-craft in the middle of a great blue lake, her eyes resting on the brilliance of the snow-covered mountains that garlanded the horizon.

The men who rowed the crossing-craft were singing.

If you row well enough the Autocrat may see/And then the Autocrat may chance to smile/And then good fortune will descend upon your house.

There was an island of gray rock in the middle of the lake, and administrative buildings glittering in the sun. Old-fashioned architecture. The Autocrat's summer residence was in the middle of lovely Lake Belanthe, which lay in the embrace of the goddess Perunna—after whom the right-most range of mountains had been named.

Then all of your sons will have eight sons/And you will have a daughter of such beauty and ability that she will come into the house, into the Autocrat's house/And there the Autocrat may see, and then the Autocrat may chance to smile.

It was an old song, by its syntax; Jils wasn't sure she caught more than half of it. Garol might have been able to translate for her. Garol was good at languages, and had an apparently solid grasp of High Aznir by report; which was a little humorous, because Garol didn't even like Dolgorukij. Garol's nature was not at base suspicious, but he had learned to be wary, and among the things to which Garol had elected to take general all-purpose undifferentiated exception was the Dolgorukij Combine and all of its works and adjuncts.

Your daughter will have sons of noble blood to grow in power and prosper in wealth/ The breeding-grounds of Geral will be yours, the seven looms of Dyraine of the weavers/ You will have the holy grain to feed your house/ And be welcomed as a guest in all Koscuisko's strongholds.

The crossing-craft drew near to the island and slowed. There was a man at the docks waiting for her. Jils tried not to be glad to see him; at this distance he could well be some other Dolgorukij than the one she was looking for, and even if he was the right man he might not have any information. Or elect to share it.

People in uniform clustered around the crossing-craft

as it tied up. Someone pushed a roll of fabric down the stone steps—a rug. An expensive rug, and though the waters of Lake Belanthe weren't salt using a hand-knotted rug of such elaborate pattern for a traction-mat was surely not the way to preserve a work of art. That was the whole point, Jils supposed. Conspicuous consumption. The Combine was rich.

The Combine was filthy rich, and had always had an agricultural surplus with which to support labor-intensive handicrafts, and as long as people could earn a decent living replacing rugs used as traction-mats who was she to think twice about it?

"Specialist Ivers," the waiting man said. It was the Malcontent Cousin Stanoczk, yes. "Good to see you. Did you have a pleasant crossing?"

The crew held the craft so still it was almost as though she was already on solid ground as she stepped out. The angle of the steps was a little awkward; she found herself glad of the extra purchase that the rug provided. The stairs were worn to a slope. They were old. On other worlds they might have been replaced, or the lake bridged; but Dolgorukij treasured old things as they were.

"Smooth as anyone could wish." There wasn't much of a breeze up across the lake, but thanks were owed to the crew as well. A rowing crew could make the smoothest passage rough if they were minded to. "These men are impressive, Cousin."

She didn't feel up to choosing the correct Dolgorukij form of the word; there were entirely too many ways to call someone *cousin* in Dolgorukij, each one with its own meaning and message about relative status, the degree of intensity with which one desired a favor, and the depth of obligation that one was willing to accept in return. Jils stuck to plain Standard. It was much safer that way.

"Indeed, Specialist. Combine-wide champions for speed as well as endurance, three years running now. Someone will take your box up to quarters. If you'd care to come with me, and have a glass of rhyti?"

If she had to. "Very kind." She didn't like rhyti. She'd learned a lot about it over the years, though. Verlaine had set her on Andrej Koscuisko to keep an eye on him, and Koscuisko drank rhyti. She'd gotten interested almost despite herself. "Thank you for meeting me, Cousin. I wonder if I could have a quick word or two with you on a personal matter."

Cousin Stanoczk reminded her of Koscuisko, if rather vaguely. The two men were related, if she remembered correctly; but Cousin Stanoczk had a very deep voice and Koscuisko was tenor, Cousin Stanoczk had dark brown eyes and Andrej Koscuisko's eyes were so pale that they almost had no color at all, Cousin Stanoczk had hair the color of wet wood and Andrej Koscuisko was blonder by several emphatic degrees.

Still, it was the same general form—not tall, deceptively slight, with shoulders whose slope belied their power and hands whose surpassing elegance belonged by right to an artist or a surgeon. What a Malcontent was doing with such hands Jils didn't know. Perhaps Stanoczk painted; it was unlikely that he practiced medicine, because medicine could be hired nearly anywhere, and Malcontents specialized in services that could not be hired or purchased at all.

Cousin Stanoczk grinned. He had very much the same surprising and open smile as Koscuisko had from time to time—one that showed a lot of small white teeth. "Be careful what you do, Specialist, the Malcontent is always at your service but will almost always find some favor to solicit in return. Sooner or later. That said, speak, I listen."

The worn stone walkway from the dock led them up a long shore of shallow steps into a green plaza where water birds were browsing in the grass like flowers on feet. Webbed feet. *How did they keep the walkways clean?* Jils wondered.

"Garol Vogel, Cousin. I don't mind telling you in confidence, as one professional to another. He's disappeared."

At the far end of the plaza there was an old wall with a high-arched gate that stood wide open. There were more lawns beyond. The guards were all in fancy dress; it was easy to overlook the fact that they were apparently also heavily armed. Once they passed through the pedestrian gate she saw yet more guards, as well as a great curving walkway paved with crushed stone, an immense stone façade with who knew what behind it, and a pretty little pavilion to one side toward which Cousin Stanoczk began to guide her.

"I've heard words spoken about it here and there, Specialist. Burkhayden, wasn't it?"

There was nothing unusual about Stanoczk already knowing. The intelligence community exploited its contacts with the Malcontent and others of its ilk, fully aware that it was being exploited right back. "Yes, that's right."

As they drew nearer Jils could see that the pavilion stood at the side of an ornamental stream, and that there were people in it. Three people not in uniform; the other three people there would be guards or servants, then. On the far side of the little stream there were musicians sitting in the shade of a large willowy tree, playing stringed instruments. The Dolgorukij plucked-lute, Jils suspected.

"Is it that you are concerned about him, Specialist? It seemed to me that Garol Aphon was more likely than even the average Bench intelligence specialist to be fully capable of taking care of himself. If I may say so to you, without giving offense."

No. She knew what he meant. Garol was professional. Some Bench specialists lost their edge over time. Garol's was one of those edges which might look dull, but if you made the mistake of presuming upon it you'd never even feel the slice as your head rolled one way and your body fell the other.

The people in the pavilion were waiting for them. One of them was seated—a young woman. The two other nonservants there were older than the young woman; that meant she had rank, whoever she was, to be sitting while her elders stood.

The Autocrat's Proxy. The Combine certainly meant to extend every courtesy to Chilleau Judiciary.

"He may have been working on something, Cousin." Jils slowed her steps, both to collect her thoughts and to finish this one. She hadn't anticipated being brought before the Autocrat's Proxy, not so soon. Did she know who those other people were? Had she seen them some-where before? "Nobody knows."

Some Bench specialist was always supposed to know what another was doing. Not all of what the other was doing; not always the same Bench specialist. But some-body was always supposed to know. It was just common sense. And nobody knew about Garol. Or else nobody was willing to say.

"So Vogel is in more deeply to his investigation than imaginable, or is perhaps simply either dead or dis-appeared?"

She'd thought about that. Dead she couldn't really believe. Accidents happened to everybody. But Vogel took a lot of killing; it wasn't as though it hadn't been tried before, on more than one occasion, and sometimes with a very great deal of enthusiasm indeed. "Call me sentimental. But I think he'd find a way to let me know if he decided to disappear."

They weren't going to be able to keep the pavilion party waiting. Stanoczk quickened his pace, but it was subtly done, not in the least bit obvious. "Let me put it to my Patron, Specialist, may he wander in bliss forever. Because for now it is my duty, as well as my pleasure, to bring you into the presence of the Autocrat's Proxy, who will receive your credentials in a while."

He had Jils worried for a moment, the quick moment between "receive your credentials" and "in a while." Her credentials were in her box, along with her dress uniform. The young woman who sat waiting for her was not in court dress, however, but in a pretty if rather plain long dress with loosely pleated sleeves and a wide skirt.

Jils climbed the few stone steps into the shade of the pavilion. There was a charcoal warmer sunk into the floor on one side, Jils noticed; welcome, because it was cool in the shadows. The others were a man and a woman, similarly not in court dress, but more formally attired than the young woman; Jils hadn't quite placed them yet.

She bowed politely, saluting the Dolgorukij Combine in the presence of this Autocrat's Proxy. There were eight Proxies in all, young people of the very best fami-lies who would spend twenty years in diplomatic service.

This one looked younger than most, but very self-assured regardless.

"On behalf of the First Secretary at Chilleau Judiciary," Jils said, "I present the greetings of the Second Judge. I am Bench intelligence specialist Jils Ivers, Proxima. Thank you for receiving me like this."

She wasn't exactly here on behalf of the Second Judge, but it was a signal honor to be thus presented informally. The least Jils could do was give the gesture as much weight as possible in return.

The young woman smiled, and waved for a chair. "Very welcome, Specialist Ivers. We will have the ritual later to repeat, I'm afraid. But we have been advised of your desire to make to my brother presentations, and I wondered, have you our mutual parents met?"

Jils stared, genuinely startled. Her brother?

How could she not have realized that this was Zsuzsa Ulexeievna Koscuisko?

She'd never met Koscuisko's parents. She'd only seen the records, stills and clips, and those were always formal presentations. She sat down.

"Haven't had the pleasure." Now that she'd sat down the others did, too: Koscuisko's mother and Koscuisko's father, the Koscuisko prince himself. Cousin Stanoczk was nowhere to be seen. Malcontents were like that, Jils supposed.

"My lord father is Alexie Slijanevitch, and my lady mother is Ossipia Carvataja. We are all wondering. Andrej comes home, it is the first time in years. You have seen him in Burkhayden where all the officers were being murdered. How does he? My brother."

Nothing like his father, that was how Andrej Koscuisko was, because his father was a tall man with black eyes and a magnificent beard. Koscuisko had no beard. He appeared to take after his mother's side of the family, because she was slim, though she was tall as well. Oh, there was no telling. What good did it do to look for people in their parents' faces?

"I'm not sure what to say, Proxima," Jils began cautiously. "Senior officer, well respected, popular with bond-involuntaries. That's a little unusual, by the way. What else can I tell you?"

The Autocrat's Proxy gave a little impatient bounce in her chair where she sat. "Oh, but he has not in all this time come home, and now. And does he speak of his family. And has he been happy in Fleet."

"My daughter does not say one thing, because she is a devout and filial daughter," Koscuisko's mother said, before Jils could formulate a response. Koscuisko's mother had a beautiful voice, rich and deep and calming to listen to. "But my son does not often write. And with his parents quarreled, when he last left, so that we find ourselves anxious. If he will not ask to be forgiven, what shall we do? So of his state of mind and temperament we seek such information as you may be able to give to us, trusting in your discretion. Even though you are a stranger. It is not worthwhile to be too proud, when it has been this long."

Her son Andrej was not filial.

Her son Andrej had quarreled with his father bitterly, and yet had been unable to convince or to prevail; had gone to Fleet Orientation Station Medical in obedience to his father's will after all, and had learned there that he was not merely exceptional in the art of torture, but enjoyed it.

The damage had already been done before Koscuisko had left Azanry. Now his family sought a strategy for reintegrating the oldest male child into his family, not knowing what Koscuisko's own attitude was going to be.

Jils didn't think Koscuisko was going to beg to be forgiven for not having wanted to go to Fleet Orientation Station Medical. Was there a way for her to get across to these three essentially sheltered people the enormity of the burden that the Bench laid across the shoulders of a thinking, feeling creature when it issued the Writ to Inquire?

It had been her errand that had caused Koscuisko to resubmit to Fleet, when he had been planning to go home. She was under obligation, in a sense. "The Bench owes more deep a debt to your son than it can readily repay, your Excellency. Excusing your presence, Proxima, I would ask that you make allowances for how much the Bench has asked from him."

Koscuisko was unlikely to ask forgiveness for anything. Koscuisko had a stubborn streak, from all Jils had studied of him, and eight-plus years in Secured Medical had only strengthened the native autocracy of his character. "There is no harder task than that to which the Bench has put your brother and your son, and he has done his Judicial duty thoroughly and well—"

If she could sweeten Koscuisko's path back to his home, it was only what was owed the man for what she'd done to him, when she had forced him back to Captain Lowden.

The courier ship *Magdalenja* was halfway between Pesadie time and the Aznir mean standard—toward the end of the day by any measure. It was late in third shift, maybe even shading into fourth by now; and Security Chief Stildyne sat in Koscuisko's cabin, smoking one of Koscuisko's lefrols and beating his officer of assignment at cards.

Koscuisko set a "hemless" playing token down across his last remaining single-loom sheet and shook the dice. " 'She was bereft and wandered on the sere hillside with none but one last lambling to console her,' " Koscuisko quoted, but it did him no good. The dice fell Stildyne's way, two "kerchiefs" and three "napkins." It would take at least a "double apron" to match Stildyne's hand. Koscuisko was doomed. Yet again. Koscuisko slumped against the padded back of the chair and shook his head.

Now it was Stildyne's turn to quote. " 'The sun rose' . . . ah . . . 'in beauty like the maiden of the middle way as Dasidar in glory rode home to claim Dyraine.' Three goslings, your Excellency, that's the rest of the maintenance atmosphere you owe me, as well as the Engineering bridge."

Koscuisko scowled, but it wasn't serious. "I have never in fact spoken to Wheatfields about wagering either, Chief, so I suppose it's just as well. How is Lek doing?"

Reaching for the tokens, Stildyne started to tidy up the board. Three games was about his limit. He had only started to read the old saga of Dasidar and Dyraine a year or two past, in order to be able to distract Koscuisko by playing cards with him. He didn't have Koscuisko's command of the couplets.

"You might want to remind yourself that he's already thirteen." Lek's Bond was that old, that was to say; Lek had survived as a bond-involuntary for that long. Koscuisko called his troops by their first names. He had never called Stildyne anything but Chief or Mister.

Koscuisko knew his name. Stildyne was in no doubt of that, but his officer of assignment had never forgiven him for having once made a mistake, not even after all these years. Stildyne was almost through being bitter about it. "He hasn't lived this long by borrowing trouble. And he's been told that the Captain ordered the substitution to keep Fleet from trying to queer the performance scores."

"So long as Lek believes it, we have no worries. Yes. And the others will look out for him." Koscuisko sounded uncertain, worried. Koscuisko liked to fret. After what had happened to Robert St. Clare at Port Burkhayden, Stildyne couldn't blame Koscuisko for worrying; a governor gone terminal meant unimaginable torment and near-certain death for a bond-involuntary. Koscuisko still didn't know exactly what had pushed Robert's governor over the edge that night, and Stildyne had no intention of ever telling him.

"No, Andrej, Lek doesn't have to believe it. He only has to focus on the fact that he's been instructed to believe it."

There was a moment's pause as Koscuisko thought about whether he was going to take exception to Stildyne's use of his personal name.

It was true that Stildyne permitted himself that degree of intimacy only rarely. But also true that Stildyne and Koscuisko alike were sitting at the table with their collars undone, and Koscuisko in rest-dress was as casual as Koscuisko ever got when he was sober: the full dark pleated skirtlike trousers, with the stiffened half-moon of starched fabric at the small of Koscuisko's back; the very full blouse wrapped closed across Koscuisko's chest; the wrist-ties left untied; and the white padding-socks on Koscuisko's feet, with the big toe gloved separately.

When Koscuisko raised his hand to push his blond hair up off his forehead, his blouse shifted to show his collarbones: and Stildyne bit the inside of his cheek to stifle his sigh of resigned and impotent desire, concentrating on packing tokens into the box. Linen-markers. This one for a hemless garment, this one for a seamless garment, this one for a single-loomed sheet of fabric, this one for this manner of embroidery and this one for that manner of embroidery, and so on.

It was a good game to play with Koscuisko. It took concentration. While Stildyne was playing cards with Andrej Koscuisko he could almost forget all about the fact that he could never have the man.

"As you say, Chief," Koscuisko agreed, finally. "Chief" was more intimate and friendly than "Mister." Koscuisko didn't reject Stildyne's advances; he simply declined to respond to them: "When we get home, I mean to call for a Malcontent. I'd rather not have to rely on just Lek's discipline to keep him safe."

It was what Koscuisko's Security did their best to do—keep Koscuisko safe. Safe from himself; safe from the sick fantasies of his dreaming mind. Before Koscuisko had come to the *Ragnarok* it had not been so bad for him. Robert had told Stildyne that. Koscuisko's former Captain had kept Koscuisko clear of Inquiry as much as possible—not from any misguided sense of decency that anyone would own to, but from simple practicality.

Perhaps the distaste commonly shared by military professionals for subjecting prisoners to torture had had something to do with it after all, but Captain Lowden had never had any such misgivings or reservations, and it took more than just Robert St. Clare to handle Koscuisko in the depths of a self-punitive drunk after yet another of Lowden's all-too-frequent exercises.

Four years of conspiracy between bonded and unbonded and Chief Warrant Officer Stildyne alike, trying to keep Koscuisko from the abyss of horror. It was no wonder that Koscuisko took such good care of his people. That wasn't the reason Koscuisko did it, though. It was effect and cause more than cause and effect.

"Malcontents have Safes, your Excellency?" This was an intriguing concept, and called for increased formality. Safes fed a signal to the governor in a bond-involuntary's brain and silenced it for as long as the Safe was within range. They were very carefully controlled by Fleet and

the Bench accordingly, because what would become of
the deterrent power of the Bond if it could be gotten
around without official sanction?

"If there is any way to obtain one, it is a Malcontent
who could accomplish the task," Koscuisko said; and
yawned. "Thank you for your company, Mister Stildyne,
I imagine I am ready to nap, now."

Stildyne closed the board around the box of tokens,
and stood up. "My pleasure, sir. We'll play for the labs
next time, maybe."

Smiling, Koscuisko waved a hand in friendly dismissal.
Stildyne didn't want to go.

He wanted to stay, to help Koscuisko out of his rest-
dress, to help Koscuisko into his sleep shirt, to put Koscuisko chastely to bed—all things that were permitted to
him when Koscuisko was drunk enough. When the fact
of Koscuisko's incapacity made the very idea of taking
advantage of it intolerable. It was Koscuisko's fault. Before Koscuisko, he would not have thought twice about
taking what he wanted so long as he was strong enough
to get away with it.

Koscuisko had ruined him. Life had been so much less
complicated before Koscuisko had come into it.

Stildyne let himself out and closed the door behind
him, nodding to Murat, whose turn it was to sit the night
watch. Murat knew. They all knew. " 'Night, Chief,"
Murat said.

In their own way they all took care of him as well as
of Koscuisko, so that they made a tidy little fraternal
community, Koscuisko taking care of Security who took
care of Koscuisko.

Was it worth it, to trade the easy and immediate gratification of physical desire as it arose for membership
in such a community, when all it cost was the pain of
unexpressed and unrequited passion?

"Have a good watch, Murat."

He had alternatives, Stildyne knew. And no intention
of exploring them. He went down the corridor to his
berth, thinking about how soon they could expect to
make planetfall on Azanry.

Chapter Four

Family Matters

Great *Ragnarok* had been built according to the plan of a cruiserkiller warship—carapace hull above, docking facilities below—opening onto the maintenance atmosphere that clung to the belly of the ship, contained by a plasma field. General Rukota braced himself as his courier approached the boundaries. There was a peculiar sensory effect associated with passing the plasma containment membrane from space into atmosphere; it made his skin crawl. He had never gotten used to it.

"Eleven eights to docking, General." The navigator was one of Admiral Brecinn's people, but carried more rank on her shoulders than a navigator usually bore. All of the team were relatively senior for their roles; it increased his suspicion that these people were committed to some ulterior purpose. Rukota didn't like it. "Thank you, Navigator. Send the request and stand by."

Yes, it was gratifying to a man's ego to be giving orders to people more accustomed to giving their own than taking anybody's. Still, ego gratification only went so far with Dierryk Rukota. No man as ugly as he had been all of his life could afford to nurture too much ego. Every time he caught sight of himself in a mirror, it reminded him. But so long as his wife didn't care, it made no difference if his mouth was as thin as the edge of a dull knife and his eyes nearly as narrow, to speak of only two of the most obviously unfortunate aspects of his face.

"Clearance is logged, General. We're expected. Well. We'll just have to hope that the evidence hasn't been compromised already."

What made the navigator suppose that there was evidence to be compromised in the first place?

Did she expect him not to realize that the mission upon which he had been sent was at least as likely, if not certain, to compromise evidence—if it was not actually bent on fabricating evidence that did not exist?

Rukota couldn't decide how best to answer, and therefore decided not to. He was technically in command of this mission. He didn't have to make nice with anybody.

The courier cleared the maintenance atmosphere with the familiar and unpleasant feeling of insects tunneling through his joints. Rukota concentrated on what the screens showed, to distract himself from his discomfort.

The entire working area of the *Ragnarok*'s underbelly lay open to the maintenance atmosphere, with the plates that would hull over the ship for vector transit stacked into a solid wall fore and aft. There wasn't much activity: some tenders, one craft in freefloat with its crew on EVA, their umbilicus tethers glinting in the powerful illumination from the *Ragnarok*'s docks.

Their destination was a slot in the hull of the ship, an envelope of stalloy big enough to park the Captain's shallop—her personal courier—in. As the navigator maneuvered toward the slip Rukota thought he caught sight of a familiar figure in the basket of a crane near the entrance to their docking bay.

Short person. Stocky. Hair smoothed back severely across a rounded skull typical of a class-three Auringer hominid, but if it was who he thought it was she had six digits on either hand, and that meant Versanjer instead. He'd thought it through one day a few months ago when he'd been in a particularly bad mood.

Twenty-seven years ago the Bench had put down a bloody revolt at Versanjer. The slaughter had been horrific. And the vengeance of the Bench had not stopped at the execution of most of the adult population; the Bench had taken the children as well. Put them into crèche. Raised them to serve the Bench with fanatical devotion, making of the daughters and sons of dead rebels paragons of everything against which the insurrectionaries had rebelled.

The navigator brought the ship into the bay, and the tow drones took control to complete the landing sequence. Rukota decided that he needed some air. Following the system engineer up through the topside observer's station Rukota straightened carefully, standing on top of the courier's back.

Something fell past the mouth of the docking slip, something big and black and silent.

"Oh, no," the system engineer said, as if someone had asked her a question. "I don't deal with those things. All yours, General."

She scurried back down into the body of the courier with unseemly and ungraceful haste. Rukota looked at the now-closed hatch for a moment, thinking about it; then he threw the catch with the toe of his boot, securing the hatch from the outside. Let the crew wait for the inorganic quarantine scans to cycle through before they left the ship. It would serve them right for abandoning him to a Desmodontae.

Something else was coming toward the mouth of the docking slip, but Rukota had an idea that he knew what this was. The crane. The basket came down across the mouth of the docking slip slowly, then slid carefully into the bay itself until it rested level with Rukota where he stood.

Jennet ap Rhiannon opened the security cage's gate and beckoned him in with a wave of her hand. "General Rukota. A pleasure to see you."

If she said so. He couldn't say the same for her, and if he had been in her place he would consider his mission to be about as welcome as the tax collector the morning after an unreported gambling coup. Rukota stepped into the basket without comment, and ap Rhiannon moved the crane out and away from the docking slip.

He could see the Desmodontae now. A great black web-winged creature out of a horror story, a giant bat, subsisting on plasma broths that replaced its native diet of hominid blood. The *Ragnarok*'s Intelligence Officer. One of the very few non-hominids with rank in all of the Jurisdiction's Fleet, her presence here on the *Rag-*

narok part and parcel of Fleet's confusion over what to do with her and what to do with the ship itself.

His wife said that Two had something on somebody, but that nobody had ever been able to decide if Two realized it or not.

"To what do I owe the honor of this meeting?" Rukota asked, watching Two carefully as she executed her aerial maneuvers. It was probably difficult for her to be confined on shipboard, rank or no rank. Rukota supposed he himself would grasp any opportunity to fly if he had been a bat.

"We'll have a formal in-briefing later on, of course," ap Rhiannon assured him. "I was surprised to hear you'd accepted the assignment, General. I'm sorry. We don't have anything for you."

Of course she didn't. What else could she be expected to claim? "Brecinn thought I'd be an impartial observer." Or a cooperative patsy. Maybe that. "Second Fleet doesn't have much work for me just now. So here I am. Don't get any ideas, Lieutenant."

There had been awkwardness, during their earlier assignment together. The gossip about Rukota's wife was widespread. Ap Rhiannon had apparently become intrigued by him, if for no other reason Rukota could guess than sheer contrariness. He had had to remind her that he was her superior officer.

Now she was the acting Captain of the *Ragnarok*, and technically outside his chain of command. Was he going to have to defend his virtue?

The Desmodontae was coming at them in full soar, gliding by very close overhead. Talking to herself, evidently, from the vibration Rukota felt in the buttons on his blouse. Maybe it was just her echolocation. Either way he wished she would stop it.

"Have you met my Intelligence Officer?" ap Rhiannon asked. Two did a spin and roll, landing on the arm of the crane and stopping abruptly. It was unnatural, that sudden absolute stop. Rukota held on to the railing. He didn't like Desmodontae. They made him nervous.

Crawling up the crane's arm to the basket Two climbed over the rim to hop down into the security cage, smiling up at Rukota cheerfully. It looked like a smile, at least; her mouth was open and the corners of her lips curled up in her face. Rukota could see her very white, very sharp teeth, set off to dazzling perfection by the black velvet of her pelt.

"Pleased," Two said. Her translator had no accent, but Rukota suddenly thought about the farce stereotype of the Briadie matron, all flamboyant hand gestures and shrill nasal tones and insatiable nosiness. "Rukota General. Seventeen thousand saved at Ichimar, and casualties held at less than one in four sixty-fours. Very impressive."

And a long time ago, but it was kind of her to mention it. "Very gracious, your Excellency. What's your take on all of this, if I may ask, ma'am?"

Ap Rhiannon seemed clearly intent on controlling the investigation from the beginning. He could appreciate that. It was her natural right as the acting Captain of this ship. If she was going to give him access to her Intelligence Officer, though, he was going to take advantage of it.

"We have nothing to give or take," Two assured him, happily. "But don't take my word on it. Take your time. Enjoy your investigation. The food is not good, by report, and accommodation cannot be said to be luxurious, but what is ours is yours."

Ap Rhiannon was not so happy as Two seemed about it all. "I'll tell you what *I* think, General. I think Pesadie wants to find someone here on board of the *Ragnarok* at fault for that explosion. The plain fact that it's incredible is not enough to stop some people. I won't have it."

There wasn't anything he could say in response to this, because she was right on all counts. "Then the audit will show that you're clean, Lieutenant. And we'll be out of your way in no time."

He hadn't convinced her. No surprise there. He hadn't sounded convincing to himself. "We've already done one assessment, General, ammunition, equipment calibration, electromagnetic emissions. Everything. Unexceptional on all vectors. So what? If evidence is not found, it can be created."

Yes. That was the way it was. "So Fleet will run a few tests, and ask a few questions. You could lose a troop or six. That's the way it goes, Lieutenant. There's a Command Branch officer dead, and there has to be an explanation somewhere."

"Pesadie can just find its explanations at its own expense. I have no intention of throwing a single life into Fleet's maw, Command Branch or no Command Branch. These are my crew now, General, for howsoever short a time, and I will defend them. Are we clear?"

Two shifted her wings with an embarrassed sort of a shrugging gesture as ap Rhiannon spoke, and it was all Rukota could do not to jump.

"I'm just here to take the baseline, Lieutenant." Yes, they both knew how easy it was to fake a baseline. But if she'd learned anything at all about him during their previous acquaintance, she would know that he didn't play games. "It doesn't matter to me one way or the other. If there's nothing here, that's what I'll tell Brecinn. If there's something here, you'll see it before she does. Can we just agree on that?"

So that he could get out of this crane basket, and away from the *Ragnarok*'s Intelligence Officer. He was probably sweating.

Ap Rhiannon glanced up into his face for a moment before she nodded, finally. "Very well, General. Welcome aboard."

Oh, absolutely. A hostile Captain and suspicious crew to one side of him, a team he mistrusted—and whom he suspected of having their own agenda—to the other: just his idea of a welcoming environment.

"Thank you, Lieutenant." Technically she was an Excellency, he supposed. But she'd been his subordinate officer, once upon a time before, and he didn't know quite how to relate to her as anything else. What did it matter if he antagonized her? She wasn't happy about any of this anyway. "Pleased to be here. Well. Actually, no. But we'll do our best with what we've got."

With luck, he wouldn't have to spend too much time with the Intelligence Officer.

But, with luck, he wouldn't have been here in the first place; so Rukota sighed and resigned himself to the fact that he was going to have an opportunity to grapple with his fears, and climbed back out of the crane basket—

when ap Rhiannon returned him to the docking slip—
to open the hatch in the top of the courier and let his
team come out.

Cousin Ferinc stood in the young master's schoolroom
with Anton Andreievitch in his arms, looking out the
tall window across the courtyard to the old wall and the
river beyond.

"There, now, that's better," he said encouragingly, as
Anton rubbed his nose and wiped his eyes. In that order,
unfortunately, but there were limits about what could be
expected of an eight-year-old—even one so self-possessed
as Anton Andreievitch Koscuisko. "Here's Nurse, young
master, time for your bath. You can tell me all about it
when I get back, but be good and don't fuss, or I shan't
bring you a wheat-fish from Dubrovnije."

Anton's bright blue eyes widened. "I shall be very
good," he assured Ferinc, solemnly. "And shan't fuss at
all. I promise."

He always kept his promises, too; at least, as well as
a child with the handicap of a developing attention span
to contend with could manage it. He was like his father
that way.

Ferinc put the child down. "Good man. Go along, I'll
just speak to the Respected Lady, and I'll see you in a
few days. Don't forget. I'll bring you a wheat-fish."

He usually tried not to think about Anton's father.
Over the years it had become easier than he would have
imagined not to think about Anton's father. He still had
dreams, but Cousin Stanoczk had reconciled him to that.
Cousin Stanoczk was not Anton's father. But he did look
a very great deal like the man, especially in the dark of
a dimly lit cell.

Ferinc watched Anton Andreievitch out of the room,
smiling gently to himself: Anton was such a little man.

Anton Andreievitch's mother spoke from behind him,
and called his attention back to where he was. "And for
me, Cousin." It was a word for *cousin* that she used only
seldom, and never except when they were alone. "What
will you bring me from Dubrovnije if I am very good,
and do not fuss?"

There was tension in her voice, and not a little bitter-

ness. But there was to be no help for it. Andrej Koscuisko could not find him at the Matredonat. It would
ruin everything.

"Surely the Respected Lady has nothing to fear," Ferinc said with tender assurance, turning to face her.
"What is it, Marana? Tell your Cousin Ferinc all."

She smiled bravely at his teasing, reaching out for him,
drawing him to her by pulling at the braids that he wore
to each side of his face to keep his hair out of his eyes.
Malcontents alone of all Dolgorukij men wore their hair
long; at least some of them did, and Ferinc had let his
hair grow as part of his way of separating himself from
his former self. There were drawbacks. This was one
of them.

"I have not seen Andrej for more than nine years,
Ferinc. Nine years. And yet he is the master of this
house, lord of the Matredonat, and all that is in it."

Master of her body, at least in principle. That was the
traditional understanding of her position here, at any
rate.

"It will probably be a little awkward. Yes." He had
his arms around her now, and the trusting warmth of
her body against his was familiar and comforting. She
was tall for a Dolgorukij woman. But he was taller. He
was not Dolgorukij, either. "Nothing I have ever heard
of thy lord would make him out to be a man to impose
himself on a lady's privacy. He is probably as nervous
as you are; consider, you know I'm right."

She raised her head and looked up at him sharply. It
couldn't be that she had misunderstood him; they were
speaking of Koscuisko in his capacity as a normal social
creature. Not as Inquisitor. "But I'm not a lady, Ferinc,
I'm a gentlewoman of yes-all-right-passable breeding—
but poor judgment—who bespoke a child from a betrothed man before his sacred wife had been bred to his
body. There are far simpler ways to say just what I am.
You know them."

Willful misunderstanding was to be his tactic, Ferinc decided. "Yes. Among them beautiful. Devoted. Precious beyond price. The hearth-mistress of the Matredonat—"

No, none of those were the words she had had in
mind, and she pushed him away from her with a smile.

" 'In the mouth of the Malcontent, excrement is honey.' You will be gone for how long, Cousin?"

Not so quickly as that, Ferinc decided, and closed the distance between them to embrace her. "Would I dare to kiss you," he asked; and did so, carefully, gently, thoroughly, "if that were true? Be fair, Marana."

She made a face at him, her hands at the back of his head, smoothing the long hair that fell unbraided down his back. "Lefrols, then, and it is very much the same thing if you would like to know my opinion. Answer the question."

"Three weeks, maybe longer, Respected Lady. I don't know for certain. I won't know until Cousin Stanoczk tells me, and he hasn't yet." Koscuisko would be home for at least that long. Anton would be reconciled to Ferinc's temporary absence after a day or two, and then six weeks would seem no longer than three to him. Marana was not likely to be as understanding, but there was nothing that Ferinc could do about that.

He was not going to Dubrovnije. But that was nobody's business but the Malcontent's. He would have to send for a wheat-fish for Anton Andreievitch.

"Think of me while you are gone, Cousin." Marana stepped away from him and back into her status; one almost saw the power descend upon her shoulders like a shawl. "Yes. I'm nervous. It's beastly of you to leave me now. But one does not expect decency from Malcontents."

She was not actually angry at him. If she knew what duty called him away from her, she would be. She would be more than angry. She would be horrified and betrayed, and would quite possibly refuse to so much as see him again, ever again.

She was right about one thing at least, though. It was nobody's business but the Malcontent's. It could be true that Mergau Noycannir at Chilleau Judiciary had no good reason to know Andrej Koscuisko's exact whereabouts: but the Saint had accepted the bargain she'd offered, and would fulfill its side of the contract. It was one way to be sure that they knew what she was up to, after all.

"The peace of the Malcontent be with you, Respected Lady. I will think of you. Depend upon it."

She was to be Koscuisko's wife, though she didn't know it yet. Ferinc was not sure she would still be his lover when he returned. "The Holy Mother has ordained that women need not bless your divine Patron. So I will say only good-bye, Ferinc."

It was in the hands of the Holy Mother. In whom he did not believe, but it would be imprudent to remind his Patron's goddess of that. "I'll be back to see you in a few weeks, Respected Lady. You have the home advantage with your lord; he is almost a stranger here. You will manage beautifully."

Women were absolved from blessing the name of the Malcontent; Malcontents, from begging leave, as from most—if not all—of the otherwise common rites of ordinary life. Ferinc left Marana in the nursery and went down the hall to make his way out to the motor stables. There was a ground-car waiting.

Marana, in the embrace of her lord, soon to become her husband as well as her master. Marana, in Koscuisko's bed—

He had to get out to the airfield in time to find his covert. He would simply have to submit the whole problem to Cousin Stanoczk, the next chance that he got to be reconciled.

Andrej Koscuisko stood behind Lek as the courier made its final approach to Jelchick Field.

The *Magdalenja* had made atmosphere, dropped out of space into stratosphere, several hours ago; it had shed the thermal load acquired in its re-entry over long, slow, high-altitude orbit, and it was ready to make planetfall in fact.

"We have for the final approach your clearance codes, *Magdalenja*. Stand by."

The Standard was precise and uninflected, but the syntax was Dolgorukij. Andrej watched the long hills, the great broad course of the river Trijan, the black-green slopes of the spacious game preserve with its old forest scroll beneath the hull of the courier: home.

There were veserts upon veserts of fields in grain, still green and silvery in the sun; it was yet midway into the growing season, and Jan Seed-of-Life had only begun to show the long black beard that marked him for a man and ripe for slaughter. Well, for harvest, but harvest was slaughter, and tradition required it be approached with reverence and care.

"Thank you, Jelchick. Final approach. Beacon scan initiated."

In all of the years that he had known Lek Kerenko, Andrej didn't think he had even once noticed that he had an accent. The blood of his ancestors in the fields below reached out to him, cried out to him—corrupted him. Lek sounded Sarvaw to him, and Andrej shuddered to hear it. If he could think such a thing—he, who owed so much to Lek for openhearted charity—if he could think the word with scorn, how could he hope to keep Lek from shame at the Matredonat?

The courier slowed perceptibly moment by moment, falling fast. Jelchick Field took a sudden approach, but it had been the most suitable airfield—the one closest to home. Andrej was not going to Rogubarachno, the ancient house in the plains of Refour where he had been born; only later would he travel to Chelatring Side in the mountains, to attend to political business with his family.

They were for the Matredonat, an estate that belonged to him personally in his capacity as the son of the Koscuisko prince, the place where he kept Marana and his child. They were going there first. It had been negotiated. It had been agreed. So why were there riders in array at the very edge of the airfield, a hunting party, and one rider on horseback sitting apart from the rest?

"Send a security query, Chief," Andrej suggested. He would not send the question himself. Let Stildyne do it. "Find us out who those people are. The airfield is secured. I want to know." He needed all the advance warning he could get, if they were who he suspected they might be.

Stildyne stepped away from beside Andrej without comment as Lek drew the courier into its final descent. Andrej could see the emergency equipment drawn up alongside the end of the travel-path, could hear Lek talking to the traffic control center; but had eyes only for those people well out of range of the courier's engines, waiting.

If he did not take care, Andrej told himself, he would convince himself that he recognized that one tall rider. And that was clearly impossible. He had not so much as seen his father in almost nine years.

Stildyne had returned. "Says it's the landlord, your Excellency," Stildyne said. "At least that's what I think they said."

"'Master of field and grain, river and mountain'? Is that what they said?"

Stildyne didn't so much nod, but merely lowered his head in confirmation. "So what does it mean, sir?"

Closing his eyes for one brief moment of frustrated fury Andrej swore, "All Saints in debauch. My father, Chief. Probably my mother. Doubtless at least the youngest of my brothers, but it was not what we had planned. I'm not prepared for this."

It was far too late to tell Lek to abort the landing, and break space again. Nor would it have been fair if he'd let himself be forced so far as that. He wanted to meet his son.

"His Excellency presents his compliments," Stildyne said, as if it was a question. "And regrets that an unfortunate desire to see you all in Hell prevents his meeting with you at this particular time or any in the foreseeable near future?"

As angry as Andrej was, he had to laugh. "Someone has corrupted you, Chief. You sound like a house-master in a bad mood. No. There is to be no help for it, and everybody knows that the prince my father left me with no choice when he elected to attend this event. I will have to go and kneel and beg for blessing."

The courier had come to a complete halt, the ventilators equalizing atmosphere. Andrej took a deep breath to calm himself. He almost believed that he could smell the hot dust of the grainlands in the summer. "When we approach them, hold the team at the same remove as my father's house-master will be standing, with my father's mount."

"We brought smoke, your Excellency." Lek surprised

Andrej by speaking up, and Murat beside him took up the skein in braid.

"We wouldn't even use irritant fog. Just smoke."

"Lay down a good field," Smath added. "Run for it. Evasive action. Just to keep in practice, sir. Just say the word."

They were so good to him. Or perhaps they simply preferred not to start a vacation with their officer of assignment in a filthy temper: so one way or another he owed it to them to face up to the coming ordeal like a man, and get it over with.

"Thank you, gentles, but the word must be 'no.' I will go and speak to my father. You may watch if you like. You will not see many Dolgorukij so tall as he is."

Meka had inherited all of their father's height, and their father's beautiful great black beard as well. Neither Lo nor Iosev nor Andrej himself stood any more near such height than the shoulder to the head. There was no telling about Nikosha, who had been a child; but even so, Nikosha seemed to take after their mother for his frame and his physique.

The ground crew had arrived. Andrej could hear Taller making the required polite conversation. A moment or two, and the passenger ramp descended, opening the side of the courier to the sight of late morning and the faint but unmistakable fragrance of sirav in bloom.

The perfume of the weeds of the country seized Andrej's brain like a drug. He could not bear to stay inside the courier breathing Standard air for one moment longer. He had to get out. Even though it meant he would have to go and confront his father, he had to get out and breathe the air, feel the pull of his own earth, the caress of the warmth of his own sun.

Nine years.

He had spent years at school on Mayon before he had gone to Fleet; he had had difficulty with Mayon's gravity as well. Off. Ever so slightly off. It had taken weeks for the uneasiness in his stomach to settle, but he had been away from home too long, and now he felt the landsickness in his stomach all over again.

It was probably just nerves.

Out there in the near distance the hunting party was moving in bits and pieces, reacting to the appearance of the courier's passengers and crew. It would be over all the sooner, and the more quickly, he engaged; therefore Andrej waited until Murat had finished his post-flight checks and spoke.

"If you please, Mister Stildyne."

He was an officer under escort, his uniform a stark contrast to the hunting costume that his father wore. Men in their family did not wear black boots in the summertime, nor boots of hard leather of any color unless they were at court or at war. The blouse of the trousers was not creased unless one's housekeeper were clumsy, stupid, incompetent, or insolent; no man of rank would fail to wear a broad belt over his jacket, from which to hang a pouch of this or a string of that. All in all, he was quite possibly as alien to them as Andrej's father and his people were to Security 5.1.

Climbing into the waiting ground-car Andrej nodded to Taller, who had taken the driver's seat. Taller knew quite well that they were taking a detour on their way to traffic control. Once Smath had hopped on board with the last of the luggage Taller headed out for the far side of the airfield, where the hunting party was gathered just to the near side of the security fence.

When the distance had shrunk to eighty paces or so Andrej stopped Taller with a gesture, and Taller secured the vehicle's drive before joining the rest of the team on the ground.

His people formed up in the standard square around him with the efficiency of long practice and the ease of clear, if unspoken, communication. Andrej started through the long grass toward the hunting party, and three riders came down from the little rise that the hunting party had invested to meet him partway.

When they had closed one quarter of the distance Andrej's father dismounted. So of course the escort dismounted as well, one of them taking the reins of Andrej's father's horse.

One half of the distance, and the two men who had accompanied Andrej's father stopped. Andrej didn't hear any word from Stildyne, but *his* people stopped too, Taller and Lek each taking a step to either side to give Andrej clear passage between them.

When Andrej was close enough to see his father's face, close enough to meet an outstretched hand, he stopped and stood and waited for his father's word. Looking up into his father's worried blue eyes Andrej wondered what there was that he could say, what there was that he could do. He knew the obvious answer: he was to kneel and beg his father's blessing. But it was not as simple as that.

This man was his father, and loved him, drinking in his face with an expression of fond thirst.

And yet Andrej's knees could not be convinced that they should bend. His father, yes, but also the man who had sent him into Hell nine years ago and demanded that he abide there, the man who—once all had been said and done at the Domitt Prison—had rebuked him for unfilial behavior in having challenged Chilleau Judiciary in so public a forum. The man whose acceptance of Chilleau's persuasions had left Andrej with no other escape from a servitude more horrible than even that which he had endured under Captain Lowden's command than to submit himself to Fleet for four years more.

At the same time, this man had not truly done much of what Andrej found to blame. His father had been an officer in mere Security, and at a time when Inquiry had been informal and field expedient, bearing no discernable relation to the Protocols in their current form. His father could have no conception of what Andrej's life had been like with Captain Lowden as his commanding officer.

This was a Dolgorukij father in the presence of a wayward son, and as much as Andrej regretted the shape into which his father had forced his life, there was no sense in reproaching a man for what he had no idea that he had done.

In the end, it wasn't his father's fault at all.

He could at any point have turned his back and stepped away from duty and obedience that required he execute sin and practice atrocity. No one had forced him to his duty but his own will to be dutiful. He had not in all of this time turned his back and said *no*, because he had not had the courage to shame his father and distress his mother.

Was that truly adequate an excuse to cover the torture and murder of feeling creatures?

Having submitted to such crimes to keep the pride of his family from stain and reproach, was he now going to shame his father in front of so many of the household by refusing the basic duty of a child in the presence of its father?

It was the act of a coward to blame another for something that was not truly their fault but one's own.

Finally Andrej's knees began to bend. He lowered his head to show his father the white of the back of the neck above the collar. Maybe it had taken all these years for Andrej to grasp the idea that he did not have to be a filial son, but so long as he was here and had committed such horrors in the name of filial piety and the Judicial order, it would be mean-spirited of him to deny his father the respect that should naturally be between father and son.

It was not his father's fault.

His father reached out to him as Andrej started to kneel and prevented him from kneeling, drawing Andrej to him instead, to be embraced both gently and fiercely.

His father seemed to be weeping, and the notion sent Andrej into a panic that he didn't really understand. So many people he had hurt so far beyond the power of tears to express, or cries, or screaming. Why should one man's purely emotional grief distress him so?

"Please, sir."

His father relaxed his grip on Andrej the moment Andrej spoke, but he didn't let go of him. Andrej stood in his father's embrace in an agony of confusion and embarrassment; too much happening too quickly between heart and mind for Andrej to be able to make sense of it.

"Please, sir, don't distress yourself. I have been wayward and unfilial, but I am your child still." And yet he was going to go from here to the Matredonat, where he would once again defy his father and insult his mother by acting as though he were an autonomous person rather than somebody's child.

His father tightened his arms around Andrej one last time, then let him go. "And yet Cousin Stanoczk has hinted, son Andrej. You know that you cannot have my blessing for your intended actions."

What was worse, his father apparently knew what he meant to do. How had Cousin Stanoczk come by the knowledge?

Was there ever any knowing, with Malcontents?

He'd spoken to a priest on their way out of Port Burkhayden, in order to be sure of the correct and complete ritual. That was perfectly true. He just hadn't expected it to get back to his father, and for the Malcontent to have transmitted the information made Andrej wonder what the Malcontent had in mind.

"I am bound for four years more at least, sir, and my ship of assignment has only recently lost two of its officers, even though we are not actively engaged." One of whom he had himself murdered, but he wasn't going to trouble his father with that surely trivial piece of information. And he had no idea whether the death of Cowil Brem was public knowledge as yet. "I must think of my son."

"As I of mine." Well, the Koscuisko prince had more than one son, and they both knew that. But Andrej was the oldest of Alexie Slijanevitch's male children; that meant he counted for more than the rest of his brothers taken together. "And I have for too many years played Sanfijer to your Scathijin, son Andrej. I don't pretend that Scathijin did not bring the most part of his grief upon himself. But Sanfijer had no one but himself to reproach for the fact that he had not been more natural a parent."

Never, never, never had Andrej ever imagined that it could be possible for his father to say such a thing to him. The surprise betrayed him to himself, and the frustrated affection and aggrieved resentment of the years brought tears to his eyes.

"I do not ask for your forgiveness, sir, as I do not deserve it." He was become unfilial. He would remain so. His father forgave it, even before the fact. "But to have your forgiveness for my fault. It would be almost as good."

It was a fault only in the context of their culture. Andrej had just realized he was no longer fully part of it; but his family was. His son would be raised here on Azanry, and have to find a way to fit himself into the society to which Andrej had been bred and born. It seemed the traditions of his ancestors had power over him that he had not begun to suspect.

"I bless thee as my unfilial son Andrej," Alexie Slijanevitch said, very solemnly, but there was the unmistakable softness of a loving parental heart within and around the words. "That is to say, my child, who has been a man in the eyes of the greater government of this Jurisdiction for these years past. Your father's blessing on your misguided, ill-advised, self-willed, and all too clearly Koscuisko head, son Andrej, with a full heart I grant it."

Something inside Andrej's chest seemed to crack open, flooding his body with grateful warmth. He bowed over his father's hand to kiss the family seal that Alexie Slijanevitch wore on his right hand; and his father embraced him once again, and held him close for a long moment as Andrej struggled for control of his emotions.

"Now. I have already violated the terms of our agreement, son Andrej. We know you are on your way to the Matredonat." His father put Andrej away from him at arm's length and looked him in the eye, lovingly. "You will perhaps forgive us in turn for having wanted too badly just to see you. Go and kiss the hem of your mother's apron, and come to us at Chelatring Side when the Autocrat's Proxy arrives."

It was almost unfair.

He was to have his father's forgiveness and his mother's understanding after all, and it was all only now. Only now that he was under some mysterious and undefined sentence of death, only now that he had already made contract with Fleet for another four years.

If he had known that his father would have softened so much toward him as to be able to cite the story of the filial son wrongly accused—the tragedy of Scathijin

the Self-Minded—he might not have done it. He might
have come home and trusted his parents' change of heart
to keep him safe from the threat of Chilleau Judiciary.

With a full heart Andrej hurried through the tall grass
of the unmown verge between the pavement of the airfield and the perimeter to see his mother, his head too
full of wonder and amazement to have a thought to
spare for anything but the moment.

They were too far away to hear what was being said,
but what Stildyne could see was startling enough.

Koscuisko's father.

Stildyne had only negative associations with the concept. His own father was a man he'd hardly thought
twice about since the day he'd sworn to Fleet to get off-
planet and away before the local authorities started to
make inquiries. The chances of anybody really caring
who had killed Stildyne's father were vanishingly small,
and the pitiful remains of Stildyne's young sister were
no more grievous a motive in the world that he had left
than other wrongs his father had done.

He'd never embraced his father that he could ever
remember, and had successfully avoided other sorts of
physical contact from the day when he'd been old
enough to hit back. His younger sister hadn't had a
chance. She'd never gotten quick and clever enough to
escape. She hadn't lived long enough.

And here Koscuisko bowed to his father.

Was about to kneel, if Stildyne read Koscuisko's body
language correctly, and he had studied Koscuisko's body
language with care and keen attention for years now.
Koscuisko was embraced by his father, and bore it; then
bowed over his father's hand.

There was something wrong. There was something altered in the slope of Koscuisko's shoulders, something
alien and unknown creeping into Koscuisko's body to
make him a different man, one whom Stildyne did not
recognize. What was it?

Koscuisko ran up the slope at a quick jog; the people
between him and wherever he was going gave way to
him, bowing, until he reached his goal.

Smish Smath had the best eyesight at distance, so Stildyne asked her, though he thought he knew the answer. "Who is that, Smath, can you tell?" He spoke quietly, moving his mouth as little as possible to preserve the appearance of waiting in respectful silence at attention rest.

After a moment, Smath answered. "Tallish woman compared to the women around her. Dark hair, fancy headdress. His Excellency takes her stirrup. Maybe—what—kissing her knee?"

"Her apron," Lek corrected, tolerantly. Lek didn't have Smish's keen sight, but he did have the advantage of knowing what went on between Dolgorukij. "He'd be kissing the hem of her apron. His mother. The sacred wife of the Koscuisko prince. A Flesonika princess, if I remember right. Old blood, in his Excellency's family."

Family. What a concept.

Koscuisko's father mounted and turned his horse's head, and the hunting party started to move. Koscuisko himself started to walk back to where Stildyne and the others were waiting for him; even mounted, the Koscuisko familial retainers backed the horses out of Koscuisko's path rather than turn their backs on him. They all seemed so much alike, in a sense; the body types were similar and yet strange to Stildyne.

In the midst of that crowd of Dolgorukij, Koscuisko seemed strange to Stildyne, and the realization was an unpleasant one.

Andrej Koscuisko was his officer of assignment, a man whom Stildyne had trained on an almost daily basis for physical fitness and to improve on the fighting skills that Chief Samons—Koscuisko's Chief of Security prior to his assignment to the *Ragnarok*—had so ably established in him. A man Stildyne had nursed through countless drunks and alcohol-induced psychotic episodes, dreams so vivid and horrible that they could not be dismissed as simple nightmares, agonies of mind and spirit that had sensitized Stildyne to the concept of guilt and sin and spiritual pain for the first time in his life.

This Andrej Koscuisko was none of those things. Koscuisko had been transformed from the man Stildyne knew and understood into a complete stranger, somebody's son, a man with a community so alien and self-contained that Stildyne could not begin to reach out to him.

These people were Koscuisko's family. All of these people were, in a sense. And here in the midst of his family, what need did Koscuisko have of Stildyne—or anybody?

Koscuisko walked down the grassy slope to rejoin them, but he didn't look the same. His posture was different. Not even his face was truly familiar; he looked years younger than he had when they had landed, and his uniform did not seem to fit, somehow. It seemed wrong on him. It was the clothes that those other people wore that would be natural on this Koscuisko's body; Stildyne had never even seen Koscuisko in anything but a uniform, or pieces of a uniform, or in no uniform at all.

Stildyne hated this.

He had anticipated Koscuisko's reabsorption into his birth-culture; he had resigned himself to the probable fact of Koscuisko's becoming so involved in personal business that he would have little time or attention to spare for his Security. But he had not realized that Koscuisko would become an alien to him, a man he could recognize only on a superficial level.

As painful as it was to be held at an arm's length by his officer of assignment, it was worse than Stildyne had expected to realize that Koscuisko might be so far away from them in spirit once he had got home that there would be no reaching out at all to make or deny contact.

Koscuisko reached them, nodding to Stildyne to signal that they should all get back into the ground-car and get on with their business.

"Blessed or berated, your Excellency?" Lek asked. Stildyne was surprised that Lek spoke, but Koscuisko didn't seem to be, so clearly it was something to do with the culture that Lek and Koscuisko had in common.

Koscuisko tilted his chin a bit, looking up into Lek's face as Koscuisko climbed into the ground-car. "Blessed as well as I deserve, and a good bit better than that. My father says he will not Sanfijer my Scathijin. So it was much better than I had feared, even though the Malcontent has been talking."

Lek could probably explain that to them all later.

"Right," Stildyne said, just to regain some illusion of control. "Let's just go clear in-processing and be out of here, your Excellency, shall we?"

What was a *scathijin*, and how did one *sanfijer*, and why was that something that Koscuisko and Lek both seemed to understand was a good thing for fathers not to do to their sons?

This Koscuisko was a stranger to Stildyne. Having Koscuisko a stranger was almost like not having him at all; and unhappiness of a sort Stildyne had never felt possessed him, as they drove off to the airfield's receiving station.

Cousin Ferinc sat in his secured observation station, watching through the heavy plate-glass window as the ground-car came across the tarmac toward the administration center where Koscuisko's people would surrender custody of the courier ship, and have their purpose and presence here cleared and documented, by the grace and favor of the Autocrat.

There was no further sign of Koscuisko's family; the hunting party was gone from view. Cousin Stanoczk—Ferinc's reconciler—said that Ferinc was to come to Chelatring Side some day, to view the Gallery. Ferinc was hungry for it, for the chance glimpse he might have there of Koscuisko's father and Koscuisko's mother and the youngest of Koscuisko's brothers, the barely twelve-year-old prince Nikolij. Nikosha. Koscuisko's favorite brother, it was said. There was no love lost between Koscuisko and his brother Iosev who was the next eldest of the Koscuisko prince's sons, and . . .

Ferinc shook his head, angry at himself, and tied his braids together at the back of his head to keep them from falling across his face. Stanoczk tolerated his obsession with Andrej Koscuisko, but only just. And without Stanoczk's charity there was no hope of reconciliation for him in the world. He dared not risk incurring Stanoczk's disappointed anger.

It was so hard.

The communications booth was fully equipped for secure transmit, but no one here would have listened in had it been open. There was no profit to be had from interesting oneself in the Malcontent's business, that was no one's business but the Saint's alone. Ferinc sent the codes that he'd been given into the relay stream with the toggling of a switch; and spoke.

"Swallow's nest, for client at Chilleau Judiciary. Transmit on schedule. As follows, confirm receipt."

He could watch. He could. It would take moments for the screen to clear, because the client at Chilleau Judiciary was suspicious and trusted no one. And was not, in fact, at Chilleau Judiciary, but Ferinc wasn't supposed to know that. Not supposed by the client to know that, at least.

The ground-car pulled up to the foot of the loading dock, almost immediately below the window. They couldn't see him. The panes were treated for thermal management. He knew they couldn't see him. They had no reason even to look.

Ferinc stared down at the party gathered on the tarmac. Security. Chief Stildyne he recognized, with pained surprise; he was a hard man to forget, and that could have been Ferinc himself in Stildyne's place, though their acquaintance dated from before Stildyne's promotion. Petty Warrant Officer Stildyne, and Ferinc. They had had some times.

Oh, he could not think of that, and most especially not—

There was Andrej Koscuisko himself, climbing out of the ground-car, pausing half in and half out to share some joke or another with one of the Security. Ferinc stared hungrily at the man who had haunted his dreams, haunted his nightmares ever since. It had been more than seven years. It felt as though it had been yesterday that Koscuisko had made his mark on Ferinc, body and soul, and left him ruined and destroyed forever.

It had been deserved. Ferinc knew that. And yet he could not shake the horror of it, and the ferocious intensity, and that slim blond officer who stood there smiling—talking with Stildyne—still owned him.

Koscuisko doubtless thought it was all over. If Koscuisko ever thought of it at all, and why should he? What had Ferinc been to Koscuisko, after all, but a man meriting punishment, out of so many that had come under Koscuisko's hand?

The transmission's chime repeated for the third, and then the fourth time. Ferinc turned away from the window.

"Confirming arrival of Andrej Koscuisko with party of Security assigned." Security 5.3 had been expected; Ferinc had made it his business to find out about them, in order to let Marana know what to expect. This wasn't Security 5.3. There was a woman there. But the client hadn't asked; she only wanted to know when Koscuisko set foot to his native soil—so it wasn't up to Ferinc to tell her.

Cousin Stanoczk said that the client was unstable, unnaturally obsessed with Andrej Koscuisko and desirous of knowing his whereabouts from moment to moment. Cousin Stanoczk was most likely to remark on the client's instability of mind when reproaching Ferinc for his own obsession.

The Malcontent made good profit from the weakmindedness of persons unnaturally interested in specific Inquisitors, however. The client at Chilleau Judiciary paid well for her reports. In kind, and in specie. And Ferinc himself was bound to the Saint on Koscuisko's account, self-sold into slavery of his own free will out of his desperate need to be reconciled with what he had seen in the mirror of Koscuisko's eyes in that cell at Richeyne, so many years ago.

It would be a moment before the countersignal cleared, because the client had been linked on redirect. That always slowed things down. Ferinc went back to the window.

The transit-wagon had come up for Koscuisko's party now. Koscuisko—having apparently stepped through to the airfield master's office for a quiet official signature or two, while Ferinc had been transmitting his report— was coming out of the building, Security forming up around him in perfect order.

Precise to the mark, a pleasure to behold, professional, competent, completely secure in their roles and who they were and what they were called upon to do at all times—

The pain of loss in Ferinc's heart was nearly physical, looking at them. And it was Koscuisko who had ruined him, Koscuisko who had destroyed him, Koscuisko who had taken it all away from him forever and left him broken and bereft.

Just as he reached the transit-wagon Koscuisko looked up, back over his shoulder. Looking up at him. Ferinc shrank back and away from the window, shuddering in terror. Koscuisko could not know. He could not.

What would Koscuisko do if he ever learned the truth behind the role "Cousin Ferinc" had come to play at the Matredonat—Koscuisko's child, and the woman who was soon to find herself Koscuisko's wife—

The relay stream's confirmation signal was noise without meaning. Ferinc reached out his hand to shut it off, barely conscious of his own actions.

Then Ferinc sank to his knees on the floor of his secured communications station and wrapped his arms around his belly to keep his stomach from turning itself inside out, and rocked back and forth in agony, remembering when.

Chapter Five

Home Is the Hunter

Marana Seronkraalya stood in formal dignity well to the front of the assembled household arrayed on the graveled ground before the great doors into Andrej's house and wished with all her heart that Cousin Ferinc could be here with her.

She hadn't seen Andrej in more than nine years.

He had sent letters, gifts, tokens, records, but she could no longer hear his voice in his letters, and when she did hear his voice—in the records that he made from time to time, the hologrammic cubes—it was not the voice of the young man she remembered. It was not the face of her Andrej.

Her son stood waiting in the forefront of the household behind her, with his nurse, wearing his best clothes. His little coat. He should have had the white and red and gold of the son of the son of the Koscuisko prince, but wore the blue-and-yellow of the son of the master of the house instead. Why should she resent the colors Anton wore? It had never been a possibility. And it had been her choice to take a child of Andrej's body before he was married. She had known that his family would resent the claim she made. She had not cared.

She had come to care. For her son's sake she was prepared to demand that the entire Combine reverse itself, and conform to her desire. She had not anticipated the effect that her child would have on her ability to accept the place of a man's second and secular wife and see another woman's son take pride of place over her beautiful Anton.

Closing her eyes against the glare of the bright sun Marana struggled for psychological balance. It wasn't Andrej's fault. It wasn't even her fault. Who had known? His letters were unfailingly kind, and sometimes all but heartbreaking. And yet his letters never really spoke to her as Andrej had once spoken to her. There was the work that Andrej never discussed; it stood between them.

This is not about me, Marana reminded herself, opening her eyes. This was about Anton Andreievitch, who had never met his father. Anton knew what his father looked like; she was careful to keep plenty of pictures. Cousin Ferinc spoke frequently and with admiration of Andrej to Andrej's son, and Andrej sent records to Anton from time to time in which it was clear to her that Andrej had no idea how to speak to a child, no idea of what Anton knew or understood at what age, no possible understanding of Anton's own personality.

She smoothed her palms against the apron that she wore, a formal apron, almost as long as her old-fashioned skirt which dropped to her ankles. There was a little breeze; it was a very pleasant day. The branches of the ranks of shieldleaf trees lining the grand *allée* leading from the side of the house at her left to the motor stables and the stables proper beyond rustled pleasingly, and sent their subtle perfume far and wide.

The house itself all but glittered in the sun, its windows washed, its pillars whitened, its black-slate roof scraped and oiled, its every odd corner and half-forgotten closet cleaned and freshened and made beautiful to receive the son of the Koscuisko prince. It was her home, after all, and he was but a guest in it—all things considered. He had lived here for only a short time out of the years during which it had been in his possession, and she had been here since before Anton was born.

There were people coming from the motor stables, a party of men emerging from the shadows of the *allée*. She knew when they'd arrived; she'd been getting the reports in series as they had left the airfield and passed onto family land and thence to the estate perimeter of the Matredonat. She had waited until the very last to call the nurse out with her young son Anton. He was a very intelligent child, but he was a child still. His attention span was limited. She didn't want him to have time in which to become frightened.

If only Cousin Ferinc were here Anton would not be frightened. Anton loved Cousin Ferinc almost as much as Anton loved his nurse, and Cousin Ferinc seemed genuinely fond of Anton. She was Anton's mother. She could tell.

Six people.

Marana watched them come. It was a long way from the end of the *allée* to the front of the house. The Matredonat was a large house, as befit the gift of the family of the mother of the son of the Koscuisko prince to that son on the occasion of his acknowledgment by his father as his father's son and heir. The cutting with the knife at the inside of the cheek, on the steps of the family's estate at Rogubarachno; the solemn declaration of blood to blood, Koscuisko to Koscuisko. Andrej had been eight years old.

Anton was eight.

Anton had had no such public trauma, nor would have. That was a privilege reserved for the first son of the Ichogatra princess, the woman who had been betrothed to Andrej since his eighth year, the woman who would be Andrej's first and sacred wife. It would be *her* son, not Anton, who would stand beneath the canopy of Heaven and submit to wounding at his father's hand, the cut, the kiss, the declaration. *Give me to drink of thee.* Andrej had not even met the Ichogatra princess more than a few times in his life, and had not thought he liked her particularly well on those occasions—at least from what he had said to her about it.

She needed to focus.

Six people. Ferinc had told her how they would be. Two in front, Security. Andrej next. Two in back, and the chief of Security last, outside of the box of secured space in which they kept their officer of assignment and one step out of alignment with his back. One step to the right, because Andrej was left-handed.

She couldn't get a very good look at Andrej, not with

those Security in the way. Her messengers had said that his family had gone to meet him at the airfield; they had never come to the Matredonat. They had never asked her to them at Rogubarachno or at Chelatring Side. She had known that she was snapping her fingers in their faces when she had decided on a child before Andrej's marriage, but she had not understood how angry it would make her for them to slight her son.

She could see Andrej's figure now, at last, as the party drew nearer. All in Fleet uniform, and Andrej wore the raven's wing. It was very odd for so young a man to wear the color of age and piety, but it was the Fleet color for a man of Andrej's rank. It had no reference to what the color signified on Azanry.

She could see his figure, but it was not familiar. Not more so than that of any man might be, familiar only in that it was Aznir Dolgorukij of the shorter run.

Something was odd. One of the Security was female.

Ferinc had not said anything about a woman in Andrej's Security; and he had said they would all be green-sleeves, all bond-involuntaries, all Security slaves except the Chief of Security who was called Stildyne. She saw only one man with the bit of green on the cuff of his sleeve and the edge of his collar. Ferinc had not known about this.

They passed in front of her at a small distance of five paces' remove, and when Andrej stepped on a magical spot that was directly in front of her they all stopped, very suddenly, without a word or gesture of command that Marana saw. It startled her. Then all at once they turned toward her, and Marana stood face-to-face with the father of her child, the loving friend of her young age, for the first time in more than nine years. Her Andrej.

The Security who stood to either side between her and her lover took a side step each, so that no one stood between them. Marana stared fearfully at Andrej for a moment, trying to see something in his face that would reveal the man that he had been and remind her that she had loved him once.

It was his figure. His shoulders, although he was filled out and hardened in some way. His hands, his booted feet, the way he carried his head, the never-quite-tidy fringe of hair across his forehead, the always-almost-smiling look to the corners of his mouth.

She could not see his heart. It was his face, but there was little she could really recognize. "You are welcome to your house, my lord."

The words were practiced; there was comfort in the ritual. She had never spoken them to him before, but she knew her lines. It was just not being able to believe that it was him that made it awkward. "Stop and take refreshment, for this house and all that are within are yours. Therefore be pleased to stay with us a while, and walk amidst these gardens green; my arms long to embrace you."

He was not looking at her. He was looking past her, to where the household stood assembled, the members of and the members in his Excellency's household. He was an Excellency in Fleet as well; Ferinc had explained it to her.

She thought that his considering gaze stopped when it fell where Anton would be standing, with his nurse. Andrej opened his mouth to answer her, but what he said was not the lines expected.

" 'How shall I come into this house when she who holds the keys is sacred to me? Not as your master, lady, but your suitor true and dedicate, to seek your blessing as that of the Holy Mother of us all.' "

She could not breathe.

There was a clattering sound that rattled in her ears, what was that noise? It was the jug of milk upon the tray that the wife of the kitchen-master held. That was it. It rattled on its tray as Geslij trembled, struggling to keep her body still.

The wrong words for a man to take possession of his house and everything that was in it, and her.

Not Powiss and Empeminij, but Dasidar and Dyraine, the end of the tale, the triumphant conclusion of the saga when the hero to whom all Dolgorukij traced their ancestry besought the beautiful and beloved Dyraine of the weavers to be his sacred wife.

The words that all Dolgorukij had used to marry ever since, but only once. No man would dream of marrying

as Dasidar had been forced to promise himself to Hoyfragen, not after the offense that Hoyfragen had given
Holy Mother and all Saints under Canopy, not after how
nobly Dyraine had suffered to prove her merit matchless
and unstained by any act in which virtue was not queen.

She knew the words to say. She just could not quite
bring herself to say them, and said to him instead "What
are you thinking of? You've got it all wrong. How could
you have forgotten such a thing?"

The rattling of the milk jug on the tray that Geslij
bore grew ever louder. In another moment, Geslij was
going to drop the milk jug entirely; that would be a very
bad omen.

"I wish I could have warned you, Marana," Andrej
said. There was the ghost of the voice of the man that
she had loved in his words; even though he still said
"warned," and not "obtained your permission." "I
couldn't risk the chance of interference. Please. Be my
bride, and make your child my son. This must be done.
I promise you."

Her child was his son. That wasn't what he meant. He
meant son and heir. Legitimate; inheriting.

He meant to spurn the Ichogatra princess for good
and all, and make her—gentlewoman though she was—
the mother of the son of the son of the Koscuisko prince.

She was light-headed with shock and bemusement.
She could get only very little meaning out of what he
said, and what meaning she could grasp seemed too fan-
tastic to be truly understood. Giddy with the unreality
of it all, she folded her hands across her apron—to
steady herself, as much as because that was what it was
to be Dyraine—and raised her voice to say the words
that she had never thought to hear coming out of her
own mouth.

" 'I will be mistress of your hearth and bed, my lord,
gladly and with my great entire goodwill, and may the
Holy Mother bless and preserve us both to serve all
Saints beneath the canopy of Heaven.' "

Reaching out to one side, not daring to look, Marana
steadied the milk jug on the tray that Geslij bore. And
just in time. Geslij's trembling had so perturbed the jug's

contents that some of the milk had slopped over the rim, and made it slippery.

" 'Will you not come and drink with me? Let us be glad and take shelter in one another, so that we may have joy and comfort all our lives.' "

House-master Chuska stepped up to the other side of Geslij with the cup, antique and priceless, shining in the brilliant sunlight. Geslij poured the milk and Chuska passed the cup to Marana for her to offer to Andrej, who received it gravely in both hands, raising his voice to begin the end of the ritual, line by line in proper form.

" 'Sacred are thy feet to me, lady, for the bearing of the weight of this my child. Sacred is your apron to me, lady, for the cradling of the frame of this my child. Sacred is your breast to me, for the nurture and the comforting of this my child. And sacred is thy mouth to me, lady, for the speaking of the name of this my child.' "

Each sentence had to be interspersed with sips from the greeting cup. Andrej conducted himself with grace and precision; he knew as well as she did that the eyes of the entire population of the Matredonat were fixed on him, how carefully they all listened to be sure that it was done correctly. Once the final word was spoken, there was no going back; he had made witnesses of them all.

When a man married his first and sacred wife before she bore his child, the words were formulae and could be gotten around; but there was no dispensation under the canopy of Heaven that could sunder her from Andrej now, nor Andrej from her, not with the fact of Anton in evidence.

It was the stuff of opera and romance, melodrama, but also law and feud and bloody warfare. For as long as Dolgorukij had told each other stories of Dasidar and Dyraine, a man who cried the full four Sacred-art-thous had made his choice public and irreversible. Andrej emptied the cup and held it out to Chuska, looking at Marana.

"And I hope to be forgiven, once I have but had a chance to speak to you." Because he made her position at once unassailable and more difficult than ever, and he who had done this thing would not be staying to help her bear up beneath his family's displeasure. There would be unpleasantness. She could not imagine that he had his father's blessing to publicly insult the Ichogatra princess and unilaterally revoke all of the complex business relationships that had been years developing—all based on the clear understanding that the Ichogatra princess would be Andrej Koscuisko's sacred wife, and that the benefit that Koscuisko's family enjoyed from the match would accrue to an inheriting son with an Ichogatra mother.

It was beyond possibility that the Ichogatra princess would accept anything less than the first place in Koscuisko's household—for herself or for her children. That was to have been Marana's place, the subordinate wife, the secular wife, the acknowledged but not-privileged children, the match a man made for pure affection and not by his father's devising. The Ichogatra princess would never consent to take second place to a mere gentlewoman.

"We will talk about it later." If he thought for one instant that he was to escape explaining, he was mistaken. "We have already upset your son, Andrej, by this unexpected departure. Now come with me and greet your child. He will be worried. He will not understand what is going on."

Anton Andreievitch had just made an unimaginable leap in status over the heads of the sons and the daughters of Andrej's brothers and married sisters. Over even Andrej's brothers themselves, conceptually. The enormity of it all should stagger Anton, but he was only eight years old, and fortunately would only understand that something unusual had occurred.

Andrej held out his hand; Marana took it. Turning around, she led her now-husband to where Anton Andreievitch stood bravely in his little blue-and-yellow coat, waiting to be introduced to the alien creature in black that was his father.

It had been so long since he had seen her that Andrej couldn't tell how angry Marana might be, or what might be going on in the privacy of her mind. Once they had been so close that they knew each other's joys and disappointments as though they had shared one mind between them; now she was a stranger. Nor could he afford to open up his heart and mind to his Marana, ever again, for fear of what she might see there.

Her legal position and that of their son was as firmly grounded now as he could make them. She would have power, but Andrej was afraid she would have very little support. The election was unblessed. Marana was to remain the anomaly, the gentlewoman, the woman who would continue to represent the loss of face and failure of contractual arrangements that this marriage entailed. He was leaving. He had the easy part.

She led him by the hand in the correct manner to where a little boy was standing, waiting with his nurse. Little brown shoes of soft brown leather. A tiny jacket of blue, and yellow trimmings; an absurdly formal lace cravat, and a face that wrung Andrej's heart because it was like Marana's face and like his own, together, and yet a face distinct unto itself.

He had seen pictures. Hologrammic records. Nothing had prepared him for this moment.

"Here is your son, my lord," Marana said. "And if he is not filial, may all Saints under the canopy of Heaven rise up to rebuke me. This is your child, whom I have named after his father to be Anton Andreievitch."

For a moment the absurdity of the situation, the tyranny of tradition, threatened to overwhelm Andrej. Filial. *If he is not filial may all Saints rise up to rebuke me.* Why should Andrej Ulexeievitch rejoice in a filial son, when he himself was not a filial son?

Why should any son be filial, when it had been in the name of filial piety that Andrej himself had sacrificed his honor and his decency and his ability to sleep untroubled by his dreams, and become Inquisitor?

"He has his father's name, lady, and I am very pleased to know him for my son."

The ritual just completed would not have been reviewed beforehand with this little boy, but they were safely returned to anticipated ground now. This piece of the homecoming speech was the same for almost any circumstance. The little boy looked up into Andrej's face with a look of relief and expectation.

Andrej didn't want to waste a moment longer with ritual and ceremony; this was his son. But his son was a child, and children could be frightened easily by the unexpected. Anton had lines that he would have been coached in and rehearsed to speak. There was no help for it but to go forward.

Andrej finished the required text. "If he can also claim his mother's courage and her strength, he will be blessed indeed. Anton Andreievitch. Do you know who I am?"

Anton was concentrating so hard on what he was to say that it seemed to take a moment for him to realize that this was his cue. He gave himself a little shake, then, that reminded Andrej almost irresistibly of a puppy climbing out of an unwelcome bath. "You are my father, sir, Andrej son of Alexie who is son of Slijan before him. Give me your blessing, sir, I beseech you, so that I may grow in wisdom and in learning to become worthy that I bear your name."

It seemed a very long speech for a little boy to have to learn. Full of archaic constructions and little-used words. It was the end of the speech making, though; or almost the end.

"With all my heart I bless you, my own son." Now it was over. Now Andrej could sink down slowly to crouch on his heels at Anton-height and look at him, really look at him. His son. His. "Come to me, then, Anton, let me have a kiss. I am so glad to finally meet you."

Anton did not seem inclined to do any such thing. Why should he run into a stranger's arms, and kiss him dutifully? Anton's nurse gave Anton's shoulder an encouraging pat that was at least one part gentle push. Anton stepped forward. Putting his little hands on Andrej's shoulders he kissed Andrej shyly, one cheek, the other cheek, the first cheek again.

Andrej held out his arms and Anton, if a little reluctantly, permitted himself to be picked up.

Andrej stood with his son in his arms. He hadn't thought Anton would be so light. "Your mother has told me so many good things about you." And people would tell

Anton things about Andrej sooner or later that were not wonderful at all. "I'd like to introduce you to my Security, because they have heard all about you. From me."

A lie. But perhaps one that could be forgiven him. Andrej didn't like to talk about Anton; he was ashamed of never having met him, though his rationalizations for not having gone home were well rehearsed and firmly in his mind to be available whenever he might need them. And what business was it of anybody's but his own? What difference did it make to anybody whether he had a child or not?

He carried his child slowly back to where Security waited, noting with amusement that the look on Chief Stildyne's unlovely face was almost one of horror. Security did not have much to do with children as a rule. Still, Anton was a brave young soul, and looked up into Stildyne's ravaged face with grave courtesy that showed no tinge of fear or horror, putting his arms out unbidden to be held by a man of whom Andrej himself could be afraid—and yet was not, knowing in the marrow of his bones that Stildyne would never do him harm.

Did Anton know that? Was there some special insight that a child's heart enabled that gave Anton the power to look into Stildyne's very ugly face—the flattened nose, the mismatched eyebrows, the cheekbone smashed up beneath the eye, the thin pale lips, the narrow squinting eyes—and see only a man who loved his father?

"My Chief of Security," Andrej explained, as Stildyne held the child in his arms and the others gathered around him. "Like unto the house-master, and these the people of his team. His crew. How do you say it in plain Standard, though? His what?"

"His watch, sir?" Anton guessed. It was the first thing Anton had said to Andrej after the rehearsed speech of welcome, and it was very apropos. Lek Kerenko caught Andrej's eye and grinned, openly and freely, with obvious approval.

"Quite so." Andrej was a little surprised, even, because it was the best word for the problem. Also because Anton had clearly been not only listening, but thinking. "Here is my good Smish Smath. Do you see many women on guard-watch here, Anton Andreievitch?"

He was going to have to cut this short in a moment. The household stood waiting; he had to let Anton lead him into the house. It would not be so very much longer, though, surely.

"No, my lord father," Anton said, with his eyes so wide that the whites showed all around. "Is she very fierce?"

And Andrej wanted his Security to know his son—because Anton Andreievitch was the best part of himself that he had left to share with people who had earned his deep regard and gratitude.

It got very late, and Marana was exhausted from the emotional strain of the day and its shocking surprises.

Andrej and his people were still on a different time, perhaps; and Andrej seemed to be genuinely besotted with his son, which more than anything endeared the stranger with the face of the friend of her childhood to her once more.

He might have become a stranger to her; he might not move or sound or even smell like Andrej as Marana had once known him. But at least he knew to cherish their son Anton. She could forgive him much for that, and save the aching outrage that she nursed with regard to his long absence for later contemplation.

She had a much more immediate situation to address. The household had to be allowed to stand down, and to sleep. The master-bedroom suite had been opened for Andrej Ulexeievitch for the first time in more than nine years. There was to be no getting around it, custom and practice and common expectation required her to wait upon her husband in his bed.

There was no escape that Marana could see. As soon as Andrej had sent word that he was coming home, she'd known that she was going to have to sleep with him, at least in the most obvious sense of the term—in the same bed. This bed was an antique, an old-fashioned Dolgorukij autocrat's bed with two tiers of steps up to the platform, its great carved headboard with the family seal of one of Koscuisko's maternal antecedents, more than twice as wide as it was long, with room for a man and his wife and the nurse and the baby.

When Ferinc came to speak privately with her he cradled her close in the dark in her own bed and slept with her in his arms, with his dark hair spread over the pillow.

Being in this bed with Andrej was almost not even being in the same room. There were two sets of curtains that marked the bed space off from the rest of the room, marked off in turn from the rest of the house by its own interior walls, like a house inside a house.

What was she to do? Engage with him? How could she?

She thought about feigning sleep. That had the burden of tradition to recommend it, a signal Andrej would understand without any potentially dangerous words exchanged. To feign sleep would only put things off, however; she would still have to face him tomorrow. And tomorrow night. And the night after that. She was expected to sleep with him for five nights running, in token of her gladness at his return—tradition. It would be awkward to feign sleep for five nights running. It would not be fair to Andrej.

Marana sat at the edge of the great bed in her dressing gown with her hands in her lap, trying to decide how she was to approach this. What she was to say. The problem wasn't Ferinc, not really; Andrej would be hurt, perhaps angry, if he ever found out, but she was well within her rights to accept reconciliation from a Malcontent in the absence of her lord. In the long absence of her lord. In the long and frequently silent absence of her lord, who scarcely spoke to her from his heart, even when he did send her some word. No.

The problem was not really so much Ferinc, and why should it even become an issue, when Ferinc was Malcontent and people minded their own business where Malcontents were concerned?

The problem was Andrej. The thought of exchanging intimacies with a man she had only just remet made her skin crawl, and yet Andrej gave no sign of any such reservations.

Andrej was coming in through the bed curtains to his bed now, in sleeping dress as she was; which for a man meant a shirt, of course. And slippers and a robe, as well, but there was no way around it—this was a man who was naked beneath his garment, and he was coming into the bed enclosure to sit down next to her.

Looking at her he smiled with a sort of defeated hopelessness, and Marana realized with a shock of icy horror that not only was Andrej stark naked beneath his shirt but so was she. She looked at her hands, and not at him.

Seating himself at the edge of the bed at a respectable arm's length from her, Andrej spoke, almost the first time he'd spoken directly to her since he'd arrived. "This bed is the size of my room on the *Ragnarok*," Andrej said. "And I'm an officer. I have twice as much space as anybody. You could put a full Security team into a room the size of this bed. I had forgotten. It is a little bit intimidating, Marana."

She didn't know what she could say. He had offered her conversation, clearly trying to solicit her reaction. She had no reaction. She was benumbed with disgust and dismay to think that she was naked in a bed with a naked man who might as well be a complete stranger.

"That's why there are curtains, my lord. To dampen the echo." She didn't want to be hurtful or cold to him, just because he was a stranger. He had a right to expect at least basic courtesy from her. He had just made her the second-most important woman in his entire family, not excepting his elder sister, not excepting Zsuzsa, the Autocrat's Proxy.

Her son would inherit the controlling interest in one of the oldest, richest, most powerful familial corporations in the entire Dolgorukij Combine. Surely that called for friendly behavior, at least, on her part.

"And the entire bed, perhaps the size of the bolster. Perhaps not quite so large as that. You have slept in decent beds these years past, Marana. Tell me, which side of the bed is it that you prefer?"

She could set that bolster between them, under pretense of desiring the support. Then it would be less like being in bed with him. "I take the near side, Andrej. When Anton was a baby, it was this side that was nearest to the nursery." Not this same bed, of course, but her own bed, in her own apartment. The bed that Ferinc shared with her from time to time, and took the far side of the mattress when he did.

Andrej nodded, but did not get up immediately to go to the other side of the bed. He was looking at the bed curtains right in front of her. Maybe he was just not looking at her, Marana thought, and the fact that there were curtains there was incidental.

"My lord father and my lady mother came to the airfield today, Marana. I suppose you heard."

Yes, she had, and she had therefore no need for him to tell her; so he meant to tell her something else.

"I do not have my father's blessing, to have insulted Lise Semyonevna. But neither was blessing withheld. I'm sorry to have put you in this position, Marana. It was only because of Anton. There are things I may not tell to even you."

A man did not take a sacred wife as Andrej had taken her today. A man sued for acceptance as a husband. She could have spurned him; he had named her sacred to him, but as masterfully as though she had been a share-owned mare. Very high-handed behavior on his part. Had it not been for what the change would mean for her son Anton she might have slapped him, instead of quoting Dyraine to his Dasidar.

At least he knew that he was in the wrong. "He doesn't seem afraid of you." She wanted to be loving. She wanted to be charitable. Maybe if she talked about their son; they had Anton in common. Only Anton. Nothing else; not any more. "I think that you have almost won him over. That gives you credit in his mother's eyes, my lord."

Andrej smiled with gratitude, but twisted his face up into a grimace of distress almost at once. "What is this 'my lord,' Marana? Must it indeed be so? I can't pretend to be the man I was. I don't know you. You don't know me. And yet we loved each other once. I believe we did. I trust we did. I'm almost certain I remember."

His cry was from the heart. "All right." It startled her to realize how close his thoughts moved to match her own. "But it's expected, Andrej, 'my lord husband.' You know that it is."

The formal language was a species of barricade that she could raise to hide behind. It was too bad that Andrej knew that as well as she did. He stood up.

"If you do I'll call you 'Holiest-unto-me,' Marana, I will. And it will be your own fault, too." The sound of his voice was mild and only humorously annoyed. "If we were to pull the pillow down the middle of the bed it need not be too embarrassing to lie together, Holiest-unto-me. So long as someone wakes before the servants come, to set the bed to rights."

Marana stood as well, and felt a strange and unexpected tremor in her belly to hear him speak. It had been her thought, too. It had been her thought almost exactly. Was there something of the Andrej she had loved still there within him somewhere after all? Kept she in any form some faded trace of who she'd been when she'd been his Marana?

"It's been a long day, Andrej." She could say it. The name had an unusual flavor in her mouth, but it was not an unpleasant one. "And you are not on home-time yet, I would guess. It would be better not to risk the scandal. Leave the pillows where they are. If we shall chance to touch by accident, it's nothing that we have not done before, once of a time."

He was untying the sash of his bed robe, and paused, resuming the task only much more slowly. "There are, after all, these years to stand between us," he agreed. "We will not need the pillows. You're quite right. They will be after me for laps tomorrow morning, Marana. You will have the room to yourself to take your breakfast."

Keeping his back to her he laid his robe aside and climbed into the bed. There was something in his body that she knew. Not in the body itself so much perhaps but in the movement of it. Something. She turned down the light.

In the dim golden glow of the votive lamp that burned within the lattice niche of the headboard before the icon that was treasured there Marana took her robe off and got into bed herself, shifting a bit toward the middle of the bed as she pulled the covers up over her bosom.

She reached out her hand, not looking, lying on her back.

After a moment she felt his hand, similarly extended at length across the expanse of the bed linen to touch her fingers—and her fingers only—with unspoken and tentative address.

Thus it was she slept.

Andrej Koscuisko awakened in the dark, not knowing what time it was, not knowing where he was for a long moment. He knew that he was safe, but it took him some thought to gather together the threads of the past day's events and decide what he was doing here in this immense bed.

He'd slept here before, but not for years.

He had made planetfall, he had done his in-processing, he had come home to the Matredonat and made his declaration beneath the canopy of Heaven, Marana to be his first and sacred wife, Anton, his son, to inherit.

This was why he had come home.

Not to astound Marana and infuriate his parents, but to set Anton firmly in place before he turned his attention to the underlying issue, the constant trouble that had dogged his waking moments since first Garol Vogel had shown him the Bench warrant at Port Burkhayden. *As regards the person of the following named soul the bearer is to exercise the solemn ruling of the Bench in support of the Judicial order.* His name.

Vogel had left the warrant with him, and Andrej had brought it. He wanted to take it to the Malcontent, but first he had had to be sure that no matter what happened Anton would be safe.

Unless he could discover who wanted him dead, he could not count on living to engender other sons; so it only made sense that he have no other wife than Marana. He had no fond hopes of convincing his parents of this. He dared not tell anyone but the Malcontent.

Garol Vogel's Bench warrant had not been for Captain Lowden. Therefore Garol Vogel had not exercised it. Then who had killed Lowden, and why had Vogel made the claim that he had, to cover it up?

If it had been Vogel, Bench warrant or no, there would have been nothing to cover up. Vogel was a Bench intelligence specialist. He had the authority to take the Law into his own hands. The existence of the Bench warrant with Andrej's name on it could only mean that someone else had killed Captain Lowden and that Garol Vogel was protecting somebody.

It would be all too easy for any intelligent person to turn their attention to Andrej Koscuisko, the man whose name was on the Bench warrant, a man much worked upon by Captain Lowden, a man whose whereabouts could not be accounted for during crucial hours at Port Burkhayden that night. A man who might conceivably have been mistaken for a Bench intelligence specialist in the dark and confusion of the service house on that fatal evening.

Andrej needed the resources of the best secret service there was. Andrej needed the Malcontent, if he was to have any hope of getting through to the truth behind the Bench warrant. But he could say nothing to anyone else about its existence, and that meant that any excuses he could offer for his behavior would be facile and unconvincing.

He was awake, now. Not just waking up—wide awake, clear headed; he even felt rested. That probably meant it was his normal rising time—early morning, on the Matredonat's schedule, time to go to exercise with Security.

Lying in the bed for one moment longer Andrej stretched himself, listening to Marana breathe. It would be less awkward for them both if he was gone when she got up. Exercise made a good excuse, one that the household could understand. He was expected to renew carnal relations, to possess himself of her body once more. And he didn't dare touch her.

Her breathing sounded deep and regular. If she was awake, she was encouraging the charade, pretending to be asleep, playing along. He had forgotten how well they had once understood each other.

Sliding carefully out from under the sheets Andrej climbed down through the double row of bed curtains into the room, leaving his robe and his slippers behind. There was little risk of waking her by disturbing the bed. It was a big bed. It had been brave of her to reach out to him in the night, but even so formal a contact as that had been almost distressing.

There was too much between them.

When he and Marana had become lovers they had

been much younger, and among the very first of each other's loves. She had not been the first woman he had known, but she had been the one he most sincerely wanted, and she had desired him. Once. Long ago. Then he had gone away, to the Fleet, gone as his father had told him to learn how to torture in the name of the Law; and found out such horrors about himself that destroyed what innocence he might have had in lovemaking entirely.

He still liked women. He could engage with them in any of the conventional manners, and have satisfaction, and even give satisfaction. But there was the other thing; there was pain.

The impact it had on him was so much more than merely sexual. The pleasure possessed him body and soul, heart and mind, terrible and transcendent, and overwhelming in its sheer power. Sexual pleasure was sexual pleasure, and it was still available, but it was an almost trivial thing set against the reaction that Andrej had learned that he could have to the suffering of souls in the torments he inflicted.

There were two problems.

One of them was that the suffering that the Bench decreed was so grotesquely out of proportion to the supposed crimes it was meant to address that there was no rational purpose to it, no excuse, no justification. It was wrong, but worse than wrong, it was ineffectual, an atrocious imposition on captive bodies that had no relation to justice or any good effect.

The second was that whether or not it was wrong for the Bench to torture its criminals, it was not right for any decent man to enjoy it. Not even if the Protocols had truly been just and judicious could it be right for the officer charged with their implementation to take so much pleasure as Andrej had in the suffering of feeling creatures fallen foul of Jurisdiction.

And Andrej took pleasure in the Inquisition, a drug so intense that his first experience had been addictive almost at once. He was soiled in flesh and in heart and in spirit by the degradation his pleasure entailed. How could he hope to strip away the years of sadistic indulgence and stand before the friend of his childhood as her true lover?

It was only decent of a man to wash before he approached his lover for intimacies. No amount of washing could remove the stain of sin that was on him. He would soil her if he touched her, because he was corrupt, and his desire had been too compromised by the helpless suffering of his victims to share with an honest woman ever again.

His pleasure itself was compromised. It would be an offense to drown in her arms who had drowned on dry land in Secured Medical, overwhelmed not by the attainment of the sacred ocean within women's bodies but by the gross lust that was within him for mastery.

He hadn't quite thought it all through before now. He'd had too many other things on his mind. But now that he had come home to be her husband, it was all too clear that he could never be any such thing in the physical sense ever again. She had been honest and true to him, even before the wedding-rite had made her holy. And he was a man too corrupt with obscenity to touch her flesh without soiling it.

He needed to think. Exercise would serve.

Andrej did not really care for exercise in and of itself, but Stildyne had a right to expect Andrej to take reasonable measures to cooperate with the efforts of the Security who would be expected to die if need be to protect him from harm. And he had come to rely on Stildyne's demands to give structure and order to his daily life, even when it could have no possible meaning.

Going through the dark bedroom to his dressing room Andrej exchanged his sleep shirt for an exercise uniform and let himself out into the inner hallway, where his people would meet him.

There was only Stildyne, waiting in the corridor, standing there talking with the porter, the elderly woman whose duty it was to sit outside Andrej's bedroom during the night in case he decided he wanted something from the kitchen. Or anything at all. Stildyne alone; Andrej looked up at him, a little confused, and as Stildyne started off down the hall with him Stildyne explained.

"You wanted to give your people a holiday, your Excellency. And they're pretty tired."

As if that meant anything. They were Security. They

were expected to execute Stildyne's will and instruction, regardless of how tired they might be. This was funny. Andrej never would have thought to hear such a thing, not from Stildyne.

"So I've put them on their honor to do their own training. It's just you and me. The house-master tells me where we could go do laps, and it will be a change to be running outdoors." Rather than on an exercise track on board of the *Ragnarok,* which ran the perimeter of the ship along the carapace hull.

It was up to Stildyne to decide on the training schedule one way or the other; if Stildyne felt his people could be excused early morning exercise, could be allowed to sleep late, it was Stildyne's business. Andrej followed Stildyne out of the master's apartments, out of the house, out toward the river past the motor stables down the long *allée* of trees, distracted by the strange and the familiar alike.

Familiar, because this place was his. These grounds, these fields, this house and everything—and everybody— in it, were his own. Possession; and responsibility.

It was a beautiful morning. The sun was not yet clear of the mountains on the horizon, and the little fog from off the river set everything into soft focus. It smelled like home, a unique and indescribable combination of dirt and vegetation, air and water for which Andrej had been longing for years without even realizing his homesickness. It was good to be back home, in his own place.

He was depraved, unfilial, a sinner. But he was a depraved unfilial sinner who was at home.

Stildyne strolled thoughtfully beside him, silent in respect for Andrej's thoughts. Stildyne was long accustomed to the fact that Andrej didn't speak much before breakfast. It took him a while to turn his attention outward in the morning. But something had caught Stildyne's attention.

Andrej sensed a change in Stildyne's demeanor, and glanced up and over at him to see what it might be. Stildyne was watching someone who appeared to be watching Stildyne through the trees, someone who walked on the other side of the ranked shieldleaf trees and kept them in view.

"Something, Mister Stildyne?"

Stildyne shifted his eyes from his target to Andrej and back in the direction of their companion in the distance, pointing without seeming to point. "He's following us. He picked us up the moment we stepped out of the building. I don't know enough about the people here to be able to say, but it seems to me that there's something out of place about that man."

There was no necessary reason why Andrej's own house security should not have a post on them. To keep Andrej's outland Security from getting lost, if for no other reason. And with Andrej back after nine years' absence there was nothing insulting—perhaps the opposite—about an impulse on House-master Chuska's part to send someone with Andrej in case he forgot his way. It would only be looking out for their master, a mark of respect and delicacy of feeling.

But once Andrej had a look at the figure who was following them he knew it wasn't house security. "Men don't usually wear their hair long here. You're quite right, Chief."

Their shadow was keeping his distance, too far off for Andrej to be able to guess whether he knew that man or not. But he could see the man's figure and the more obvious details of his dress. Decent Dolgorukij men wore beards, yes, if they grew beards at all and were old enough. But no decent Dolgorukij male ever wore his hair long down his back. That was no decent Dolgorukij.

Andrej explained, because Stildyne was waiting. "That is a Malcontent, Chief. A religious professional of a particular sort. You've heard of Malcontents?"

Maybe he had and maybe he hadn't. Stildyne was a Security warrant, and had had contacts in intelligence fields, once upon a time. "Heard about them, yes, your Excellency. What do you think he's up to?"

Shaking his head, Andrej smiled. "There's no use even wondering, Chief. The Malcontent does as the Malcontent pleases, and the Malcontent's business is for the Saint alone. You needn't worry."

"Looks familiar somehow," Stildyne remarked, as if clearly aware that a Malcontent shouldn't be. Andrej had to grin.

"If you'd met a Malcontent you'd remember, Chief, trust me on this. We approach the river. Shall we run?"

He didn't know what the Malcontent might be about and he didn't care, because there was no way he would ever find out unless the Malcontent should reveal the information for the Saint's own purposes, and there was therefore no sense wasting the energy.

"Very good, sir. After you."

Just he and Stildyne, in the early morning, on a worn old track that ran alongside the river down to the nearest bridge. The Security they had brought with them were on vacation, Stildyne had said, and came alone. Stildyne had Andrej all to himself. Stildyne was on a holiday of a sort as well, Andrej mused, and this was one of the treats he had granted to himself, morning exercise alone with his officer.

Andrej could see no objection to so harmless a self-indulgence on Stildyne's part. And he did owe Stildyne laps. He always owed Stildyne laps. He would die owing Stildyne laps.

But not before he laid that Bench warrant before the Malcontent and asked the Saint's assistance in identifying who on the Jurisdiction's Bench wanted him killed, and why.

Chapter Six

Disquieting Undercurrents

It was four days into his investigation, six days now since the accident. General Rukota stood on the flight-prep line in the *Ragnarok*'s maintenance atmosphere with the Ship's Engineer louring beside him, watching Pesadie's preliminary assessment team work through an operational audit on yet another Wolnadi.

"Willful obstruction of an authorized Fleet investigation," Rukota pointed out. "As has characterized the approach of this entire Command from the date of the incident. I have never encountered such a concerted effort to be unpleasant in any situation into which I have had the misfortune to be placed in over twenty years of service of the Judicial order."

Rukota himself was a tall man, unaccustomed to the company of people who could look down on him. Wheatfields was slender, but unquestionably very tall, and rolled a little twiglet of wood from one side of his mustachioed mouth to the other before condescending to favor Rukota with a response.

"Flatterer." There was no hint of any personal animosity in Wheatfields's voice. There was no hint of any emotion whatever. "I suppose you say that to all the people you're trying to screw."

Closing his eyes in a momentary spasm of frustration, Rukota reminded himself that it was nothing personal. Wheatfields just didn't like strangers getting into his Wolnadis any more than Wheatfields was likely to tolerate strangers taking more personal liberties. Rukota was right with him, on that. He didn't like the Pesadie team either. They were too obviously looking for something. They weren't finding it, but they had no business coming here with any preconceived ideas on the subject of whether there was anything to find in the first place.

"No, your Excellency, I usually take a more traditional approach: 'Hello, what's your name, did you know that artillerymen can do it on a full three-sixty transit?' You know. Why don't you just go ahead and tell us whose Security it was?"

Wheatfields glanced sideways at him for a thoughtful moment, as though he was carefully evaluating Rukota's facetious overture. Rukota felt a twinge of uncertainty: he didn't want Wheatfields. He didn't care for engineers; he'd always found their approach to intimacy to be entirely too focused on technical details to make for an enjoyable engagement. If he was going to try men at all a Chigan would be the place to start—there was no question about that—but when Wheatfields answered, Rukota realized with disgust that Wheatfields had been having him on. Making him think. Playing games with his mind.

"No, I don't like the psychology of it, Rukota. The minute we say 'Look here for a malfunction, if any,' we've introduced the concept, and there isn't any malfunction to find. The best way we have of proving that is to let your people run a really thorough test on everything here. If they can't identify the subject craft on empirical evidence alone—you have your answer."

In more ways than one. Wheatfields's reputation should have warned Rukota that Wheatfields was teasing. It had been years since the Judicial mistake that had resulted in the horrible death of Wheatfields's lover, spouse, partner, whatever it was that Chigans called each other when they mated.

Chigans didn't necessarily mate for life—the peculiar population dynamics of Chigan society encouraged a rather more fluid approach to intimate relationships— but Wheatfields himself had by report been deeply scarred by the emotional trauma. It had been an exceptionally egregious lapse of good judgment on whoever's part to have let Wheatfields look at the Record of his lover's torture.

At any rate Wheatfields had been as celibate as a woman in a Chigan enclave ever since, by all reports, and had a reputation for being unpleasant. Rukota supposed he was lucky that Wheatfields was speaking to him at all. Part of the investigation, yes, but that didn't mean that Wheatfields would have acceded to an interview if he'd been feeling difficult.

Wheatfields had been daring the Fleet to discipline him for years, and Fleet to its credit had turned its back on behavior that could easily have meant Wheatfields's dismissal in disgrace. It was his death that Wheatfields was looking for, anyway.

"At the rate we're going it'll be weeks before we're finished, your Excellency." There were twenty Wolnadi fighters in the *Ragnarok*'s inventory, twenty-three if you counted the reserves. And Wheatfields probably was. Just to make his point. "What's your investment in hanging on to a bunch of admin types from Pesadie Station for that long? I'd think you'd want us off as soon as possible."

Four days, and this was only the second Wolnadi that Pesadie's team had worked on. Operational audit took time, especially when the Ship's Engineer held so close to his principles and absolutely declined to offer assistance from the *Ragnarok*'s resources—all in the name of ensuring a true and pure result, of course.

Wheatfields smiled. Rukota noticed with astonishment that Wheatfields could actually look pleasant, when he smiled, and really very engaging when he almost laughed.

"Operant behavior," Wheatfields said. "We haven't had staff to run audit on everything. This is an opportunity, Rukota, free labor for as long as it takes. I'm sorry about the environment, though. The stores are pretty low. Nothing personal."

Wheatfields was right about the quality of life on board of this ship. Worse, there were maintenance issues that could only result from increasing starvation for replacement articles and consumables. The *Ragnarok* hadn't been at Pesadie Station above two months; there had to be a more pernicious reason for the state of its stores than just the timing of its depot visits. Somehow or other the *Ragnarok* had simply not been getting its stores in.

"You want me to believe that your people weren't out there on overtime to sanitize that exercise craft?" Rukota demanded. Because if Engineering truly hadn't done an operational audit on the craft before hazarding the findings of the assessment team, the *Ragnarok* was naïvely convinced that innocence was adequate protection against harm. That would be deeply troubling, because of its stupidity, but also because the *Ragnarok* could only think that if they already knew that there was a reason that would be revealed, and from outside its boundaries.

"Just enough time to satisfy ourselves on the fighter in question."

Wheatfields's candid response made Rukota feel better . . . and then made him feel worse. Wheatfields was confiding. Wheatfields was extending the handshake of truce, and inviting Rukota to become complicit in the *Ragnarok*'s cover-up. It was a risk for Wheatfields to take. Rukota was supposed to be an impartial observer. He had a duty to the Bench.

What duty?

The people that Admiral Brecinn had sent along with him were not in the least bit neutral. They almost didn't even pretend to be. So why should he hold himself to a higher standard, when everything around him was so corrupt?

"Well. You've got to grab resources where you can find them, I suppose."

Because it was his honor, that was why. He couldn't quite turn his back on Pesadie and ally himself with the *Ragnarok*. He couldn't. He had a duty. And his own integrity to consider—at least what was left of it. "No chance of a stash of good bean tea on board, is there? I mean decent stuff. The bean tea in mess is enough to drive a man to desperation. By which I mean khombu."

With clear regret, Wheatfields shook his head. "Sorry, Rukota. Don't even try it. You'll never find my supply. You'll just have to suffer."

That was right. Chigans drank bean tea. He should have remembered.

Wheatfields went off for a word with one of the Security warrants and Rukota stayed behind, watching the assessment team work on the Wolnadi and wondering if he could get a word through to his wife. *Desperate straits. Please send bean tea.*

There had been some stores with them on the courier ship when they'd arrived, the standard issue and survival rations. Meat broth, for one, which had been the only thing that had saved him thus far. When that was gone, they would have no choice but to share the *Ragnarok*'s common mess: and Rukota did not know how he was to face that prospect, and survive.

In all of the years that Ferinc had been here, he had never been so reluctant to approach the Malcontent's cell in the Brikarvna safe house as today.

He was usually happy to be called to open his accounts for examination, because it meant that Stanoczk would be there, and Stanoczk would not deny him reconciliation. This time it was different. Stanoczk would be angry with him. He had transgressed.

That Stanoczk would deny him was unthinkable. The all but certain fact of Stanoczk's disappointment was almost as horrible as the thought of being sent away alone, unblessed, uncomforted, unreconciled. Ferinc knocked.

It was an old place. It had doors made out of wood, heavy and hung on actual hinges, and when they closed behind one the report of their impact was muffled against the wood that lined the walls into a dull, thudding sound of very oppressive—or promising—finality.

"Step through," Stanoczk called from inside the cell, but Ferinc hesitated, wondering if he should not turn around and go away. He had not done as he had been supposed to do. Stanoczk would be unhappy with him.

And still he was a man, and would stand evaluation like a man. Koscuisko had ruined him, destroyed him, annihilated him, but Koscuisko had not yet made him into a coward.

Ferinc went in, closing the door behind him with quiet resignation. Stanoczk was there, sitting at the long low table, drinking a glass of rhyti. There was only one chair at the table. Ferinc bowed over Stanoczk's hand to kiss his knuckles, a formal and traditional greeting that he had learned to give with affection. Stanoczk did not take Ferinc's hand in return. Stanoczk was that angry.

Sitting down on the floor at a polite distance Ferinc folded his legs for compactness's sake, and waited. He had been in the wrong. This would not be easy. But Stanoczk was his reconciler, and would not let him suffer so long as the peace of the Malcontent was within his power to grant.

Had it not been for Stanoczk, Ferinc believed that he would have killed himself years ago. After Koscuisko.

"What news do you bring from the Matredonat, Ferinc?"

Cousin Stanoczk's deep voice was low and level. He didn't look at Ferinc. Ferinc could be grateful for Stanoczk's candor; he would not draw the painful confrontation out.

"All seems well, Stanoczk; the child learns not to fear the stranger, the lady grows accustomed to his presence. They say that they sleep in the same bed, but not together."

He wasn't supposed to know. He was supposed to have kept clear of the Matredonat until Koscuisko was summoned to Chelatring Side.

"Tell me, Ferinc," Stanoczk suggested. "Explain. You haven't been reckless in the past. Sometimes almost I have heard praise for you. Talk to me now. Why did I have to seek here for you, when I expected you in Pirlassins?"

Resisting the temptation to solicit reassurance, Ferinc concentrated on the report Stanoczk required. To keep things from one's own reconciler was as much as to shut one's own mouth against sustenance when one was starving.

"I met the party at the airfield, Stanoczk, as I was directed. I sent the report to the person at Chilleau Judiciary. It was acknowledged."

Stanoczk had set his glass of rhyti down, and was preparing to smoke a lefrol. The simple ritual always made Ferinc shudder. Andrej Koscuisko had been smoking a lefrol. "You also had acknowledged your instructions, Ferinc."

That cell had been bigger than this one, better lit, much colder; but it had been as bleak and comfortless, and the stone floor had been as hard.

"It was an error of judgment. I looked out of the window. I knew that Chief of Security, Stanoczk, before he was a chief warrant officer. Oh, I could ruin him—I know things about Stildyne that Koscuisko would not tolerate—"

"We aren't talking about the warrant officer," Stanoczk reminded him. "Go on, Ferinc. I am hoping to be able to excuse you. Help me."

Stanoczk was angry. And Ferinc was heartily sorry for it. Sorry that he had betrayed his discipline; sorry that he had seen Koscuisko; and sorry that he had made Stanoczk angry. There was no way to make it right.

"Oh, I went to look out the window, Stanoczk, and he looked up. Him. As if he knew that I was there. Marana was so unhappy. To think of him in her arms, in her bed, I couldn't stay away. I had to see for myself that she was all right. And then I saw them by the river, Koscuisko, and Stildyne, and . . ."

He didn't want to say this.

He couldn't keep the truth from Cousin Stanoczk.

"I think he may have recognized me. Stildyne. Koscuisko wouldn't. I don't think that he would, not from a distance, not like this. Surely he didn't know—he couldn't have guessed—"

"You let yourself become distracted, Ferinc, and I do not tolerate being disregarded." Stanoczk's warning called him back from the edge of the abyss—as Stanoczk had so many times before. Stanoczk's voice. And Stanoczk's touch.

And the skillful, loving passion of Stanoczk's caress, which had the power to turn the self-punitive fury harmlessly into the emptiness of the past, the power to turn him back from the edge of madness toward a species of fury of a more benign sort, raging in his mind and his desire, quieted to Stanoczk's word in the embrace of the Malcontent.

"I'm sorry, Stanoczk." At least Stanoczk would know he was sincere. "I should have fled to this place and cried for mercy. And instead I went back to the Matredonat. Are you very angry with me?"

Rising to his feet Cousin Stanoczk began to pace, smoking his lefrol, his head bent to regard the floor very thoughtfully.

"After all these years, Ferinc, and to be put back into that place in your mind so suddenly and so completely. It is as though we have not helped you find any healing, at all. If I can't reconcile you to your past they will excuse me from the exercise and try to fit you to another man, one who can better share the true peace of the Malcontent with thee. I don't want that."

Ferinc heard Stanoczk's language drop into the familiar, intimate mode of address, and felt fear gripping his heart. He hadn't stopped to think about that. He hadn't stopped to consider the effect his selfish action might have on Stanoczk at all.

"I don't want another reconciler." He had come much closer to the mystical understanding of the Malcontent with Stanoczk as his tutor than he had ever hoped. "How shall I beg to be forgiven? Do not deny me reconciliation, Stanoczk. I couldn't bear it."

Stanoczk turned so sharply on his heel that for a moment Ferinc saw Stanoczk's cousin, and not Stanoczk himself. Koscuisko had had a quickness about him. It had been very unnerving.

"You do not ask forgiveness of any Malcontent, Ferinc, surely you know so basic a thing as that by now. Nor may I deny you reconciliation, even if I wanted to. It is as much as my soul is worth. But neither your wishes nor mine will change the fact that you are not of the Blood. The Malcontent has taken you on trust and out of compassion for your suffering because of the man who is responsible for it, and should I fail to help you to find peace, I fail our divine Patron. May he wander in bliss."

In bliss and in intoxication. The Malcontent had been a very famous lover of liquor, in his life: liquor, lovemaking, and laughter.

"What happens now?" Ferinc asked, looking at his feet folded beneath him, on the floor. "I want to go back and see him again. I want to be sure Marana is all right. I love Koscuisko's child, Stanoczk. What am I to do?"

He watched the ash fall from Stanoczk's lefrol to the

floor, and shuddered. Stanoczk turned back toward the table, and sat down.

"I will bring the Bench specialist to the Matredonat, Ferinc, she will an interview with Koscuisko conduct. You may during that time speak to the lady. The Second Judge still believes that she needs this Judiciary to win her bid, and has offered concessions that we want. We particularly need to secure them before Chilleau Judiciary comes to understand that it need not sue to the Combine for victory."

Was Stanoczk speaking of neutral issues to calm his nerves, to avoid an unpleasant necessity?

"If she has so much support, it bodes well for the transition, doesn't it?" Clearly the more people that supported Chilleau Judiciary, the fewer who would be rioting when the Selection was announced.

Stanoczk shook his head, however. "The transition may run well, Ferinc. You will be glad that you are sequestered and here before too much longer, though, I think. Will you speak to Koscuisko, and seek peace?"

Yes.

No.

He'd had fantasies. But after what had happened to him at the airfield, Ferinc had to admit to himself that he did not have the nerve. "If you think I ought, Stanoczk. What shall I say?"

Stanoczk shook his head. His expression had grown less serious, less stern, and he was leaning back in the chair with his knees splayed at a very informal angle, a very much more relaxed picture indeed. "It was a question, not a challenge, Ferinc. I see it all so clearly. 'Hello, you may not remember me, but you had cause to discipline me once, and since then I have been providing comfort to your wife and a role model for your son. I only thought that you should know because I have no hard feelings.' Yes. I can imagine."

When Stanoczk put it that way, it did sound funny. Not a threat at all. Encouraged, Ferinc put what he could only hope was an expression suitably mild and innocent on his face, and shifted on the floor so that his knees were underneath him, and he was that much closer to Stanoczk. He was taller than Stanoczk. He was almost eye to eye with him, and could set his elbow to the table to look up into Stanoczk's skeptical face confidingly.

"Shall I just go and get started on a suitable speech, then?"

It was a very cheeky thing to say to one's religious teacher, the official representative of the religious order that had taken him in those years gone by and made the Fleet forgive the charges brought against him for desertion. Ferinc was counting on that.

And Stanoczk laughed. "You'd be better advised to give some serious consideration where you are here and now, if you hope to avoid falling into error. It is my opinion that you have gone too long without adequate reconciliation, it will take days to sort you out, and that will have to wait. Still. We have some hours. And so you may be confident that I mean to examine you with the strictest diligence, within the limits of the time that we have here and now."

Oh, he could write his speech for Koscuisko tomorrow, then. Because when Stanoczk was minded to be thorough the process of reconciliation could go on and on. Rigorous though it was there was no substitute for the deep and profound peace, the inner security, the sense of calm and well-being that resulted from the reconciliation of the Malcontent.

There was water and a warmer, rhyti and food. The cell was small, but it was a secure safe place, and there was a thick pile of bearskins in the corner to guard against the chill as the hours wore on. He was alone with Stanoczk, whom the Malcontent in his mercy had granted to Ferinc to reconcile his pain with the mysteries of the Holy Mother's Creation. There was nothing he could say to Stanoczk that would surprise, shock, or offend him; he was safe to open the dark agonies of his soul, and know that Stanoczk would handle him gently.

For these few hours he could be as happy as if he'd never even met Andrej Koscuisko.

Another day, General Rukota told himself, swallowing back his sigh of resignation. Another hostile and combative communiqué from Pesadie Training Command.

"Acting Captain ap Rhiannon." The voice of the recorded image of Admiral Brecinn on view in the Captain's office gave every ounce of the venom doubtless intended to the word *acting,* to emphasize ap Rhiannon's tenuous claim to any rank at all. "We all approve of thoroughness. In theory. But it has been eight days."

"I fully endorse Pesadie Training Command's desire for a careful and complete investigation." Ap Rhiannon's own voice on record was smooth and validating in turn, for all the world as if she had believed that to be what the Admiral was saying. Rather than exactly the opposite. Rukota looked to ap Rhiannon, who was sitting alone in the briefing pit. She was drawing circles in spilt shirmac tea on the table in front of her, not meeting his eyes.

Rukota could appreciate that. It was one thing to say the words once; quite another to maintain that brazen composure the second time through, listening to herself. Knowing how confrontational the words had been. "It is for this reason that we so much appreciate the continued support of Pesadie Training Command, Admiral Brecinn. The investigation is well under weigh. We hope for completion within seventy days."

The Admiral, to her credit, had not actually sputtered. "See if you can't find some way to hurry things along. I have no intention of allowing the monopolization of my valuable personnel resources. That will be all, Lieutenant."

Rukota couldn't really blame Brecinn for "Lieutenant." Ap Rhiannon had provoked her. And yet ap Rhiannon hadn't done it to be provoking; she appeared to have a genuine motive that Rukota had not yet been able to decide if he could credit.

The record stopped. Ap Rhiannon looked up from her artwork with an expression of anxious tension on her face. "I don't like her," ap Rhiannon said, as though there had been any doubt. "I don't suppose that you could shut her up for me."

Rukota shook his head, walking slowly to the briefing pit to sit down. "You know better than that, your Excellency." He didn't mind giving her the rank. She had to deal with Brecinn, after all. "And in every conflict, there is usually a point on either side. With respect. But your Engineer is a very difficult man. And it's catching."

Don't shoot me, I'm an artilleryman. I only fire the cannon. I don't even know what's on the other end of the round. It was an old joke. Rukota wondered if he dared make it.

Ap Rhiannon frowned. "Difficult, how do you mean 'difficult'? You know what he's been given to work with. If he hadn't had an attitude problem to rub off on Engineering, Engineering's attitude would have rubbed off on him. And I don't blame them either. You can see the environment Fleet expects this crew to deal with."

Rukota stretched his legs out in front of him and studied the toes of his boots. What was on ap Rhiannon's mind? She was crèche-bred. Troops were disposable, for crèche-bred. Duty to the rule of Law was everything. "That's no excuse for failure to cooperate, your Excellency. We all have our own challenges."

The look she gave him was equal parts confusion, anger, and disappointment. "Some of us more than most, General, and none of which include volunteering for martyrdom. Brecinn is not going to turn this into a training accident. The training accident was strictly coincidental."

That was stating things a little strongly. He knew what she meant, though. But how far was she willing to take it? This was a side of ap Rhiannon he hadn't seen before. She appeared to have personal feelings about the matter. He hadn't thought crèche-bred were issued any personal feelings.

"It's a reasonable suspicion, your Excellency, be fair. I'm not Fleet's most particular officer. You know that." He was in fact not very keen on rank and protocol unless he needed them to get the job done. Ap Rhiannon did not insult him by pretending to protest anything to the contrary, so he continued without any such hypocritical interruptions.

"But I've seen things on board of this ship that could make even me wonder. Another officer might easily decide to call the complaints seditious. And Brem *was* the third of the *Ragnarok*'s officers to go. It's only been a few months, hasn't it?"

She stood up suddenly, with a gesture whose angry violence startled him. "No, General. Any such expressions of discontent are more than understandable. You should have a look at the *Ragnarok*'s transfer history sometime; it's fascinating. Fleet has been packing us with problems for years. I don't like feeling like a target, General, but if this ship hasn't been set up as a fireship, I've never seen a fireship in my life."

Fireship. It took him a moment, then he understood. She meant that Fleet was using this ship to warehouse its undesirables until such time as Fleet could wipe them all out in one swift conflagration.

"I'll grant you that the mess has fallen to near-punitive levels." There was no point in mentioning that ap Rhiannon herself fell into that category, because ap Rhiannon was thickheaded and stubborn and difficult but she wasn't stupid. "But that doesn't mean Fleet's willing to throw lives away, your Excellency. Your concern gets the better of you."

As soon as Rukota said it he wished he hadn't, because that was clearly exactly what Brecinn had in mind, and what ap Rhiannon was resisting with every weapon at her disposal. Ap Rhiannon had few weapons compared to the commanding officer of Pesadie Training Command, so perhaps it was inevitable that her deployment lacked finesse.

How had the Bench failed Jennet ap Rhiannon?

She was crèche-bred. She had been raised to show no tolerance for disloyal behavior or qualified opinions on anybody's part. Anybody—peers, subordinates, superiors. But the crew of the *Ragnarok* sounded like a crew with serious problems of disaffection, and ap Rhiannon was defending them. Not calling in a Fleet Interrogations Group to conduct a purge.

She smiled at the wall where the image of the Admiral had been. "You're very right, General. Nobody's throwing any lives away. These are my lives. I'm responsible to the Bench for them. And I'm not letting a single soul on board of this ship pass into Fleet's hands without a fight."

There were in some ways some aspects of ap Rhiannon's own behavior that could possibly be potentially interpreted as giving the appearance of mutinous intent.

Rukota stood up slowly, but with determination. He had to get out of here. Something in the atmosphere was clearly affecting his brain. The atmosphere scrubbers were failing. Yes. That had to be the explanation.

"By your leave, your Excellency. I'll be getting back to trying to ignore my preliminary assessment team."

If one of Fleet's own prized paragons of devotion to the rule of Law could sound like a battery with its primer gone bad, there was no longer any sense nor reason in the world.

The plasma-sheath generators near the leading edge of the *Ragnarok*'s upper hull spooled their atoms-thin gauze in a ceaseless churning. Filament-tissue, invisible to the average hominid under Jurisdiction, fabric flowing like water up over the carapace hull and down along the maintenance atmosphere in constant motion, the sheath both protected *Ragnarok* and fed its great fusion converters, pulling the trapped dust and debris of both planetary and interstellar space into the ship's engines.

Passing through the energy inferno, the sheath was constantly cleansed of matter and cycled back to the outer hull once more. Self-healing, tolerant of whole shuttlecraft passing through, and yet capable of absorbing the constant bombardment of subatomic matter, the plasma sheath fed the *Ragnarok* on whatever space had to offer, guarding the hull jealously—guarding the lives within.

Feeding the ship, and cleaning it, the sheath carried the industrial waste of the furnace process itself the entire circuit of its rounds to pass the dross back through the fusion converters and abandon it to nuclear disassociation.

The entire process was below the level of the *Ragnarok*'s consciousness, like breathing. Engineering was aware of it, in the background, and kept a close watch on the rate of spool and the yield from the outside, but for the most part, plasma-sheath generation was entrusted to ship's computers.

Like the normal breathing of the average animal, occasionally something irritated one of the generators, and it coughed.

There was a little remote traveling in the plasma stream, as if dropped there through the cyclers at some point after that portion of the fabric of the sheath had left the furnace. Just a little smaller than one of the spooling-ports, perfectly round and smooth—catching on nothing—it fell from the ship embedded in the plasma, like a piece of grit surrounded by a protective layer of mucoid tissue.

Once it had left the ship, however, the little remote took surprising action, kicking itself away from the *Ragnarok*'s hull, tearing itself free with a sudden convulsive gesture.

Away from the ship, it dropped, inert and silent, traveling on the inertia of its escape until its sensors told it that it was clear of the ship's communications intercept net.

And then it began to transmit.

It was too small, too primitive, to do anything but send its tiny packet of information. It was preset for one exact target receiver, burning its limited power supply with reckless profligacy in its urgent need to make its message heard.

It had things to say, to the right people. It knew who had been on board of the ship nearest to the observation station when the station had exploded. It knew which team it had been, and which Wolnadi. The names were required; the Warrant could not be written without the names, and without a Warrant, there could be no serious challenge to the *Ragnarok*'s custody of the individuals in question.

It sent the names on transmit, and fell silent.

Ap Rhiannon had asked Dierryk Rukota to join her in the Captain's office. He wasn't much occupied this forenoon, tired of watching the assessment team go through one Wolnadi after another and sensibly resigned to the futility of trying to talk to the Ship's Engineer; so he'd come directly.

He beat her to it, finding himself when he got there

with nobody but the First Officer for company. The First Officer, however, was apparently too absorbed in some documentation to more than acknowledge his presence with a polite, if uninterested, nod.

Rukota looked around. This had been Captain Brem's office. It looked unoccupied—as though Brem had only begun to move in before his unexpected death. None of the décor looked particularly like ap Rhiannon to Rukota; had she moved in at all? Or was she still operating out of a Lieutenant's office, being punctilious about her rating? It'd be like her.

"Well, if the Captain isn't going to use this space, I wish she'd loan it to me," Rukota said to the room. The Captain's office was one of the larger administrative spaces on board of the *Ragnarok*, and it was quite emphatically roomier than the squad bay that Mendez had allotted to the Pesadie team. "I could fit my whole crew in here. With some space left over for a bean tea service," he added, a little unfairly, eyeing the quite obviously unused service set to one side of the room. If there was any hope at all for good bean tea it was nowhere on board but here, since Wheatfields had declined to share his.

Mendez set his flatform docket aside as the admit warning sounded. "Haven't had it fumigated yet, General. And my Captain needs the space to talk to your Admiral."

Rukota was minded to object to Mendez's assumption that Brecinn was "his" Admiral, but found the First Officer's unself-conscious reference to ap Rhiannon as his Captain too interesting to interfere with. And ap Rhiannon was here, now, after all. No bickering amongst the troops in the presence of Command Branch, Rukota reminded himself.

"General Rukota."

She came into the room with a precision of Security whose posting of themselves at the door was beautiful to watch. Rukota had noticed that, about the *Ragnarok;* all of the normal morale indicators were absolutely topnotch as far as crew demeanor went. He'd been trying to convince himself that they were all simply on their best behavior with outsiders present; but the ability of a pair of troops to post in perfect synchronicity was not something that could be turned on and off for company. It was either a consistent habit of living, or impossible.

Bowing his salute in response, Rukota felt it better not to speak until spoken to. She clearly didn't have a great deal to say to him. Seating herself at the Captain's desk, she gestured for him to come and stand behind her. Mendez took a position beside him, at her right shoulder, and petrified without a moment's notice into an archetypal image of a First Officer present for a Captain's transmission.

Rukota didn't think he could match the pose. Moreover, he could not help but feel that he would only look pathetic if he tried. At least he understood why he was here, now; ap Rhiannon had some sort of an official communication to make.

"This is Acting Captain Jennet ap Rhiannon, Jurisdiction Fleet Ship *Ragnarok,* for Admiral Sandri Brecinn. Pesadie Training Command."

The usual preliminaries, and then Admiral Brecinn appeared in holographic projection at one-and-four-eighths' life-size in the room in front of them. It was a good deal closer than Rukota had ever gotten to her, and the experience was not an entirely pleasant one. She looked rather older, and very tired.

She also did not look to be in a very good temper. "You have results to report, ap Rhiannon?" Granted, Brecinn had no motivation for observing the niceties of Fleet protocol; she seemed to be alone in her office, and ap Rhiannon was only acting in the capacity of Captain. Rukota thought her choice of words unnecessarily short, all the same.

"Preliminary results, Admiral. I am calling to report that the Wolnadi fighter that was nearest to the scene of the accident when it occurred has been identified by the preliminary assessment team. My Engineer has transmitted the information to me. I will be asking General Rukota to prepare an in-depth analysis."

Rukota heard her, but he didn't believe it. He kept his face clear and his expression serene by main force of will. It was times like these that being ugly was useful; people generally spent as little time as possible looking at him, and were less likely to notice a continuity glitch accordingly.

If the Wolnadi had been identified, it was news to him.

"And not before time, Lieutenant." Brecinn sounded gratified, almost gloating. But not surprised. Suddenly Rukota had a very unhappy feeling that something even uglier than anticipated had occurred. Had one of the team come by information by stealth, and transmitted it?

It was hard to imagine. There was a genuine coherence to the crew of the *Ragnarok* that Rukota found intriguing, and that would be hard to reconcile with treachery on the part of any of the souls assigned.

Admiral Brecinn addressed him directly, calling his attention back to his immediate environment. "I was beginning to wonder what you were taking so long at, General. When may I expect my report?"

He could answer this one honestly, which always helped. "I'm unsure as yet, Admiral. The information is just in. I haven't had a chance to consult with the team."

And yes, he *would* play along with whatever it was that ap Rhiannon had in mind. It was poor policy to contradict Command Branch in front of other officers. He could afford to wait until he knew what she was up to before he decided what his considered response would be. He didn't owe Brecinn anything in particular, one way or the other.

"Well. Fair enough, I suppose. Don't keep me waiting. Anything else to report, Lieutenant?"

Brecinn's insistence on ap Rhiannon's junior status was beginning to grate on Rukota's nerves. The crew of the *Ragnarok* didn't seem to mind "Captain" ap Rhiannon; they corrected themselves easily enough when they said Lieutenant, or at least they had in Rukota's limited experience. If the crew of the *Ragnarok* didn't mind, why should Admiral Brecinn?

Whether or not ap Rhiannon experienced a like sense of aggravation, there was more than a touch of asperity in her voice as she replied. "Yes, Admiral, in fact. I have shortages to report, and it's impacting health and welfare. We were to have been at the resupply station days ago, Admiral. I have got to go and get some of these requisitions filled."

Brecinn had not been expecting anything of the sort out of ap Rhiannon, either in subject or in delivery. It was all too clear from the momentary wobbling of her stream-snapper's beak of a mouth. "You've already been told three times that there simply are no replacement converters available for that secondary fusion. I've told you, there's a shortage on, or don't you believe your own supply reports?"

What shortage? Rukota wondered, hoping his face was appropriately blank. Shortage of converters for fusion furnaces? That was ridiculous. Why would Fleet tolerate a shortage in such a critical area? Motivation and weapons systems had the very highest priorities. He must not have caught something, somewhere.

"Understood, Admiral Brecinn. But I have other requisitions against existing inventory for nutritures. Meds. On-board recycles. Some of these have been outstanding from the beginning of the recent exercise."

Oh, really? That could explain why the bean tea was as bad as it was. If he'd known ahead of time, he could have packed an extra store for his personal use; although that might not have been interpreted as a friendly sharing gesture.

"General Rukota? What do you have to say about all this?"

Brecinn's abrupt, direct address startled him beyond his ability to cover it up. Was she calling ap Rhiannon a liar? Or simply a poor judge of logistical requirements? Did it matter? Brecinn clearly did not care how she spoke to ap Rhiannon, Command Branch or no Command Branch. It made a man feel very uncomfortable: apart from the gratuitous rudeness of the gesture, what made Brecinn think that she could get away with it?

"The scope of the assessment team's brief does not extend to the *Ragnarok*'s requisitions-in-holding." He could hear his own stiff outrage in his voice. And he was trying to be polite; because he believed that discipline and courtesy were supposed to move up, as well as down, the command chain. "As far as anecdotal evidence is to be trusted I can personally vouch for the generally depressing lack of required sensory characteristics in Ship's Mess."

But Brecinn was already pulling her head back beneath the bony shell of her figurative carapace. "Well, as long as it doesn't interfere with the investigation, I suppose you may as well go resupply," Brecinn said, with a dismissive frown. "Rukota, I'll be waiting for your report."

Ap Rhiannon had given her what she wanted, the promise of a report. Brecinn clearly felt she could afford to play from her rank. "But I don't mind telling you, Lieutenant, that to my mind identifying the saboteurs responsible for the murder of Captain Brem should be somewhat more important than stocking up on sweetener for your fast-meal mush."

"Thank you, Admiral Brecinn." Ap Rhiannon for her part sounded absolutely unmoved, as if she had not even noticed Brecinn's rudeness. "For my part, I was raised to believe that the health and welfare of the souls entrusted to my Command under the rule of Law was much more important than playing pointless political games with anyone. I state once again for the Record that the evidence will show that the *Ragnarok* had no part in the death of Cowil Brem. Departing for resupply, by your leave, Admiral."

Admiral Brecinn waved ap Rhiannon off with a cavalier gesture of her hand. "Do what you must, Lieutenant. I need by-name identification of the crew of that Wolnadi, General, so that the documentation can be prepared for a formal Inquiry. The sooner we can complete the necessary reports, the better off we will all be in the long run. I trust you take my meaning. All of you. Pesadie Training Command, away, here."

It was a mistake on the Admiral's part, an error. Rukota knew it in his bones, even though he did not yet know exactly why it was an error.

Cutting the signal with a decisive gesture ap Rhiannon stood up; and remained for a brief moment with her back to them, leaning on the table's surface as though she was tired. Rukota supposed that it was abstractly possible that she was, but there would be no getting such an admission out of her.

Then she straightened up, and looked back over her shoulder at them. "Let's get out of here," she suggested.

"Before we run into any interference. You know what to do, First Officer. General Rukota, thank you for coming. I felt you would wish to be present."

"Tell me about this information your Excellency has just provided," Rukota suggested, unwilling to go away quietly. "Does the preliminary assessment team know about this?"

Ap Rhiannon smiled. Mendez didn't. They were in this together, Rukota realized; and he was complicit as well, at least by implication. "It's possible," ap Rhiannon said. "We think we've had a leak. But as long as she thinks she's got the names coming, we can win a little time to maneuver."

Well, to the resupply depot at Laynock, for instance. Except that the Laynock depot wasn't the only depot that was accessible from the Pesadie exit vector. And he wasn't going to think about it. It was none of his business. "If she's got the names already, it's all academic, your Excellency."

Ap Rhiannon shook her head. "It's not official. She can't admit to having the names until your report transmits them. And once she has the names, she'll want the troops. I don't know how we're going to protect them, exactly. But we've got to think of something."

A vision from the recent past rose up on the mind's eye of General Dierryk Rukota. A shuttle. A courier. Clearing for Azanry, if he remembered correctly. Hadn't the technician said it was the *Ragnarok*'s Chief Medical Officer, going home? One of the Ship's Primes. Traveling with Security.

Ap Rhiannon was playing more dangerous a game than Rukota would have imagined, if she had done what he suspected. Her career was at risk, at the very least; and for what? Reluctance to surrender four souls to Inquiry, to torture?

Or educated expectation of how the scope of Inquiry would widen with its own inexorable logic from four to sixteen to two hundred and fifty-six?

"What's my place in this mess, then, your Excellency?"

Ap Rhiannon almost smiled. Almost. "Let that assessment team do what they came for, General. Ask them when they'll have information for you to prepare your

report. It's their job, after all. With respect. General."
Stay out of it. You aren't part of it anyway. Keep clear.

Rukota was disgusted enough to do just that. He bowed in salute. "Very good, your Excellency. Returning to assigned offices as instructed."

She hadn't a prayer of making it work, whatever it was. But he understood her motives and her rationale. And he liked them better than he liked Pesadie, with its corrupt Admiral and its opportunistic staff of reasonable people.

If Brecinn was going to enforce her will against the Jurisdiction Fleet Ship *Ragnarok,* it would be without aid and comfort from General Dierryk Rukota.

Well satisfied, Admiral Brecinn toggled into her on-station braid for Dame Noycannir to share the news. Not just the news she had just gotten from that tiresome little petty officer on the *Ragnarok,* but the other news as well, the news that had made ap Rhiannon's call welcome but not exactly a surprise.

Names. Names and identifications, received just this morning from remote. "Mergau. Yes. If you would come and pay me a visit, please. A note from a mutual friend with news that may be of interest."

They'd had two weeks to prepare. Noycannir had everything she needed to conduct a valid, legal Inquiry; with the names, she would be able to start to set up her strategy. Her interrogatories. Her in-depth personal file analysis, looking for the evidence of disaffection and corruption that would explain what they had done—and support the confessions that Noycannir had promised.

Sacrificing four lives to the rule of Law was not something to be done lightly. And yet Chilleau Judiciary would need Pesadie's support, in the coming weeks. The Second Judge would surely make her declaration soon. Pesadie had to be ready to defend the Second Judge's claim against any challenges, had to be in position to move against civil unrest; for the greater good.

She couldn't do that if Pesadie was compromised by an unfortunate, ill-timed accident. She could not afford the compromise. She had to be ready to deploy all of her resources, to stabilize the sector should the Selection be contested, to achieve the privileged position in the new administration that the reasonable people with whom she did business expected her to gain and maintain for the mutual benefit of all parties.

It was only four lives.

Noycannir would find a way to hold it to four. Surely. Noycannir was a reasonable woman herself. And four lives were as nothing, compared to the greater good, compared to the lives Pesadie would save by being there and being ready to act to restore order.

Forty lives were not too much to pay for that. So four were not worth mourning. It was to be their glory to give up their lives to ensure a safe and stable transition when the Selection was announced. Theirs would be a sacrifice no less noble for being hidden for all time. Yes.

It was only six days to Laynock and back. It would be at least three before ap Rhiannon would force herself to release the official report with the names. By the time the Warrant had been endorsed at Chilleau Judiciary and returned, the *Ragnarok* would be back at Pesadie Training Command.

Noycannir had enough to worry her. There was no sense in cluttering her mind with unnecessary details. Brecinn had the names; that would be more than enough information for Noycannir to start to work.

Chapter Seven

Thresholds

Mergau Noycannir looked over the list of names that
Admiral Brecinn had handwritten out for her, realizing
with joy in her heart that this was even more perfect
than she could have hoped.

"These are to be the prisoners, then?" she asked, hoping the note of admiration in her voice was suitably
transparent. Brecinn was vain; it was not difficult to handle her. "Your team is to be congratulated. When must
I be ready to begin processing?"

She'd presented Brecinn with a conflict of sorts, between Brecinn's desire to bask in her acclaim and the
fact that she didn't have a good answer for the question.
"I don't mind telling you that the *Ragnarok* is not being
reasonable at all, Dame Noycannir. Why am I not surprised? I'll be able to get a Warrant as soon as the official report is released, and we'll have the prisoners very
shortly after that. Four days?"

Impossibly optimistic, Mergau was sure. But that
suited her purpose just as well. She didn't need the prisoners. She just needed to know who they were going to
be to mount a coup that was so daring it would win her
power and influence beyond her fondest hopes.

"Very good, Admiral. I've got some preliminary data
pulled on the *Ragnarok*'s Security. I can start to bring
it all together. Shall I get started?" Mergau stood up as
she spoke, to indicate her eagerness to be on about her

part of this important task. To tell Brecinn that she was leaving, now, but doing it politely.

"You have everything you need, Dame?" Brecinn asked. "Good. Yes, thank you, we can't be on top of this unfortunate situation too quickly. It's gone on for far too long already. Ap Rhiannon will be sorry. I promise you that."

Mergau didn't care about ap Rhiannon. She had her own agenda to put forward.

The fact that the named Security were all people assigned to Andrej Koscuisko only made her task more poignantly appropriate.

"No matter how clever these little officers think they may be, sooner or later they all pay, eh, Admiral?" Mergau agreed, and bowed. Leaving the room on a graceful note of conspiracy. Not bothering to point out that Admiral Brecinn herself might well be one of those "little officers" who would eventually pay.

Not before Koscuisko paid. And Koscuisko had so much to pay for. Everything that had gone wrong with her life went back to him; but she would have revenge—all the more sweet because his own people, his own precious and famously cherished Security, would be the instrument of her ultimate victory.

Hurrying through the halls, Mergau made her way to the out-of-the-way storesroom that had been configured for an interrogation arena, a theater of inquiry.

Had she everything she needed, Brecinn had asked. The instruments of torture were here, the drugs from the Controlled List, restraints and implements, shackles and chains; all secondary, though Brecinn did not know it.

What was truly crucial to her purpose was the Record: and the equipment Mergau needed to effect her plan. She'd told the Admiral that she would gain confessions to whatever Brecinn decided the story should be; she hadn't lied. She'd only stretched the truth a little.

She had realized what she could really do with this opportunity only gradually. Pesadie Training Command was a testing facility; its judicial records were naturally weighted in just the direction she needed to go—insubordination, sabotage of training exercise, failure to comply with instructions received from exercise commanders, mutinous intent.

She could hardly have hoped for so generous a field from which to choose had she been free to survey all of Chilleau Judiciary's records. Koscuisko's people. She would send a message to her spies on Azanry. She would know exactly where to find him.

Koscuisko was no match for her in cunning or in strategy; it was only the unfair advantage of his medical training—the product of the privileges of wealth and rank—that had made her look bad in front of her Patron, that had persuaded the First Secretary to devalue her worth and her abilities.

Mergau checked her secures and engaged the privacy barrier. "Smish Smath," Mergau said to her voice-trans. Secure. No one could forge her voice. She had to be very careful. Nobody had done what she planned to do in all the history of Jurisdiction. "Murat Spodinne. Taller Archops, Lek Kerenko."

More luck, on top of luck. Kerenko would be easy. He was one of Koscuisko's Security slaves, a bond-involuntary troop. There was no need to create a confession for Lek Kerenko; all she needed there was a simple "expiration of a Bond during the process of Inquiry, without prejudice."

The others would have misled him all along, of course; by definition, a bond-involuntary could not plot mutiny. The governor would not allow it. Once she began to probe and test for what knowledge he might have, his governor—the story would go—would so work on him, in combination with her keen interrogation into matters that he should have seen and noted and reported to his First Officer, that he would die of self-inflicted punishment.

She would be sure to specify that he had not been at fault in any way. That way, his family would not have to repay the Bench for the costs of his training and his keep. Andrej would be grateful to her for that. She would see to it.

Three confessions. Only three. Smath would be the most challenging. There were relatively fewer women in Security; they tended to be absorbed in Engineering instead because of their superior skills in operating under pressure. They were disproportionately underrepresented in Brecinn's records accordingly. Women were more logical, better at covering their tracks, harder to catch up doing something stupid.

She'd make do. She had the Record here.

"Index on class of hominid. Sex. Physical characteristics." She'd preselected the data files on the cases that would match any of the *Ragnarok*'s Security; this would be a much swifter search. "Execute."

Andrej Koscuisko had been there at Fleet Orientation Station Medical when Verlaine had sent her to take the Writ to Inquire, and come home as Inquisitor to Chilleau Judiciary. She had done the best she could. It had been hard. And Koscuisko had done better.

In an evil hour she had commended Koscuisko to her Patron while she was still at Fleet Orientation Station Medical, to spite the station's administrator and her Tutor, to put them all on notice that she was a force to be reckoned with and had the immediate ear of the First Secretary. That they had good cause to be careful how they misused her, because she had more power than they seemed to realize. It had been a mistake.

Verlaine had compared her to Koscuisko and found her wanting. No matter how hard she tried when she returned to Chilleau Judiciary, Verlaine had Koscuisko always in the back of his mind, pointing out her every small miscalculation, jeering at her every failure. Every defeat.

Koscuisko was a rich man from a powerful family; he had education and a certain degree of personal charm. People were so easily impressed by superficialities. They ascribed talent to Koscuisko that no one could hope to match, and built him up into a sort of legend against whom a mere mortal was powerless to compete. But just because she did not have Koscuisko's medical education did not mean that she lacked for knowledge of the Record . . . and how it could be used.

She had technical knowledge of Bench Record devices that few other people could hope to touch. Her access codes had never been revoked—Verlaine had thought he could yet find a use for her access, she supposed, as legal cover for some desperate act.

Now she would make use of her Writ against them all. She would use her knowledge of the Record to create a false history of interrogation and confession for three of the four Security troops who were on that Wolnadi fighter.

It would be a daring piece of work. The technical integrity of the Record was the cornerstone of the rule of Law and the Judicial order. No one had ever forged a Record. No one would ever dare reveal that she had done it. If the Record lost credibility, the Bench lost credibility. For the good of the Judicial order, Chilleau Judiciary would be forced to formally accept her forgeries as the truth.

She would take the Record to Azanry to confront Andrej Koscuisko. He was the Ship's Inquisitor on board the Jurisdiction Fleet Ship *Ragnarok*. It would be his duty to accompany her to Chilleau Judiciary to conduct the investigation. He would have no choice. And once she but had him in her hands, he would have no choice about anything, anything at all, ever again.

She would bring Koscuisko to Verlaine, a very special gift, captive, revealed as a coconspirator in the death of Cowil Brem—and who was to say that he had not been involved in that of the *Ragnarok*'s other recently dead officers as well? Was there to be no limits to the depth of Koscuisko's guilt? Verlaine would be gratified.

If he were not grateful, he would have to seem to be. He would be unable to reject her gift, not unless he was willing to risk not only his career, but that of his Judge as well. Verlaine would be forced to keep Koscuisko secured, concealed, hidden away, her prisoner; or be destroyed. And she would be secure.

She would have knowledge that could destroy the new First Judge and destabilize all of Jurisdiction space: knowledge that the Record could be forged, knowledge that Chilleau Judiciary could be blackmailed into compliant silence. She would be First Judge, because Verlaine would not dare deny her anything.

Pesadie Training Command would get its just reward. And Mergau Noycannir would be revenged at last on Andrej Koscuisko for all of the humiliations she had suffered in the past because of his wealth, his education, his position, the unfair advantage he enjoyed as an Inquisitor, putting her to shame in the eyes of her Patron.

Andrej Koscuisko walked hand in hand with his son in the garden, feeling the warmth of the afternoon sun like a blessing on his face. His home sun. His body knew this air, this gravity, this light. It was almost physically painful to be here in his own place, the world that had bred him, the sun that ruled the chemistry of his blood. Home ground.

Anton looked up at him from time to time, strolling with him, but said little. Andrej didn't mind. What did he have to say to this young boy?

"Do you like the summer, Anton?" Andrej asked.

He knew there were other things that fathers were supposed to say. Studies. Saints. Obedience. Hunting. Things a young lord had to learn and know. Andrej didn't care. And he didn't have time. He would be leaving soon. If he was lucky, he'd be coming back; but if he wasn't, he would at least know something of the person his child was. Someone else would teach Anton who he was supposed to be.

"Summer is empty, sir," Anton replied, after a moment's apparent thought. "I like harvest. Harvesttime is full. I see people I only sometimes see in summer. I like harvest."

What was he to make of such a claim? Andrej wondered.

It was true, wasn't it?

In the summer the house was empty. Everyone was dispersed out into the fields, all across the estate. There was so much to do, and so much day in which to do it. Wasn't part of what made harvest glad the knowledge that the heavy work was done until the spring?

"Harvest is good," Andrej agreed. "I also like snow. Not wind. But snow. I never liked the wind, Anton."

Now Anton smiled up at him with an open, candid expression that wracked Andrej's heart, for reasons that he wasn't sure he understood. "Ferinc says it's words in the wind, sir."

Yes, that was what Andrej had been taught. Words in the wind, messages gone astray, and if you could catch the whole of the message the soul who'd breathed it would be free at last. "Who's Ferinc, son Anton?"

"Cousin Ferinc, sir. I love him very much. If he hadn't gone to Dubrovnije I would show you to him." Malcontent, then. Anton would show his father to his friend?

Andrej frowned up at the clear blue sky, surprised to feel the pain in his own heart. He shouldn't feel pain; he should be grateful. Anton had a special friend that he loved. It wasn't as though that would have been different had Andrej lived at home all of this time; Dolgorukij fathers and their sons were never friends. There was too much to stand between them. Anton called him "sir" with grave and unfailing respect. What might it be like to be called "Papa"?

The sun caught on the glass panes of one of the garden gates in the distance. Someone had come in from the other side of the garden, the side that faced the motor stables. Andrej sighed. "Yes, I would like to meet him, Anton. Since you love him, I must love him also. Now you must go with Lek. He'll take you back to the house. I have company come."

Anton stood waiting on the garden path, and after a moment, Andrej realized that Anton was waiting to be kissed.

Crouching down on his heels, Andrej kissed Anton on the cheek, and Anton put his arms around Andrej's neck to hug him. It was peculiar behavior for a Dolgorukij son, to hug his father. Whoever Cousin Ferinc was, he had taught Anton to be a loving child.

Suddenly Andrej felt overwhelmed with gratitude that Anton felt free to offer him affection. Of all things. Had he ever, ever hugged *his* father? Or had they been too formal with each other from the start?

Anton went away hand in hand with Lek, whom Andrej particularly wanted to show to his household as someone to be trusted with the most precious thing he had. His child. And coming down the garden path was his cousin, Stanoczk, and the Bench intelligence specialist, Jils Ivers.

"The peace of the Malcontent is with you," Cousin Stanoczk said, formally. "You know the Bench intelligence specialist, your Excellency?"

Of course he did. He had spent some very unpleasant moments with Ivers in his office on the *Ragnarok;* but it was not a question of personal fault. He had seen her within the past year. He hadn't seen his cousin Stanoczk for far longer than that. "Bench specialist," Andrej nodded. "But, Stoshik, how long?"

Now Stanoczk grinned at him and relaxed. "Some time, Derush. Do you embrace the Malcontent, or have you too much dignity?"

There were two kinds of joke there, whether or not Stanoczk meant both rather than just the one. The first was that Andrej would embrace a Malcontent who was his blood relation, but he had not yet "embraced the Malcontent," which was quite a different proposition.

The second was that he himself, Andrej Koscuisko, might pretend to disdain the Malcontent, whose moral turpitude was strictly relative to Combine mores—when his own sin was atrocity under the laws of almost any well-developed moral community.

Andrej held out his arms for his cousin, and embraced Stanoczk with a full heart. He and Stoshik had been playmates when they had been children, never minding the gulf of rank that stood between them. Before Stoshik had elected the Malcontent. It was a very comforting embrace; but that was Stanoczk's business, after all—comfort, and reconciliation.

Finally Stanoczk pulled away, and laughed, holding his hand to his eyes for a moment. Stanoczk had brown eyes, brown hair, a deep voice; but otherwise he and Andrej alike were—the very types of the blood of the family of their mutual maternal grandmother. The Kospodar line. Chuvishka Kospodar, in fact, from whom the Sarvaw nations had yet to recover.

"It's good to see you, Derush." Stanoczk used the childish diminutive rather than the more formal adult pet name. It *had* been a long time. "I need to speak to you on the Malcontent's business. Later. Is the Bench specialist to stay? Because I could to Beraltz go and speak."

House-master Beraltz, Stoshik meant. Andrej turned to Ivers, who had watched him greet Stanoczk with reserved good will. "If you have no other business, Specialist, you are welcome to a place at my hearth."

Perhaps "welcome" wasn't quite the word for it, and it was only *his* hearth in principle. It was much more Marana's hearth, Beraltz's hearth, the hearth of the people who had lived here and seen to the estate these nine years past; but still, in point of protocol, it was "his" hearth.

"Cousin Stanoczk says we're expected at Chelatring Side in eight days' time," Ivers said. "An expedition in force, I've been told. Thank you, your Excellency, you're very kind."

That was right. He had to go into the mountains. The Autocrat's Proxy would come to take the pulse of the Koscuisko familial corporation, and though Zsuzsa would doubtless know their father's prejudice already, it was all part of the play of the Selection for the grand rounds to be made.

The Autocrat called her people to herself when she wanted to issue a decision, to let them know her will. The Autocrat came to her people one by one when she sought their advice and their opinion: and so it had been since the days of the Malcontent's life beneath the canopy of Heaven.

"Go and tell my Chief of Security," Andrej suggested to his cousin. Stoshik took himself away on Andrej's not very subtle suggestion, and Andrej turned to Ivers. "Stildyne says he has worked with you before, Specialist. But since you go to Chelatring Side to hear my father's will, what use do you have for one mere Andrej? Walk, and talk to me."

It was a beautiful day. It would be midsummer soon. The breeze from the river smelled of growing things, the bosom of the Holy Mother, the skin of the great green-gold fish of the Matredonat. Someone would bring refreshment. A man could not walk five paces in his own garden without someone turning up with a laden table.

"First I have to tell you that the First Secretary at Chilleau Judiciary sent me in full knowledge of the fact that you might feel that he's attempting to bribe you."

She didn't look at him, but at the great hedge at the far end of the garden, well beyond the maze. She took a very formal tone with him, one that made the word *bribe* all the more unusual in context. "Chilleau Judiciary can't do anything just now without a political interpretation being cast on it, after all, your Excellency. So it's important that you understand that what I've been sent to tell you is independent of your family's advice to the Autocrat. And of the final decision at Selection."

The gravel on the path was crushed pink rock quarried in the hills around the Serah. It had been so long since he had felt it crunch beneath his feet. "Yes?" He didn't know what she was talking about.

She seemed to realize this with a sigh. "When I saw you last, your Excellency, it was to bring you an offer from First Secretary Sindha Verlaine. You took an unexpected action to assert your independence, your Excellency. The First Secretary regrets his ill-considered action. I have with me fully executed Bench documents for relief of Writ, sir."

Relief of Writ?

Andrej stopped in the middle of the garden path with the late morning sun warm on his shoulders, squinting toward the river. "I don't understand what you're trying to tell me, Specialist." He was afraid to believe what he thought she was saying.

"Your reengagement with Fleet was essentially coerced. It can be put aside. I have the legal instrument. Stay home, your Excellency. The Bench regrets its lapse in judgment. Sir."

The words made no sense. She spoke Standard, not Aznir, but he had been tutored in Standard from a young age, he knew the language. It wasn't that.

Andrej shook his head with violence. It was as though he had gotten water in his ear sinking too deeply into the bath, and couldn't find his balance. "Your humor is ill chosen, Specialist Ivers." He wanted to believe that it was possible, and it couldn't be, because he wanted it far too much. "Why have you come?"

"I've brought the documentation with me, your Excellency," she insisted firmly, but as if she was fully sensitive to the confusion it created in his mind. "Since you have been so generous as to offer me your hospitality, sir, perhaps I could meet with you later today or tomorrow, and display my proofs. I know it must be difficult to credit. But I'm telling you the truth. The First Secretary is not playing games."

She almost said "*Any more games.*" He knew she had. Could it be true?

"Why?" Andrej asked, wonderingly. "Why, after all these years, would Verlaine have come to such a conclusion? Does my old schoolmate Noycannir no longer have his ear?"

Ivers looked confused. But Ivers knew Noycannir; Ivers had brought her to Port Rudistal, years and years and years ago. Noycannir had thought that she was to assume control, but the Domitt Prison had already been taken off-line, and under Andrej's personal command.

"There are political implications." Ivers's tone was grave and reserved. Of course there were. They could not escape them, not under the current unsettled circumstances. "But I've spoken to the First Secretary, your Excellency. I believe his motivation to be genuine. If opportune."

The house-master's catering party had come into the garden from the gate nearest the kitchens, and he could not discuss this matter in front of the house staff. They were discreet; they would keep it in the family—but the family in which they would keep this news comprised every soul at the Matredonat.

"Freedom?" he asked, watching the house-master's party nearing with tables, hampers, linen.

"It is the judgment of the Court that your extension was only solicited as a result of improper pressure. 'Unreasonable duress,' I think it says. There is more."

Could it be true? Did she in reality offer him the escape he had believed denied him? Was he to stay here on Azanry, in his home, with his child, and never be the instrument of atrocity again?

"Too much, Specialist Ivers," Andrej said finally, putting one hand to her shoulder to communicate the depths of his emotional confusion. "I cannot grapple with this suggestion here and now. We will take rhyti. There is to be no help for it. Tomorrow in the morning, after breakfast, come to me in the library, and show me the documents you have.''

She wasn't playing games with him. Bench intelligence specialists didn't play games. She knew what she was saying, as she had not more than one year ago when Captain Lowden had sent her to speak to him on board of the *Ragnarok*.

A full banqueting-hall of local gentry was coming to the Matredonat for dinner; there was to be dancing in the gardens after dark. Her offer needed more concentration than he would have to spare until tomorrow. He needed time to think about what she had said, and make up his mind about whether he had interpreted her correctly or not.

"At your Excellency's disposal, sir, entirely." She knew that what she brought was world-shaking for him. If *she* believed that he was to be free, how could he doubt?

He would be free. He could stay home. He would learn to be a husband to Marana, if she would permit it. He could become a father to his son, in place of some unknown Malcontent. And he could engage with the Malcontent to see if there was anything a man could do to atone for such sins as he had committed. He could be reconciled to his family, his father and his mother.

All he would have to do then was discover who it was that had wanted him dead; and if Chilleau Judiciary offered him freedom, did that mean that the threat had not come from Chilleau Judiciary, or was being withdrawn?

He would never see his Bonds again, not until the Day dawned for them and they came to him. If the Day ever dawned. If they ever came to him after that. Yet when last year he had believed that he was going home at the expiration of his tour of duty, he'd known that he could not take his Bonds with him.

The fate that had faced them then had been far worse than it was now. Captain Lowden had been in command of the *Ragnarok*. Andrej had shuddered to think of people for whom he was responsible, of whom he was fond, suffering Lowden's whims and jests without him to protect them. But now Lowden was dead.

Andrej didn't know much about Jennet ap Rhiannon, but she was nothing like Griers Verigson Lowden. The bond-involuntaries assigned to the *Ragnarok* were as close to safe as they could be. First Officer would look out for them. Stildyne would be there.

And they would want him to be free, even at cost to themselves—as he would wish for them. He couldn't let that become an issue in his mind: or not an insurmountable barrier. Once he had seen Ivers's documentation with his own eyes, he would know whether he was to send Stildyne back to the *Ragnarok* an orphan.

Dierryk Rukota was lying on his back on the bench in the squad-bay that First Officer had assigned to the preliminary assessment team, chewing on his thoughts and trying to digest his mid-meal, when the admit at the door sounded with unexpected urgency, and the *Ragnarok*'s Intelligence Officer came storming through in a great rustling of wings, with four or five Ship's Security behind her.

"I have no intention of tolerating, no, it is not prudent!" she shrieked at him, her momentum carrying her clear to the far wall of the squad-bay where she scrambled up onto the surface of the desk-ledge and glared at him horribly. "At the very least a formal protest, and you will be very lucky if the Engineer does not have you simply locked off. I would not regret seeing it."

He couldn't speak for the shock of the surprise, the clear sense of assault and the fear he had of predators with such sharp glittering teeth. Half-stupefied, he could only freeze—still lying on his back—and wonder, for the crucial moment that it took her to find a foothold at the top of the empty equipment locker. Clambering up, she inverted herself, wrapping her wings around her in a thunderous gesture of high dudgeon and rocking sullenly back and forth in expectant silence.

For a moment he considered whether the particularly nasty bowl of soup he'd gotten for his mid-meal had poisoned his brain somehow. It could be a bad dream, couldn't it? Delusions. Why would the Ship's Intelligence Officer, one of the Ship's Primes, have come down to the dismal space that Mendez had assigned to them, in person? And—in the unlikely event that she had decided to indulge a taste for fresh raw Rukota—what conceivable reason could she have for bringing witnesses?

He sat up carefully, taking stock of the situation. He was trapped in here, alone, with her. Security was at the door, but by the looks of them they were not inclined to intervene should Two take it into her head to tear his throat open for a snack.

"Your Excellency. A very great pleasure, ma'am. To what do I owe the honor?"

Her great black leathery wings filled the room like an explosion as she gestured. "I am not mollified; you are not in order. I am keeping all of them. Confined to courier. You will have to sleep in some room else."

All right, it was Pesadie's team. They'd done something; or something that they'd done had been traced back—the information ap Rhiannon had announced to Admiral Brecinn, perhaps? "If her Excellency would be graciously pleased to explain, ma'am."

Two was still muttering, and how she managed that with a translator Rukota could not fathom for the life of him. Not that he wanted to dwell on that particular phrase—*the life of him*—with an obviously angry Desmodontae in the same small room as he was.

"As if you think that I am stupid. Lax. Remiss in procedure," she accused, shifting her wings with an angry sort of irritated restlessness. "As if you think we are to be simply walked in on and queried by any uncleared parties. As if you have no knowledge of plain Standard or good discipline. It is intolerable, I remind you!" she shouted yet again, her wings an agitated scrim against the back wall.

"Yes, ma'am, but if you'd just give me the worst of it. I am responsible for the conduct of the team, after all." Technically, at least. In fact, they'd made it all too clear that he was only there for show: but at least the Captain and crew of the *Ragnarok* seemed to understand that as well.

Two dropped from her perch; Rukota shut up. Scuttling forward on her strong little feet, using the primary joint of her wingtips to hurry her along, she paused before Rukota on her way out of the room, lifting her sharp black face toward Rukota's with an expression of immense dignity, only somewhat weakened by the fact that she surely could not see him.

"Members of your party have been found using guest-code to access ship's computers."

Rukota closed his eyes with involuntary pain. Violating Security protocols was a willful endangerment of Fleet resources, not to speak of lives.

"And once members of your party had accessed ship's computers, they tried to command-prime to the First Officer's administrative log. It is just as well that our Captain did not notice. For myself I do not care, but there is a default penalty, yes?"

Indeed there was. The default penalty for compromising administrative security was six-and-sixty, and dismissal from service without benefits. Jennet ap Rhiannon was entirely capable of invoking it; she would probably not make dismissal stick, but nobody on board would stand between those people and the whip. Rukota set his teeth against a grimace of disgust.

"Thank you, your Excellency." They had put him in an absolutely unacceptable position, that of being responsible for an act that he had not authorized and of which he deeply disapproved. "I'll see to it that it's so noted in the official report. Confined to courier, you said, your Excellency?"

She glared up at him for a few breaths longer before apparently making up her mind. "We will not speak of it again. First Officer has found a place for you, we are short a Ship's Third Lieutenant. It is at least a clean berth."

It occurred to Rukota that for the second time Two had rather pointedly excluded him from the well-deserved quarantine of the preliminary assessment team. He was grateful, if surprised. He didn't like those people.

"I'm very much obliged, your Excellency. I'll take them off your hands as soon as we return to Pesadie. From Laynock, am I right?"

She was between him and the door, with her back to the Security troops she'd brought with her. Looking up into his face, Two laughed.

It was unmistakable. She opened her sharp-muzzled mouth wide, affording all too clear a view of her very beautiful, very sharp white teeth; curled the corners of her black lips back happily, and panted, the tip of her cunning tongue quivering with genial hilarity. He couldn't hear a thing but he knew that she was laughing. This was something she had learned to do, apparently, to communicate with hominids, and it communicated very well.

"Impertinent," Two said, and with a sudden movement of one wing sent Rukota staggering back against the wall to collapse onto the ledge where he'd been sleeping. "My Captain will have a word to say to you, Rukota. Someone will come to show you to quarters. Good-bye."

Tucking her head down to her chest abruptly, Two scuttled rapidly from the room, and all of the Security went with her. The *Ragnarok* was not going to Laynock at all. They didn't care if he knew it. What was a man to make of all of this?

Third Lieutenant's billet. So ap Rhiannon had not vacated the First Lieutenant's quarters, and Seascape was logically in the Second Lieutenant's berth. Was that where he fit into all of this? Impossible.

Impossible that they should think to add him to the crew of the *Ragnarok*. Impossible to think that they could use an artilleryman. Impossible to imagine any set of circumstances within the realm of possibility that would enable such a situation. Warships did not select their own officers. Officers did not select their own assignments.

Ships released to resupply went to resupply and returned to their Command of assignment. Or they were in violation of standard operating procedure. In the jaundiced view of Pesadie Training Command, violation of standard operating procedure could all too easily be interpreted as—

He wasn't going to think about it; he was going to wait and see.

My Captain, Two had said. Not "acting." Captain ap Rhiannon.

He'd wait to see what ap Rhiannon would tell him:

and then he could decide how soon he should get seriously worried about what was going on, on board the Jurisdiction Fleet Ship *Ragnarok*.

Morning at the Matredonat.

As accustomed as Jils Ivers was to moving in circles at all levels of society, the luxury of Koscuisko's house rather stunned her. It was not so much a richness of food and drink and bed linen and appointments, though those would not shame a First Secretary—or even a Judge herself. This was a more profound wealth than material: all of these people with nothing whatever to do but wait upon her hand and foot, figuratively speaking, and Jils had no doubt that it would be literally speaking had she been inclined to accept a more extreme degree of body-service. All of these people.

Things that could be done by machine, by automated process, were done by hand here at the Matredonat, because Koscuisko had the money to afford to support human souls to do work that machines could do at less cost and in much less time. It was a species of conspicuous consumption that she had only very rarely encountered elsewhere in her travels on behalf of the Bench, and then only in much more primitive societies.

Koscuisko's private library was on the ground floor of the master's private house-within-a-house, a great, cool room with an immense hand-loomed carpet of considerable antiquity and value beyond price, tall massy shelves stacked deep with old-format printed texts bound in the tanned hides of animals, and an immense long study table in the middle of the room the approximate size of a one-soul courier. Jils looked at the shelves of books and scanned the titles, some of them unreadable from a distance, the gilt rubbed black with handling and age.

Garol should be here. He could probably read some of that.

Koscuisko closed the flatform docket and pushed it away from him a little space, turning toward her in his chair and taking up his flask of rhyti. He'd asked her to sit just at the end of the long side of the table, so that she was on his right, and there was not the great span of the table between them. It was almost intimate.

"This represents an unimaginable reversal on the First Secretary's part, Bench specialist. Does it not?"

The rhyti server was near at hand; she had her flask as well. She preferred almost anything to rhyti, but she hadn't let on, yet. She was waiting to see how long it would take for the house staff to come up with that particular piece of intelligence from other sources. It was an experiment. "It may seem so, your Excellency. But from my point of view it's a consistent stage in the development of Verlaine's thinking. That's one of the things that convinces me that he's telling us the truth with this offer."

Not the Bench order for relief of Writ. There was no controversy there; Koscuisko would execute it. There was no hesitation on Koscuisko's part over the Judicial order that would make him a free man. It was what else the First Secretary had sent that gave Koscuisko pause, and rightly so, because the implications were staggering.

"Speak to me, Dame Ivers. Permit me to share the benefit of your insight, because I do not trust this damned soul further than a starving wolf in the dairy, and yet I cannot but respect your professional opinion."

The Domitt Prison. Verlaine had not been to blame for that atrocity, perhaps, not directly; but he was responsible. Jils had never heard him try to pretend otherwise. It was one of the things that most annoyed Verlaine about Koscuisko. Verlaine had been in the wrong and Koscuisko had told the world. Regardless of what the formal decision of the special Court had been, Verlaine knew his honor to be justly tainted forever by what had happened to Nurail prisoners at Port Rudistal in a prison to which he should have paid more careful attention.

"His Excellency will recall from his orientation that the First Secretary had sent a Clerk of Court to qualify for the Writ."

Mergau Noycannir, whom Verlaine had pulled out of a gutter somewhere and nurtured as his protégée. Ruthless. Determined. And willing to do anything for the First Secretary's approval; a potentially very useful person to have on leash if only she could be kept on leash, because such people had no sense of proportion.

"You came to Rudistal with her, as I recall, Specialist. Yes."

Noycannir had no formal medical background, and proved ultimately incapable of mastering the intricacies of the Bench's Protocols. There had been no way to tell before they'd tried, and the sacrifice asked of Noycannir had been extreme. "The First Secretary's choice of representative was not perhaps fortunate." Verlaine had had no one else from whom he could have demanded so stern a proof of dedication as to go to Fleet Orientation Station Medical and become a torturer.

"If you will however consider the motives behind the attempt. He wanted an Inquisitor not under Fleet controls, to break the monopoly Fleet had over Inquiry and reclaim the Judicial function for the Bench. This was his motive. The First Secretary became interested in you because of your ability. I respectfully suggest you consider two aspects of that instinct on his part."

Koscuisko stood up and began to pace, but he was listening. Perhaps he was remembering things. Jils knew what sort of pressure Verlaine had put on Koscuisko, in his attempts to force Koscuisko's cooperation.

As many special field assignments as Fleet would tolerate, making Koscuisko's life as difficult as possible while he was assigned to *Scylla*—to make the point about Verlaine's influence, and how much easier Koscuisko's life would be with Verlaine as his friend.

Assignment to the *Ragnarok* under the command of Fleet Captain Lowden after Koscuisko had cried failure of Writ at the Domitt Prison, knowing what Lowden's record with Inquisitors was like—perhaps the single most ignoble, pettiest, and least worthy action to which Jils had ever known Verlaine to stoop.

Verlaine had hoped month by month that Koscuisko would yield to the strain of serving Lowden's corrupt interests, and petition to be called to Chilleau Judiciary. Koscuisko had not. Whether it was sheer stubbornness on his part, or whether Verlaine had underestimated Koscuisko's sensitivity to the plight of the bond-involuntaries under Lowden's command, Koscuisko had lasted out his full tour of duty; at what cost to himself Jils could hardly even guess. His determined resistance had frustrated and angered Verlaine—emotions tempered by the special heat that came from Verlaine's knowledge that he was in the wrong.

Finally Verlaine had backed Koscuisko into a corner with a threat to annex his Writ, and Koscuisko had kicked the bottom out of the box in which Verlaine had thought to trap him, and put the entire Jurisdiction Fleet between them. Again.

Now Verlaine had finally decided to admit that his behavior had been inappropriately motivated, and worse, it had been—there was no other word for it—unjust. Cruel and unjust.

Jils kept talking, because Koscuisko was clearly still listening and thinking while he paced. "Your reputation, your Excellency, maximum results with only the minimum amount of force required, no more. Even your Tenth Levels, sir, shockingly effective demonstrations, maximum invocation of deterrent terror where the verdict of the Bench called for the extreme penalty. Surely you can see that you are the man that Verlaine would want if he had begun to have reservations about the entire concept of forced confession. You do it so well."

Verlaine was conservative; he hated waste, of any sort. Koscuisko was the single most efficient Inquisitor in the entire inventory. Koscuisko didn't waste pain or blood, lives or limbs, not when he was given his own head. And in those instances in which Koscuisko had been handed a life out of which to make a public example, he hadn't wasted that, either. He'd exploited the resource to its absolute fullest, so that it was Koscuisko's work that people remembered when they called to mind the extreme penalty under Law for treason.

"I won't be pushed, Bench specialist," Koscuisko said. "I have been sufficiently imposed upon, to my mind. And behind the First Secretary's crude bullying I cannot but suspect I catch a whiff of a bitter old acquaintance."

It was true that Noycannir had carefully presented Koscuisko in the most annoying light possible before Verlaine. But Noycannir's influence had waned over time.

"He is not accustomed to being defied or resisted,

your Excellency. You brought out the worst in him, and
there's no excuse for it. But you win. There is nothing
more that he can do to make you his for the use of the
Second Judge. His realization sheds too strong a light
on the deficiencies in his own behavior. He perceives his
clear duty to make what amends he may. And he is truly
of a mind that Inquiry is a waste of lives, and no longer
in the best interest of the Judicial order."

"Do you believe this to be a genuine statement of
policy, Specialist Ivers?" Koscuisko asked, standing at
the table behind his chair, nodding at the flatform
docket. "Because if it is genuine, I must endorse it. The
personal history that I have with Chilleau Judiciary and
its people would not deter me for an instant. If I but
knew."

"He's convinced me of his sincerity, sir. And an en-
riched sense of cynicism is part of our initial issue when
we sign on." It wasn't as though Verlaine was the only
person within the Judicial structure who had come to
believe that the system no longer served a useful purpose, if it ever had. Inquiry had been an experiment
that had taken on a life of its own; the initial result of
institutionalizing torture as an instrument of State had
been very positive, but those results had been short-
term. Terror could stabilize a population for a few years,
but then it began to create a complex of destabilization
all its own.

Koscuisko sat down. "I will faithfully consider it,
Bench specialist." He had clearly already made up most
of his mind. It was only the possibility of duplicity on
the First Secretary's part that troubled him. "For the
rest of it. I will of course accept the offered relief. But
how are my people to be managed, if I have become a
private citizen?"

Koscuisko felt somewhat less strongly about his unbonded troops, perhaps, if only because they did not
need as much protection. But it was still obviously an
issue in his mind.

"Once you have countersigned the document, sir, I
will transmit it to Sant-Dasidar from the nearest Bench
offices. It will take two to three weeks after that for all
your voice-clearances to be purged. Until such time as

you can no longer invoke the Record you remain a Judicial officer, your Excellency. Although with these documents on record your status will clearly be in the process of changing."

If Verlaine had been able to break Koscuisko's bond-involuntaries free from Fleet and bring them to Chilleau Judiciary years ago Koscuisko would have come with them, almost certainly. Jils kept talking. "Until then the Bench will wish to continue to protect its officer. Your people can return to the *Ragnarok* once your clearances have all been purged, your Excellency, and at your instruction I will leave immediately for Bench offices, if you should wish it."

Because otherwise she was scheduled to travel to Chelatring Side with Koscuisko seven days from now, to be present when the Autocrat's Proxy took her formal poll of the Koscuisko familial corporation. She had intended to leave for Bench offices afterward; that was what Cousin Stanoczk had arranged. But if Koscuisko was impatient she would not be surprised, nor was she unwilling to change plans. Koscuisko thought about it.

"It is only a few more days, Bench specialist, and I am at home already. If I am to trust the First Secretary, I will trust that this is a done deed. No, do not change your plans on my account. It would only call attention. I need to think and plan how to reveal this to my family. Give me the document. I will make my mark."

Koscuisko's signature, holograph endorsement, and his seal. The thing was done. All that was left was for it to be recorded, and that was the merest technicality.

"Thank you, your Excellency. As you wish, sir."

Koscuisko was pale. And yet looked so much younger. "Thank you as well, Bench specialist, and now excuse me if you will. My heart is full. I need to be alone here for a while."

To offer a salute by way of courtesy was not appropriate; he was no longer an officer, except for the formality. Something Jils had heard came to her mind, instead.

"According to his Excellency's good pleasure," Jils agreed. A Dolgorukij formula, for a Dolgorukij autocrat. Her mission was accomplished. Andrej Koscuisko had come home at last; and now would stay.

Chapter Eight

The Malcontent

On the morning of the ninth day since Andrej Ulexeievitch had returned to Azanry, Marana pulled open the great curtains that draped the windows of the master's bedroom and looked down into the gardens below. It was well past breakfast; she had lain sleepless for long hours in the night, struggling with her sense of fairness and duty, and consequently slept later. The light in Andrej's bedroom was different than in her own and provided few clues as to the time.

As Marana looked out over the garden in the mid-morning sun, Andrej Ulexeievitch himself came out of the house below her, rushing into the garden like a man in pursuit of some elusive goal. She frowned.

He had had an appointment with his guest, the Bench specialist, in the morning. He had seen Specialist Ivers for a few words in the garden yesterday as well. He hadn't said anything to her about the meat and matter of the conversation; he hadn't seemed disturbed or unhappy—yet who was she to say?

His outland Security were there, spreading themselves well out along the perimeter of the garden. But Andrej was headed for the maze. Security would not be able to track him there, unless he wore a blip; it was an old maze, and very cunning. Nor would she be able to see where he was, because the latticework of living centuries of shrubs had roofed the maze over solidly. In the winter, yes, she was able to see her son Anton running through the maze with his pet mas-hound, if there wasn't any snow and he wore something brightly colored.

She wanted to know what was on Andrej's mind. Shrugging into her robe—glad that her woman wasn't there to insist she dress—Marana hurried down the private stairs and out of the house, into the garden. Nodding at Andrej's master of Security, Marana went straight for the maze, and in. She knew the maze. She didn't know which way Andrej had gone, but she could guess. They had once had a favorite place to go and be lost in—

Turning a corner, Marana caught sight of him as he went around the crisply trimmed edge of the shrubbery hedge, trailing his left hand across the green leaves as he went.

"Andrej!"

He had found the bench in the arbor that had been their trysting-place of old, and sat there with his face in his hands, rubbing his eyes. Something was wrong. She flew to his side and took his right hand in her own, and he let her carry his hand away from his face without protest. He would talk to her, then.

"Andrej, what's the matter?"

His hand worked in her anxious clasp, his fingers fluttering with emotion. "It's not wrong at all, Marana, but it's so far from right. I don't know what to do."

She waited.

After a moment, Andrej turned to her and took her hands between his. "Marana. When I came home, and so far abused your goodwill as to marry you. It was not because I thought you might still love me, or had pined for me in solitude for years. But to protect our son."

Someone must have told him about Ferinc. Marana felt a chill in the pit of her stomach: she had thought she could explain—but she had yet to broach the delicate subject, and now it was too late.

Andrej spoke on, without asking or apparently expecting a defense from her. She was under no obligation to defend herself. She knew her rights, and Ferinc was one of them.

"And only then because I have had warnings, Marana, of a powerful enemy who wants me dead and has the means to accomplish this. I was almost assassinated at Port Burkhayden, Marana, and I place my life in your hands to tell you even so much as that."

He didn't want to go into details. She could sense it. She agreed. She didn't want him to go into any details either. She didn't want any knowledge that could be used against him. "Tell me, Andrej," she encouraged. "Has something changed?"

"Everything is changed except that." Releasing her hands with a gesture of hopelessness he pleaded with her, palms up, as if gloomily convinced even before the fact that he could not express the enormity of it. "Chilleau Judiciary offers me freedom. And more than that, in return for my voice in my father's ear, but freedom without qualification. Marana. I would never have dared bind you to me in such a way if I had thought that it would mean imprisonment for you."

She was safe to ignore the latter half of his speech; she thought she understood the former. He was being yes-or-no again. It was so very Andrej of him that she felt her heart soften with remembered love. "Relieved of your duties, you come home to be a husband to your wife and a father to your son. How can that not be right, Andrej? Speaking of the portion that regards our son in particular."

Andrej resettled himself on the cool stone bench, at a little farther remove than that at which Marana herself had sat down to speak to him. "Had I only known that I had time. I might have won your permission beforehand. I might not have flouted my father's will, again."

Marana hid her smile of recognition. Yes, he had behaved in a very high-handed manner. Yes, he had been arrogant and self-willed, and focused completely on his own agenda to the absolute exclusion of anything else. That was what an autocrat was expected to do. And Andrej's aim was the protection of his son; surely he could understand that that fact won him some consideration from his son's mother.

"Surely to have you home is a good thing," Marana encouraged him, gently. "You have a child. He will grow to love you. You so often wondered whether you were doomed to inspire only fear and filial duty." That there were issues between Andrej and his father was a fact of life unchanged in the years Andrej had been way from home. "You will have work to do. To repair relationships with the business interests of the Ichogatra."

He looked at her almost reluctantly with his head lowered, grasping the edge of the seat of the stone bench in either hand. "But do we have a future to make between us, Marana? If I am to be home. I would like to know if we might try to see if we can remember what it had once been to have loved one another."

Her heart went out to him, trying so hard to do the thing that was right, trying so hard to determine what that might be. She slid across the bench closer to him, and this time he did not stir. "When Pellarus came back to Osmander, he was changed," Marana pointed out tenderly, not minding if her own uncertainty sounded in her voice. "And it was time before she knew him for her lord. But she did come to know him."

Andrej nodded in apparent acceptance of the offer, or at least of the spirit that had inspired it. "Pellarus was changed by ordeal and honorable battle," Andrej objected regardless, stubborn for all his clear understanding of what she meant to offer to him. "Osmander had not made a life for herself. As another woman very properly might."

Marana had made up her mind now, and was determined. "I am your wife, Andrej; you my husband. It's not for you to say whether Ferinc should be an obstacle. I say we should approach it as Pellarus to Osmander, and see if there is truth for us in the story. Else, we will negotiate. But I would like to try, because sometimes when I am not paying attention it seems that I remember loving you."

Turning to her Andrej raised his hands to take her by the shoulder and caress her face with trembling fingers. "It is so much to think about," Andrej said, in a voice that was heavy with tears and wonder. "And all at once. It's been so hard to meet Anton, knowing I was going away, that to think I need not go away is almost too much happiness. I cannot deserve this, Marana."

What could he mean? " 'If happiness were deserved how few would ever be.' " It was an old adage, no less true for its antiquity. "Strive only to be worthy of it. Not to deserve it."

She leaned her forehead against his, and in a breath remembered with so forceful a rush of shared delight that it nearly overwhelmed her. His face had changed, his manner subtly altered, his language edged with harsh experience, his eyes grown weary from looking upon alien visions. But his smell was Andrej.

It was Andrej with some overlay of age and maturity; his personal linen did not take the scent that she remembered, he dressed his hair with different toiletries than those he had once been accustomed to use.

It was still him. Beneath the influence of soap and cloth, the underlying truth of his body was the one that she remembered. It was so easy to put her mouth to his and taste his kiss, drunk in the moment with the certainty of her senses.

There was an alien flavor to his mouth. He was an older man than he had been, his kiss was not as sweet as when they had been children. But she could recognize enough. His smell, the taste of his mouth, the remembered shifting of his body against hers—Andrej.

He would come home, and stay. Anton would learn to love him. With Andrej at her side, there would be nothing to fear from the spite of his family.

With Andrej home it would be different, now.

There was someone on the grounds of Koscuisko's manor house that Chief Stildyne thought he recognized, and Lek was not the man to argue with his Chief. Their officer had gone into the maze in his garden; his lady had gone in after him, and so far as Lek was concerned anything he could find to focus his attention away from what was likely to be happening in the maze was all to the good.

Smish Smath chirruped, her little trill a very creditable imitation of a local warbler. Lek recognized her accent all the same. Leaning away from his post just enough to catch her hand signal, Lek read the signs. *Quarry bearing Taller to Murat. Intercept at twenty-four eighths. On one. Two. Three. Four.*

Taller to Murat told Lek what direction to seek;

twenty-four eighths gave him the distance. It would be a stretch at the sprint, but he could do it. There was a relatively clear field between the maze and the outermost perimeter, but once past the gravel track of the promenade there were trees and plantings to muddle the pursuit.

If the quarry gained the garden wall, they would lose it. There were too many directions in which a man could run to hide, and no way to alert the house security in time. Perhaps that was best. Perhaps Stildyne was crying the alert. It was in their best interest as Stildyne's team on site to ensure that Stildyne not find himself in need of outside help.

Lek ran for the goal as though the Aznir were on his heels with the dogs, and the Devil after. Taller had flushed the game. Lek could hear someone running, and altered his course to intercept, pushing for each extra bit of speed that he could muster. This was for Stildyne's face. He couldn't let Stildyne down in front of all of these Aznir. He would not.

Lek could hear the quarry, but still could not quite see it. Whoever it was ran very well and very quickly, but Lek had had the advantage of direction. Lek knew where he was to look for his prey; the quarry didn't know where to expect Lek. Seeing his chance, Lek shifted his pursuit track in a wide arc to cut across the fleeing man's path and terminate his flight.

The target saw his danger and veered off toward a break between two trees, but the shift in direction cost him time. Lek launched himself for the quarry and landed him, crashing to the ground against the base of a tree trunk, with his arms wrapped around the waist of Stildyne's prey.

The others were with him, now—Smish and Murat and Taller—wrestling with the man Lek had brought down, subduing him by degrees as he struggled. Once he felt sure that the others had a good grip on the man, Lek pushed himself away from the prone body to stand up.

What he saw froze his blood. The man was Malcontent.

He wore his hair long down his back, but worse than

that, as Taller and Smish pinned his shoulders to the ground Lek could see the crimson halter around the prone man's throat, exposed, revealed by the struggle that disarranged his clothing and pulled his collar wide.

Lek leaned into his shoulder and struck Taller as hard as he could to shake him free, pushing at Smish at the same time. He'd startled them. They went down.

Lek reached down to embrace the Malcontent, to help him up, to beg forgiveness for the error they had made and explain that his off-world companions had not known that they were making such a terrible mistake. Murat landed on his back, flattening Lek across the Malcontent's body.

Lek started to become confused. This was a Malcontent. The person of the Malcontent was sacred. He couldn't let these off-worlders abuse a Malcontent. He was one of these outlanders, though. He was supposed to do as his Chief ordered, and his Chief wanted this man stopped and secured. But this man was Malcontent. He couldn't let them impose violence on the person of the Malcontent; it was a sin, and yet—

"That'll do," the Malcontent said firmly, but it wasn't a Malcontent's voice. It was some warrant officer or another, speaking plain Standard. Maybe not a warrant officer. But it was Standard. And it certainly sounded like a warrant officer to Lek. "Disengage, and terminate your exercise. Very well done indeed, and me with the advantage of knowledge of the terrain. Where is your Chief?"

Lek helped the Malcontent to rise, while Smish and Taller came up on either side, predictably confused. Lek didn't blame them. He was confused himself.

"He's Malcontent," Lek explained, as Chief Stildyne joined them. "No man may touch the sacred person of the Malcontent. Well, not without leave and permission. We almost made a horrible mistake, Chief."

He was confused and uncertain, and beginning to be afraid. He knew that the person of the Malcontent was not to be approached with violence. But did Stildyne? And more to the point—did his governor know that?

Stildyne shook his head. "He's not Malcontent, Lek," Stildyne said, with absolute assurance. "He's not even Dolgorukij. I know this man, or at least I used to know him. He's a deserter from Gotrane. Not Malcontent at all."

"That was then," the Malcontent said. "This is now. You, troop, Lek? Don't worry. It's all right. Do as your Chief tells you. And the peace of the Malcontent be with you. It's all right."

The Malcontent wasn't moving, wasn't giving anyone any reason to have to hit him. That helped. What the Malcontent said was confusing, but Lek thought he could make sense of it if he tried. Stildyne thought he knew the man. Maybe Stildyne had. An outlander, electing the Malcontent? Because he didn't look like any kind of Dolgorukij to Lek, let alone Aznir. Stildyne was right about that.

Stildyne came forward, keeping a wary eye on the Malcontent. "We're sorry, Lek, we didn't realize. But I do know him. And I do need to know what he's doing here. Is this going to be all right for you?"

There was no time like the present for the Malcontent to escape, because Lek's team was paying attention to him to the exclusion of anything else. But the Malcontent wasn't fleeing. The Malcontent simply stood with his back to the trunk of the tree, waiting calmly. Lek shook his head vigorously, to shake out the confusing thoughts that warred within him.

"You can't push him, Chief, you can't. He's Malcontent. He's a sacred person. Please."

"There'll be no pushing, Lek, put your mind at ease," the Malcontent said kindly. He had a soothing tone of voice whose combined accents—warrant officer, Malcontent—were very comforting. "Your Chief has questions, fine, we'll talk. That's all. He's telling you the truth. Come on, then, let's go to the house, but I don't want your officer to see me."

Taller and Smish were at Lek's sides, watching him. Murat stood behind him, and put his hand out to Lek's shoulder. Lek stood for a moment, letting things settle out. Yes. He was going to be all right. It was not going to be a problem. It could have been. It had almost been. But it was all right now.

"Ready, Chief," Lek said. Now he was curious himself: an outlander, bound to the Malcontent? He wouldn't have believed it possible.

Whatever Stildyne might have to say, Lek hoped he'd get to listen in.

Marana took her leave with a tender kiss, and Andrej leaned back against the hedge that surrounded the bench and watched her go. It had been their bench. Perhaps it would be their bench again, someday.

He waited several moments to give Marana time to gain the house, to go up to their room and finish dressing. It was mid-morning; soon there would be mid-meal. He would see Anton during the break from daily studies.

He was going to have to talk to Chief Stildyne.

A year ago, when he had first thought he was going home—before Jils Ivers's embassage from Chilleau Judiciary had turned his life in such an unexpected direction—the single thing he had found to regret in the prospect of freedom was that he could not take his troops with him. Bond-involuntaries belonged to the Bench. Un-bonded troops could make their own decision to stay with Fleet or follow him into private service in his House, but the bond-involuntaries had no such flexibility.

He was going to have to tell them that he was leaving; it was not going to be easy. Standing up at length— stretching himself, a little stiff from long sitting—Andrej started for the entrance to the maze. He would find Stildyne nearby, or someone who knew where Stildyne was.

Right now there were only four people at the Matredonat who knew what Ivers had brought: himself, and Jils Ivers, Marana, and almost certainly his cousin Stanoczk. But Stoshik hadn't been at dinner last night, though he'd said that he and Andrej needed to meet. Andrej wasn't sure Stoshik was on the grounds at all; Malcontents were like that. They came and went on their own schedule, taking and asking leave of nobody.

One of the house-master's people was waiting, well clear of the mouth of the maze itself. Not one of Andrej's own Security. That was odd.

"Prosper all Saints," Andrej said, giving the man leave to speak to him.

"To his Excellency's purpose and the profit of his House. Your outland Security are anxious to speak with you, your Excellency, in the library in the master's quarters."

"Is something wrong?" Andrej had intended to look in on the schoolroom, but that was in another part of the house altogether.

"It's not for me to say, your Excellency. It's the Malcontent's business."

Andrej frowned. Was Stoshik returned? What would Stoshik be doing with Stildyne in the library? Well, there was the obvious, of course, since Stildyne and he held a sexual preference in common, and Stoshi's sacred duty was to offer reconciliation to unhappy souls. But if it were so simple as that it was unlikely that Stildyne would welcome company. Stildyne might not know about Malcontents, who could be much more aggressive on their home ground than outside of Combine territory; there was only so much Lek was likely to have explained.

Taller and Murat were at the door to the library, which meant that Lek and Smish were within. Nodding at them to keep to their post Andrej went through into the master's library, closing the doors behind him. What was going on?

Stildyne had a man seated in front of Andrej's great desk that fronted the tall windows overlooking the garden. Smish and Lek were there.

The Malcontent was not Stanoczk.

The Malcontent was some tall, slender creature with green-tinted eyes and dark hair, whose long-fingered hands lay still and calm on the arms of the chair in which he sat, but whose fingertips were white with tension. Andrej spared only a quick look at the Malcontent on his way past to confront Stildyne, who stood beside the desk. "There is a problem, Chief?"

The Malcontent had given a start when Andrej entered the room. Was it the man Stildyne had called to his attention at exercise several days ago, on the morning after his arrival at the Matredonat?

"I'm not sure if it's a problem, your Excellency." Stildyne sounded more uncertain than he usually did. Andrej wasn't sure he liked the implications. "This man has been keeping an eye on you ever since we got here, and we caught him trying to observe you in the maze. Lek says he's Malcontent. I say he's a deserter from Chambers at Gotrane. I used to know this man. There's a discrepancy here that concerns me."

Lek was in the room, but he didn't look distressed to Andrej. He looked a little dusty, yes. Andrej beckoned Lek to him; Stildyne stepped away. "You say Malcontent?" Andrej asked. Lek nodded, very confidently.

"He wears the braid, your Excellency. And gave me peace."

Both convincing from the worldview of a Dolgorukij who had never been off-world; but not conclusive proof, particularly where Security warrants were concerned. Stildyne was a suspicious man. It was his job. "What is his name?"

"He says Ferinc, your Excellency, Cousin Ferinc. Chief says differently."

Lek and Andrej both knew that what a man's name had been before he elected the Malcontent had no particular relation to what he would answer to once he came to be called "Cousin." But if this was Cousin Ferinc, of whom Anton spoke . . .

"Really," Andrej said with interest, pitching his voice to carry to where the Malcontent sat under Smish's observing eye. " 'Cousin Ferinc'? The man my child loves. You were to be at—where was it?"

The Malcontent didn't want to speak, it seemed. Andrej could be patient. There was something odd going on here; he would call for Stanoczk if he had to. This was his house. He had a right to know what Malcontents were coming and going, and for what reason, at least approximately. "You can tell me, Cousin, or I will ask my Cousin Stanoczk. It is all the same to me. You have distressed my Chief of Security."

The Malcontent raised his face, so that the light caught his profile. Rather fine features, but not particularly Dolgorukij. Very strange. Some outlander's bastard, hounded into the Malcontent by his exotic looks?

"Dubrovnije," the Malcontent said. "I promised to bring him a wheat-fish. Your Excellency."

Dubrovnije was the right answer; Andrej started to

turn back to Stildyne and the next question, before his mind quite caught up with his senses. "A man may desert and throw himself upon the Malcontent for protection, Chief. It is the right of every child—"

Under Canopy. Stildyne knew that. Stildyne had been newly assigned, he to Andrej, Andrej to the *Ragnarok,* when some Sarvaw mercantile pilot had elected the Malcontent to evade prosecution for piracy. Years ago. But suddenly Andrej was convinced that he recognized Cousin Ferinc's voice, and it had been even longer ago than the incident with the Sarvaw mercantile pilot.

"He's not Dolgorukij, your Excellency," Stildyne said, watching Andrej's face. Stildyne would know that Andrej had realized there was a problem. "I think he may have been Amorilic. Maybe. Petty warrant officer."

"Girag," Andrej confirmed. Stildyne's eyes widened marginally in surprise; Stildyne hadn't expected Andrej to recognize him. And yet Andrej knew who he was, now. "Petty Warrant Officer Haster Girag, wasn't it? Cousin?"

That was the man. The Malcontent shifted uneasily in his chair, as if to hide himself from Andrej, turning his face away.

"You know this person, sir?" Stildyne asked. Carefully. There was a layer of inquiry in Stildyne's voice that Andrej could not quite interpret, but it would keep.

"Haster Girag," Andrej repeated, and closed the distance between him and the Malcontent to stare down into the man's pale face implacably. "You. A deserter. And you come into my house? You endear yourself to my child? Why should I tolerate this obscenity, 'Cousin'?"

He knew who it was. He remembered. Girag had taken liberties with prisoners in his custody, liberties outside the Protocols, unsanctioned and unlawful. Andrej had punished him. It had been at least seven years. Possibly longer.

Cousin Ferinc stood up, finally, but it was only by way of putting some distance between Andrej and himself. "It wasn't meant to go that way, your Excellency." He made Cousin Ferinc nervous, Andrej noted, and followed Cousin Ferinc step for step across the room, stalking his prey without mercy. "And I don't blame you for having questions. But I don't have to explain myself to you. I'm under direction from my reconciler. And if you don't mind I'll be going. I've promised to bring Anton Andreievitch a wheat-fish. From Dubrovnije."

This was intolerable cheek. Haster Girag had been a bully. An abuser of prisoners. A sexual deviant, or if not a sexual deviant, then at least a man who found amusement in sexual perversion. It was beyond imagining that the Malcontent knew this man's history and still tolerated his cultivation of a friendship with a child, any child. No. Not any child. *His* child. Anton Andreievitch Koscuisko.

"You will not give any such thing to my child, Cousin Ferinc—not until I have had a chance to be sure that your reconciler knows just what you are. Who is it to whom I must appeal? Name this man, Ferinc, if you please."

Cousin Ferinc had his back up against the library bookshelves and stood there trembling, with the stink of the fear-sweat upon him. There wasn't anyplace farther for him to go. He was afraid of Andrej; Andrej could tell. He had good reason to be afraid of Andrej. It was prudent and proper, just and judicious that it should be so.

But Andrej was not going to threaten Cousin Ferinc.

Cousin Ferinc wore the halter of the Malcontent, and Andrej knew as well as Lek how much genuine immunity hung by that red ribbon around the neck of the slaves of the Saint. "It is his Excellency's cousin Stanoczk," Cousin Ferinc replied, in a voice that spoke volumes of shame and of humility.

Andrej saw it all in a sudden flash of insight, and closed his eyes. Of course. He had turned Girag's perversion back on the man, as suitable punishment for Girag's misuse of prisoners. Now Girag enjoyed reconciliation in like form from Cousin Stanoczk. Andrej's own cousin Stoshik. The obscenity of it was almost too much to be borne.

"I understand." He wished he didn't. "Give my good Lek peace, Cousin Ferinc, and go. Do not let me see your face again. And have no contact with my child until I have had a chance to explain to Stoshik why your hands should be taken off at the wrists before you should be allowed to so much as touch such innocence."

Girag's offense had not been against children, no. Not against women either. It had been the constraint of people otherwise his match or more that had seduced Girag. Grown men. But it was bad enough at that.

Ferinc bowed his head. "By your command, your Excellency, under your roof." He seemed to master himself moment by moment as he spoke, and gave Lek peace very prettily. "The peace of the Malcontent is with you, Lek, be easy."

There was finger-code passing between Stildyne and Ferinc, but Andrej ignored it. It wasn't any of his business. He didn't even want to know. When Ferinc had left, Andrej turned back to the room from staring at the backs of the books on the shelves of the library. "Chief. I need to talk to you. Gentles, if you would leave us, for a moment."

Lek was apparently secure, though quite possibly confused by the crosscurrents raised within this room by a Malcontent who was not Malcontent at all. Or who was not Dolgorukij. It was all right for Lek to be confused, so long as he was not in conflict within himself. It was with internal conflict that Lek became vulnerable to his governor.

Stildyne seemed confused as well, but determined on something. Once the doors had closed behind Lek and Smish, Stildyne spoke, to have the initiative. "You also knew this man, your Excellency?"

That was right. He was someone Stildyne had recognized. Girag and Stildyne had had history together of some sort.

No, Andrej thought suddenly, with a spasm of apprehensive fear. *Not that sort of a history. Surely not.*

Yet why not? Was it impossible that Girag and Stildyne had been lovers? It was still a far cry from abuse of prisoners outside of Protocol—"He was senior man on a detachment at a holding facility in Richeyne." He would simply have to lay the whole thing out, and let Stildyne say what he would about it. What did it matter? He meant to break the bond that was between them; he would leave Fleet.

No.

He would leave Fleet, but that would not break the

bond between them. He owed Stildyne honesty. "My Captain had been forced to second me to some Judicial investigation there. That man liked to play with prisoners, Stildyne. It was his practice to demand sexual favors in exchange for food and water. It is abuse of prisoners outside of Protocol."

Any Inquisitor could demand sexual favors, on pain of torment. It was recognized, if not codified, as useful in eroding the self-respect, and contributing to a good outcome accordingly. That wasn't the point. The point was that even an Inquisitor was expected to observe the Protocols. Rape wasn't part of accepted protocol until the sixth level of Inquiry; and any demand for sexual services was a species of rape, so far as Andrej was concerned, regardless of whether or not an assault went with it.

What Girag had done was perhaps not so unusual a thing for a man with power over prisoners to demand. Andrej had not been naïve then; he was not naïve now. But whenever Andrej stepped into a prison, he expected to have absolute control over what abuse his prisoners were to be required to endure, and Girag had violated the sole right of an Inquisitor to inflict atrocity under cover of Law.

"I very much wanted to deliver him to those same prisoners, Mister Stildyne, but it would have been inappropriate. I found willing recruits among station Security instead. I am ashamed to explain what I did to him, Chief, but I don't think I'm ashamed of having done it."

Certainly compared to other things that he had done, his afternoon's sport with Haster Girag paled into all but absolute insignificance. Except for Haster Girag, perhaps. Perhaps he *was* ashamed.

Perhaps the imposition had been excessive. Something had clearly shattered Girag's life; perhaps confronting his own hunger and being forced to admit it for what it was had been too much for him. It had been too much for Andrej, after all, if the specific nature of the thirst was not the same. He had never recovered from the realization that he was a monster.

After a moment's thoughtful silence Stildyne spoke. "Well. You should know, though." There was an unusually grave note of deliberation in Stildyne's voice, as though he faced the Court. "My previous acquaintance. We used to have parties. We used bond-involuntaries for entertainment. You would not have approved of my own conduct. Sir."

Andrej stared up into Chief Stildyne's ruined face with shock and horror. He knew perfectly well that prior to his arrival on the *Ragnarok* Stildyne had been in the occasional habit of exploiting his access to bond-involuntary troops for sexual purposes. He couldn't change any of what Stildyne had done; only what Stildyne did ever after, as long as he was responsible to Andrej for the welfare of those troops. It was unthinkable that Stildyne would revert to previous abusive behavior once Andrej was gone. So why was Stildyne telling him this?

"To you I would trust my child in a heartbeat, Chief." He knew perfectly well why Stildyne was telling him such things. And he had no cause to scorn Girag as diseased. His own hands were far more deeply soiled than Girag's had been, though his sin was sanctioned by the Bench in support of the Judicial order. What were the games of pain and sexual dominance that Girag had played, compared to gross and unjustifiable murder? "But Girag has cause to bear a grudge. I cannot risk him next to my child."

Stildyne looked skeptical. "I see. Thank you, your Excellency. But if you did. Trust me with your son, I mean. What would he call me? Chief? Or Mister?"

The question made no sense. Too much had happened today, and it was still short of mid-meal. Andrej needed to go into a dark quiet room, and think. It was the wrong time to tell Stildyne that Andrej was not going back to the *Ragnarok*.

"He might very well mistake your worth, and call you Brachi," Andrej admitted. "Being a child. And not understanding the respect due to a man in your position."

There was a flicker of surprise in Stildyne's eyes, but it went very quickly. Stildyne bowed. "I'll see about Lek, your Excellency. And ask the house-master to send your cousin Stanoczk, when he can be found."

Yes, that would be good. Andrej sat down at the great desk in the library and buried his face between his hands. This had been unexpected. Unnecessary. And he had not told his people. He would have to tell them. Soon. Not now. It would raise too many issues of judgment and abandonment if he told Stildyne now, in the face of Stildyne's painful revelation about his past.

"Thank you, Mister Stildyne. I will sort myself out between now and mid-meal." It was going to take him much longer than that; so there was no time like the present to be started.

What could have possessed Haster Girag to elect the Malcontent? What could have possessed the Malcontent to accept him? Who had made the decision to permit Haster Girag to come to the Matredonat and cultivate Anton Andreievitch, and who was Andrej Ulexeievitch to judge?

But Anton was his child. And the thought that Anton should admire such a man as Andrej knew Girag to be was more than he could rationalize, even him.

Ferinc bent his head and made for the escape of the library doors with all deliberate speed, struggling to maintain control of himself. Koscuisko was furious with him; Koscuisko had a right to be.

But Ferinc was Malcontent. He could not be threatened; the degradation of his status as a slave of the Saint gave him immunity. No casual punishment assessed by any layman could compare to the humiliation of the red halter.

He was not even legally a person, but an object. Slavery was illegal under Jurisdiction, but there were exceptions for religious observance, and the Malcontent was one of them. Koscuisko could not touch him. He was an object belonging to the Saint.

And yet it was his doom—as Stanoczk had regretfully suggested—to remain outland and fundamentally un-Reconciled in his heart of hearts, because one black day years and years ago Andrej Koscuisko had mastered him, and he had been a slave ever since. Not to the Malcontent.

I can explain, Ferinc signaled to Stildyne, as he forced himself to walk across the room rather than running. He had not used the finger-code for years, but he was confident that Stildyne could still understand his accent. *No threat to the officer. Truth, Stildyne.*

Stildyne need not be angry at him for being here— he was no threat to Koscuisko or to anything that was Koscuisko's, and among the things that were Koscuisko's were the woman and the child that he had grown to love for their own sakes, and no taint of Koscuisko about them. Koscuisko himself had disappeared from Ferinc's mind here, years ago. He had been almost at peace, and now he was damned.

Cousin Stanoczk would be disgraced in Chapter. Ferinc had been disobedient, undisciplined, but worse than that had revealed by his behavior that despite the most concerted efforts Stanoczk had made on his behalf he was still fundamentally unReconciled. What would become of him?

He cleared the threshold and gained the outer hallway, but Koscuisko's Security were not stepping away. The bond-involuntary Lek Kerenko had one hand to his elbow, but very gently, as if to give support; the woman cocked her head at him, gesturing down the hall.

"Chief's room down this way, Cousin," she said, and she used a Standard word for *cousin* that sounded oddly in Ferinc's ears. "Come on. You can have a drink. You look as though you might not mind one, if I can say so without giving offense."

Of course. They read finger-code as well. It had been bond-involuntaries who had invented it, after all, as a means of communicating between themselves without compromising their discipline. Ferinc had bullied the knowledge out of bond-involuntaries, knowing how to exploit their vulnerability to their governors; that was how he'd learned it. Lek's fellows clearly had the knowledge, as well, but Koscuisko would not have permitted his Bonds to be coerced into teaching it.

It was a telling detail that spoke of the exceptional trust Koscuisko had earned from his Bonds, more evidence to Ferinc of what he'd lost. He couldn't speak. He let them escort him down the hall to a room near the end of the corridor, where the house-master had placed Koscuisko's chief of Security. He knew these rooms. There was more familiar here than not.

Lek poured out a drink for him, fully half a glass of cortac brandy; Ferinc took it with a nod of thanks and had drunk half of it down before he realized that the house-master had given Stildyne the good stuff. The really good stuff.

The liquor calmed his nerves. He took the balance of it with more respect and consideration, listening to the voices in his mind drop off one by one into a drugged stupor. After a while, Stildyne came into the room, and the Security left.

Stildyne sat down. Ferinc looked up at him a little stupidly, feeling the liquor. He didn't usually drink. "What did you tell him?"

Stildyne looked thoughtful, and much older than Ferinc remembered him. "You and me. Parties. Bond-involuntaries. He would have tortured himself, trying to guess and never just coming out and asking."

Ferinc shook his head, regretfully. "You needn't have, Stildyne. You owe him no explanations. Surely." Even as he said it, he knew better. He knew things about Stildyne that he had not guessed before Andrej Koscuisko had come into the library. It was only more evidence of the fact that Koscuisko was a terrible and corrosive sort of metamorphic agency. Stildyne. Of all people.

"You're right, of course." Stildyne's agreement was amused—on multiple levels. "But it doesn't make any difference. You'd better leave. He doesn't want to see you."

Ever again. "Let me have a word with his lady, Chief," Ferinc asked humbly. "Just so she knows. In case there's gossip. I had leave from Cousin Stanoczk to make sure she was all right, not to spy on Koscuisko. I wasn't to have been caught skulking in the garden."

Stildyne nodded. "If you do it now, you should be all right. Himself is in a state; he'll not be stirring. But I don't understand, man. Why are you here?"

"I truly mean no harm, Stildyne. I came looking to make up a lack, years ago. I thought that I was doing well, really. Stanoczk says that he has failed me, but it's not his fault."

Nor was it Koscuisko's.

What Koscuisko had done to him had not made him the moral cripple that he was. He had always been a moral cripple. Koscuisko had only put the fact in front of him, where he could not avoid recognizing the truth of it. That was all. For that, Koscuisko deserved his thanks; and yet Ferinc could not imagine trying to explain any such thing to him.

Maybe to Stanoczk. Maybe. If Stanoczk would speak to him. If the Malcontent did not send him away from Cousin Stanoczk forever, and try some different approach to the reconciliation that was his right—even though he was a slave.

"Some lacks are never going to be made up," Stildyne said, in a voice that was almost sad. Almost. But this was Stildyne. On the other hand, Koscuisko had Stildyne, too. "The dogs in this house are cherished more tenderly than I ever was, Haster. Ferinc. Sorry."

As if Stildyne was thinking about his past, and not his present.

"I'll be away." Ferinc needed to see Marana, and then he needed to run. He would go to the chapter-house at Brikarvna. Stanoczk would know where to find him there. "I'm sorry for the trouble I've caused you, Brachi. I should have known better than to try to steal a glimpse."

It was an echo from a long time ago. Warrant to warrant. Stildyne smiled. "Yes," he agreed. "You should have. But it's lucky for the troops that they caught you, all the same, or I'd have had them on remedials for months."

And he could have been in Stildyne's place. He could have been Stildyne. Chief Warrant Officer. Trusted and valued, and rejoicing in the care and tutelage of professional Security troops, only one step short of the Ship's First Officer.

To be Stildyne, he would have had to have been Stildyne all along, though. Stildyne hadn't ever minded taking advantage of opportunities. But he'd taken much less advantage than Ferinc. Stildyne had always been a practical man. Ferinc had been a bully—he knew that—and bullies were trying to conceal the fear within themselves, and Koscuisko had opened him up and laid it bare in front of the entire world.

So he could not have been Stildyne. There was comfort in that realization that Ferinc took with him to go to see Marana, and say good-bye to her.

Someone came quietly into the room, closing the great double doors behind them. That was odd. Andrej hadn't heard anybody ask for permission. Maybe he'd been too caught up in his own misery to have noticed.

"For one day merely I leave you to your own devices," someone said, in a deep voice that was both distressed and bantering at once. "And what do I return to find? You have ruined my poor Ferinc, Derush, and I particularly wanted to beg you to forgive him, and grant him peace."

Cousin Stanoczk.

Andrej raised his head from his palms and blinked, trying to focus. What time was it?

"Have you called for rhyti, Stoshik?" Andrej was thirsty. It was probably past mid-meal. "Sit. Talk to me. I need to speak to you. But what is this of so-called Cousin Ferinc, first of all."

He couldn't keep the disgust out of his voice. The shock had been too great. Stanoczk went back to the doors and let the servants in to lay the table; Andrej watched the process dully.

Stanoczk poured a flask of rhyti and sweetened it with a liberal hand. The servants left. He brought the flask of rhyti over to where Andrej sat behind the desk and set it down at Andrej's hand, seating himself on the desk's surface beside it.

"He is a deserter, Derush. He came five years ago, no, six years ago, about a year after you had taken his discipline on yourself, and spared him legal sanctions. We intercepted him on his way into Azanry as a tourist. Fleet said that we might keep him or send him back. And we had learned the story from him, or as much as he was capable of telling us."

It was good rhyti. Andrej took another drink, and his mind began to sharpen. "Why deserter?"

Stanoczk shrugged. "His life had become intolerable to him, Andrej. You proved him to himself all too effectively. We considered that it was your intervention that had sent him to us, and made the offer, and were accepted."

An outlander, taken in to the embrace of the Malcontent. It was unheard of. "Nothing that was done to him was worse than he had done, Stoshik. The Saint owes him nothing. He is a corrupt man."

Cousin Stanoczk shrugged again. "Yes, but it was you, Derush, and you are so much better at it than he ever was. Your impact was all the more shattering. And the Saint's proper business is with damaged goods. It is our holy charge, you know that; those who are pure and uncompromised have their choice of Saints, but for Ferinc there is only the Malcontent or to be damned."

Andrej couldn't argue with him on that. Cousin Stanoczk was the expert, after all. So instead Andrej said the thing that troubled him most deeply about finding Girag here at the Matredonat.

"Knowing what he was, though, Stanoczk, you let him come here, to this house, and endear himself to my son. To my son, Stoshik. How could you put my child at such a risk? Girag should hate me. The Holy Mother only knows what such a man might do to be revenged."

Marana had said something about Ferinc earlier, when they had spoken together in the garden. What had it been?

"You would be happier if he did hate you, I think, Derush," Cousin Stanoczk said gently. "He does not. You terrify him still. He knows that he has been a sinner. He has learned to do the Malcontent's work here honestly and honorably. He teaches Anton to love you every day, Derush, you will not deny his worth once you have come to know him better."

Andrej didn't like the way this conversation was trending. He stood up to distance himself from what Stanoczk would say, taking the flask of rhyti with him. "Well, I am home, Stoshik," he said. "And mean to remain here. I have told no one but Marana. So there is to be no need of Malcontents to teach my son to love his father. You can have him back. Take him away. I don't want to see him here. Ever again."

Stanoczk stayed where he was, sitting on the desk with his back to the room. "Perhaps it is so," Stanoczk said. "But for the goodwill he has nurtured in your child there are thanks owing, Andrej, and the Malcontent has a word to say to you about your household. Will you hear me?"

Andrej wasn't interested. Still, Stoshik was a Malcontent, a religious professional of a particularly dangerous sort. Starting his life once more at home here on Azanry by setting himself at odds with the Saint was not good precedent. A man could have all Saints against him and prosper under the protection of the Malcontent; and if a man outraged the Malcontent, all Saints could not protect him from ruin.

"To you, Stoshik, I listen," Andrej agreed. "And also to Cousin Stanoczk. Out of my respect for your divine Patron, may he wander in bliss." Stanoczk was his cousin, and Andrej loved him, Malcontent or no. Stoshi nodded solemnly, as if accepting the terms Andrej laid down—such as they were.

"You will stay here at home, you said, Andrej?" Stanoczk asked, as if he didn't know. Perhaps he didn't. It was always safest to assume that the Malcontent knew everything, except what one was going to do next. "We seek an understanding with you, Derush, you are your father's son. For the sake of your soul you should forgive Ferinc, and thank him for the good service he has done here these years past."

There was no man free from the Malcontent, no soul without some hidden shame in the past that the Malcontent could use against it. Or was there? Was any of his own shame hidden, shameful as it was? He had never sought to deny the horror of his crimes to himself or to anyone.

Yet he did not want to contemplate the day when his son should start to understand just what he was. Perhaps that was what the Saint held over his head. "You go too far, Stoshik." It was worth consideration—how a man without shame might be invisible to the Malcontent. "Thank him?"

"For the good service he has done you, Andrej, in making you a hero to your son. And strengthening the spirit of the lady your wife, to face her daily trials."

The flask of rhyti Andrej held dropped to the carpeted floor and bounced, splashing hot sweet liquid all over the rug.

Marana.

That was what she had meant when she had said it. *It is not for you to say whether Ferinc should be an obstacle.* He hadn't understood. He had been thinking about other things. Not only Anton, but Marana, was there no end to this nightmare?

But Stanoczk was just telling him. So that he would know. So that he would not be surprised. So that he could rule his household wisely and with benevolence and charity. No man might raise his hand against the Malcontent. Stanoczk was only warning him, for his own good.

"If a man is to thank the enemy that comes into his home and woos his child and corrupts his wife, then a man is not the master of his household." This was beyond all imagination. Stanoczk could not be serious. "Suppose instead I hunt this person down and scourge him naked from my boundaries, Stoshik, what penance must I pay for such a crime as that?"

Stanoczk stirred himself from the desk to come and take a napkin from the table that the servants had laid, crouching down at Andrej's feet to blot the spilt rhyti up from the rug. "You will do nothing of the sort, Derush," Stanoczk scolded, but very gently. "If you spoke again to Ferinc, you would know it is not revenge on his part. It has been the ordeal we set him to in order to test the quality of his obedience, to send him here. It is our fault if he loves your child. Promise to consider that you might forgive him, Derush; it is deserved, I attest it to you in the name of the Saint himself."

To consider the possibility of forgiving Girag for coming here was distasteful, but at least Andrej could agree to do so much and still be honest. "I have said he is not to show himself to me again, Stoshik. But I will talk to Anton. Perhaps Marana also. And I will consider my debt accordingly. Yes. I promise."

Stanoczk was done mopping up rhyti, and fixed himself a flask. "Good, it is well. Thank you. Now also your Stildyne. You have no cause to hold him so far from you, Andrej. You owe so great a debt that you cannot repay."

Outrageous. "When was it that I invited you into my bed, Stoshik? You exceed all bounds of propriety."

Stanoczk turned to face Andrej, very serious. "Well. We were told that there was an issue, Derush, that required the intervention of my Patron. And it is my only pleasure in life, to meddle in the private lives of other people, having none myself. You cannot blame me."

Stanoczk had hardly ever been serious a moment in his entire life. It was how Stanoczk managed the pain that had propelled him into the embrace of the Malcontent. Had Stanoczk not been Dolgorukij, it could have been much simpler; he need not have suffered for desiring men if he had been born to a more liberal culture. Stoshi could have been born Chigan, and been happy.

"True enough." Stanoczk looked at him; Andrej could only admit to the plain fact. "Have you been told also what it is, this issue? Or does the ritual require that I lay it at your feet in plain language?"

"That would be telling," Stanoczk said. "Speak to me, Andrej, in what way can my divine Patron reconcile you to the life that the Holy Mother has decreed for you beneath the Canopy?"

Maybe it was just as well to do it now. He was already benumbed by shock and distress. What better time to talk about his own death?

"You brought to me Specialist Ivers yesterday, Stoshik." The document was in a secure drawer in the library desk, along with the other things he had for his cousin. He had put them there this morning, when he had come down for his interview with Jils Ivers. "Did you ever know another Bench specialist who worked with her? Garol Vogel."

"Garol Aphon Vogel." Stanoczk nodded. "Yes. A sour and suspicious man, Andrej. I like him." *Like,* not *liked.* That was potentially interesting. Ivers had said that Vogel had not been heard from.

"I saw him last at Burkhayden, it has been some months. The last time I spoke to him he gave me this, and suggested that I seek the advice of the Malcontent."

The Bench warrant. Andrej drew it out of its secure place and passed it to his cousin, whose dark eyes widened at the sight of it. Yes. Stanoczk knew what a Bench warrant looked like.

"In the shortest possible statement, Stanoczk, someone wants me dead, and has the means to get the Bench endorsement. I must know how to protect myself, if I can. If I cannot, there is no sense in asking me to forgive Haster Girag, as I will not be available to do any such thing. Help me, Stoshik."

In silence Stanoczk took the Bench warrant and opened it out in careful hands, looking thoughtfully at what elements Andrej could not guess.

Andrej could wait for Stanoczk to meditate on the document, and its meaning. He had something else in his desk. While Stanoczk turned the Bench warrant over in his hands and held it up against the light, Andrej took the notebooks out of the secured drawer, stacking them in chronological order.

He had almost forgotten all about them. But in Burkhayden he had had a dream that had reminded him of what a treasure he possessed, and how little he deserved it, and what his responsibility to posterity was with regard to it.

Finally Stanoczk sighed, and put the Bench warrant away in his blouse. "We cannot allow it, Derush, we rely on you for the future. I will submit the problem. What else?"

"I might ask you, Stoshik," Andrej countered. "A man does not seek aid from the Malcontent without paying the price."

Cousin Stanoczk shook his head. "My Patron does you no favors, Derush. This is a question of Combine politics. You have the natural right to demand the Saint's protection, without prejudice. I can't pretend to extort concessions. Unless you would be kind to my Ferinc. I've become fond of him, Derush."

Andrej could only shake his head in wearied wonder. "You are all surprises today, Stanoczk. I have these documents. I need them to be safe and secured, if I am dead. They will be worth much more than money, in a generation's time."

And the Malcontent would know best how to conserve the information for the Nurail, still forbidden access to their own cultural heritage by the bitter and unreasoning enmity of the Bench. What Andrej had belonged to them, and had to be cherished carefully till it could safely be returned.

"This is then what, Derush?" Stanoczk asked, curious, picking up one of the notebooks to leaf through it. "Your penmanship has not improved with time, I must say."

Andrej had to smile at that. "The circumstances were challenging. It was at the Domitt Prison, Stoshik. The Nurail there had no chance to pass their weaves except to me who was their torturer, but were willing to use even their own murderer as the tool to see the weaves remembered. Written down."

Stanoczk let the leaves of the notebook riffle through his fingers. "It explains the hurried hand, I suppose. Does anybody know? They are proscribed under Jurisdiction, Derush, on pain of offense against the Bench itself."

Yes and no. "Nurail may not sing their weaves, Stoshik, but there is no law that says a Dolgorukij may not write them down if it suits his fancy. Also I hold the Writ to Inquire, and may do many things with impunity forbidden other men."

"Such as to my Ferinc," Stanoczk agreed, but as if it was by the way. "I should not grudge you that. You did not ruin him. Had you not destroyed him he might never have reclaimed his sweet humility, which I love. Only you are not to tell him that, because I have little enough influence with him as it is, and should he realize that I am fond, he will take advantage, and be misery to deal with. More misery, rather."

Andrej didn't want to talk about Ferinc. He didn't want to think about him. "Will you take these? There will come a time when the Nurail will have leave to come and find them, and they must be safe till then."

Stanoczk nodded. "I will go to Chapter, Derush, and put these in trust for the future, and ask about the warrant. When I return to go with you to Chelatring Side, I will tell you what the Saint may have found out."

There was nothing more that Andrej could do about it until Stanoczk came back, then. And he needed to speak to his Security before the sun set on the day. The news would come out. He had a clear duty to his people that they should hear of it from him.

"And I in turn will sound out my child and his mother, and give careful thought to if I should tolerate that your Ferinc breathes the same air as I do. It is my pledge to you, Cousin."

Stanoczk came to embrace him, but informally, as his kinsman rather than as a Malcontent. "It really is so good to see you, Derush," Stanoczk said. "You have been away for so long. Your family has missed you. I have missed you. Save a place at supper for me, in six days' time."

Andrej nodded, unwilling to speak, feeling overwhelmed by a species of nostalgia for the place where he was, the place where he could stay, the place that was his place. Stanoczk let himself out, with the notebooks—and the Bench warrant—secure in his custody.

An hour. He would take an hour to compose himself. Then he would have to tell Stildyne that he was not going to go back with him to the *Ragnarok*.

Chapter Nine

The Appropriate Channels

Marana had gotten a late start to the day, late in rising, much later in dressing, and only now was sitting down in the nursery office to review the status of Anton's lessons with the house's master of children's education.

"The lesson plans have fallen a little behind, Respected Lady, but it is only to be expected," Housemaster Janich said, but comfortingly. "Under the circumstances. Our young lord's father does not come home every day."

Marana closed the schedule log carefully. Nor would their young lord's father be coming home ever again; he was here to stay. But it was for Andrej to make the announcement.

"Still, this is a lag of three days." The single most pernicious fault that Aznir culture found with the members of its hereditary aristocracy was in the tendency of many to substitute privilege for perception. "How are we to recover?"

Anton Andreievitch had needed the very best education because he had been fated for a life as a bastard child, who could reasonably expect a good position within the Koscuisko familial corporation, but whose performance would be under constant scrutiny by the partisans of legitimate children jealous to ensure that no undue special favor was shown him. Now she didn't have to worry about that any longer.

Now Anton needed an even better education, because

he was to inherit the controlling interest in the familial corporation one day. Then history would judge her worth as a mother, and the value of her love for Andrej Ulexeievitch, by the prosperity that Koscuisko should enjoy during Anton Andreievitch's tenure as its master.

Therefore she would have to pay twice as much attention to Anton's lesson plans. The family would do its best to intervene, to take control of so important a task away from her. She would be ready to defend her primacy; she would accept help, but she would not yield control. Anton was her son.

Janich frowned. "The young lord does well with his languages, Respected Lady. Perhaps some time could be found in the schedule for Standard grammar and syntax. I will create a recovery plan, if this suggestion meets with your approval."

And above all else Anton had to be allowed to be a child. It was lucky that he was intelligent and biddable; he did his lessons with as much diligence as one could ask any child his age, and learned them well. Ferinc helped Anton with his language. How was that going to work, with Andrej home?

"Thank you, house-master. We might find a way to do a science lesson outside of the classroom as well. If it can be worked into Anton's play."

Ferinc was here, standing in the open doorway to the nursery office, looking very pale. Janich had noticed Ferinc as well. "Very good, Respected Lady, until next time. With your permission."

Janich had gotten more formal with her. Before Andrej had come home, she had been "Respected Lady," but no one had taken leave of her "with her permission."

Ferinc stood aside, smiling in wordless response to Janich's greeting as the house-master left the room. Marana stood up and waited for Ferinc, who closed the door.

"What is it that they say about Malcontents, Respected Lady? That there is no trust or honesty in them?"

Something had happened. Ferinc was much worked upon by some emotion or another. Andrej knew about Ferinc; he had told her so in words that implied without accusing, earlier today, in the maze in the garden. Had there been some terrible sort of confrontation?

"They say such things about all Malcontents." Not Ferinc. Ferinc was her very great comfort. Almost her friend. "What is it, Ferinc?"

Ferinc reached into his blouse for a case of some sort, as long and as broad as her hand. No, as *his* hand, and Ferinc had long hands. Wincing slightly. "I'm lucky these boxes are as crushproof as they are, Marana, or else it would have been all over. Has the fish survived?"

Marana opened the case. A wheat-fish, secure in a padded container, carefully wrapped to avoid breaking off any fragment of the long whiskers in the beards of the heads of grain that had been used to plait the ancient good-luck charm. "How is that have you been scuffling? Ferinc."

He was looking at the wheat-fish, not at her. "I'm glad. You must give it to Anton for me, Marana, and tell him that I love him, but I have to go away on the Malcontent's business. The thing I never told you was that I had known your husband, once, under different circumstances. He has forbidden me to see his son."

In all this time, Ferinc had given no hint— "He has good reason, Marana," Ferinc added hastily. "The Malcontent knew, of course, but there are personal feelings. And. To be honest. I never meant to love either of you."

It was worse than just that Andrej had discovered Ferinc to be her lover, before she had been able to come up with a good strategy for telling him. She had been the lover of a man whom Andrej had known, and did not like.

There were so many questions that she wanted to ask. *Were you a criminal? Why doesn't he want you to see Anton? Is he jealous? What is it? Doesn't he realize that Anton loves you? Not that I—*

Ferinc was Malcontent, and any such questions were not to be asked. Marana swallowed hard, instead. "You deserve better for your care of Anton." He had been as tender a parent as any woman could wish, and Anton was not even his son. "Is this to be forever, Ferinc?"

Too much was changing too fast. She had not thought far enough ahead, perhaps. There had been too much to do to cope with the immediate changes resulting from Andrej's declaration of the Sacred-art-thous to leave her any room to think on more than the issues that lay directly before her.

Ferinc stood very close, and touched the hair beside her face. But not her face. "It's his concern that makes him stern. So if Cousin Stanoczk can speak for me perhaps I'll be allowed to see Anton. But you, Respected Lady, you owe your husband duty and honor, and a chance to be your husband. You know it's true."

Yes. She knew. It didn't make it any easier, though.

"What becomes of us, if Andrej and I marry?" In the true sense, rather than the formal sense. "Ferinc. All of this time." He had been so great a comfort to her. She was torn between the duty that she owed Andrej, both as a man and as her husband, her duty to be honest and true; and reluctance, inability, to discard five years and more of Ferinc's quiet support.

"I will think about you on cold lonely nights, and wonder if you miss me," Ferinc said. But wickedly. There was a streak of play running throughout his personality that took much of the sting out of even so melancholy a thing to say as that. "And tire my lover with I-remember-when until she kicks me out of bed, and bids me go hang myself. And then it will truly be a cold and lonely night."

She'd known that it was going to come to this. Part of her had known that, anyway. She took him by the braids on either side of his face and kissed him, very carefully. *Good-bye.*

They didn't embrace. The kiss was enough. He looked at her for a long moment, as if he was committing her face to memory and smiled, fondly, without much pain.

Then he kissed her nose. "Give Anton his fish," Ferinc reminded her. "And my excuses. I've got to go. Thy lord has sent me away, and we don't like to provoke the inheriting prince, because we have to apologize and it's the wrong direction for the Malcontent's preferred mode of operation, isn't it?"

It was the end for them, one way or another. Andrej was to stay. If they were lovers ever again, it would be different. That was unavoidable. " 'Till later, Ferinc."

Nodding, Ferinc left, and closed the door again behind him. She was alone. She owed Andrej a chance to be her husband in a modern, Standard way, as well as the traditional manner. She'd see what he had to say to her about Ferinc, and then decide.

But now she would carry a wheat-fish to Anton at his lessons, and interrupt his day just to tell him that Cousin Ferinc had loved him.

Stildyne set a watch on Lek to be sure he remained at peace with his governor, and went back to his room to see whether the bottle of liquor that was there was alcoholic throughout.

In time he began to sense a particular fragrance in the corridor through his open doorway, and knew that Koscuisko was on his way. Lefrols. Koscuisko's smokes. A peculiar weed, and foully odiferous, but it meant Koscuisko to Stildyne, and that was usually a good thing. Even when it was a bad thing.

Koscuisko hadn't changed since the morning, and it was late afternoon. He looked as though he had been sleeping on the desk, with his head buried in a pile of bound text—his face was creased, his eyelids falling half shut.

Coming into the room Koscuisko closed the door, and sat down, and reached for Stildyne's glass. There was only one glass on the table. That would explain it. For a moment Stildyne was alarmed, because Koscuisko could drink him under the table and tended to run through bottles of liquor at a phenomenal rate when he was minded to self-medicate; then he relaxed. This was Koscuisko's home ground. He probably had barrels of the stuff.

"What is it," Koscuisko asked, holding out the emptied tumbler for a refill. "About what name you should be called. Talk to me about this, Mister Stildyne."

Why not? Haster Girag had raised hard truths about Stildyne's past that he'd never shared with Koscuisko; and he had been drinking. Koscuisko was doubtless already skeptically disposed toward him after the morning's revelations; if he was going to quarrel with Koscuisko, he might as well do it when he didn't have to compromise a period of amity and good communication to say what was on his mind.

" 'Chief,' " Stildyne said. "And 'Mister.' Never Stildyne, I suppose I could understand that, not without a 'Chief' or a 'Mister.' Robert you love. Him you call Robert. Lek maybe you don't love so much as Robert, but you call him Lek anyway."

Koscuisko watched his face, as though waiting for him to make his point. "Mister Stildyne. I call my orderlies also Heron and Diris and Lupally. A man should not call responsible people by their first names. It is not of due respect showing."

Koscuisko's dialect was deteriorating. They'd been here for some days now. The house staff spoke Standard, by and large, when they were talking in front of Koscuisko's Security, but Stildyne strongly suspected that they all spoke their own language when they were alone. Or speaking to Koscuisko.

"Well, where I come from, you call a man by his last name when you have no relationship. But people that you know you call by first name."

That wasn't exactly true. He didn't come from anywhere in particular. It was just a conflict between styles—his style, Koscuisko's style—and Koscuisko had the rank, so it was not unreasonable for Koscuisko to assume that his style should define the terms of the relationship. It was all just the issue of whether there was a relationship. Of course there was a relationship. Stildyne was a Chief Warrant Officer. Koscuisko was his officer of assignment. That was a relationship.

"Were you with Girag then on the basis of Brachi and Haster?" Koscuisko asked, thoughtfully. It was not a challenge or a taunt; it was just a question. It was very, very good cortac brandy; it seemed to slip down almost by itself.

To everlasting confusion with it all. Stildyne poured the glass Koscuisko sought and kept it for himself, passing the bottle back. Less effort that way. The bottle needed refilling less often than the glass. "I'm not sure I remember. There was a crew of us at a Fleet base at Gotrane. We probably didn't know each other all that well."

Koscuisko took the bottle but didn't drink from it, looking around him absentmindedly—for the glass. Stildyne knew that was what Koscuisko was looking for. "One is on intimate terms with one's house-masters, but one does not call them by their private names, Brachi. Unless it is in private. And I dared not ever use Chief Samons's name but once in my life that I can remember, because it was so important to try to avoid noticing what a spectacular beauty she was."

Brachi. Koscuisko had said it. Koscuisko was not drunk—or nothing like as drunk as he had to be before he started to get sentimental. He was not teetering on the brink of total psychological collapse. No one held fire to the soles of his naked feet, and that was just as well, because Stildyne would have had to kill them had anyone tried. Stildyne himself was more drunk than Koscuisko, and on only a little more liquor.

"Nor wished ever to use mine. For fear of being misinterpreted," Stildyne said sourly, being drunk. Rising to his feet, he went to the drinks cabinet and took out a clean glass for Koscuisko. And another bottle of something. Just now he didn't care what it was, exactly, so long as it had alcohol in it. "Now you are three times as determined. Now that you've heard about my past."

Koscuisko looked at the empty glass Stildyne set down before him for a long moment. Sighing, Stildyne plucked up the bottle from Koscuisko's hand and poured; then at last Koscuisko seemed to realize that it was meant for him.

"Your past distresses me, Brachi, but it is past. And means you are more greatly to be honored for that you have changed your manner."

No, it didn't. He hadn't left off taking the occasional bite out of a bond-involuntary because he had developed any moral scruples. He had learned not to take advantage of them because Koscuisko disapproved. And that was all.

If there was more to it, Stildyne didn't even want to know. He'd heard about morality. It seemed an unnecessary complication to life in an unjust and uncertain world. Koscuisko had opened his mouth as if to say something, and then closed it again. Stildyne waited.

"And I have struggled this day with how to say this to you, Brachi. But I also have a chance to step away from abuse of those within my power. It is the message that Ivers has brought."

What was Koscuisko saying? Koscuisko had never abused his Security, nor any member of his staff—except the orderly who'd been caught stealing drugs. Koscuisko had beaten her very thoroughly for that, and then forgotten to report the crime to the Captain or the First Officer, to keep the woman from prison. So far as Stildyne knew, there had never been any further problem with the orderly in question.

"You meant to come home last year, sir." So there was only one other thing else that Koscuisko could possibly be talking about. And only one thing it could mean. "Has there been some movement on the part of Chilleau Judiciary?"

Chilleau was expected to put a bid in for First Judge, and it would be a solid bid. As far as Stildyne's limited interest in politics went, he understood it to be a very real candidacy. Koscuisko was Stildyne's officer, but—though it had been easy to overlook on board the *Ragnarok*—Koscuisko was in fact a great deal more. Chilleau Judiciary would want Koscuisko's voice on their side. Stilled, if not raised in active support.

"I have executed documentation. It was this morning. I only heard last night. And I so much regret leaving the people behind, Brachi, but I am to be relieved of Writ and sin no more against the natural laws of decency."

I so much regret leaving you behind, Stildyne thought to himself. A fantasy; but an appealing one. When what Koscuisko meant was Lek, and Smish, and Pyotr, and Taller, and Murat. Godsalt. Robert St. Clare.

Stildyne knew what Koscuisko's people would feel when they found out. It was pure selfishness of him to wish Koscuisko bound to his Writ, in order to have him back on the *Ragnarok*.

"Revocation of Bond, then, in a sense." Freedom unimagined and wonderful. "We'll all be very happy for you, sir. I'll write to you. If you would like to hear."

Lowden was dead, and unlamented. Stildyne didn't

know anything much about ap Rhiannon, but he knew that First Officer had been taking careful notes, over the years, of the ways in which Koscuisko had protected his people. First Officer was a very intelligent man, for an officer. It wasn't going to be the same with Koscuisko gone, but it was never going back to Lowden days. Stildyne was sure of that.

Koscuisko nodded, in apparent appreciation of Stildyne's calm acceptance. Calm on the surface, at least. He had believed Koscuisko to be going home less than a year ago, he had had practice in imagining his life without Koscuisko in it.

Whomever they assigned as Chief Medical Officer could hardly be one-eighth the trouble that Koscuisko had been. If they assigned a new Chief Medical Officer at all, with senior officers in such demand these days.

"I should speak to the gentles," Koscuisko said. "Do you tell them first? Or do I?"

"I'll do the dirty deed, sir. Let it alone. You can make a speech when we say good-bye. When do we leave?"

If Koscuisko had accepted relief of Writ, Stildyne's people didn't have an officer of assignment any more. Technically speaking, they probably should be on the next courier out to rejoin the *Ragnarok*, bringing the news with them.

"You shall not, before time," Koscuisko said, decidedly. "The Bench specialist says that there will be some days before the documentation is complete. And that until my codes have been revoked, I am still entitled to the Bench's protection as a Bench officer rather than a private person. And it was to have been a holiday."

A good story. It would probably work, too, especially with the backing of the Bench specialist. If Chilleau Judiciary wanted Koscuisko's goodwill this badly, they were unlikely to risk tainting the enthusiasm of his endorsement by petty insistence on the proper allocation of Fleet security resources.

"I'll tell them," Stildyne repeated. "It's my job. You'd better go and dress, your Excellency—it will be dinner soon."

Koscuisko nodded, accepting both direction and the reasoning behind it. The simple gesture went to Stildyne's heart; would he ever again have an officer who listened so well to him? Rising to his feet Koscuisko went to open the door, to leave the room; but paused with his hand on the latch-lever.

"Will you come to me, when you retire?" Koscuisko asked. "I would welcome you to join my household. Though you would almost never hear yourself called Brachi, even then."

There was no point Stildyne could see to it. But no sense in giving gratuitous offense. Koscuisko doubtless meant well, even if it was plainly guilt that had inspired the offer.

"Thank you, your Excellency. I'd be honored." He was years short of being able to retire, if he lived that long. Koscuisko would have forgotten all about it, when the time came. Or if Koscuisko hadn't, Stildyne would have come up with some good excuse, by then.

Still, why not? Since he had nowhere else under Jurisdiction to be, why not find a comfortable berth among the many members of his Excellency's household in which to spend his declining years?

Because he wouldn't take favors from Koscuisko. He'd die sooner than turn into Cousin Ferinc, never recovered from Koscuisko's mark on him, obsessed and distracted to this day.

Koscuisko bent his head and left the room. Stildyne sighed, and put the bottle away from him, and left the room himself to go to find some rhyti in the kitchen. To give himself time to think, and sober up, and make up his mind on how he was to tell Koscuisko's people that they were going home to the *Ragnarok* without Koscuisko, who had taken such good care of them over the years.

In the summertime the light lasted beyond the hour at which a young lord should properly retire to his bed, making the young master of the house fractious with reluctance to go to sleep.

Marana sat in the master's parlor after dinner stitching a piece of fancywork, waiting, listening. Andrej sat at the desk next to the double-harp and read over accounts. She knew that it was not because he was concerned, but

THE DEVIL AND DEEP SPACE

because he was expected to review the journals when he came back to his house, and assure himself that the books had been honestly and honorably maintained in his absence. He would have to call an assembly within a day or two and thank the house-masters in each department for their good husbandry of his resources, and distribute tokens of his appreciation and approval. Tradition.

Not all of the traditions of family life were in church records or the acts of saints, however. Andrej had been away for years. She owed him her decision, and she owed it to the love that they had once borne for each other to make it soon.

There was a pounding of young feet down the carpeted corridor outside the room, a gleeful shriek of slightly manic excitement; it was Anton, pursued by his devoted but distraught nurse, coming flying into the room with something in his hand.

When Anton saw his father in the room he stopped, visibly taken aback, unsure of how he was to proceed without error. Anton's delight in his treasure was too much for his dignity, though, even in the presence of his awesome and alien father; smiling, Anton advanced upon Andrej, holding out his prize.

"Look what I have here, lord father, Cousin Ferinc has brought me a wheat-fish. From Dubrovnije."

Andrej had half turned from the desk to face his child, holding a stylus in his left hand, arrested in mid-notation by Anton's unexpected appearance. She could not read his face. Ferinc had told her that there'd been history between them; but Anton loved Ferinc. Now, which would rule? The personal disgust that Andrej had for Ferinc, or a true father's willingness to be tender of his child's passions, and handle them with care and with respect?

"Indeed?" Andrej asked Anton, his voice soft and affectionate. "May I see?"

Anton stood at his father's side as Andrej admired the wheat-fish, with its fine black beard and its gleaming body of woven golden straw. Two blond heads bent over a wheat-fish, Anton gazing up at his father's face with transparent adoration, Andrej's own face shadowed by the tilt of his head but concentrated clearly on his son. She had never seen Andrej so strongly in Anton, ever before. The visceral reminder of who Anton was and why it was that he should be so like Andrej caught her by surprise, a movement in her belly as though Andrej's hand lay across her womb where Anton had been cradled as he grew.

"I was having my lesson. He gave it to my lady mother. I must write him a note." No, Ferinc had brought it to her and fled, because Andrej had told him that he wasn't to see Anton ever again. But he had kept his promise to Anton. "Isn't it fine? I have never seen so nice a wheat-fish in my life."

Marana smiled, but she was still waiting to know what Andrej would do.

"This is very special, I think," Andrej said, playing his fingers delicately along the long beard of the grain heads. "No common wheat-fish has so black a beard. I am impressed. Ferinc must have picked it out for you very carefully. I'd better give it back to you, though, and you must take very good care of it, and tell him your thanks for his kindness."

Black-bearded grain was the most holy. Andrej was right; it was a special fish. Andrej would have been within his rights as a Dolgorukij parent to have taken it away and destroyed it; Anton had not asked Andrej's permission to accept gifts from a man who was not related to him. Andrej did not. Andrej praised the wheat-fish and its donor and Anton's keeping of it instead. It was his pledge. There were to be no recriminations.

"Ferinc is very good to me, sir. I wish I could have taken him to meet you. But I didn't have the chance."

"Perhaps next time, son Anton. I am sure he must be a very good friend to you to have brought you this fine gift. Go and show your lady mother. And then you must go with your nurse."

Anton took his wheat-fish and kissed his father's cheek with spontaneous affection, pure and true. Andrej had passed. Andrej had declined to slander Ferinc to Anton who loved him, though Andrej himself, by Ferinc's report, despised the Malcontent. He had earned the right to try with her, to see if they could be wedded again as fiercely as they had once been, before they were married.

Marana praised Anton's treasure, kissed him, sent him away; and stood up. Andrej had turned away from the desk to look after Anton and watched her now, his attention apparently arrested. Setting her needlework aside, Marana closed on Andrej across the floor of the parlor.

When she was less than an arm's length from him she put her hand up to her hair, slowly, keeping her eyes fixed upon his face all the while; and pulled one of the long bone pins that kept her headdress secure, loosing a thick braided strand of her heavy, wheat-colored hair. His pale eyes were darker by the moment as the pupils widened; an encouraging sign. Holding out the pin, she waited for Andrej to raise his hand to receive it, dropping it into his open palm.

One moment longer she stood, looking at him. He'd said nothing to her about Ferinc. If he said nothing now, he never would. She turned around. Slowly, she walked out of the room, doing her best not to strain her ears to hear if Andrej had got up to follow her. She was willing to try to reach out to him. Was he willing to meet her midway?

He was behind her.

He followed her down the hall to the bedroom. Marana plucked the pins out of her hair one by one as she went, Andrej following after to gather them up as they fell, and her hair draped ever more loosely around her shoulders with every discarded pin.

The bedroom door stood open; the servants had been here. The curtains were drawn back from the great bed, the lamps turned to a welcoming yellow glow, the windows open to the deepening twilight to let the cool air come into the room. Andrej shut the door.

She was too shy of him to turn around, and that was humorous, because she was the one who had laid claim. Andrej was close behind her, at her back; he put the thick hair away from the back of her neck with a careful hand and kissed her there, thoughtfully. It made her shiver.

Andrej seemed to find that an encouragement. Lacing

his fingers through her hair he kissed her neck, her throat, at the back and the side of it, with contemplative moderation. Pressing his lips against her skin; tasting the salt of her body with a considering tongue, slowly.

She turned around, with her long hair trailing slowly through the open fingers of Andrej's right hand. He wore country-dress, very informal. She had not seen his body in all this time, and yet his body was her property, in a sense. She had a right to assess its condition.

She opened the front plaquet of his simple smock, the embroidered band that ran down the front of the garment from shoulder to hem, offset from the collar by the traditional hand's span. Since it was summer, the garment that he wore beneath was as thin as gauze; the heat of his skin beneath her fingertips, even through his undergarment, brought the blood to her cheek, as though she stood too near the fireplace.

Smoothing the open smock back along his shoulders, she put her palms flat to his undershirt and felt the flesh beneath. Andrej. There was something still familiar about the fall of his ribs as they belled toward his diaphragm, the contours of his skin stretched over them; her hands remembered.

She needed the heat of him. She was cold. She put her hand to the back of his neck to draw his mouth down to hers for a kiss, but there was something at the back of his neck that startled her, and she drew away from him with her mouth still half open as it had been to seek his mouth. There was a line, there, across the back of his neck, beneath his skin, between the back of his ears and his hairline at the nape of his neck.

A scar. She touched it with her fingers, and Andrej stood with his hands at her waist and waited for her to be satisfied. Scars. Why was he scarred there? Where else was he scarred, that he had never mentioned to her in his letters?

Sliding his hands up from her waist Andrej gathered her to him and kissed her mouth. She could feel the tension gather in his body. There were his fingers at the back of her shoulders pulling the knot of her kerchief free, pulling the kerchief itself away from her shoulders, uncovering her bosom. It was summertime; her dress had no sleeves. There was no obstacle to interfere with Andrej's unbuttoning her bodice and peeling the fabric open, down her arms, to the floor.

He held her with an arm around her waist and slipped his fingers beneath the garment's neckline to touch the naked skin of her softly rounded shoulders. The sensation made her catch her breath. Andrej's breath seemed to come a little shakily on his own part; he turned the neckline of her undergarment back to bare her shoulder and kissed her where her neck met her body, and shuddered with desire.

Skin. She wanted skin. He was distracted; he was not paying attention. Taking a fistful of linen in each hand Marana tugged up and away to free his undergarment from the waistband of his full trousers. The undergarment had no fastening; it wrapped across the front of Andrej's body, and in the winter it would close with ties—but for now, once she had the hem free, it was easy to pull open and away.

Marana backed away, toward the bed; Andrej watched her go. She looked into his face, wondering if he had second thoughts. She felt so naked, with Andrej watching her. It was intolerable that she should be timid in front of him.

Marana shook her head, and her hair settled like a fine spun shawl across her shoulders. Andrej closed his eyes and bit his lip, the fish that had carried his half of their child into her ocean stiffening visibly beneath his wrap even at several paces remove. Yes. That was better.

She climbed onto the bed, unfastening her hip-wrap as she went. Andrej followed her, his mind apparently focused on her shoulders. Rolling beneath him on the bed's surface, Marana tucked her thumbs beneath the band of his hip-wrap, and then that was gone, too.

Here was the fish in which they had both once delighted. Marana embraced it between her palms and stroked it with affectionate greed; she had not had Andrej's fish since the night before Andrej had left the Matredonat, more than nine years ago. It had been a brisk fish, then.

Andrej knelt on the bed and trembled while Marana

beguiled herself by caressing him; then he caught her hand away and carried it to his lips to kiss her palm. Taking control of the encounter, prisoning her hands in his to protect himself from the distraction of her touch while he tested the curve of her flesh with kisses, tasting her, drinking her fragrance, relearning the feel of her body against his cheek.

He touched her as carefully as though they had never known each other. In all the years that he had been with Fleet, Andrej had been unlikely to have been celibate; what did his hands remember? Was it one woman? Any five women? Or simply the knowledge of alien woman-flesh?

She had known no other lover but Ferinc while Andrej had been gone. But Andrej had been her first love and her first true lover. Even after all of these years, her body remembered that, and craved the caresses that she and Andrej had practiced together to increase their pleasure in one another.

"Andrej," Marana whispered, hoarsely. "Come to me. I want your fish, Andrej. Let me feel him wriggle to his place."

He raised his head, he shifted his body, he half lay over her with his arms straight to the bed on either side so that she felt the heat of his bare flesh, but had no contact with it. His face was flushed, his mouth gone ruddy, his eyes glittering with erotic intoxication beneath their half-closed lids.

"Come to me," Marana urged him. Using small words, speaking to his fish. Her own minnow, the fishlet between her thighs, surged for the pressure of his body; she was not thinking very clearly herself. "Now."

He settled himself against her. In small and careful steps his fish tested the straits of passage, venturing ever more deeply within her with each trial. He had forgotten what it was to lay with a woman of his own race, perhaps.

She ran her fingers down his back with fierce hunger, pressing as deep into the long muscles on either side of his spine as she had strength. The bending of his back in reflex beneath her hands caught at his hips like pulling at the string of a longbow to bend its tip, and Andrej's fish was at home within her. Hers.

Every thrust of Andrej's fish maddened her minnow

even more; the passion that consumed her was beyond naming. It was hot in the room; her skin was on fire, she could feel the sweat on Andrej's belly against hers as his fish strove within her, and the salt scratch of his fish's beard against her body worked upon her flesh like the judgment of Heaven.

He destroyed her.

He was her lover and her husband and the friend of her childhood, and even so he destroyed her without mercy, utterly and entirely, and completely. She screamed in terror and in ecstasy as her entire body caught fire and was consumed from the inside out with living flame.

The bed would burn. The room would catch the blaze, the house would be destroyed. The roof would come down through the blackened structure; they would be buried alive in fire and smoke—

Slowly, very slowly, Andrej collapsed in her arms, and fell over onto the surface of the bed to one side of her. Drowned. The fires cooled as the tides retreated, the bed's cover damp with sweat and exercise. The house would not burn. She carried the ocean within her; they were safe.

Andrej reached out a hand behind him and pulled the bedcovers up from the far side of the bed, pulling her limp body to him away from the rumpled portion of the bed to cover them both with the draped coverlet and rest in the middle of the bed now, together, and for the first time since Andrej had come home. Nestling his face against the back of her shoulder, Andrej slept almost at once.

She rested with him for a little while, her body still shaking within itself in the echoing reverberation of the pleasure he had given her. It was different than when Ferinc loved her. But it had worked. She could still be Andrej's lover; she could be his wife. She could adjust, adapt. There was strangeness to his body—exciting as well as intimidating—and he was not the man that she had known. But neither was she the woman that he might have remembered. It was not impossible that they should begin again, and perhaps be happy.

His sleeping smell had something in it still of the Andrej who had once been hers. Marana set her mind on hope for the future, and slept.

Chapter Ten

Alternate Means of Procurement

Cousin Ferinc sat at the receiving station, watching the traffic analysis reports; he didn't pay much attention to the fact that someone had come into the intelligence station until a hand came down on his shoulder. By then it was too late.

"What interests you, Ferinc?"

It was Stanoczk. And Ferinc was to have met with Stanoczk, almost an hour ago. He had let himself become distracted. How could he do that? Stanoczk was his reconciler. And his reconciler was the single most important person in the world to him . . . after Anton Andreievitch, and Marana, and perhaps Andrej Koscuisko.

Turning in his chair Ferinc stood up quickly, taking Stanoczk's hand away from his shoulder to kiss Stanoczk's knuckles in greeting. "Stanoczk. I'm sorry. You startled me."

"You should not have been startled," Stanoczk pointed out. "You should have been waiting for me. Elsewhere. I despair of you, Ferinc. What have you found?"

Sometimes his gratitude for Stanoczk almost overwhelmed him: Stanoczk's patience and forbearance, equable temper and genial goodwill. The hand of the Malcontent rested lightly on Ferinc, because it was Stanoczk's.

"If it's Noycannir, she could have done it." No, wait,

that didn't make much sense. "I've found something interesting. It's proximity, but it's suggestive."

Ferinc nodded at his analysis screen, wanting Stanoczk to see, hoping Stanoczk would find the information interesting. Maybe interesting enough to overlook Ferinc's lapse in leaving his own reconciler to wait, and wait, and finally come find him. Malcontents were beaten for lesser faults; more or less frequently, as the need and inclination required.

Stanoczk scanned the screen and raised an eyebrow. "What does this mean to me, Ferinc?"

Stanoczk had to see it. It was that obvious. "Just look how depressing a person she must be. Over the last three years. Five suicides. Five."

A Clerk of Court on the Second Circuit; an evidence disposition manager at a sub-court headquarters; a Security troop on detached assignment for debriefing of troops at a Fleet station under the Second Judge's aegis. A third-level communications specialist at Chilleau Judiciary.

And his favorite: a documents release controller at Fontailloe Judiciary itself, where the First Judge presided. That one had been carefully investigated at the time, because of the sensitive nature of the dead woman's job. Everything had cleared. Ferinc didn't think they'd looked hard or long enough.

"Ferinc, despair is more bitter a pain than many can bear. Surely you know this." But Stanoczk was still looking at the screen; the cross-tracking, the time elapsed between a personal contact with Mergau Noycannir and the unfortunate death of an officer of the Court by her own hand. "None of them murdered?"

That was the question, of course. In one instance at least, the cause of death had been recorded as due to an overdose of a recreational drug; there had been a record left. The drug had been of such exceptional purity that a pharmacy audit of the Court's administratively attached medical personnel had been conducted. There had been no findings, and the investigators had left it at that.

There was no recorded curiosity about the chemical

signature of whatever batch the drug had come from, and Ferinc thought that was a shame, because he was almost ready to convince himself that such a trace would have led far away from the actual site of the incident and back to Chilleau Judiciary.

Maybe the trace *had* been done. Maybe it *had* led back to Chilleau Judiciary. Maybe the investigators had assumed a political assassination, and elected for prudence over justice.

"The pattern intrigues, Ferinc," Stanoczk admitted. Ferinc had been confident that it would.

What would one have to do if one set out to accomplish the unthinkable, and subvert the justice of the Bench? Bench warrants did not come out of nowhere. They had to be validated and cross-validated at every step of the process of issue; at any given time, somebody knew where it had come from and where it would be going.

And the further along the process of issue moved, the fewer obvious questions were likely to be asked about the integrity of the validations that the warrant had collected.

When a man came before the Court to argue in the face of the grieving widower's tears that he was guilty of manslaughter, but not murder, for the death of the security guard during an attempted robbery by cause of temporary intoxication depriving him of the use of his reason, it rarely occurred to anyone to ask whether the security guard was dead.

"There is a flaw in the argument, of course," Ferinc pointed out, as Stanoczk frowned over the data. "I am starting from a supposition. So I may be entirely mistaken. But why is it worth so much to her to know exactly where Koscuisko is?"

Stanoczk nodded, but Ferinc hadn't asked a question in a form that Stanoczk could answer with a nod. "I think we need to prefer the question, Ferinc. And also. I have sent the Malcontent's thula to Chelatring Side."

The two halves of that did not quite connect, but they came close enough together that Ferinc could draw the bridge between them. Andrej Koscuisko would arrive at Chelatring Side within five days' time to be present as his father gave the Autocrat's Proxy the wishes of the Koscuisko familial corporation as regarding the Selection of a new First Judge.

The Second Judge was scheduled to announce her candidacy within the next ten days. Now that Verlaine had bought Koscuisko off, there was little doubt that Koscuisko would support the Second Judge.

It was the Malcontent's mission to maximize the concessions that the Combine could demand in return for its support, before Chilleau Judiciary realized that it would win its bid—and no longer needed to purchase the support of member worlds.

"I could tell Noycannir that Koscuisko stays at home," Ferinc suggested. "There's no telling but that I might be marked for a convenient suicide myself, in the near future. I can feel no particular sense of obligation, with that in mind."

Grinning, Stanoczk shook his head. "There is no such word as *suicide* in the Malcontent's vocabulary, Ferinc. No. We will fulfill our contract. We do not yet know that her motive is sinister. And . . ."

Ferinc waited. Stanoczk seemed to reconsider what he was about to say. Shaking his head as if to clear it, he continued.

"And she is at Pesadie Training Command, and expected to remain there. Those deaths, they have all occurred after she had been physically present. But you will see to it that the thula is ready should we need to bring news with speed. And open up the Gallery for me, Ferinc. I want to take your Stildyne on a tour."

Ferinc paled. He couldn't help himself. "What business does Stildyne have with the Malcontent?" Even as he asked it he knew the answers, both of them. He knew. And it wasn't his to ask. Stanoczk put a hand to Ferinc's shoulder kindly, but didn't answer; Stanoczk changed the subject, instead.

"You have spoken to the lady?" Yes, several days ago. He hadn't seen Stanoczk since. He hadn't wanted to. He'd had permission to see Marana, but not to create a disturbance in the garden and arouse the wrath of Andrej Koscuisko himself.

"She knows where her duty lies. And accepts it." Willingly, he could have added, except that he wasn't sure how willing that acceptance was. Or how willing he might be that Marana could turn her back on him, and seek the embrace of her lord. "I'm going to miss Anton. Worse than poison."

Not the best choice of phrases, considering the several drug-accomplished deaths—murders, or suicides—that he had just been reviewing. But the point was made. Why did Stanoczk shake his head, as if in wonder?

"What has happened to you, Ferinc?" Stanoczk asked. "You speak as a man with no feeling about the other man, in your life."

What did that mean? Koscuisko? "Did you talk to Koscuisko about me?"

Now Stanoczk snorted in apparent disgust. "Egoist. Have I nothing better to discuss with my own cousin? As though he could be bothered about you, with other issues on his mind."

That was true. Koscuisko had given Stanoczk the Bench warrant on the same day that Ferinc had given Anton's wheat-fish to Marana and fled. Perhaps Koscuisko had been distracted when he'd seen Stanoczk.

"I only wondered. I am forbidden to see Anton until he's had a chance to consult with you and ensure that you know what sort of a depraved creature I am. The sooner you and he have that discussion, the sooner I may seek for visitation rights."

Stanoczk gave him a shove that sent him staggering, but it was pure affection on Stanoczk's part. Ferinc could smell it. "Visitation? And rights! You are Malcontent, Ferinc, or at least we have pretended that you may someday be a Malcontent in fact, and you can speak such a word? You are impossible. Shut up. Get out. Go to Chelatring Side."

He'd forgotten.

"Visitation privileges?" he asked meekly, with a grin he could not quite repress and a sharp eye out for Stanoczk's boot. Stanoczk was quick with his feet, when he was provoked. "Opportunities, options, avenues, potential approaches—"

"Shut up, shut up, shut up!" Stanoczk cried, almost helpless with laughter. "May all Saints witness what I have to do, to treat with such a donkey. Out. Get out. Go. And I will meet you."

Stanoczk was right. Something was changed. He had seen Andrej Koscuisko, and lived. Open up the Gallery, for Stildyne's benefit?

He had a lot of work to do. He needed to get his reply through to Noycannir at Pesadie, still pretending that she was at Chilleau. And then he needed to bestir himself and get into the mountains, to the Koscuisko's stronghold at Chelatring Side on the breast of mighty Dasidar himself, to see to it that the thula—a Kospodar thula, one of only twenty-seven ever made, the fastest ship of its size or any larger under Jurisdiction—was ready to serve the Malcontent's purpose. Whatever that would turn out to be.

He had faced Andrej Koscuisko, and Koscuisko had been angry at him, and he had not fallen to his knees and begged for mercy. The peace of the Malcontent was his at last.

He could even share his reconciler, without too much distress; and hope that Stildyne might find a share of that peace, in the Gallery.

There was no signal at the door, and yet it opened. Admiral Brecinn looked up from her desk with surprised displeasure: who dared enter her office without signaling?

More to the point, who could? The door had been secured—

Mergau Noycannir. Standing there in the now-open doorway with a flat-file docket under one arm. Brecinn could not read Noycannir's expression; the office was dim by choice and the light coming through from the corridor beyond put Noycannir's face into shadow.

"I beg your pardon, Admiral," Noycannir said. She certainly sounded confused and apologetic. "They told me you weren't in. I meant to leave a message."

An important message, no doubt, or else she wouldn't have forced the door's secures to leave it on Brecinn's desk. Brecinn smoothed her involuntary grimace of irritation away with an effort. "Come in, Dame. Close the door."

Yes, she'd had her people say that she was unavailable—especially to Noycannir. Noycannir might ask questions that Brecinn wasn't interested in having to avoid just at the moment. It had been five days since the *Ragnarok* had left for resupply at Laynock. Brecinn had told Laynock to expect the *Ragnarok*, and ensure that its resupply contained every surplussed ration and expired supply set they could get rid of.

It was an opportunity to take the garbage away and shut ap Rhiannon up at the same time. The redirected stores might not be very exciting in terms of market value, but what was the sense in wasting an opportunity? She hadn't heard back from Laynock. The *Ragnarok* was evidently dawdling.

Noycannir approached the desk, but didn't sit. Just as well—Brecinn hadn't invited her. "I wanted to let you know," Noycannir said. "I feel I should make a short visit to Chilleau Judiciary to see what's become of that warrant. It must be caught up in processing somewhere. We haven't received it, have we?"

It was not surprising that the Bench warrant for those troops had not come back from Chilleau. She hadn't requested one yet. She needed the official report from the preliminary assessment team; she hadn't gotten it. The *Ragnarok* was not merely dawdling, but dragging its feet, and there hadn't been a sound out of the assessment team for days. That was the only thing that stopped her from sending a corvette after them: if something was wrong, she would have heard something.

Could ap Rhiannon have detected the leak, and plugged it?

Possible, if improbable. For that to happen, ap Rhiannon would need the cooperation of Ship's Primes, and Ship's Primes were very unlikely to cooperate with any one mere junior officer, especially one as abrasive as ap Rhiannon. Besides which, even with the cooperation of Ship's Primes, ap Rhiannon could not plug every leak.

"No, we haven't gotten our warrant approved. Thank you, Dame Noycannir." The *Ragnarok* would be back soon; there was a natural limit to how long they could make a simple supply run last. She'd see to it that the report was suitably back-dated, and make a stink about

Chilleau Judiciary's loss of an important Fleet disciplinary document.

It would remind Chilleau of Pesadie's importance to the successful transition of the Bench to its new First Judge . . . because Chilleau could not afford to treat the investigation into the death of Cowil Brem, a Command Branch officer, with anything less than the utmost discretion.

So it wouldn't matter, in the end, that ap Rhiannon was dragging her feet on her report. Brecinn would have names and a warrant. Ap Rhiannon would have only the extra demerit marked against her name in the intangible register of Fleet and reasonable people everywhere. "I appreciate your assistance in this matter. When will you return?"

Noycannir frowned slightly, as if in thought. "Well, that naturally depends on what the problem with the warrant might be, Admiral. It could take days. Shall we say—back in nine days, to get to work?"

Brecinn stood up. "Well, good travel," she said, extending her hand. "And good hunting. I hope I don't need to tell you how important your effort is to our readiness as we stand by to support the Judge at Chilleau." She wouldn't say "Second Judge," and it was too soon to say "First Judge." Noycannir would take her point. "Nor how deeply we all appreciate your energetic pursuit of mutually productive goals."

Noycannir's smile was a little cynical, but Brecinn didn't mind. "Just as you say, Admiral. I'll see you in nine days' time or less, then."

Well, it would probably be longer than that, but Noycannir didn't yet know that she would be staying to see the new request for a Bench warrant through channels. That was all right, too. Noycannir would be expecting to profit for her intervention. Let her work for her profit.

And ap Rhiannon just dug herself deeper into her own obliette day by day by day. There would be a reckoning. Admiral Brecinn was not a vengeful woman, but ap Rhiannon's intransigence was an insult to Fleet itself. Fleet would settle with Jennet ap Rhiannon.

And the *Ragnarok* would be transferred from a draw on resources to a source of tremendous profit, once the new First Judge cancelled the program and forgot all about the ship's existence.

"With Security as well, Dame?" courier ship captain Gonkalen asked, reading the documentation that Mergau had presented. "With respect, it seems a little odd to take Security to Chilleau Judiciary."

Gonkalen looked a little uncertain, but Mergau was sure of her documentation. She hadn't spent all of the past several days creating her forged Record. She'd found time to ensure that she'd be able to get what she wanted when she was ready to make her move.

"Can't be too careful in uncertain times, Gonkalen, and Chilleau Judiciary's own resources are probably fully deployed just at present. It's a mark of thoughtfulness on the Admiral's part, really. Is there a problem?"

No. There was no problem, not unless this Gonkalen meant to argue with Fleet Admiral Sandri Brecinn about her disposition of her own resources. He passed the dispatch order back to her, and bowed. "Of course not, Dame. When do you wish to leave?"

"How soon can we leave?" She knew the correct answer to that question; she had chosen this ship with care. A fast courier, with transport for a Security team, and a storage area that could be secured. That was for Koscuisko. He would board the courier as a Bench officer on detached assignment; he would arrive at Chilleau Judiciary her prisoner, her slave.

Gonkalen shrugged. "At your convenience, Dame. There is a Security team on standby at all times."

That was the right answer, fortunately for Gonkalen. Mergau nodded. "Here are my effects, Ship Captain. I'd like to leave immediately, if you please."

Once they'd cleared Pesadie, they would start to spin for vector transit—but not for Chilleau. Gonkalen would be surprised, but she'd be his superior officer by virtue of Admiral Brecinn's delegated authority. It would be a secret mission. There would be no questions asked, or at least none answered.

Azanry, in the Dolgorukij Combine, and Koscuisko would be at the old fortress known to the locals as Chelatring Side. She had the flight plan. She had the administrative clearance codes, for use when the time came. Her appearance would be sudden, unannounced, surprising. He didn't have a chance.

"As you direct, Dame Noycannir. Within the hour."

By the time it occurred to Brecinn to wonder where she was, she would be on her way to Chilleau Judiciary with a prize under lock and key that would render her position unassailable for the rest of her life.

Silboomie Station experienced a fair level of activity during a given shift, but a visit from one of the big battlewagons in the cruiserkiller class was unusual enough to be an event. They'd had a day or two to anticipate it, as well; once the loading drills had started to pool into the supply set to be ready for the gaining ship's barge, it had been clear that the size of the ship was to be extraordinary.

That the ship was not only a cruiserkiller class warship, but an experimental model—a test bed for the still-developmental and controversial black-hull technology—had only added excitement upon interest. Half the station was out upon the dispatch apron, high above the loading area, to watch the slow descent of the ship's barge down to the loading level.

The clear-space of the station was clearly marked with illumination globes for the entire hemisphere, so that there would be a constant source of light, even when the station's orbit carried it through the night shadow of the cold dead world that anchored it in Silboomie system. The ship's marks were clearly visible, once in range; great *Ragnarok* itself, whispered and gossiped about as much because of the people on board as the innovative promise of the black hull.

Scanner Habsee, the Supply Officer on shift, counted the people who were watching the spectacle, and shook her head. Nineteen heads, and only thirty-six on Station. It was just as well that theirs was an oversight function, restricted to maintaining the automatics and administering the appropriate releases and secures. Because if the work relied upon the living, rather than the mechanical, it would have come to a standstill just now, to watch the *Ragnarok*'s barge come in.

From Habsee's post in the control pillar, she could see the pilot platform on the barge as it sank past her line of sight. There were three people on it, and one of them had to be the Engineer, since he was required to attest to the receipt and valid need for supplies transferred.

One of the people on the pilot platform was tall enough to be the Chigan engineer Serge of Wheatfields, notorious throughout Fleet not so much for his own accomplishments—which were respectable—as for what Fleet had accomplished against him. There was a question to be raised though, over whether the adjective *notorious* could be applied to any of the *Ragnarok*'s officers in comparison to its Ship's Surgeon, whose reputation outshone that even of the late, unlamented Fleet Captain Lowden for dreadfulness and horror. Supply Officer Habsee wondered if the Engineer was ever jealous of Andrej Koscuisko.

With the Engineer at the wheel on the pilot platform the barge slid into its preprogrammed docking slot without a single jolt or jar, not so much as a flash of proximity warning lights. Locked off, ready to commence loading, the barge engaged its interface protocols with the Station's cranes, and the transfer process began.

Descending the ladder set into the side of the barge, the three people who had ridden it down began to make their way across the tarmac to the lifts. And suddenly something fell out of the upper atmosphere, something huge and black, erratic in its movements, swift and sudden in its turns.

Habsee could hear the exclamations of the onlookers over the monitors: fear, confusion, wonder. Recognition. It wasn't a huge black awful thing falling from the underbelly of the *Ragnarok*. It was only the *Ragnarok*'s Intelligence Officer, taking advantage of the joined atmospheres to fly the extra distance rather than ride on the barge.

The Desmodontae came in swift and low, heading straight for the control pillar; to climb up the outer wall, Habsee supposed. It disappeared from sight below the lip of the tower's balcony, only to reappear—climbing up over the outer railing—even as the lift doors opened to discharge the other members of the *Ragnarok*'s supply party.

Habsee went to her post, to greet them formally from behind the transfer-desk. There on the desk's surface was the supply manifest, complete and cross-checked, ready for receipt signatures and release of responsibility.

It was rather a full manifest, she'd noticed. Maybe the ship had been out beyond range of resupply for the months since the death of Captain Lowden. Some of the staff thought that the *Ragnarok* had been on training maneuvers at Pesadie Training Command, though, and not out in the Fringe at all.

It wasn't any of their business, really. They were reasonable people. The ship requested the support; Silboomie Station supplied it. That was their job. Their mission. Asking questions about clients' recent active postings was not included in the mission statement.

"Welcome to Silboomie Station, gentles," she said. She could hear a scrabbling sound behind her, to her left, as the Desmodontae let itself in from the outer balcony. "Your manifest has been prepared. I think you'll find everything in good order. I'm Scanner Habsee, the shift Supply Officer."

The Desmodontae had scuttled past the desk to take its place with the other crew from the *Ragnarok*. "Ship's Engineer," the tall Chigan said, confirming her previous guess. "Serge of Wheatfields. Logistics Control, Pinapin Rydel. Stores-and-Replenishments, He Talks. The Intelligence Officer, Two."

Logistics and Stores-and-Replenishments nodded politely in turn, but the Desmodontae only stared. What was it doing here? Logistics and Stores-and-Replenishments one expected, but what did an Intelligence Officer have to do with a routine resupply? Had there been an undiscovered shortage of the nutrient broth that Desmodontae used for food? What?

"As you'll see from the manifest, we're ready to validate," Habsee replied, a little nervously. "Will you be wanting to spot audit prior to acceptance, your Excellency?"

Many Engineers did, as part of good prudence, and to ensure that they were receiving what they had requested. It was different for commercial transfers, of course. Smaller orders could be more easily verified, and commercial transfers involved money. If the *Ragnarok* didn't get what it expected, they'd just reorder. Silboomie Station was a chartered Fleet support activity; they took what Fleet paid, and were grateful for that much. They had their own ways of making sure that the margins were acceptable.

"Won't be necessary this trip. We're all reasonable people, after all, aren't we? And Two has validated the audit trail." The Engineer's response was a little confusing, but he kept talking, as if what he'd just said had been easily understandable. "There are some additional stores we're particularly anxious to pick up, now that we're here. They weren't on the pre-trans manifest, we'd like to do an ad-hoc add-on."

Happened all the time, especially where reasonable people were concerned. As long as there weren't too many last-minute requests, they could usually locate and load the desired commodity before the barge had finished clearing its original manifest.

"Of course, sir. Material class code?"

The Engineer glanced down at the silent staring Desmodontae at his side, and the Intelligence Officer turned its black-velvet muzzle up in the Chigan's direction and spoke.

"Standard deck-wipes, by the octave, each," the Intelligence Officer said—and its voice was female. Female, and oddly cheerful, somehow. "But a particular lot, if you please. It should be located at encrypt serio trevi-spikal-conjut-seven. Sector four. Line two. Crane access seventeen."

Deck-wipes weren't an acquisition item, under normal circumstances. They were as easy to come by as they were easy to dispose of, by the octave, each. Scanner Habsee didn't wonder; she knew how to mind her own business, and she had to scramble to get the matrix coordinates loaded, because by the time she had grasped what she was being told, "Two" was already halfway through the location sequence.

"I confirm encrypt serio trevi-spikal-conjut-seven. . . ." The information came up slowly, the cross-reference seeming to require longer than usual to complete its search. "With respect, ma'am, according to the register it's a shipment of tallifers, special hold for experimental—"

Two raised one clawlike hand in a swift gesture of warning, and most of one wing came with it. Habsee shut up, startled into silence.

"There is a very good reason for such an entry," Two said, solemnly. "We, however, have strict instructions to receive deck-wipes from that coordinate. We are not to leave without them. It would, of course, help immeasurably if you could slip the package into mid-manifest, and excite as little notice as possible."

As long as there were no inadvertent misunderstandings. Habsee invoked standard handling on emergency override, to get the package moved without the flag-action of a special transfer. Fortunately, the index location was only one or two processes deep; it had been placed quite close to the loading apron—doubtless deliberately.

Two was the Intelligence Officer, after all. If there were Intelligence issues involved, Habsee rather wanted to get rid of it as soon as she could.

"It will be one moment." Habsee frowned in concentration, working the problem on-line. Pull a heavy lift off a mid-process, get it to the closest entry site. Find the package—there; load the package. It was remarkably heavy, for its size.

Habsee adjusted the counterbalance resists. The load stabilized; she keyed the global-domain. "Attention on observer. Maximum load limit on dispatch apron has been exceeded, return to post." She was expected to run the idlers off from time to time; and they had already had the better part of the treat—the *Ragnarok*'s barge docking, with the dramatic appearance of the Intelligence Officer as an unexpected thrill. "Repeat, maximum load limit exceeded, return to post."

Clear the area. By the time the lift with the special consignment cleared the front end of the massive stacks to make its slow ascent from two levels down, the dispatch apron was effectively deserted. Not that the movement of the special requisition was really hidden or

concealed in any sense, no. It was just as not-obvious as
it could be, given the restrictions under which she had
to operate.

Then it was done. The special consignment was placed
forward, and the loading barge took it up as if it had
been waiting for just that. The next four packages in
their dull gray, featureless containers slid onto the barge
immediately afterward, hiding the special package from
sight. The Engineer stepped forward and set his mark
against the manifest, bending his head to the ident scan
with solemn, bored gravity.

"And that's that," Habsee said, as the ident came
back true blue and the manifest ticket faded into SHIPPED
from STORES. "Pleasure to be of service to you, gentles.
And good-shift."

Special packages and cruiserkiller-class warships aside,
it was just the same thing that she did shift in, shift out,
for shift after shift after shift. It was all either SHIPPED
or STORES to her, and once shipped, it was no longer of
any interest to Scanner Habsee whatsoever. She sent a
standard notification to Pesadie Training Command to
confirm disposition of the special consignment, and went
back to her daily tasks without a second thought.

Jennet ap Rhiannon stood on a loading apron in the
maintenance atmosphere, watching as the maintenance
crew unshipped the case of deck-wipes that Wheatfields
had brought up from Silboomie Station. Two had traced
its provenance through avenues known only to her; Two
said it would be evidence. If it was a shipment of tallifers, it would mean one less hope for making their case
against Pesadie Training Command.

"What good does it do us, your Excellency?" Mendez
asked, from beside her. Mendez to the right of her, Two
hanging from a support beam to the left of her, and
Wheatfields standing—as was his habit—apart, watching
the crew, chewing on a twig of something or another:
Command and General Staff, Jurisdiction Fleet Ship
Ragnarok.

Only Lieutenant Seascape was missing; she was up in a
crane where she could watch the crew work from above.

It was a big case of deck-wipes. Twice Wheatfields's height. Three or four times as long as Wheatfields was tall. One Wheatfields deep.

"I'm hoping it will be ammunition, First Officer." She appreciated the fact that he called her "Excellency," even though she knew he knew it was merely a courtesy title. She could not bring herself to call him "Ralph." "It should prove that Pesadie is corrupt, and trading in armaments. Therefore there is also a strong possibility that the explosion that killed Cowil Brem was related to black-market munitions."

"Wait," the Ship's Engineer said suddenly, then lapsed back into his customary sullen silence. Jennet waited. On the crane overlooking the platform, Lieutenant Seascape leaned over the top of the crate as the crew winched its top cover clear.

For a moment Seascape remained just as she was. When Seascape raised her head to look across to where Jennet stood with the other officers, it seemed that her expression was a mixture of horror and delight. Then Seascape urged the crew to hurry as they took down the great side panel that concealed the contents of the crate from Jennet's view.

Bending over the crane's basket, Lieutenant Seascape hooked the cable onto one of the lift points on the crane. Jennet hoped she was tethered into the basket; it was a long reach.

The winch started to work, the great side panel lifted, the maintenance crew guided it carefully across the platform to where it could be laid flat. The outline was clear, but the blanket was still in place, and a person could still tell herself that they were mistaken.

The blanket lifted clear. There could be no mistake. It wasn't a case of deck-wipes; so much had been obvious from the first glimpse they had gotten of the contents of the crate.

"Sanford in Hell," First Officer swore, but reverently.

It was the main battle cannon for the forward emplacement of a cruiserkiller-class warship, beautiful, deadly, and efficient beyond measure.

Jennet waved at Seascape, calling out to her. "Thank

you, Lieutenant." She needed to know exactly what else was in that container, now that the basic fact was confirmed and undeniable. "Carry on."

"Somebody will get the Tenth Level for this," Mendez observed. "Selling off Fleet armament. What's next?"

Jennet looked up to where Two hung from the crossbeams, scratching her neck with her wing. Mendez knew. Mendez had to know. "At least it gives us some leverage," Jennet said. "But it means going to Taisheki."

That was where Fleet Audit Appeals Authority had its base. And so far she had left Pesadie Training Command on false pretenses, though the action could be excused as a misunderstanding if Fleet was generous and willing to overlook it; but once they left Silboomie Station for Taisheki, they were at war with Pesadie. There was no other way around it.

"What exactly do you mean to appeal to Fleet, your Excellency?" Mendez asked, but calmly, without challenge. Playing the Devil's advocate. "What has Pesadie done? Except for demanding some troops and, oh, been implicated in black-market profiteering with Fleet's battle cannon, just a little."

"Demanded surrender of Fleet resources to face the Protocols based on illegally obtained information, demonstrating a clear preconception prejudicial to the rule of Law. Two's found Brecinn's marks all over this case of deck-wipes, which proves she's corrupt. The last person who should be investigating the death of Cowil Brem is an officer who has something to hide. What was she storing on that station, anyway? Why did it explode?"

Wheatfields raised a hand and took the twiglet out of his mouth. "Taisheki," Wheatfields said. "Three days, your Excellency, maybe five, First Officer."

Mendez hadn't asked, but Wheatfields was answering anyway. Jennet felt something in her gut relax. It was only an implicit agreement to go to Taisheki, but it was enough, and it heartened her more than she could say. They'd challenged her decisions, but they'd accepted them; this was the closest they'd come to an endorsement yet—and she needed their support, if she was to have any hope of making this work.

"What about the Bonds, First Officer?" Six bond-involuntary troops were on board, assigned to support Koscuisko at torture work in Secured Medical, governed to obedience. And Koscuisko wasn't here to keep them comfortable with the situation, to assure them that they were not to blame for the fact that the ship was operating well outside its normal range of procedures. There could be trouble with their governors.

If Wheatfields had agreed and Mendez was not objecting, they believed that the crew would accept the decision. It wasn't value neutral. Making an appeal to the Fleet Audit Appeals Authority had consequences. If their appeal was not sustained, there could be disciplinary action, loss of rank and pay; disciplinary action that should properly be restricted to the ship's officers—but the odium attached to having made an appeal that was not sustained would attach itself to the entire crew. Transfer out would be difficult, if not impossible. Nobody wanted troublemakers within their Command.

And there was more. If an appeal was not sustained, it opened the possibility that Fleet would elect to investigate the *Ragnarok* for mutinous intent. There was only one reason why so desperate a course of action as an appeal could be contemplated: the fact that Brecinn had made it clear that "mutinous intent" was exactly where she was going anyway.

Mendez did not quite shrug. "So far, so good, your Excellency," Mendez said. "And making an appeal is within your authority. Medical will keep an eye out. And there's Koscuisko's influence to consider; he's corrupted them to a significant extent."

This was an intriguing claim. "How do you mean, corrupted?" Jennet asked.

"Gained their trust, your Excellency. Convinced them that nobody's going to get unreasonable on 'em without going through him first. Ruins the whole effect, but there you are."

She'd heard gossip about Koscuisko's relationship with his Bonds; she hadn't thought it through, but Mendez was right. The whole idea was for bond-involuntaries to be incapable of transgression, because punishment was so horrible and so immediate. But the governor reacted to internal stress states to make its determination of whether punishment was in order; without those cues, the governor did—nothing.

"Will you go on all-ship, First Officer?"

Mendez nodded. "I'll make the announcement, your Excellency. Serge. How long to vector transit?"

Wheatfields did something peculiar, even for him. Raising one arm high overhead, he drew a great looping circle in the air, three times, five times, before he dropped his hand to tuck his twiglet back between his teeth. "Twelve hours," Wheatfields said.

She could see movement at the far end of the maintenance atmosphere. Engineering was already moving to hull the maintenance atmosphere for vector transit.

"I'd better get, then, your Excellency. With permission."

Jennet returned Mendez's bow with grave precision. Wheatfields nodded and excused himself, and she couldn't tell whether he had actually saluted her or just been momentarily distracted by something underfoot.

Two hopped down from her perch and scurried off after Wheatfields, her bow over and done by the time her translator got to the end of "By your leave, Captain." Jennet ap Rhiannon stood alone on the apron, watching Seascape strip the coverings off that beautiful cannon.

Maybe once they were on vector she could send Rukota to Engineering, to help install the battle cannon in its place. She wanted the cannon in place. She thought that they might need it. The *Ragnarok*'s own armament was on the light side, always had been. It was an experimental hull. It had never been equipped to defend itself. Until now it had never faced an environment in which it might be required to.

Defend themselves—against even Fleet? If it came to that. She was not going to throw anybody's life away without a fight. The rule of Law would be upheld. It would. She looked at the battle cannon, and shuddered.

But she had work to do, if she was to be prepared to transmit an appeal to the Fleet Audit Appeals Authority at Taisheki Station. She would need to have her Brief in order. And request Safes, for the bond-involuntaries.

She left Seascape to supervise the birth of the battle cannon and exited the maintenance atmosphere for her office, to get to work.

General Rukota hadn't seen much of the officers of the *Ragnarok* since the preliminary assessment team had been confined to quarters. He looked in on Pesadie's people once a day because it was his duty, but he wasn't any more interested in talking to them than they to him, and the visits were short accordingly.

Something was clearly in the air; he'd known that since Two had not-told him that they were not going to Laynock for resupply. But the crew of the *Ragnarok* had discipline: whatever it was, he wasn't hearing gossip. He spent his day in the Lieutenant's quarters they had set aside for him, writing letters to his wife and children for some future and possibly never-to-come date when he would be able to transmit them.

He worked on his official report, the one that Admiral Brecinn was expecting, the one with the by-name identification of the troops who had been on the Wolnadi at the time of the explosion of the observation station. But he didn't spend too much time on it. He saw no particular point: ap Rhiannon was not about to surrender those troops, so taking his time was doing her a favor, really.

The longer it took him to prepare the official report, the longer it would be before ap Rhiannon would have to stop defying Admiral Brecinn and start defying a Bench warrant with the full weight of Chilleau Judiciary behind it, which was going to be much trickier than merely refusing to cooperate with Pesadie Training Command.

He worked on his memoirs instead. Some of the officers he had known in his career deserved commemoration, some of the battles he had fought had been worthy of preservation for the lessons they could teach, and he had his theory of armament to propose and develop. Plenty to do.

Twice a day he went to exercise. Individual training in the morning; group combat drill in the evening, when he could find someone in the arenas to spar with him. He could almost always get a bout with one particular team of Security that was apparently on its fifthweek duty, in Medical.

Individual members of any Security team—the Captain's Security 1-point, Intelligence's 2-point, First Officer's 3-point, the Engineer's 4-point—could be and were posted to Medical to maintain their basic field medical skills; but the only time an entire team did fifthweek duty in Medical was when they were bond-involuntary, and the only place bond-involuntaries could be assigned was to the Chief Medical Officer, because he was Ship's Inquisitor. Security 5-point.

But Rukota had seen the Security manifests. There were only six bond-involuntary troops in all on board of the *Ragnarok*, and four of them were to have gone home with Koscuisko on leave. Therefore Jennet ap Rhiannon had switched Security teams. So she couldn't surrender the troops that Brecinn was demanding, because they weren't even on the *Ragnarok*.

That was ap Rhiannon's business, though, not his; and was certainly nothing to do with the troops themselves. They gave him a good workout. They pressed him hard enough, but not too hard. They worked so well together. Good people. It would be a shame to let Pesadie Training Command torture them to death.

He was just getting cleaned up after his evening's exercise, toweling off his thinning hair, getting dressed, when Security came for him. "General Rukota?"

One of the senior Warrants, Miss Myrahu; he'd interviewed her about the audit problem. She was standing in the doorway of the dressing room, but it was nothing personal; there was no segregation of the sexes in Security arenas and he was more clothed than not anyway, by now.

"Speaking. Excuse my state of undress. What do you want?"

Maybe Brecinn's people had tried a breakout and been shot down. A man could fantasize. If they had, though, wouldn't that cause damage to the courier? And it was a nice courier. It deserved better. When this was all over he would have it fumigated. Exorcised. Apologized to, at the very least; as far as he could tell it was an honest ship.

"If you'll come with us, sir. Captain has requested an interview."

Had she, indeed? Well, why not. It wasn't as though he had any urgent business of his own; he was curious, too, to see what ap Rhiannon might tell him—if anything—about what was going on.

"Very well. At your disposal, Miss Myrahu, lead on."

His escort took him down to the engineering bridge in the very core of the ship, the single second-best-shielded area on the *Ragnarok*. Was it his imagination, or was the atmosphere in the corridors a little more tense than it had been earlier today?

They stopped him at the entrance to the observation deck, signaling for admittance; when the door opened, Security turned around and went away, leaving Rukota alone—or as alone as a man could get, on board a cruiserkiller—to step across the threshold on his own.

The observation deck over the engineering bridge was a gentle curve of clearwall, railed off, but otherwise with a full range of sight—and sound. Ordinarily they would be able to hear everything that was going on, but the feed seemed to have been turned off temporarily.

Either way, the people working below in the engineering bridge couldn't hear *them*. It was better not to distract ship's engineers while they were concentrating. A momentary distraction could have serious consequences during a vector spin, and what might earn an inattentive Security troop an especially pointed thump on the head on the exercise floor could cost the entire ship its very existence, if it came at the wrong time.

Pausing on the threshold, Rukota took it all in. It was dark on the observation deck, to cut down on distractions. But the command structure of the entire Ship was here, the Captain—acting Captain—ap Rhiannon, the Ship's First Officer, the Intelligence Officer, even the one other Lieutenant who had been unfortunate enough to be assigned here. Command and General Staff, Fleet Jurisdiction Ship *Ragnarok*, with sauced-flats and—so help him—bappir. Bappir, on the observation deck of the engineering bridge.

He was dead, and gone to his reward. Or he was dead, and for his next task—a few octaves with Jennet ap Rhiannon, trying to teach the mulish young officer about self-preservation and protocol.

"General Rukota." Ap Rhiannon beckoned him in, waving him to a place at the rail where he, too, could look down over Serge of Wheatfields's dark close-cropped head to the great visual field that occupied one wall of the engineering bridge. "Come in, sit down. Have a flask of bappir. Have two, you may as well."

He couldn't see well enough to be able to read the mechanicals' displays from their removed vantage point. It didn't help if he squinted. The First Officer handed him a slice of sauced-flat, adding an extra handful of ponales across the top in a gesture that was apparently intended to be friendly.

Santone could eat ponales; their mouths had all been cauterized from the inside out by a steady diet of the acerbic fruit from childhood. If First Officer expected *him* to eat ponales, however, he was going to need more than two glasses of bappir.

"What's this all about?" *Your Excellency*. He'd forgotten the "your Excellency." He remembered in the middle of a mouthful of sauced-flat, and by then it was too late.

"Well, in the simplest possible terms, it's this." Ap Rhiannon hadn't seemed to notice. She was leaning on the railing with a flask of bappir in one hand, tracking a scan somewhere down in the pit of the engineering bridge as if it meant something to her.

"We're being set up to take the blame for something we didn't do, and there are lives at stake. That preliminary assessment team had cleared the craft implicated well before anyone broke into Security. And Brecinn's been telling us we can't get resupply on critical goods, but once you leave Pesadie Training Command's sphere of influence, the shortages don't seem to exist."

Once you leave Pesadie Training Command? Of course. Why not? It was major resource deployment contrary to standing orders, that was all, unless anyone really believed that Brecinn had had some place other than Laynock in mind when she'd released the *Ragnarok* to go to resupply. A little spot of failure to obey lawful and received instruction. Oh, maybe a little mutiny. Just a little one.

"I'm not about to give away four crew. As nearly as we can tell"—glancing at First Officer for confirmation—"most of the rest of the crew doesn't like the idea either. Either that, or they realize that four is never enough for Fleet. We feel the only real option is an appeal."

Much good that would do her. An appeal could be accepted or rejected at the Pesadie level, and that would be that. What was she talking about? The only "appeal" worth making would be to the Fleet Audit Appeals Authority. And that was clearly out of the question.

"I've never seen the *Ragnarok* do a vector spin," ap Rhiannon concluded, straightening up, standing away from the rail. "And we know we haven't been providing you with much by way of entertainment. Are there any ponales left?"

The Intelligence Officer was keeping to herself, eating a custard. Two wouldn't be able to get much out of watching, not glassed-in as they were. Perhaps she was hearing transmissions. Or perhaps she was simply enjoying the custard, in the company of the *Ragnarok*'s other officers. The *Ragnarok*'s soon-to-be-cashiered officers. The *Ragnarok*'s lucky-if-they-weren't-all-summarily-shot officers.

"You're going to Taisheki." He might have known, the moment she'd started talking about vector spins. She would hardly be making so much fuss out of simply returning to Pesadie Training Command. "You are out of your mind. Individually and collectively. With respect. More bappir in that jug, is there? Lieutenant Seascape?"

Grinning, the Lieutenant pushed a full jug of bappir across the curved rail-table toward him. Ap Rhiannon laughed, but it didn't sound as though she had much pleasure in it.

"General, either I go to Taisheki, or Pesadi helps itself to the *Ragnarok*'s crew as it sees fit. And for no purpose, no valid purpose that supports the rule of Law."

Maybe ponales on sauced-flats weren't quite so bad. Maybe it was strong bappir. They all looked as though they hadn't had much rest over the past few days; even Two's pelt betrayed a suspicion of dust, around the feet.

The hands. Whatever. He had done nothing but rest. The bappir went past them, and right to his head.

"Well, it's your career. And your career. And his, and quite possible yours as well," he noted, glancing around him at ap Rhiannon, the First Officer, and Wheatfields, in the pit of the engineering bridge below them, and the solitary Lieutenant left on board. "Can it really be worth hauling the entire ship to Taisheki? For what? All right, four lives. All right, four innocent lives." The enormity of the undertaking rather stunned him, bappir or no bappir. "Seven hundred people on board this ship, Captain."

And each of them willing to accept the blame and the burden, the permanent brand of a troublemaker and a dissident, to go crying to the Fleet Audit Appeals Authority at Taisheki over a mere four lives? Howsoever dirty the plot, howsoever innocent the lives, there were just four of them, and there were more than seven hundred people on board the *Ragnarok*.

"None of them with a great deal to gain," ap Rhiannon countered, somberly. "And all of us with entirely too much to lose." Yes, advancement, promotion, hope for the future in Fleet. A career. No, that wasn't what ap Rhiannon had been getting at, at all. "If we don't fight it, we may as well have colluded from the beginning, as though we're the kind of crew that really would sell ourselves just to stay out of trouble—"

"Attention to the Engineer, with respect, Captain," Mendez interrupted, gesturing toward the pit of the engineering bridge with his flask of bappir. "Might want the sound up. Lieutenant?"

Ap Rhiannon looked confused for a moment, but Mendez wasn't talking in her direction. It was Lieutenant Seascape who made the necessary arrangements, plaiting them into the braid.

"—increase spool rate on plasma sheath," Wheatfields was saying. The plasma sheath was the ship's respiration, and the faster the ship was to move, the more quickly it had to breathe. "Cassie, reduce your rate of acceleration. We're going to come up on it smoothly. I said reduce your rate, Cassie—"

There was urgency, but little sharpness, in the Engineer's voice. "Thank you, Cassie, sorry about that. Sela. We should be starting to cook in tertiary furnace."

And the plasma sheath had to thicken to catch the increased rate of particle bombardment, as well. Which of course implied that the ship's engines would start to run hotter than the usual tolerances. The only thing that could draw the extra energy off the furnace before the activity level began to reach critical parameters was to thin the sheath and slow the ship down—or take the energy and turn it into speed, enough speed to take a mass of the *Ragnarok*'s dimensions and shoot it like a projectile into the vortex of the vector, where even the *Ragnarok* could experience something akin to faster-than flight.

"Tersh and quat both coming along nicely, sir. Preparing overflow energy dump to the pintle batteries."

Space was mostly empty, and the vectors were the fastest way through it. The vectors were characterized by the absence of large objects in their vicinity; some speculated that they were pinholes in the fabric of space of some sort, formed long ago by the passage of a mass so dense that it had left a relatively stable deformation in the universal fields behind, clearing out most of the existing matter from the area as it went. They had to be old, if so, because enough minute particulate matter had accumulated in the area over time to feed the *Ragnarok*'s engines.

"All right. Watch it, Cassie. Ilex. Start the spin. Don't forget that we've selected left-helical twist, and get ready to set your mark."

The vector was clearest—fastest—in its center, the vortex, but getting there and staying there could be a bit complex. They needed the correct trajectory to counter the characteristics peculiar to the vector itself. The *Ragnarok* had to line up on the vector and gauge its approach just right to ensure that they would hit the vortex and go straight through to Taisheki.

"Begin your offside roll, mark. Four. Five. Six. Seven. Mark."

They didn't feel a thing, of course. They wouldn't. If they were out in the maintenance atmosphere standing on the hull, perhaps they would feel some vibration, but no more than that. But the blank star field on the massive display at the far end of the engineering bridge cleared, and reimaged on a vector dynamic that made the speed and character of the ship's maneuvers graphically accessible, even to a mere Fleet Ground Landing Forces officer like himself.

"We hit that one just a shade too hot. Cassie, you're going to have to back down just a slice. Pumet, give me a fractional retard and second and third."

There were machines here to do to work of setting the ship on vector spin. It could be done without the help of mechanicals, but only theoretically, and only with smaller craft—with correspondingly less complex characteristics.

The fact remained that even the expert systems on this experimental model failed when confronted with the combined effects of seemingly unrelated factors. The mechanicals, the expert systems, the professional machines—*Ragnarok* relied upon them to maintain life support, motivation, respiration. It was more of a job than a mere seven-hundred-plus organics could manage between them. But only organics could manage the chaotic interplay of multiple events at the extreme limits of the on-board systems' tolerance.

"Stay on acceleration. Perfect. Coming up on second mark. Are we pulling any extra drag on that hull-flap section we had to seal manually?"

All of which taken together meant that although the Engineer might not be able to get the *Ragnarok* on vector without the mechanicals, the mechanicals alone could not get the *Ragnarok* on vector as well as they could with the Engineer to make adjustments.

The mechanicals only knew whether or not there was extra drag on hull-flap section whatever. They had no way of knowing why it might be so, or what kind of other effects the manual seal was liable to have.

The ship's spiral hit the second glowing graph point on the screen's display. Serge of Wheatfields was tapping the rail on his console, clearly deep in concentration. "That's good. Pumet, left retard. Sela, check the spool to speed, how are we doing?"

The third mark was coming up on-screen, and Rukota

almost thought he could see the fourth—still faint and dim. "That's as it should be. Cassie, we're feeling a little sluggish—do you agree? Pumet, let it warm up a couple of layers."

They hit the third mark, and the spiral path on the display screen was beginning to make Rukota dizzy. The fourth mark was up within a scant eighth of the third, and the marks came ever more quickly as the *Ragnarok* gained momentum and the spin it needed to hit its mark on vector.

"Lift those retards, Pumet, keep it as smooth as you can." Wheatfields had less to say, and was speaking softly and quietly—careful not to disturb concentration. "All right, now, gentles. Seven eighths to vector spin. Go for it."

The cruise-marks on the display screen blurred into a single point of light that circled around the screen's perimeter, spiraling ever inward. Rukota took hold of the railing to keep his equilibrium. Watching the target blips as the ship's course proceeded was like watching a sleep-spinner. He didn't want to embarrass himself by falling over.

"This—is—going to be—the smoothest—sweetest— vector spin, in the history of the Jurisdiction Fleet—"

And the single point of light that was all Rukota could see of the ship's course markers circled closer and closer to the center of the screen, each rotation tighter, each period shorter and shorter and shorter.

"Two eighths to vector spin," Wheatfields said.

The light point was a throbbing pool in the center of the screen, the target blips too close to one another to distinguish them individually. Then—as Rukota stared in fascinated wonder—the light point shuddered and condensed into a single solid point dead center in the screen that fixed and held and shrank into oblivion.

The Engineer turned at his post and looked up at the observation deck, to where ap Rhiannon leaned over the rail in tense concentration.

"Captain, we have the Recife vector."

Unclenching her hands from the railing, ap Rhiannon took a few deep breaths—as if she had been holding her breath, and hadn't realized it. There were subdued gestures of triumph and relief from the crew down in the engineering bridge pit; ap Rhiannon keyed the cross-transmit.

"Thank you, Engineer. The First Officer and I have taken the liberty of asking your relief shift to come on early. I hope that you may all join us in Mess area next forward for bappir and sauced-flats. It isn't much, but it comes with our sincere thanks."

Nodding, Wheatfields turned back to the pit. "Thank you, Captain. Well done, all. Let's just braid our loose ends, and let the next shift on, shall we?"

Mendez turned off the cross-transmit, and the Lieutenant shut down the transparency factor so that the observation deck no longer offered the view of the engineering bridge that they had recently enjoyed.

Ap Rhiannon drained a flask of bappir, staggering just a bit; the Intelligence Officer, behind her, steadied her unobtrusively, without seeming to have noticed anything. Ap Rhiannon wasn't drunk; Rukota knew better than that. Ap Rhiannon was probably just exhausted. For all he knew she'd been sitting up shifts, fretting about her people, trying to convince herself that going to Taisheki was the right—or not merely the right, but the best and only—thing to do.

"I've got a favor to ask you, General Rukota." There was no uncertainty in ap Rhiannon's voice, however. The *Ragnarok* was on vector for Taisheki; there was no changing that now. And therefore no reason to waste any more energy on worrying the issue. Obviously. "We found a beautiful piece of armament at Silboomie Station, hiding out in a case of deck-wipes. Main battle cannon. Would you advise the Ship's Engineer on installation, once he's had a bit of recovery time?"

She'd taken the *Ragnarok* and left Pesadie without explicit clearance; she'd taken resupply—so that she could run without access to Fleet stores for a while—and she had taken the Recife vector for the Fleet Audit Appeals Authority at Taisheki Station. And she had convinced the Ship's First Officer, and the Ship's Intelligence Officer, and of course most importantly the Ship's Engineer, to do as she said, and go.

It was a fearfully desperate thing to do, for a mere

four lives. A crew that would consent to hazard careers and pensions for such a slight piece of principle—had no place in the Jurisdiction Fleet of Admiral Sandri Brecinn.

A crew that would agree to defy authority and jump the chain of command to appeal for the lives of four Security was either a working unit with clear common goals and an awesome sense of self-respect, or it was actually, honestly, two steps short of the kind of mutiny that even he would have to acknowledge. Perhaps the *Ragnarok* was both things, at once.

"Battle cannon, you say." Contraband, clearly. Ap Rhiannon didn't like black marketeers. "Of course. At your Excellency's disposal entirely." He didn't like black marketeers, either.

She was looking up at him directly, with a curiously forlorn expression buried deep, deep, deep in her professionally unreadable black eyes. "Maybe we can talk again," she suggested; there seemed to be something more that she wanted to say, but had thought better of. She was right to suppose that she had some explaining to do, but he could wait. "But for now you'll have to excuse us, General."

"Wanted in Mess area next forward. Of course." He bowed in salute, carefully, rather more respectful of "Captain" ap Rhiannon than he had been inclined to feel before.

She in turn nodded, her own gesture somewhat less of an acknowledgment of courtesy offered a temporary position and more an acceptance of acknowledgment of rank. She wasn't thinking about it, no; she seemed too tired to be thinking on so deep a level—or so trivial a one—as that. She was getting comfortable with "Captain." Maybe she was earning it.

"Later, then. Security, return General Rukota to quarters—Wheatfields will want to know where he can find him. First Officer, Two, if you would please come with me."

He would much rather have gone with the *Ragnarok*'s senior staff to Mess area next forward.

And beyond?

Chapter Eleven

The Procession of the Sirdar

And when the last piece of sauced-flat had been eaten to its crust, and the last half-a-flask of bappir had been swallowed, Jennet ap Rhiannon left the last of the mess areas she had been visiting since they'd made the Recife vector and returned to quarters. She was so tired that only the wake-keeping drugs she'd gotten from Medical were keeping her going, so tired that she nearly lost her way twice, so tired that she kept forgetting that the people behind her were her own Security escort—or the acting Captain's Security escort, at any rate. She felt no sense of ownership or identification with them.

She felt very little.

When she got to her quarters it was a moment before she realized that they were her quarters, and not someone else's, because there was a Security post outside the door, and the only time Security was posted outside an officer's quarters was when it was the Captain's quarters.

She was so tired that the door was coming open and she was already moving into the room before she realized that the Security post was 3.4, not 1.-anything, and what that implied about who was within the room and what he was doing there.

And then quite suddenly she was wide awake. Security 3.4 was the First Officer's. Ralph Mendez was sitting in the room, at the worktable, leaning his forearms against its edge and pushing an empty cup of what had probably been konghu from side to side between his hands.

Mendez was responsible for Security, as well as for Operations. If an officer offered an act of sedition or mutiny, it was Mendez's job to take the officer into custody until such time as the question of guilt or innocence—error or intent—could be placed in the hands of a Ship's Inquisitor for discovery and investigation at the Advanced Levels of the Question.

The door slid closed behind her, and they were alone. She could take him, from this distance; she wore knives, and she knew how to use them. But she could not take the First Officer, and the Security at the door, and the rest of the Security on board. And it was better not to jump to conclusions, no matter how obvious it all seemed.

"First Officer. A surprise. Have you been to bed at all, your Excellency?" She'd approached the Engineer first; there had been no other option. The Engineer was the person who was ultimately responsible for where the ship actually went, and how it actually got there. And she'd seen the Intelligence Officer next, because once she could feel confident that Wheatfields would at least listen to her, she had needed to be sure that no one was paying any particular attention to the *Ragnarok*'s movements.

By the time she'd got past the two of them, the *Ragnarok* had already reached Silboomie Station, and Mendez had seemed comfortable enough with developments—if not exactly enthusiastically supportive. Enthusiasm was not to be expected. Nobody wanted to do this.

Well, she'd known it had been a gamble, from the start. They couldn't all be successful. An unsuccessful gamble had only one possible outcome for crèche-bred, and that was death.

Stretching in his seat, Mendez yawned and set his empty cup upside down on the tabletop. "With respect. You should ask, your Excellency. I have an authorization from Dr. Mahaffie, here—"

He didn't need an authorization. He could arrest her on his own authority. That he would arrest her was obvious; they had already cleared out all of her personal effects—they were that sure of her. Her quarters were as featureless as though she had never slept here.

"—and Dr. Mahaffie says that if you don't shut yourself up in quarters, your Excellency, and get at least a shift-and-a-half's rest, he will issue a dose. Enough sleeper to stop even Jennet ap Rhiannon in her very determined tracks. And I've got the handgun here to make the delivery, too. I'll shoot you down in the corridor, that's a promise."

Dr. Mahaffie did not hold the Writ. Andrej Koscuisko did. She had no illusions about what awaited her. She knew what the punishment was, what it looked like. Her entire class had watched, day by day, hour by hour, for the two and a half days it had taken the assigned Inquisitor to execute Yordie for failing in his field test.

Koscuisko was better than any borrowed Inquisitor. It was widely acknowledged that Koscuisko was the best there was. But Koscuisko wasn't here, and Mahaffie didn't hold the Writ, so what was First Officer talking about?

"What do you think the feeling is amongst the crew, First Officer?" She'd pretend that she had no idea why he was here. She'd pretend that she had no idea that he was not in with the rest of them, all the way. She could kill him, rather than let him net her for Andrej Koscuisko.

There was no point in killing him.

He had dealt honestly with her; he had not said anything, one way or another, that would be inconsistent with arresting her. And she could not escape from the *Ragnarok* with just a knife or two. Or rather, although she could, she would only escape at the cost of one or more of the lives that it was her business and her sacred duty to preserve, not to destroy.

She hadn't thought about Yordie for years, except for nightmares. The last Tenth Level Command Termination that Andrej Koscuisko had performed had taken nearly seven days. . . .

"You've got to understand, Captain. Nobody on board this ship wants trouble with Fleet. On the other hand most of us on board are already in trouble with Fleet. I believe Serge mentioned something like that to you before."

She didn't know what he was talking about. She

leaned her back against the closed door and waited for him to start making sense.

"And most of us have been kicked in the face before, and we're tired of it. Most of our people are with you. And the ones that aren't with you, aren't against you. There is only one little thing."

What little thing was that? It had lasted forever, Yordie's dying. It had gone on for so long that it had ceased to be horrible, and become boring, tiresome, tedious. She could remember hoping that each scream would be his last, and no longer because she had been his crèchemate, but because she was sick and tired and disgusted at him for screaming. For his weakness. And that had only been two and a half days.

Koscuisko could make her scream like that; she had no doubt of it. Somehow the humiliation of ending her life so meanly, her pathetic puling recorded for all time in the Record, was even more horrible than her appreciation of the kind of pain that it had taken to make Yordie so shamelessly frantic with sharp unbearable agony that he had not been able to preserve a single shred of the dignity that had been his birthright.

As long as there was no active resistance, there need be no loss of life; except for her own, and that would not matter. Within the space of a very short time her life would mean nothing at all, and her death would be merely inconsequential. "What 'little thing' is that, First Officer?" She would play along. She would not make things needlessly difficult. It had been a good effort. It had almost worked.

"You have insisted on your prerogatives as a Second Lieutenant, your Excellency. It was one thing when you were acting First Lieutenant, and even understandable when you became acting Captain. But the Recife vector has changed all that."

As a prisoner she had no privileges. She knew that as well as he did, if not better. What was the point of all this?

"If you're going to ask people to follow you to Taisheki, you've got to acknowledge their agreement. You've got to live up to your end of the contract. These people aren't going to Taisheki with any Fleet Second

Lieutenant, not even a crèche-bred one. They're going to Taisheki with Captain Jennet ap Rhiannon. I want you to lose the 'acting' bit."

She'd already lost her Captaincy, her First Lieutenancy, her basic rank of Second Lieutenant. "Very well, First Officer." She was tired of waiting for him to say the words, to come to the point. She just wanted to go to sleep.

"You will occupy the Captain's quarters, and you will use the Captain's office. We've moved your personal possessions. If you will follow me."

Captain's quarters? That was an unusual way to characterize a prisoner holding cell. Unless it was a phrase left over from the days of Captain Lowden, since Lowden had tended to handle prisoners as though they— and Andrej Koscuisko—had been personal possessions, rather than Bench resources.

Something was just not adding up.

Rising to his feet, Mendez gave the signal, and the door slid open again behind her. She waited for the Security to seize and secure, but nothing happened. Mendez merely came forward, and gestured toward the door.

The Security she'd brought with her were still posted outside, and saluted as she stepped across the threshold. Security fell into formation behind her, and Mendez himself took the subordinate-escort position at her left elbow.

She started walking, because it was habit, because they were not to initiate movement on their own; unless she was a prisoner, of course, in which case they would carry her at their own will in their choice of direction. She'd forgotten. She let First Officer direct them, remembering that she was a prisoner. But they weren't going toward the holding cell out in Secured Medical, forward. They were heading back down into the shielded heart of the ship, instead. The Captain's quarters.

Ship's Primes had sleeping space within the shielded core, rather than toward the upper hull where more disposable Lieutenants were assigned to sleep. Ship's Primes had two entire rooms at their personal disposal, outer and inner, and the things in the outer room of the Captain's quarters were her things.

Her personal shrine to the rule of Law, the religion of her childhood. The trophies she had taken—the weapon that had wounded her at Atrium, the ship's pennant from her first Vorket command, her personal commendations.

There was no way they meant to secure her in these quarters, rather than in a cell. So they didn't mean to secure her at all. They only meant for her to be their Captain.

She lost control over the terror and the tension, the relief, and the fearful weariness within her. She staggered toward the table, and First Officer was right with her, making sure that she sat—rather than falling—down.

"Thank you, First Officer." And the entire ship, by proxy. She could not refuse the honor, not if she meant to have their continued cooperation. "You don't know what this means to me."

It meant that she was not going to die. Or not just yet. The greater meaning was beyond her, at the moment. She was very tired. And the wake-keepers were wearing off, and all at once.

"Only what you've earned, Captain. Now get some rest."

She put her head down on her crooked forearm resting on the table's cool polished surface, and went to sleep.

The message had been laid casually atop the day's stack of administrative notices, by design. It wasn't the sort of thing to draw attention to itself, but her aides knew what it meant and that it meant a problem.

Pesadie Training Command modular packet released from storage to Jurisdiction Fleet Ship Ragnarok *on direction, receipt executed by Ship's Engineer, Serge of Wheatfields, countersigned.* Dated, validated, two days old.

While she had been talking to Noycannir, while she had been calculating turnaround and reissue time, the *Ragnarok* had gone to Silboomie Station—not Laynock Station at all—and they had absconded with the single most valuable item in her private inventory.

It wasn't her item. She held it in trust for reasonable people, because she had the means to arrange secure storage and document an audit trail that would cover disposition when the highest bidder had been selected, payment received.

It was immeasurably worse than when she had lost all of those munitions when the observation station had blown up with the *Ragnarok*'s Captain on it. How had the *Ragnarok* known?

Wasn't it obvious?

She had underestimated the *Ragnarok*. Somebody— maybe Jennet ap Rhiannon, unlikely though that seemed—had turned out to be reasonable after all. Someone had been found to surrender the information, because reasonable people could be relied upon to know what was reasonable to do. Ap Rhiannon wanted that module for herself.

Was she going to sell it? Hold it for ransom to force Brecinn to cancel her planned recovery from the training accident? Use it as a bribe to acquire position within the informal hierarchy of responsible people?

If there had been a sellout in the works, Brecinn would have heard about it by now. Surely. Wouldn't she have?

Or had someone on her staff already sold her out?

Had that been how ap Rhiannon had known to go to Silboomie for the special module? Were reasonable people already making arrangements to abandon Brecinn as last year's hero, and do business with ap Rhiannon instead? She'd been an idiot not to see it. Who was better placed to part out the *Ragnarok*, to sell off its assets, to skim its stores than ap Rhiannon herself?

This called for an immediate reconsideration of plans. She needed to see where Noycannir was in her process. What was ap Rhiannon going to do? Silboomie Station. Not Laynock. Where could you get to, from Silboomie Station?

Fleet Audit Appeals Authority. Taisheki space. Maybe that was all right. She had contacts at Taisheki.

Signaling for attention on her voice box, Brecinn called up the central communications deck. "Send a message to Chilleau Judiciary. Priority transmit. Dame Mergau Noycannir, sole recipient." She'd see what Noycannir had to say to her, and then she'd decide what to do.

Who could have guessed that a minor training exercise could explode into a fight for her very survival?

Lek Kerenko stood at attention-rest with his team alongside the transport craft, listening to the voice of his ancestors shouting for attention in his brain.

Chelatring Side. The Autocrat's Proxy. Chuvishka Kospodar, the rape of Prishklo, the slaughter of the Sivarian innocents, the walls of Erchlo, the dead lake at Immer. The blasted remains of Chatlerin, on the coast.

Koscuisko was the enemy, had carried him here into the heart of the enemy's territory, was carrying him farther still to Chelatring Side to see the Autocrat's Proxy and to meet the great-great-granddaughter of Chuvishka Kospodar himself.

Koscuisko was the three-times-great-grandson of Chuvishka Kospodar, the doom of the Sarvaw, the man who had unleashed the Angel of Destruction against an unarmed and defenseless population, a defiler of women, a murderer of children—

Koscuisko was the enemy, but Koscuisko was his officer of assignment. And Koscuisko himself was not Lek's enemy, but had been a good officer to him, the best man Lek had seen assigned as Ship's Inquisitor in thirteen years of bond-involuntary service.

Koscuisko was coming, walking slowly down the track to the motor stables with his lady at one side and his son at the other, talking to the Bench specialist while the Malcontent Cousin Stanoczk brought up the rear. Andrej Koscuisko, hand in hand with Anton Andreievitch. The four-times-great-grandson of Chuvishka Kospodar, who broke away from his father when he saw Lek standing there waiting and came running over the graveled apron with his arms outspread to embrace him.

Don't run, little lord, you'll fall, and scrape your hands.

Crouching down on his heels, Lek watched Anton Andreievitch come. He could not frown at the child, anxious though he was. This child was the enemy of his blood. This child's ancestor had drowned children as beautiful and beloved as he was for the crime of being Sarvaw, born of a Sarvaw mother and a Sarvaw father— vermin by definition; nor had those children been any the less dear to their parents than was Anton to his Excellency.

Was it Anton's fault that his blood was tainted?

Anton Andreievitch put his arms around Lek's neck and kissed him. Lek held the child in his arms, and the voices in his blood murmured in confusion as Lek spoke.

"There, now, little lord, you do me great honor, but we're only going to Chelatring Side after all. You've heard of Chelatring Side, I know you have, and you're to come next time, you told me so yourself."

In all of Anton Andreievitch's life, he had never met his own grandparents—not his father's parents. Things were changed now. The Koscuisko familial corporation would receive Anton Andreievitch as the inheriting son of its inheriting son; Koscuisko had seen to that.

Chelatring Side was not ready to receive its new master-to-be, not ready to receive its new princess. There would be rank conferred on Koscuisko's Respected Lady before that happened; it was too awkward that the mother of the Koscuisko prince should be a mere gentlewoman. All very complicated, but the only thing that mattered right now was that Andrej Koscuisko was going to Chelatring Side and his child was bereft.

"Be well," Anton Andreievitch said with careful precision, kissing Lek one last time before he stood away. "Have care for yourself, Lek, until such time. As . . ."

It was a formula. Anton Andreievitch had to learn an entire catalog of new formulae, now that he was no longer merely an acknowledged son, but the inheriting son. Lek kept his face as carefully clear as possible, willing the words into Anton Andreievitch's mind. *Until such time as we shall see each other. Until such time . . .*

". . . um, until such time as we shall see each other once again, and all Saints keep you in the heart of the Holy Mother."

The Holy Mother was an Aznir whore. But that was beside the point. Surely. "Thank you, my lord, and all Saints under Canopy prosper thy purpose till we meet again."

He knew some formulae as well. He'd just never imagined that he might ever say such a thing with affection. Shifting his weight, Lek put one knee to the ground so that he could bend his neck in solemn and traditional salute; the grave bow that Anton returned to him in response almost broke Lek's heart. Anton would learn. Someone would teach him. Anton gave him face as a respected family retainer, and he wasn't; he was a mere Sarvaw, which was to say a brute animal.

"Load courier," Chief Stildyne said, with a note of amusement and tolerance buried so deeply underneath the layers of rubble and broken glass in his ruined voice that it was almost imperceptible. Koscuisko had taken leave of his Respected Lady; she came forward to take custody of her son.

Lek loaded courier with the rest of his team. This time he was not flying; the courier had its own crew. Chelatring Side was deep in the mountains of the Chetalra range, named after the goddess who had been sovereign here before the Aznir had come and their Holy Mother with them. Dasidar the Great—from whom all of the oldest, noblest families of Aznir Dolgorukij claimed descent—had set his name on the mightiest peak among the Chetalra, Mount Dasidar himself. Navigation at altitude through such a mountain range was difficult enough for a practiced crew. Lek was just as glad he didn't have to drive.

Koscuisko boarded next to last with the Bench specialist before him, as befit his senior rank; and laid his hand on Lek's shoulder as he went forward to take his place at the great windows that lined the courier's skin. "You are very kind to my son," Koscuisko said. "He is very fond of you. His mother asks that I praise you particularly for your care, and I thank you for it also."

It sounded a great deal more formal in Koscuisko's Aznir dialect than it was meant, Lek was sure. The Dolgorukij dialects in general did take on a formal sort of tone when translated into Standard, and Koscuisko with his Security spoke Standard without fail, even here. Even at home.

Lek smiled and nodded in appreciation of the compliment, while the voices of his ancestors raged in his blood. *Can you be bought as cheaply as that, Lek, and this the man who is Kospodar's child.*

Maybe there was something that his ancestors didn't

understand, Lek mused, watching out the windows as the courier traveled forward slowly down the graveled drive toward the launch field.

He was only Sarvaw in an Aznir context. Outside of the Dolgorukij Combine he was Dolgorukij, and a bond-involuntary. Koscuisko did not honor him by treating him, a Sarvaw, as though he were actually a human being. Koscuisko treated bond-involuntaries as though they were human beings, when what they were was instruments of torture for Koscuisko's use. That was how Koscuisko had purchased him. Not with praise as Aznir to Sarvaw; but with respect as man to man, in context of the Fleet.

At the launch field the courier idled for several moments as the flight engines were engaged, the fuel adjusted, the change from ground to air travel modes completed.

Then it took a short run down the launch corridor and leaped into the sky on a sharp angle of ascent that was so unexpected and extreme that Lek grinned almost despite himself, as though he was on a carnival ride and headed straight for the cold hard ground.

It was not very long by airborne courier between the estate of the Matredonat in the grain belt of Azanry's largest continent and the mountains where Koscuisko's family had first established itself in the days of the warring states long, long ago. A few hours, and the courier had covered the grain-growing regions of the continent; another short period of time, and the landscape began to rise to meet them.

Steep slopes. Barren crags. Long lawns of green at impossible angles, and grazing animals navigating all but the most extreme slopes; old-fashioned buildings, low and gray and thick walled with black slate roofs pitched at an angle to shed the accumulation of snow during the winter. There were dire wolves still in these mountains, Lek knew. They could no longer be hunted except by the permission of the Autocrat and by a member of the ancient blood, because they were a last remnant of what had once been an enemy as savage as the Dolgorukij themselves.

The courier flew steady and straight, but the mountains did not level off. The mountains continued to rise beneath them.

The pilot switched the propulsion mode of the courier from thrust to float, so that they could continue the approach at a much reduced rate of speed. Lek was just as glad. The rock grew closer by the moment—great jagged peaks that looked hungry to him. They made him nervous. He didn't want to knock into any mountainsides.

It was quiet in the courier.

Nobody was particularly enjoying this but Koscuisko. Lek could hear Koscuisko making conversation with Cousin Stanoczk and the Bench specialist, noting the points of interest, naming the landmarks. Arguing with Cousin Stanoczk whether the battle of Mingche had been fought at the ford at Vsalja or on the bridge of Girnos, because *the song said stone but the bridges over the river had been wooden till well after the event but they were stone by the time the song was written down and the poet had realized that calling them "wooden" would just confuse people but people knew that they had been wooden and people weren't stupid but the song also said the banks with the high-water so it had to have been the ford, and you just stay out of this, Stildyne, whose side are you on, anyway?*

Lek couldn't imagine the Bench specialist being unnerved by the nearness of the mountains. But he was. He wasn't accustomed to land-based flights. His training had all been for engagements in deep space. That was his job, to defend the *Ragnarok*, and he couldn't have defended the *Ragnarok* here, because there hardly seemed to be enough room to maneuver for a single Wolnadi, let alone a battlewagon.

They were flying between mountains, now, following the course of a river back toward its birthplace. And the terrain was rising fast, or they were sinking fast, skimming over a ferocious and forbidding landscape of sharp black peaks whose wind-scoured flanks were like obsidian-edged knives; heading straight for the great shield-wall of the Chetalra Mountains, whose steep peaks pierced the clouds.

The black peaks rose up into the visiports of the transport, as if eager to examine its contents for a meal as the courier worked its way into the body of the goddess Chetalra. From what Lek could hear, Koscuisko was saying they had had reached the flanks of awesome Dasidar, towering above them and before them steep and frightening. The valleys were all filled and hidden with mist; there was no seeing how deep those valleys were. As they flew steadily onward toward the mountain, they ran through alternate stretches of ice and snow that shut their visibility down to nothing with brutal suddenness.

But the variant text says glassy slope. Glassy slope. Not grassy slope. So it was higher up than the bridge, there would have been grassy slopes, so it had to be the fort. Stildyne, name of all Saints, you haven't been reading the revisionists, have you? Holy Mother. Just when you think you know a man.

They were going to run into the wall.

The mountain filled their vision on three sides, with an unfathomable chasm on the fourth; the walls of Dasidar's fortress rose into the very heavens, and they were continuing to make straight for them, rising as they went. The side of the mountain was as smooth as stalloy here, polished over the ages by wind and snow and cold, and the sheer size of the rock—the closer one came to it— was terrifying, in its way.

Lek braced himself, biting his lip to stifle his cry of fear. They were going to crash. Why hadn't the officer noticed? Because the officer knew where he was going. The courier made straight for the wall, closer and closer, and Lek slowly began to realize that they were not as near to the wall as he had thought. The scale of that great wall was almost unimaginable.

Rocks he had taken for boulders were great towering crags, bits of green that he had taken for moss or lichen were clumps of trees as large as small forests, and the courier just kept heading on steadily toward the wall. But continued to climb. The wall fell away beneath them, but it did not end. There was more and more and more of it; and then the courier topped one final rise, and Lek gasped in involuntary shock.

Chelatring Side.

The ancestral seat of the Koscuisko familial corporation, set into the side of the mountain like a babe against its father's bosom, curved close into the embrace of Dasidar himself where he sat in majestic glory looking out over his conquered world, a stronghold huge and invincible, dwarfed by the rock around it for all its size.

Chelatring Side.

The walls went on forever, and the towers could not be counted. Its fortress walls were monumental, and its ranks of solar panels glittered forever-long in the bright sunlight. There was nothing beneath them now but clouds, and of the peaks that stood sufficient tall to stand in array with Dasidar the nearest was veserts upon veserts away, even by direct flight.

This was not a fortress, this was a city. This was a large city, and that such a piece of work should be the personal possession of any one man or even group of men was almost obscene. No. It *was* obscene. There was no "almost" about it.

The courier cleared the first banked wall, and there were walls behind walls behind walls, each rising higher and higher into the sky with the weathered gray of the stone of the fortress almost the same shade as the mountainside itself. Wall upon wall, and tower upon tower, and Andrej Koscuisko sighed happily where he sat. "Home," Koscuisko said. "What do you think, Specialist Ivers, do you like it?"

The Bench specialist was staring out the window, as transfixed as any of them. "I don't know what to say, your Excellency. Description fails to capture the actual impact of the place."

"I suppose when one grows up in such surroundings, it seems more homely. Also one was accustomed to approaching it in stages, when one was a boy, before the entire installation was sealed for supplemental air. And still my brother Iosev got the nosebleed. Every year. Finally they let him stay at Rogubarachno, but he was the only one left there of my brothers; he learned bad habits."

Supplemental air? Well. Yes. Altitude. How high were they? Lek didn't want to know. Was it his imagination that he could see the curvature of the planet itself, on the horizon?

The courier cleared the second set of walls and settled

to a halt in a motor court. They were well to one side of the fortress itself, but there were fortified corridors, and transport waiting. Fortified? Lek wondered. Or were those obviously thick walls, the steeply pitched roofs, the half-buried foundations simply accommodations for the winter? There was no snow on the ground within the compound, but outside the walls it lay undisturbed. How much of it was there?

"Your Excellency. That," the Bench specialist said, and pointed. "That. What is that. Is that what I think it is?"

What was she looking at? There. Not alongside the courier, but at a near remove, its glittering lines elegant and evil in the bright thin azure light.

The Malcontent Cousin Stanoczk coughed. "Yes, Bench specialist," he said. "She is. Kospodar thula."

Kospodar. There was no escaping the beast, in all of the Combine.

"Cousin Stanoczk, I thought the Arakcheyek Yards only built twenty-seven of them. What is this one—" She almost asked *What is this one doing here?* She almost did. Lek could hear the unspoken words clearly in the quiet cabin, though she had stopped herself in time.

"And this is one of the twenty-seven, Bench specialist. You would like a tour? Andrej. Permit me. Let me show off this pretty little animal. You can stand and talk to Ferinc if you do not care to see her for yourself."

The courier had been secured. Lek could hear the opening of the cargo bays. Someone was working the secures to the passenger landing ramp, and let a blast of air come in. Hot air. Lek was surprised that it was not cold, but they did lie in full sunlight.

"I have nothing to say to thy Ferinc," Koscuisko said, sourly. "Except for, 'be damned.' Here is supplemental, gentles, you must each wear one until you are indoors. You will want one to tour the thula. Go with Stoshik."

Supplemental atmosphere generator, a little soft packet that sat on the shoulder, a supple tube that lay along the cheek below the nostril and clung there of its own accord. Lek took one; the courier's navigator helped him to adjust it. His headache went away. He hadn't realized he'd had a headache.

The Malcontent broke from his place and down the

ramp as soon as it was cleared, and the Bench specialist after him. Stildyne nodded; Lek followed eagerly. A Kospodar thula. He had only ever heard of them. He had never hoped to see one.

It would be something to tell the crew when they returned to the *Ragnarok*. Without their officer . . .

Lek put that unhappy thought aside. It was to be. There was no help for it. And he needed all of his attention to spend on the thula.

Talk to Ferinc, Stanoczk had said. Insufferable cheek, Andrej decided. Nobody had said anything to him that would change the fact of who Ferinc had been, nor had anybody a satisfactory explanation for why Ferinc should be tolerated at the Matredonat. He was home now. He was to stay. Ferinc had no place left in his house.

That Marana had taken comfort from Ferinc in Andrej's absence he could understand, so long as he declined to think about it.

Yet Anton loved his Ferinc, and Andrej didn't know what he was going to do about that. The Ferinc that Anton loved was very little to do with the man Andrej had disciplined so many years ago; it did no good to tell himself that it was for Anton's sake that Ferinc should be denied him. Anton was a loving and trusting child. Children learned what they were shown, rather than what they were taught. To be fair, Andrej could not deny Ferinc credit for the beautiful spirit of his son, the openhearted affection that he had found so surprising and so endearing. How could those two Ferincs be the same man?

He was not particularly interested in Cousin Stanoczk's thula. Unless he missed his guess, Specialist Ivers would imagine that this was the only one that the Malcontent owned; and she was impressed enough at that, because the Bench itself could not afford any more of them. That had been why the program had been cancelled. Andrej suspected that the Malcontent had more than one thula at his saintly disposal; not because he knew, but because he—unlike the Bench specialist—had the native child's grasp of the money that the Malcontent held in safekeeping for the Saint's purposes.

He stood outside the craft at the side of the loading ramp and looked at the sky, instead. They were so high into atmosphere at Chelatring Side that everything looked crisper, brighter, sharper in the thin air. Sometimes he thought about the old times when Koscuisko had lived at Chelatring Side and only gone down to the grain fields to raid or to marry, and wondered whether his ancestors would hold him in contempt for that he had to use a supplemental atmosphere generator when he came to his own home.

He knew that he'd looked down on Iosev for chronic bleeding of the nose, as if it were a moral weakness. There were many more reasons than just that to find his brother wanting, that was so.

Someone came around from the nose of the thula toward him, and stopped dead in his tracks when he caught sight of Andrej. Andrej sighed. "Come to me, Cousin," he suggested, knowing that it was not a suggestion. "Stanoczk says that I am to have a word with you."

Ferinc looked a different man, in this thin light, than he had in the library at the Matredonat, which had been comparatively dim. There was more gray in his long fore-braids than Andrej had noticed, but his gaze was clear and level. When Ferinc dropped his eyes to bow it was with professional self-effacement, not the fear that had possessed him before. "If Cousin Stanoczk says, your Excellency, I am bound to obey."

Oh, be that way, Andrej thought to himself with irritation. *And your soul to perdition on top of it.* "My child loves you very much, and speaks of you often. Someone has taught him to be so openhearted as to gladden the heart of a long-absent father. How are we to manage this between us?"

"We" was owed Ferinc, regardless of how Andrej felt about the man personally. Marana had not approached him to moderate his ban on Ferinc, but every time Andrej heard Anton mention the name it reminded him that there was an issue to resolve.

"Permission to speak freely, your Excellency," Cousin Ferinc said, but it wasn't a Malcontent talking, it was the petty warrant officer that Ferinc had once been. Andrej didn't care to be reminded of who Ferinc had been, but that was the problem whole and entire right there, wasn't it?

And who was he, of all men, to disdain Haster Girag for what Girag had done, when he himself was so much the more depraved a beast? "Granted."

It took Ferinc a moment to collect his thoughts, but then he licked his lips as though they were dry and spoke. "I was sent for duty, your Excellency. I didn't mean to grow close to the child. I didn't see it happening. I am the slave of the Malcontent. His Excellency knows how little I have to say about where I am next to go. But, your Excellency, if I could be permitted, even if only to write from time to time."

Andrej knew that he was Anton's biological parent, his genetic sire. Ferinc was the man who had been Anton's father—the realization was liberating and agonizing, at once.

"Stanoczk is right." Andrej said it out loud, and heard the somewhat confused wonder in his voice. "A duty is owed to you, Ferinc. I don't want to see you. Deal with Marana. I withdraw my prohibition. Anton loves you. How could I love him, if I kept you from him?"

Liberating: because what he had done to Ferinc when he had punished Haster Girag—rather than reporting his criminal behavior for Fleet to punish—had not destroyed Ferinc's capacity for happiness, Malcontent or no. Ferinc could still feel and share a parent's love for a child, love that was untainted by the corruption of the torture cell.

Agonizing: because Andrej despaired of ever taking Ferinc's place in the heart of his own son. He did not deserve it; he could not truly begrudge it to Ferinc; and yet, and yet, and yet. Ferinc reached out and took him by the sleeve, as if overcome. Loosened his grip, then straightened up. "Thank you," Ferinc said. "I won't give you cause to regret it. I promise. Thank you."

And yet he had only done the right thing, because the pure parental affection in Ferinc's voice was unmistakable. Undeniable. How cruel would it have been to deny Ferinc to Anton? To deny Anton to Ferinc?

It was the Malcontent's business; so Andrej did not have to think long or hard on it, nor could he bear to. He merely nodded, and Stildyne came down out of the thula to rescue him from awkwardness, pausing in apparent confusion to see him and Ferinc together. "Your Excellency," Stildyne said. "Your assistance, sir. Lek's bonding. We may not be able to pry him loose. We need your help."

No, Stildyne had only wondered where he was, but Andrej was glad to take the offered escape route. Andrej nodded yet again; and went up the ramp into the courier to see what had gotten into his good Lek, hoping he'd done the right thing for his son.

Admiral Brecinn stared at the little ticket in front of her on her desk, her hands flat to the desk's surface as though she could stop the room from spinning by main force of will.

The treachery was unspeakable.

Dame Mergau Noycannir was not at Chilleau. She hadn't been there, she wasn't expected, and so far as Chilleau knew she was at Pesadie. Mergau Noycannir had taken the finest, fleetest courier at Pesadie and left days ago, but she hadn't gone to Chilleau at all. It all made too much sense, all of a sudden.

Noycannir had come from Chilleau to observe the exercise. When the accident had happened, she had offered her services to Brecinn as though motivated by nothing more than an eye toward her own advantage and a desire to ingratiate herself with the network of reasonable people. She had counseled patience, subtlety, tact, but it had all been a trick.

The *Ragnarok* had stolen the cannon from Silboomie Station and left for Fleet Audit Appeals Authority at Taisheki. Mergau Noycannir had disappeared.

It was a conspiracy; Brecinn couldn't quite puzzle the exact framework of it out, but she knew a conspiracy when she smelled one. There was no time to sit and beat herself for her stupidity, her trusting nature, her gullibility.

This had gone beyond a simple issue of lost profit. The loss of the battle cannon was a serious compromise. Reasonable people did not tolerate being compromised. She needed a good story and she needed it fast, and she needed to get it to Taisheki Station before the *Ragnarok* had a chance to log an appeal. She had to get her word in first.

There were reasonable people at the Fleet Audit Appeals Authority. And the cannon was worth a very great deal of money.

The *Ragnarok* was clearly trafficking; they'd killed poor inoffensive Brem because he'd discovered something inconvenient, perhaps because he'd been reluctant to participate. They'd used their stay at Pesadie Training Command to forge documentation for stolen munitions, using her own validation codes. Now they intended to present the gun to Fleet to incriminate Pesadie and divert Fleet's attention away from their own corrupt dealings.

It was not the most convincing story in the world. But it was all she had. And if it cost her everything she had left to buy credibility at Fleet Audit Appeals Authority—poverty was better than death. Poverty she could hope to recover from. Assassination was much more permanent a handicap for an officer's career.

She would see to it that ap Rhiannon, not Sandri Brecinn, paid the price for this treachery, if it took the last resources she had at her command. She would be revenged. She could no longer hope to profit from the *Ragnarok*'s decommissioning, but she would see to it that ap Rhiannon died for her duplicity.

There were only fifty people at dinner, sixty at most, but Stildyne couldn't get a decent count for the glittering of jewels in the bright lights. They hurt his eyes. And he was drunk already: not on any alcohol, but on the luxury that clothed his body and beguiled him with unimaginable sensuality.

They hadn't brought dress uniform with them.

Koscuisko's people hadn't said word one, but Koscuisko's people had been busy at it since the day that they'd arrived here on Azanry. Stildyne could only guess that garments had been borrowed, checked for size, when he'd thought they were merely being laundered. Because on gaining crew-quarters here at Chelatring Side earlier today, they had found dress uniform ready for all of them.

The fit was exact and the detail was precise, from the formal version of the service marks that Taller wore on his collar—from the Abermarle campaign—to the exact shade of green that marked Lek for a bond-involuntary. Of course, the shade of green had to be precise; not all hominids under Jurisdiction had the same sort of color vision, after all, so tone and saturation were as important as hue.

Perfect. But so much more than perfect. The boots had been shaped to the wear of the foot, but they were lined with glove leather so soft that it was almost like sex to set foot inside them. Koscuisko's personal linen had always been that, linen, and Security had handled it often enough over the years while managing drunken officers; Stildyne had never imagined the luxury of wearing a linen hip-wrap on his own part.

And the boot stockings were silk. And the uniform blouse was a wool spun so fine that it made a man afraid to put it on, but it lay so lightly across his shoulders that he almost felt naked. It was unnerving. His under-blouse alone was worth three weeks' pay, and the kit was complete. It was astonishing. And it made him angry, in a subtle sense; how dare Koscuisko's people treat them with so much contempt as to casually clothe them with a year's wages, and not even bother to mention it?

Stildyne stood by the side doors into the great dining room, brooding about it, watching his people. House security had posted Security 5.1 in visible positions around the officer, a guard of honor. Koscuisko's people were particularly fascinated by Smath and Kerenko, to judge from their placement, because they were to either side of Koscuisko himself, with a clear corridor between down which the servers might pass.

Koscuisko would never wear his uniform again. He wasn't wearing his uniform now, sitting at the table, talking with Specialist Ivers to one side of him and a boy-child on the other. Not that much older than Anton Andreievitch, Stildyne thought, and nudged Cousin Stanoczk in the ribs with his elbow.

"Who is that?" The boy-child looked like Anton Andreievitch, come to that. Or like Koscuisko. That meant nothing. Chelatring Side was filthy with people who

looked like Koscuisko. He had thought that Cousin Stanoczk looked like Koscuisko, at the Matredonat. There
were closer matches here everywhere he turned.

Cousin Stanoczk frowned, apparently confused; but
his face cleared quickly. "Young prince. The youngest of
the family, Nikolij Ulexeievitch. Your officer's youngest
brother. Who else?"

The servers were carrying a meat course down the line
behind the seated guests. Stildyne caught a glimpse of
the Bench specialist's profile as she turned her head to
consider the offer; she looked a little panicked, Stildyne
thought. Yes. It had already been several courses.

"Father. Mother. Autocrat's Proxy." Stildyne named
them off as he knew them, and Cousin Stanoczk filled
in the rest.

"Thy officer's sister, actually, did you know that?
Fourth born and second eldest of daughters. Younger
than Iosev and Meka, but older than Lo. There's another
sister. And the oldest sister is not here tonight, because
it is too awkward in today's environment, after all."

Whatever that meant. Stildyne counted them all up in
his mind; Koscuisko had four brothers, then, and three
sisters as it seemed. More family than Stildyne had ever
had. In Dolgorukij terms, Stildyne had never had family
at all, he supposed. "Why do they keep staring?"

That the guests were intrigued by Smish in uniform
Stildyne could understand. Koscuisko had warned them
to expect that, and the experience of their stay at the
Matredonat had only confirmed the exotic appeal Smish
had on Azanry. He wasn't sure he understood what was
so interesting about Lek. Lek was tolerably well put together, yes, and Security were expected to maintain an
appropriately lean and menacing physique. But so were
Taller and Murat, and Murat was quite possibly abstractly the more attractive of the three. Being younger,
for one.

Now Cousin Stanoczk shoved him, as Stildyne had el-
bowed Cousin Stanoczk earlier. "What do you think?"
Well, if he'd known what to think, Stildyne thought a
bit resentfully, he wouldn't have asked "And do you
mean to watch all through the dinner, Chief?"

"No, Cousin, I think he's safe enough with his own

people. These troops look like they mean business to me." The house security who staffed the room were as fine troops as Stildyne had ever seen; he could smell their edge. It was subtle. They more than just looked impressive. They had the juice.

"Then come with me. I've got something to show you."

Cousin Stanoczk drew him away from the room, walking backward, sidling through a panel door in the wall that Stildyne hadn't noticed being there. "He's Sarvaw, Chief," Cousin Stanoczk said, and after a moment Stildyne remembered having asked the question about Lek. "Imagine that. A Sarvaw security troop. Assigned to the son of the Koscuisko prince. The mind, it absolutely boggles."

Stildyne couldn't see what was so particularly boggling about that. "It's all Combine one way or the other, Cousin, isn't it so?" All right, so he'd heard that there was bad blood in the history. History was history. And if it wasn't history, it ought to be, once it was history. "How can they tell, anyway? You all look alike to me."

Cousin Stanoczk snorted, apparently taken by genuine surprise. "Say such a thing to either Aznir or Sarvaw and insult them equally, friend Stildyne. You will perhaps consent to trust me on this. We can tell."

The corridors through which Cousin Stanoczk led him were emptier by the moment; the area into which they were descending seemed almost deserted. There were locked doors. Cousin Stanoczk had the keys.

"But *how* can they tell?"

And where were they going? "If you had the history of this family, you might have cause to understand, Chief. I would almost say that Sarvaw children know Aznir for their enemy in their mothers' wombs. And my cousin and his Lek, they get on together?" The corridors were narrowing, and they kept climbing down stairs. Cousin Stanoczk stopped in front of one particularly large wooden door to work the secures.

Lek was a bond-involuntary. He had no choice. That wasn't what Cousin Stanoczk was asking. "His Excellency respects and values Lek equally as his other Security. Maybe there's even a community feeling between them, both Combine—what?"

Stanoczk had rolled his eyes in exaggerated exasperation, leaning into the door to open it. "If you only knew what nonsense you were talking, Chief. But, at any rate, that is why they are staring. Andrej has been playing his Lek up from the moment he arrived, to give him face. I'm not surprised that the family are fascinated."

That was all to the good. Stildyne found Cousin Stanoczk a little fascinating for his own part. Stanoczk was very like Andrej Koscuisko in some ways that had nothing to do with his physical appearance; and so completely unlike Koscuisko in others. Cousin Stanoczk flirted with him. Andrej Koscuisko had never kissed a man with amorous intent in his entire life, not in any context that counted.

"Where are we going, Cousin?" He didn't mind taking a stroll with Cousin Stanoczk. But he was beginning to wonder what was going on.

"Going, we go nowhere, we are arrived," Cousin Stanoczk said, somewhat confusingly. "You and my Ferinc had history, I understand. I thought that you might be intrigued by some of what it can mean, to be Malcontent."

Cousin Stanoczk turned and closed the door behind him, and secured it. Stildyne stood and stared.

It was just a corridor, but it seemed to be a long corridor, and there were pictures on the walls the likes of which would have been startling enough in almost any other context but which were truly amazing in a Dolgorukij one.

"What's this?"

Cousin Stanoczk took Stildyne's arm encouragingly, and started down the corridor. "It is the Gallery—technically, the Great Gallery at Chelatring Side. Or more technically, it does not even exist. This part of the house belongs to my holy Patron, Chief. Some mysteries cannot be written, but they can be shown."

Visual documentation. Pictures. Ways in which a man might discover that he was Malcontent. "Reconciliation," Stildyne guessed, trying hard to look without seeing. It was hard. They were persuasive pictures.

"In one form or another." Cousin Stanoczk's voice was cheerful in agreement, seeming unmoved by the explicit and arousing images on the walls. *Why not?* Stildyne asked himself, in despair of ruling his own flesh. Cousin Stanoczk probably saw them all the time.

"I'm not Dolgorukij, Cousin." And nobody would know that better than an Aznir Dolgorukij, because that was as Dolgorukij as they got. "Why have you brought me here?"

"I wish to take advantage," Cousin Stanoczk said, enthusiastically. "In an attempt to seduce you. Say that I may succeed, and I will be a happy man. One of these in particular I think you will especially like, Stildyne, if you would put your eyes back in your head and follow me."

This was not a dialect of Dolgorukij that Stildyne could grasp. Cousin Stanoczk was speaking plain Standard. But Dolgorukij—didn't. That was why they were so expensive in service houses, after all. Dolgorukij *didn't*, not with other men. Were those expensive Dolgorukij all Malcontents?

He couldn't think. The lovingly detailed sexual images in the paintings that lined the walls had stacked themselves firmly between his cerebrum and his brain stem, so that the only processing that was going on in his brain any longer was direct and visceral. Eye to brain to spine, and down.

His entire body was following Cousin Stanoczk with avid interest, eagerly curious about wherever it was that Stanoczk was going and whatever it was that Stanoczk might have in mind. His entire body, less his brain, which was still only slowly processing the things that he was seeing on the walls.

He had to hurry to catch up. When he did, he put his hand to Stanoczk's shoulder, and left it there; turning his head Cousin Stanoczk grinned back at Stildyne over his shoulder, and led him deeper into the Gallery.

Chapter Twelve

The Great Gate

Jils Ivers had known torture, hardship, and privation in her life, and no ordeal that she could think of at this moment could be compared to a Dolgorukij formal banquet. Not because she wasn't comfortably seated; she was. Not because there were after-dinner speakers; there weren't, though the toasts had been difficult to get through on account of the amount of drinking that they involved.

There was simply too much food. And she hated to not eat every bite of it, because she never knew for sure when exactly she'd have a chance to eat again. It was torture. It was all so good. Agony.

And when the Koscuisko princess—Andrej Koscuisko's mother—rose from the table at last, with everybody else in turn rising in order of precedence to progress out into the great hall of Chelatring Side, Jils Ivers heard an orchestra tuning, and groaned inwardly. It was too much. She had to go lie down. Nobody took exercise after such a meal as this.

But Dolgorukij went dancing, and she was on the arm of the son of the Koscuisko prince, Andrej Koscuisko himself. He looked so different in civilian dress. Dolgorukij aristocrats wore fancy clothing, brightly colored, frothing at the cuffs with lace. Exotic animals, as unlike a man in the black of a Ship's Chief Medical Officer as could be imagined.

"It is only a darshan to start," Koscuisko explained,

encouragingly, clearly sensitive to her distress. "My brother is shy. But would very much like the honor. If you would permit, Bench specialist."

Figures of eight, many of them already in motion. Koscuisko's youngest sister was waiting for them, with a young man; the boy Nikolij Ulexeievitch bowed to her very prettily, with almost no trace of anxiety on his face, and Jils had to smile and give in.

She had never thought of Koscuisko as a man with brothers and sisters. As odd as it had been to see him at his ease at the Matredonat with his wife and his young son, it was stranger still to see him here in a darshan-eight, dancing with his young sister, and his youngest brother serving as her squire.

Inquisitors were without family; they existed only in the thoroughly adult context of the Law, the prison, and the torture room. Andrej Koscuisko was the single most notorious pain-master in the entire inventory, and here he was the older brother in the middle of his cousins and his brothers and his sisters and his parents as well.

By the end of the figure she was beginning to feel much less uncomfortably full, but she was still grateful to be ushered to a chair behind that of the Koscuisko princess to sit down. Nikolij was an attentive host, bringing her a glass of punch and a fan with which to cool herself. He yielded up his duties to his brother with good grace when Andrej Koscuisko appeared from out of the press of people to sit down beside her.

Koscuisko's mother looked back at her son over her shoulder and raised an eyebrow. Koscuisko rose swiftly to bow over his mother's hand, but sat back down almost as quickly, smiling.

In the lull in the music between the conclusion of the darshan and the beginning of whatever other dance it would be next an elderly woman came through the mingling guests, and the crowd made way before her. Very straight she stood, very short, almost as small as young Nikolij, who was still growing; her hair was thin and yellow, but her face was youthful in its appearance for all the wrinkles at her eyes and forehead.

When she was five paces or so in front of where Koscuisko's parents sat, she stopped and planted her walking stick firmly on the ground in front of her, and waited. The room got quiet.

"The son of the Koscuisko prince has returned home," she said, her voice clearly meant to carry. "It grieves me to be the one to say, my prince. But he brings neither plunder nor slaves. And therefore, according to the ancient rules of your House, must pay a forfeit."

"Saints," Koscuisko swore under his breath, beside Jils. But he seemed to be smiling. It was some form of hazing, perhaps?

"True enough," Koscuisko's father agreed, with a rumbling undertone of amusement in his voice. "Be merciful, I beg you. He is my son. What shall his forfeit be?"

The elderly woman took another step forward. The great hall was so quiet that Jils could hear the scrape of a chair across the wooden stage as one of the musicians adjusted his place. "Family jeweler," Koscuisko whispered to her, not moving his lips. "Savage woman. I am terrified."

"He brings neither plunder nor pelf," the elderly woman repeated. "And yet has at least one thing to show for his long absence, my prince, something above price. As forfeit we think that we should be allowed to examine his items of adornment. Perhaps to contest with him at target."

"It is worse than I had thought," Koscuisko said quietly. "Do they know that Lek is my knife teacher? I am sure of it."

Lek? What was it about—then she remembered. Yes. That was right. Koscuisko's Sarvaw bond-involuntary. People had been whispering about him all night, and as far as Jils could tell he was enjoying his notoriety thoroughly. It made Jils a little uncomfortable, but she supposed that if it amused the man himself she was not the one to find fault with it.

Koscuisko stood up, moving around to stand in front of his mother and bow to his father. "In truth I am improvident and thriftless," Koscuisko said. "And yet possess treasure. If my father's jeweler will name her time and her champion, I will maintain my honor; or call her 'Younger Sister' for a year."

People seemed to be having a hard time keeping their

faces straight. It was a hint to Jils that none of this challenge and rebuke was serious.

"Tomorrow, after breakfast. At such time as your head will have had a chance to clear from your night's debauch, young master."

Now people had started to laugh. The jeweler continued. "We will meet you here, upon the field of honor. And your father and your mother will bear witness, young master. May we hope to see all five?"

A different note, suddenly, some kind of hunger—genuine, and sincere. Five-knives. Koscuisko's Emandisan steel. That elderly woman wasn't the family's jeweler; she was the house armorer. Maybe for Dolgorukij it was the same thing. *Items of adornment,* the old woman had said, and she was talking about Koscuisko's knives.

"Dame Isola, you have rebuked my poverty before my mother and my father, and I will be avenged. You will have to fight to see all five. I put you on your guard."

Now everybody in the entire fortress who did not have to be somewhere else would come and watch, and cheer for one side or the other. This was a family, a familial corporation, not a military installation. But in some ways, its gestalt was not unlike that of an elite, ground-combat troop unit.

The music had started to pick up again; the show was apparently over for now. Koscuisko came back for her, holding out his hand with transparent expectation that she would want to dance. "Bench specialist. This is the procession-step, very sedate. Perhaps you would consent to honor me."

Procession-step. That sounded safe enough. Giving him her hand Jils rose and went with him to dance, making a note to be sure to come to the great hall in the morning and watch Koscuisko contend with his house troops for face and credibility.

The knife flew clean and true to target, and the crowd cheered. Andrej turned to face them—his parents and his sister Zsuzsa, seated at her father's right in token of her proxy rank—and bowed, smiling. Yes. He was a good shot. Joslire had always praised his natural eye, and said that the blood of the hunter was in his veins. Joslire.

"I think my son shows his worth, Dame Isola," Andrej's father called. The chairs had been moved back to a safe distance, along with the carpet that defined the privileged space. "Do you dispute it?"

Dame Isola, for her part, had stood to one side to watch the progress of the contest. Now she bowed her head. "The son of the Koscuisko prince does his blood honor. I admit it." She seemed to take it in good part, even though she had to know that the coach with whom Andrej trained—now that Joslire was dead—was Sarvaw. "The challenge is well met, my prince. And still."

Lek stood well apart, with Andrej's other Security; they were in uniform, as he was not—they still belonged to Fleet. They had been kept late, last night, and no one had come to take him to train this morning, which was just as well. Supplemental atmosphere or no, the altitude was debilitating; they all felt it, Andrej was sure. Even Stildyne. Andrej had almost never seen Stildyne walk with such hesitation, except when he had been injured in one leg on an assignment—to Ropimel, Andrej thought it was.

"Still?" Andrej's father prompted. "You have further tests to propose? Take care, Dame, this is the man who is to be your master. Do not press him over-hard."

It was an affectionate and insincere rebuke. Dame Isola bowed. "Yes, my prince, and still. The son of the Koscuisko prince has demonstrated his ability." She turned to Andrej, and her bow was respectful, but not nearly so deep as that she had made his father. "It is Emandisan steel, your Excellency, and I would very much like permission to handle it."

Of course. It hadn't been just to see whether Lek was to be granted their respect, and him Sarvaw. It was the knives they wanted. This whole thing had been a setup. She wanted to get her hands on Joslire's soul.

She was the family jeweler; she had maintained steel and adjusted sidearms for Koscuiskos for an octave, almost, almost eighty years. She had served his father and his father's father before that. Joslire might have recognized such a soul; Andrej was curious to see what she might make of Joslire's knives.

"For that you must sue to my son Andrej," Andrej's father said. Andrej could hear the possessive affection in his father's voice as he had never before in his life. *My son Andrej*. Had it been there all along? Did he only recognize it now because he had learned what it was to say *My son Anton*? "He shall decide. Thank you, my son, you vindicate your honor, and you make us proud."

Andrej bowed to his parents with his heart full of gratitude and love.

There would be discussions still when it came time to start to adjust the business considerations consequent to his having forced his father's hand and married Marana. He could never explain about the Bench warrant, not to his parents, because of the relation between it and the question of who had killed Captain Lowden if it had not been Specialist Vogel.

But he had not been more than moderately rebuked for it. He had been afraid that he would be decisively rejected, having only then won forgiveness of a sort for past misdeeds; instead, it seemed that his father understood better than Andrej had imagined that he might.

Maybe Cousin Stanoczk had told him something about the Bench warrant, Andrej decided, waiting for the houseman to carry the tray back to him with his knife. He hadn't seen Cousin Stanoczk since last night.

The houseman brought the knife he'd just thrown back to him on a fabric-lined tray; Andrej loosed its mate from the forearm sheath on his right arm and laid it beside its twin to be shared out, passed around, admired.

Dame Isola was watching him, waiting, and the look on her face was an almost hungry one. He knew what she wanted.

Reaching up over his shoulder, Andrej pulled the mother-knife from its sheath at his back, and passed it to her direct. She held it up to the bright morning light that streamed through the windows at the far wall, fingers delicate to the blade to avoid smudging, her wrist flexing subtly as she tested its weight and its balance.

"He was taller than you are," she said. "And very

quick in his movements. But less restless. And also his shoulders, they were more square than yours." Joslire, whom Andrej had known as Curran. Joslire's people had come for the knives when Andrej had gone back to Rudistal to execute the sentence of the Bench against Administrator Geltoi, who had been found to blame for the Domitt Prison.

Andrej had refused to give them up. They were his knives. Joslire had said so. Dame Isola frowned. "But the balance is wrong for such a man," she said. "There is no inner core to these other knives, young master, what is it?"

Thy knives, Joslire had said, pushing the knife that Dame Isola held through the back of Andrej's hand and his own hand to sew their lives together. *Thy knives and my knives, from the first that I came to understand your nature. To the end with thee, my master. And beyond.*

Andrej held out his hand; Dame Isola passed the knife back with evident reluctance. "It was not always so." The knife slid back into its place between Andrej's shoulder blades as easily as ever it did, and it always gave him anchor there. Security. A feeling of protection.

Chief Samons had had to pull the knife from Andrej's hand. Because he'd needed it. Joslire had claimed the Day. It had been Joslire's right to die. If anyone could understand, it should be a jeweler, a woman whose whole life had been in steel. "It became heavier. After Joslire died."

The soul of a man was an intangible. It had no weight. Andrej could not explain it; he had no theological grounds for making any such claim. But he knew. The knife was heavier now. There was some part of Joslire in the knife that had never gone away from him, nor ever would.

Dame Isola waited in respectful silence as Andrej set the knife back in its place. Then she leaned forward, just a bit, with an inquiring and beguiling expression on her face.

"And the other two, young master?"

Andrej smiled. It was, to an extent, a trick question. Because there were two more knives that he wore. One of them he usually wore in his boot. But the fifth of five knives was a secret, one to which Andrej himself was not privy. He could not show all five knives. He didn't know which one was the sacred one. Joslire had never told him.

Joslire hadn't told him till Joslire had been at the point of death that Andrej was wearing Emandisan steel, and had been all along. Andrej suspected that the sacred blade was the mother-knife, because that one was the one that held Joslire's soul; it was the holiest of Joslire's knives to Andrej. But he didn't know. And he had no one to ask.

So it had been his practice to show off four knives when the occasion called for it, but never all five at once. Not always the same four. Just never all five at one time. That way at least he could respect the spirit of the Emandisan steel, because his undoubted violation of its sanctity was due to ignorance on his part.

And he had loved Joslire, loved him still, honored Joslire in his heart and took comfort in Joslire's knives. "The other two were not required for target practice, with respect, Dame Isola. I trust you will forgive me."

Dame Isola looked for a moment as though she would make another remark; exposing his secret, perhaps. There was a definite light that spoke of arcane knowledge received in her clear eyes. But as she seemed on the verge of opening her mouth to make some roguish comment, the great doors at the far end of the hall opened with unexpected suddenness, and a squad of house security came through.

House-master Jepson was in the lead—the senior security man here at Chelatring Side. Andrej's father stood up, turning to face Jepson; who bowed.

"Special envoy from Chilleau Judiciary," Jepson said. "She demands an interview with the Koscuisko prince, on behalf of the Second Judge and the rule of Law."

There was someone with the security squad that Andrej thought he recognized. A woman. Who was that? Glancing over to catch Jils Ivers's eye, Andrej found her frowning at the woman, with an expression of open skepticism.

There were Fleet security troops behind the house

troops. "I'm not expecting any such honor," Andrej's father said. "Who is this person?"

Some of the house-master's men had materialized to either side of Andrej's sister Zsuzsa, the Autocrat's Proxy, and vanished into the background with her. There had been a bit of a crowd assembled to see whether Andrej would acquit himself well in response to Dame Isola's challenge or suffer defeat; there was plenty of background into which to disappear.

The woman under escort stepped forward smartly, but she did not salute. She nodded her head, but that was all. "I am Clerk of Court at Chilleau Judiciary," she said. "Dame Mergau Noycannir. And I hold the Writ in whose support the Writ of the Koscuisko prince is to be annexed, on direction."

It made no sense. But Andrej recognized her now. What could possibly have brought Mergau Noycannir, of all people, to Chelatring Side?

Mergau Noycannir strode proudly into the great hall of the fortress place that Koscuisko's people kept in the mountains, her sharp eye missing nothing of the power and the wealth that this place displayed with such offensive opulence.

There had been a Kospodar thula in the shipyards where she had landed. The Arakcheyek shipyards had built them on Bench contract. How could there be Kospodar thulas in private hands? In Koscuisko's hands? Such wealth could not have been gained legally. She would have to call for an investigation. Later. Once she had become Queen of the Bench.

The great hall was the size of a maintenance hangar in stone, whose floors were carpeted with knotted wool, lighted by great windows and large fixtures in the ceiling; and it was full of people—a small crowd at the far end, people in chairs, more people standing. One person stood up as her escort neared.

The head Security man bowed. "Special envoy from Chilleau Judiciary," the man said. He didn't sound very respectful, to Mergau; he sounded in fact as though he didn't exactly believe her. He should know better, Mergau told herself. He would in time. She would see to it, but for now she was so close to her prize that she could almost taste the fear and despair that she would have from Koscuisko. Soon. Very soon.

The man who had risen to his feet was looking at her with an amused expression on his face. The chair beside him had emptied. "I'm not expecting any such honor," he said. "Who is this person?"

It was time to take control of this. Mergau stepped forward. "I am Clerk of Court at Chilleau Judiciary." Who was he to ask? "I hold the Writ in whose support the Writ of the Koscuisko prince is to be annexed, on direction."

The tall man shook his head. "I am the Koscuisko prince," he said; there was a note of mild amusement in his voice that Mergau found hateful. "I hold no such Writ. You seek my son, Dame Noycannir." Gesturing with his hand, he waited; and Andrej Koscuisko stepped forward from behind him.

Andrej Koscuisko. In his shirtsleeves, and looking at her with wary confusion. How she hated him. How she had waited for this moment.

"This man." She pointed. "You. Andrej Koscuisko. You are required to come to Chilleau Judiciary to pursue the investigation into the death of your Captain and the subsequent discovery of mutinous conspiracy, on board of the Jurisdiction Fleet Ship *Ragnarok*. Under the provisions of Bench disciplinary codes, your Writ is annexed for the duration of the investigation. I should like to leave immediately, if you please. There is not a moment to waste."

Koscuisko looked confused. But he was alone; he had no choice. "I don't know that the Captain is dead," he said, but it was a weak attempt. He might think that he was challenging her, standing there in the middle of a target range with his arms folded. But he could not deny her evidence. "Still less that there is any such mutiny, Dame. If Chilleau Judiciary truly means to annex my Writ, I am very much surprised."

Whether he were surprised or not was not material. He would learn soon enough not to take such a tone with her if he did not wish to suffer the consequences.

Mergau advanced on Koscuisko where he stood, past Koscuisko's father, to confront him face-to-face. There were security troops at this house, but she had brought Fleet resources with her, and Koscuisko would have no choice but to go with her once she had made her case.

Where were Koscuisko's own Security, the Security he would have brought with him from the *Ragnarok*, his Security slaves? She wanted those people. She wanted to make Koscuisko kill them one by one, in fearful agony; and that would be the start of Koscuisko's punishment. But just the start. They were bond-involuntary; they could not disobey a direct legal order. Koscuisko would be forced to give the order. They would even subdue Koscuisko himself if she said the word.

"You force me to a disagreeable display." She meant there to be no chance of misunderstanding. They would all see. Koscuisko would be left entirely without recourse. "Since you insist. Here is the Record. You of all people understand the implications of this evidence."

Putting the Record down on the empty seat of the chair that Koscuisko's father had vacated, she set the Record to scroll through her evidence. The space between the chair and the far wall had been cleared; Koscuisko had apparently been showing off his combat skills of one sort or another. The images that the Record projected were clear and sharply focused in the air.

Murat Spodinne. Taller Archops, Lek Kerenko. Smish Smath.

Current assignment Jurisdiction Fleet Ship Ragnarok, *skill class code mission engineer Wolnadi prime. Suspicion of conspiracy to commit illegal and insurrectionary acts. Confession as accused and execution in due form.*

The Record broadcast the official language of confession and condemnation, but Koscuisko was not listening. "Explain to me, Noycannir," Koscuisko said. "How can Verlaine have sent you to bring me back to Chilleau Judiciary for whatever purpose. Having previously sent Specialist Ivers to me with fully executed documents for relief of Writ?"

Taller Archops. Skill class code weaponer Wolnadi four, current assignment Jurisdiction Fleet Ship Ragnarok, *suspicion of conspiracy to commit murder of senior Command*

Branch officer, insurrectionary assassination in the first tier. Confession as accused and execution in due form.

Noycannir stared. What was Koscuisko talking about? Relief of Writ? Verlaine would never do that. Verlaine hated Koscuisko as much as she did; Koscuisko had disdained and humiliated Verlaine personally and professionally before Fleet and the public alike, at Port Burkhayden. And if anyone had heard hints of a relief of Writ, someone would have told her about it. There would have been gossip.

"You confuse me, Koscuisko, and I suspect you seek to evade your sworn duty. No matter. We will clear it up soon enough once we arrive at Chilleau Judiciary. I trust your kit is packed. Be so good as to summon your Security and we can be on our way."

Murat Spodinne. Confession denied at the Eighth Level, obtained at the Ninth Level under the provisions of emergency legal code subsection suspicion of mutiny. Conspiracy to commit murder and mutinous intent. Conspiracy to undermine the Judicial order. Confession as accused and execution in due form.

The pre-interrogation pictures, the identity validation shots, were focused a few eighth's distance from the chair, displayed in a format large enough for the assembled crowd to see them. Mergau was taking no chances.

But Koscuisko was not moving.

"Tell her that," Koscuisko said, and pointed. Mergau's vision blurred with fury: Bench specialist Jils Ivers. That bitch. Ivers had never liked her; she would say anything Koscuisko wanted her to, just to discountenance Mergau. "Tell her that the documents she carries are illusory. I'm waiting."

"No, *I'm* waiting, Koscuisko." She didn't care what any eight Bench specialists said. Bench specialists supported the Bench. They would have to defer to her, now, because she had the power to shake the entire Jurisdiction to its foundation, and she would. "Aren't you listening? You know these people. How can you pretend to deny the evidence of your own senses?"

Mergau could destroy it all with a single word: forgery. Bench specialists weren't stupid. If they wanted to save their skins and protect their privileges, they would learn quickly enough to take their orders from her.

Lek Kerenko. Skill class code primary helm navigator Wolnadi three, current assignment Jurisdiction Fleet Ship Ragnarok, *suspicion of conspiracy to commit murder and mutiny by indirection, failure to refer incriminating evidence to proper authorities. Expiration without confession of a Bond.*

Koscuisko started to speak, but he was forestalled.

"I know *that* person." It was a young woman's voice. Mergau turned her head, startled, shocked; there was a young woman standing beside Koscuisko's father, and she was pointing. "We saw him at dinner last night, very handsome. He's Sarvaw."

"The Serene Proximity is right," Koscuisko said, pointing at the image displayed large behind him, holding out one hand with an expansive and contemptuous gesture. "Lek isn't dead. And hasn't confessed any such thing, because it isn't true. Nor are Smish or Murat or Taller. Noycannir. What have you done?"

How could he ask such a thing?

Was he so stupid that he could not understand that she, and she alone, had dared to forge the Record?

Then a Security troop stepped out of the crowd that was gathered there watching, and bowed; and the impact of what Koscuisko had said hit home. The Malcontent had lied to her. Koscuisko had switched Security teams.

She'd forged the Record for nothing: these people were alive. They were worse than alive. They were here. They were visibly present for everybody to see, so everybody knew. After everything that she had done. Everybody knew that this was not a true Record. Andrej Koscuisko would not come with her to Chilleau Judiciary.

"Mister Stildyne," Koscuisko said. "Secure this supposed Record, if you please. House-master Jepson. If you would assist my people in taking Dame Noycannir into custody—"

With a scream of frustrated rage that had been building for nine years Mergau drew her glasknife and sprang at him, hearing his cry of startled agony as the knife went home and shattered in his body. Flooding the wound with neurotoxin. Incapacitating him—if not killing him outright—and she had another glasknife.

She was a dead woman here and now.

Yet if she could not have the vengeance that she sought she could still take Koscuisko down to death with her, and die happy at last.

Listening in horror to the insane claims that Noycannir made, Andrej Koscuisko clutched at whispered voices in the wind to find an anchor and hold fast. If he was swept away he would be lost.

Evidence of mutiny on board of the *Ragnarok*, and he had seen no such evidence, but it was all too likely to be true. The ship had been treated shabbily by Fleet all along, but it had gotten worse with Lowden gone. There could be mutiny, and it was his duty to root it out and punish it.

These were his people. He couldn't quite grasp what it was that was wrong with the evidence that he was hearing, but he knew that those were his people, and it was up to him to execute the vengeance of the Bench. Tenth Level Command Termination. His own people.

People to whom he owed his life, if not his soul. He couldn't think. He took hold of the first thing that occurred to him and threw it at Noycannir as hard as he could manage to push her away and shut her up.

"How can Verlaine have sent you to bring me back to Chilleau Judiciary, having previously sent fully executed documents for relief of Writ?"

He could no longer be made to punish people, any people, let alone the *Ragnarok*'s crew. He was separated from the crew of the *Ragnarok* by Judicial decree. Jils Ivers had the documents. They had not been transmitted, no, but she had them and they were fully executed. But did that still mean that his people were to be tortured, even if he was not to be the person who did it?

How could he bear to let any ordinary butcher mutilate the bodies of people to whom he owed so much in love and duty and good lordship?

Noycannir simply sneered. "We will clear it up soon

enough once we arrive at Chilleau Judiciary. Be so kind as to summon your Security and we can be on our way."

Andrej's panic deepened. Could it have been some kind of a joke on Verlaine's part, after all? No. It could not have been a joke. Verlaine had sent Jils Ivers. Not even the First Secretary would dare deploy a Bench specialist on a mission of petty vengeance, just to make a spiteful joke. Raising his hand to point at Ivers in the crowd, Andrej struggled to keep his voice level; if he should show Noycannir the slightest trace of weakness he was lost, he was certain of it.

"Tell her that." He could hardly choke out the words; because it could be true, it could be a plot for revenge. It was even possible that Ivers was in on the scheme. "Tell her that the documents she carries are illusory. I'm waiting."

No. It could not be possible. Not a Bench specialist. If a Bench specialist was in on a plot on Verlaine's part to hold out false hope of escape and freedom—only to take it all away at the last minute—then there was truly no justice left under Jurisdiction; and the entire galaxy was damned.

"No, *I'm* waiting. How can you deny the evidence of your own senses?" And yet Ivers did not speak. Was she as stunned by the enormity of Verlaine's betrayal as he was? Or—was it possible—

"I know *that* person," Zsuzsa said, and her clear voice cut through a fog in Andrej's mind. "He's Sarvaw."

What?

Noycannir's evidence. It was the crew of the Wolnadi that had been involved in the training accident, yes. Jennet ap Rhiannon had sent these people home with him to keep them from the Bench. The crew on Record were here, alive and well.

"The Serene Proximity is right." There was more wrong here than any possible joke on Verlaine's part. "Lek isn't dead. Nor are Smish or Murat or Taller. Noycannir. What have you done?"

She had brought a Record with her, or at least it looked like a Record to Andrej, and he should know. It carried the counterseals, it showed the codes, it seemed genuine. But if the Record were genuine—then Noycannir had forged evidence.

The rule of Law depended upon the sanctity of evidence.

Oh, this was astounding treachery, and if Chilleau Judiciary were behind it, Chilleau Judiciary had to be destroyed. But if it was just one mad woman, it had to be exposed without mercy and without delay.

Andrej decided. "Mister Stildyne." This was far beyond any personal considerations; he had to take this Record into custody, and place it in evidence. "Secure the Record, if you please. House-master Jepson. If you would assist my people—"

He never finished his thought.

He had not been looking at Noycannir; it was a mistake. She was on him like the weight of blind remorse, she stabbed him with a knife that seemed to explode within his flesh into a fireball of anguish. Below his right shoulder, toward his side, missing the upper lobe of his lung if he was lucky, why did it hurt so much?

He was going to die. The sharp blow that his head took when he hit the ground settled his wits back into his consciousness, somehow, and Andrej knew that he had moments at best.

Her attack had taken them all by surprise. The room was full of people. Stildyne had been at the back of the crowd with Security, and prudently so; Stildyne would have moved Andrej's Security to the back of the room the moment he had realized that Noycannir had brought Fleet Security resources, just in case those troops had come to arrest Andrej's team. House security was on the other side of his father and his sister Zsuzsa. It would take seconds for any of them to intervene. He did not have seconds to spare.

Neurotoxin. The knife had carried veniwerk poison. The tissue of his body would start to dissolve within moments. Andrej rolled away from Noycannir, onto his left side, avoiding the pressure on his wounded side by instinct—but the move crippled him, because he had only the one good arm with which to defend himself, and now he was lying on top of it.

She swung at him savagely with another knife in her

hand, and as Andrej ducked away from the threat he wondered how she had got them past the weapons scan. Glass knife. They would want to revise their search protocols. He rolled away from her and she rolled after him.

Andrej pulled away across the floor as best he could with one half of his body searing with agonizing pain, digging his left elbow against the floor for traction, straining with his neck bent and his head down. Trying to get away. Hoping against hope to win enough time to let his people react, and save him, but it all happened so quickly, and he knew it was only the adrenaline surge of pain and terror that made it seem as long to him.

He heard a sound. Noycannir crouched over him with her weapon raised to strike. The sound had been steel hitting stone. Emandisan steel, he knew it by the ringing of it, the stone of the floor. The mother-knife had slipped its catch and loosed itself and fallen. How could that have happened? He had no time to wonder about it.

The knife had fallen from the gaping neck of his blouse and followed the line of his arm down onto the floor at his elbow. He swept it into his hand with an awkward scraping grab of desperation and sank it into Noycannir's chest as deeply as he could manage, twisting away from her glasknife—which shattered against the stone floor and spread its poison. Rolling over and on top of Noycannir's body, using his own weight to press the blade home because he had no strength left with which to stab.

The hilt of the knife was hot now in his hand, and slippery. It seemed to resonate. Was it the sound of his own screaming? Was he maybe dead?

Not dead enough.

The rest of the world had caught up with him at last, but it was too late. They took him by the shoulders to move him from where he lay, and Andrej shrieked in agony, and passed out.

Coming to himself again after some unknown while Andrej opened his eyes, which declined to focus. He couldn't raise his head to shield his eyes from the bright lights that surrounded him; someone held a big broken gnarl-knuckled hand up carefully between him and the direct glare of the floodlights, and Andrej recognized Stildyne.

After a moment Andrej raised his left hand—inefficiently, but a man could only do as much as he could do—and gestured for Stildyne to come down to him. He wasn't quite sure where he was, on a gurney or on the floor, but he knew by the dazed fog in his mind that he was doped to the lips before and the dorsal fins behind, and he could guess that they were flushing the wound in which Noycannir's glasknife had shattered for all they were worth.

"Record," Andrej croaked. It didn't come out very promisingly, but this was Stildyne. Stildyne was accustomed to making sense out of the muttered and incoherent ravings of drunken Dolgorukij—how different could this be?

Stildyne dripped a little stream of fluid into Andrej's mouth and waited. Andrej tried again. "Record."

This time it came out almost normally. Stildyne nodded solemnly, with what looked like a smile of grim amusement on his face—though it was a little difficult to tell, against the brilliant halo of the emergency lights behind Stildyne's head.

"Secured," Stildyne said. "On lawful authority directly received. Not a problem, sir. Next."

Good. Stildyne apparently grasped the importance of keeping the Record out of Specialist Ivers's hands. Not because Ivers was in on any double-dealing; but because Ivers's duty to the Bench could well be in conflict with what Andrej knew he had to do to see justice done—or more precisely, to avoid an injustice. "Noycannir?"

It took him longer to get the longer word out, and Stildyne wasn't so familiar with this one. But Stildyne caught it and shook his head this time, rather than nodding. "Dead as dead, your Excellency. I've never seen that catch to slip on you. But it's a good thing that it did."

These things always happened so fast. They were still happening too fast for Andrej; the drugs were clouding over in his mind, moment by moment. He had to concentrate.

"Thula." He needed to get back to the *Ragnarok* as

quickly as possible. There might be other elements to Noycannir's plot of which he was still unaware, elements that could continue to work themselves out on their own momentum even after Noycannir herself was dead.

That was the way of it with poisonous reptiles, or so Andrej had heard. Had Noycannir been behind the Bench warrant for his death? "Stoshik. Cousin. Stanoczk."

Stildyne moved his head to look around him, and Andrej winced at the sudden assault of the light. He needed Stildyne back to block the glare.

"Ferinc's gone for him." It was odd to hear Stildyne call Girag by that name; but perhaps it was only fair, after all. Regardless of who the man had been, he was Cousin Ferinc now. And Andrej was going to have to count on him to comfort his son for a little while, until Andrej could get home again.

There was just one more thing, then, and Stildyne would make the connection, Stildyne wouldn't need to hear it all spelled out for him. Stildyne would know.

"Uniform." He had to get the Record back to the *Ragnarok*. So he had to travel in uniform; very few people under Jurisdiction were legally permitted to transfer a Record. But once Ivers logged her documentation and his codes were revoked, he would no longer be technically entitled to wear the uniform of a Ship's Prime officer on board of the Jurisdiction Fleet Ship *Ragnarok*, let alone that of a Ship's Inquisitor.

Therefore Ivers could not be permitted to transmit the documentation that Andrej had endorsed until he had brought Noycannir's forged Record safely to the *Ragnarok* and placed it into evidence in due form, legally, lawfully, uncontrovertibly.

Maybe they should offer Ivers a ride back to Pesadie Training Command, Andrej thought; and closed his eyes. It was a mistake. He had only enough time to realize the error before he was unconscious once again.

Andrej lay with his mind adrift for what seemed to be a long time, half-conscious of what was happening around him, thinking.

Mergau Noycannir had forged the Record. That was

shocking enough on its own, but there was more. She had registered confessed guilt on the part of three of his Security, three people who were not dead and had not confessed. The Record had no tolerance that Andrej knew of for reversing receipt of a confession. Once the identity codes were cross-validated, the confession had legal status; it became its own object in law.

It would be all too easy for Chilleau Judiciary to turn its back on the forgery of the Record. The woman who was responsible for the crime was dead. It would be simple prudence on the part of the Bench not to introduce the shocking fact that evidence and confession could be so egregiously forged; the Bench had stability concerns enough already.

And yet Ivers had said that Verlaine questioned the usefulness of torture in upholding the rule of Law. Couldn't he use this instance as a shocking example of the fact that the Inquisitorial system was no longer entirely in the Bench's best interest?

If Andrej did not challenge the legitimacy of the forged Record, he could not reject the confessions it recorded. Smish, Murat, Taller, Lek, they were legally dead in that forged Record; how long would it take for someone to make them really and truly dead, out of the way, silenced, no longer a potential embarrassment and reproach to Jurisdiction?

People held his body, moved his body, and Andrej paid almost no attention to what they were doing. They'd flushed the wound. Yes. And were restoring fluid, swiftly, to minimize the strain on his circulatory system. Andrej could hear them talking, but the words made no sense, and he had issues of his own to ponder.

In order to protect his Security he had to get the forged Record into evidence as a forgery, and have its so-called evidence purged. He had no way of telling whether the information had been transmitted to any other Record, as for instance at some local Court.

He had been hearing the familiar sound of the pumps, but they shut down now. The flush was complete. How much damage had he sustained? How much of it was permanent? Had the neurotoxin destroyed lung tissue or merely muscle? He could open his eyes and find out, but for that he would have to open his eyes, and he wasn't done thinking.

He had to get the Record back to the *Ragnarok*, and that meant as an officer, a Ship's Inquisitor with possession of a Writ to Inquire. He had to ensure that his people would be safe. And if anyone should somehow force the issue and refer one of them to torture—

He would not. So long as he was the Ship's Inquisitor, he was the officer who would perform the interrogation of any assigned resources. And he would not. Drug assist, speak-sera, that he might consent to; but no more, Writ or no Writ.

The Bench could remove him only by accusing him of treason. Failure to obey lawful and received instruction was mutiny. That would compromise the son of the Koscuisko prince in an environment in which the political stability of the Dolgorukij Combine was needed to stand as a balance against civil unrest during the coming transition of power; maybe that would work in his favor, if it came to that.

But it didn't matter any more. They couldn't make him. He was the only one who could do that. Jils Ivers had offered him freedom, relief of Writ. A chance to come home and be father and husband, to enjoy the power that entailed to the inheriting son of the Koscuisko prince. He had so wanted to come home and meet his son. The offer of escape from Inquiry had been a huge and staggering opportunity, but he could not trade the lives of his people away for wealth and power.

And it didn't take relief of Writ to free him from the horrors of Inquiry. It only took a decision on his part. That was all. He had for so long told himself that he had no choice. He had for so long bathed in blood and torture, and done atrocious and obscene violence to helpless souls to rob them even of their last secrets before they died. He had believed that he had had no choice. He had been wrong about that. All of this time he had been wrong. Of course he had a choice.

It was so simple. He could do as he was bidden, or he could die. Yes, it was rational to be afraid of that death; he knew better than any man alive under Jurisdiction what a Tenth Level Command Termination could mean. But by the same token, he knew what it was not; nobody could do what he could do with pain at such a level. He knew that. It was not vanity. It was only fact.

Not very long ago he had faced in himself the fact that he had played Captain Lowden's game and tortured souls in Inquiry beyond the limits of their crime to placate his commanding officer, so that Lowden would leave the bond-involuntaries alone. Not beyond the limits of their guilt—all of Inquiry was beyond the limits of any guilt—that had been part of the problem from the beginning. But beyond even the limits of the Bench's ferocious list of torments to be invoked per the seriousness of the crime suspected.

He had done it to protect his people, but he had been wrong to do that. He had no right to beat a prisoner to save a bond-involuntary a beating, he had no right to make such decisions, he had been wrong. And had killed Captain Lowden, not because he had been wrong—there was no help for what crimes he had done, they were done, he could not call them back—but in order to protect his Bonds from imposition.

All this time he had been guilty of so far greater a confusion of the mind. He had always known that Inquiry was evil, and that he was committing sin each time he implemented the Protocols. He had known that from the beginning. He had believed that he had no choice. Now he could see it. All of this time he had traded torture for his own security, his own pride, his own parochial and misguided set of values.

How could filial piety require that he sin? Why had he ever thought that his father and his mother would be more honored in a son who committed gross atrocity than in one who refused the obscene torture of sentient souls? In what way could his duty to the Holy Mother require that he mutilate the flesh and bone of souls that were of Her own creation?

There was the old theological question, of course, of whether hominids who were not Dolgorukij had souls. It didn't matter. He knew well enough that souls who were not Dolgorukij suffered as horribly as Dolgorukij did when they were tortured. The Holy Mother Herself would cry out in anguish to witness such suffering; and if She did not, how could She be holy?

If he returned to the *Ragnarok* he could lose everything, and he had so recently been given everything: his parents' forgiveness, if not their understanding; the chance to be truly married with Marana; and a beautiful and loving child who was his son. The power of the Koscuisko familial corporation. Freedom from Secured Medical's horrible requirements, forever after. Everything.

He could not turn his back on his people. There was nothing that he owned or had enjoyed that was worth the lives of his Security: and it would only begin with the lives of his Security. He knew how Fleet inquiry was executed, after all. He better than most.

Lek Kerenko was a bond-involuntary. Lek had nothing that was his; even his body belonged to the Fleet, and the Fleet could do whatever it wanted with him, its absolute power moderated only by rational considerations of efficiency and replacement costs.

Lek had given him the only thing that Lek had left to call his own—his trust, and perhaps even a portion of affection. How could he reject so great a gift as everything from a man who had nothing for the sake of mere fields and houses, money, wealth, and the domestic comforts of a hearth to which he was still yet a stranger?

Brachi Stildyne had had nothing all his life. Stildyne had no cause to return anything to the world that had given him so little; and yet, Stildyne, who had grown up comfortless, uncomforted, tried to give comfort to a man from so different a background that he might as well have been an alien species.

Stildyne, to whom nobody had ever extended charitable kindness or sought to understand, had saved Andrej's life and helped preserve his sanity by exercising charitable kindness, trying to understand, efforts all the more remarkable coming from a man who'd never had the luxury of caring for another soul in his life.

And when Stildyne had found someone to care for, how had Andrej honored that regard—except by declining to reject it outright? How great a sinner would he be if the best thanks he had for Stildyne's strength over the years was to turn his back on his own crew and let them fall to torture, one by one?

The people here on Azanry were his by birth and blood and familial affection. But his people on the *Ragnarok* were his because they consented to enter into the relationship, and not with the son of the Koscuisko prince, not with their sibling or son or father, but with a mere man, and a more than ordinarily flawed one. He had to go back.

He'd live if he could but he'd die if he had to, and if he had to, he'd do it defending the people to whom he owed his life and his sanity. Andrej opened his eyes and started to sit up. It didn't work.

Stildyne held him as he fell back the few fractions he'd been able to raise himself off the surface of the diagnostic bed, and Andrej's body knew better than to try to argue with Stildyne. Someone adjusted the shades on the nearest light and raised the level of the bed; Andrej cleared his throat.

Stildyne was there with a flask of rhyti. The room came back into focus. Medical personnel, looking pale and very severe. Stildyne, more sensed than seen, at his side. Stoshik. Bench specialist Jils Ivers, and his father, leaning up against the wall with his arms folded and reminding Andrej suddenly and incongruously of the First Officer.

"Can Lek fly the thula?" Andrej asked, looking at Cousin Stanoczk. Cousin Stanoczk looked rather pale himself. Andrej wondered what Stanoczk might know about Noycannir's scheme that he could not reveal; or could it be that the Malcontent had not anticipated her attempt? That would truly be unnerving.

"He will have to," Stanoczk nodded, with grim amusement. "If you are to reach the *Ragnarok* at Taisheki Station."

What?

Fleet Audit Appeals Authority was at Taisheki Station. Had ap Rhiannon been unable to defend herself against Pesadie on her own? Why else would the *Ragnarok* go to Taisheki, except to file an appeal? It was a worrying indication. The only people Fleet could lay a claim to this early, without evidence, were here; but Noycannir had produced false evidence. Had ap Rhiannon been forced to surrender collateral witnesses?

He needed to review the Record; he needed to know exactly what Noycannir had placed into evidence. And then he needed to know if she'd transmitted that so-called evidence anywhere, anywhere at all. He could review the Record once they were in transit.

"When do we leave?" Andrej asked, to find out what the parameters were. Cousin Stanoczk bowed.

"At his Excellency's convenience entirely," Stanoczk said. "But you have to take my navigator." And why did Andrej think he knew exactly who that was? Later. Andrej nodded thanks and acceptance at once.

"Stildyne, I need to get dressed. Meet me at the thula as soon as you can. Specialist Ivers, would you care to accompany me?"

She was in an interesting position. It all came down to the documents, didn't it? Ivers nodded, a gesture that was almost a bow. "Delighted, your Excellency." With rank. So they understood each other. "I may never have a chance to travel on a thula again. They cost money, after all."

A note of warning, there. The Bench had evidence in hand of how much money the Malcontent commanded. There would unquestionably be an inquiry, over the coming years, into how deeply the fingers of the Malcontent truly reached. That was the Malcontent's lookout, though, and the Malcontent was more than adequately qualified to protect its interest. Andrej looked past Ivers for the medical people.

"Prognosis, Doctor. Status, please." He himself was a surgeon, not a soft-tissue specialist, and his experience of traumatic wound management was almost completely limited to the care-giving side of the equation. The house physician stepped forward and bowed.

"Gross physical trauma to the upper right-hand portion of your chest, sir, the muscle beneath the front part of your shoulder. Some of the lymph is damaged, potentially some of the lung. It's too early to tell. We got the flush-and-neutralize started in good time, but there is danger."

Of course there was danger. Every muscle in his back and side and belly on the right side of his body hurt, and a good representative sample of the corresponding elements on the left were protesting in sympathy. There was a huge empty space in his body where the upper portion of his chest was supposed to be—local anesthesia, Andrej presumed—and his mind seemed to be floating at some few measures' remove from his body in a comforting narcotic haze.

"Stabilize for transport, please, Doctor. I've got to get out of here. My duty absolutely requires that I return to my ship immediately." He recognized the expression of condescending superiority on the doctor's face; it was one of his own favorites.

"I'm sorry, sir, it's out of the question. I cannot permit it. Your wound absolutely requires immobilization while the neutralysis completes, and a single wrong move could set muscle regeneration back days. Weeks. No."

As a matter of principle Andrej always unfailingly deferred to his general practitioners when he was the patient, whether or not he agreed with them. It was simply good protocol. Just as well that he was at Chelatring Side, and not on board of the *Ragnarok*, because he would never have dared pull rank on one of his subordinate physicians. So arrogant a misstep could undo years of careful building of relationships.

"I hear and comprehend, Doctor, but I insist. It is absolutely necessary that you stabilize for transport immediately. The alternative is not cancellation of transport but transport without stabilization, and we both know that to be a much more dangerous proposition. You are master in your own infirmary, Doctor, but I have a duty to the Bench which must override even your authority."

He knew his argument was persuasive, as far as it went, and that it was unlikely to be acceptable. Andrej would have respected the house physician less if he didn't object strenuously to any such suggestion. The doctor looked across the room to Andrej's father, scowling.

"Your Excellency," the doctor said. "This is an imprudent suggestion. I will not answer for the consequences. Your son faces serious and permanent injury, your Excellency, and possibly a fatal outcome. Relieve me of this requirement."

Andrej's father straightened up, crossing the room to come to Andrej's side. "He is my son," Andrej's father agreed. "I know this man, in a manner of speaking. So I believe what he has said, that his duty requires that he travel. As dangerous as it may be for him to travel with such a wound, it will be much worse if you will not consent to do what can be done."

The point exactly. Andrej could have smiled, but he had already annoyed the doctor, and who knew better than he that a physician was not to be challenged in his own infirmary?

"I therefore lay the blame on *his* head," Andrej's father said kindly, but implacably. The expression on the doctor's face reflected his clear realization that he had no choice; he would have to comply. "You are to accept no portion of the blame, Doctor. It is my son's decision. Stabilize for transport, if you please."

It was an order even a physician had to obey. The doctor bowed. "Going for transport kit directly," he said. "According to his Excellency's good pleasure."

He left the room. That left Ivers, Cousin Stanoczk, and Andrej's father, if one disregarded the technicians for the moment.

"It is necessary?" his father asked. Andrej nodded.

"It is crucial." That didn't make it easier; just explained why it had to be done. "To save the lives of my Security, and possibly many more beside. I am I regret still your unfilial son. And will challenge the Bench if I must."

It was a reference to the letter that his father had sent him after the trials at the Domitt Prison. His father did not rebuke him for the reproach, however; it was almost as good as an apology. "Come back soon, then, son Andrej," his father said. "I want you home. And you have explaining to do to the Ichogatra."

Yes. He did. And if his punishment for marrying Marana was to be the negotiation of reparations and new contracts in light of the prejudicial cancellation of the planned contract of marriage—he was still ahead of the game.

Andrej held out his left arm—with some difficulty, because his muscles ached. His son had embraced him. He could not embrace his father, not under these circumstances. But he could indicate his desire to. "I will come home when I can, sir," he said. Promised. "Depend upon it."

A long handclasp, a paternal kiss, and Andrej's father turned around and went away. There was nothing more to say. Maybe his father couldn't say anything more anyway.

He'd have to say good-bye to his mother, if he had time, but now there was only Stoshik to get through and he could leave. "Who is to beg forgiveness from Marana?" Andrej asked. "As I am taking Ferinc with me, Stoshik. Somebody must go and explain. This is the last thing anyone could have expected."

Stoshik was very pale. "It shouldn't have happened," he said. "I blame myself. Derush, we are supposed to have better care for you than to allow you to be assaulted by madwomen. Specialist Ivers, what do you know of this?"

Stanoczk had to know that Ivers knew nothing. He was just playing the scenario out; Ivers was an envoy from Chilleau Judiciary, after all. Noycannir had belonged to Chilleau. It could be made to look ugly. The Combine would make Chilleau pay dearly for the potential of the appearance of a conspiracy to assassinate the son of the Koscuisko prince.

"I probably know even less than you do." Ivers seemed to have no stomach for the play; or else her blunt frankness was her role. Perhaps that. "I will report to the First Secretary as soon as is prudently possible. But I feel completely confident in this much: Noycannir was on her own. Chilleau Judiciary has no hand in this."

Maybe Chilleau Judiciary was going to have to leave the issue of the thula alone, after all. Andrej didn't feel that he had much time; the drugs were fast overtaking his consciousness. "Stoshik, I'll come back as soon as I can. If I can. Speak to Marana for me, I beg you. This is grotesque injustice to her. But I can see no option worth considering."

"Taisheki space," Stanoczk said, his reply indirect but obvious enough. "Ferinc will have the briefing. Good travel, Andrej, Bench specialist. We can speak again when you've come home, Derush."

Stanoczk wouldn't tell him anything about the Bench warrant, not in Ivers's presence. Had he got everything? The doctor was back with a medical team, and they had brought a stasis-mover with them, an inclined sort of a mechanized bed—they meant him to be as thoroughly stabilized as possible.

How many days to Taisheki, even in a thula, and confined within a stasis-mover? Andrej closed his eyes wearily, overcome with dread at the prospect. Once he closed his eyes, they stayed closed. The drugs pulled him down into the darkness, and he was lost.

Chapter Thirteen

Order of Battle

The thula was compact and very efficient, but it had clearly been built for speed rather than comfort. Jils wasn't quite happy with the prospect of spending two or three days alone on this thula with Andrej Koscuisko—alone as far as medical resources went—but neither had Koscuisko's own family physicians been; they had trammeled him up so thoroughly that the odds of his doing injury to himself were minimized. The odds of him doing anything at all were minimized.

There were Security in the wheelhouse with the Malcontent Cousin Ferinc, learning the thula; more Security in the narrow corridors outside the low-ceilinged cabin in which Koscuisko rested. She'd heard Cousin Stanoczk say that the Malcontent would have a briefing for Koscuisko. But for that, Koscuisko had to be awake.

Andrej Koscuisko hadn't awakened in the day since the thula had taken the vector for Taisheki. The house physicians would have put his medications on time-release. It was what she would have done with Koscuisko under the circumstances, but was she to sit and watch an unconscious invalid all the way to Fleet Audit Appeals Authority? She needed to talk to him.

She sat in the little cabin and waited, sharing the time with the others on board. Rank was no respecter of duty rosters, and they all needed Security to fly the thula, which meant that every waking moment she could spend on watch freed one of the Security to learn the operational characteristics of this elegant and fearful machine. Familiarity with fast spacecraft was a good thing. It decreased the chances that someone would make a wrong move and kill them all.

Toward the end of the shift Chief Stildyne came into the cabin with two flasks of something steaming and hot and offered her one. "Rhyti," Chief Stildyne said, as though he was apologizing. "Nothing much else by way of stimulants. Dolgorukij, you know. How's the officer?"

"About the same." Exactly the same. The wound was well dressed, but it still smelled like raw flesh, and Koscuisko did not move. Koscuisko couldn't move. That stasis-mover was a piece of work. "Either it's much worse than they let on, or he really annoyed them."

The latter, she thought, and Chief Stildyne by his smile seemed to agree. She wished he wouldn't smile. His lips were thin to begin with, and when he smiled they disappeared entirely, so that his face looked even more like a fleshless skull than it normally did. It was nothing personal. She liked Stildyne, he was among the best Warrants she'd ever worked with. But he was ugly.

Stildyne stood looking at Koscuisko in the stasis-mover; Koscuisko opened his eyes, frowning. Just like that. How long had he been awake? "Brachi," Koscuisko said. "Where am I?"

Stildyne made a peculiar face that Jils couldn't exactly interpret. He fit his flask of rhyti into Koscuisko's good hand before he spoke, guiding it with care. It wasn't easy for Koscuisko to drink. Stildyne adjusted the stasis-mover's indices more toward the vertical; Koscuisko drank again. "On vector for Taisheki Station, sir. Two days out. Cousin Ferinc wants to talk to you, now or later."

Koscuisko's eyes wandered, but he focused on Stildyne's face with an apparent effort. "In one day and sixteen hours, Chief, you are going to find whatever drug delivery system they have me plugged into, and you are going to pull it. I'll want to be awake. Ferinc is where?"

Stildyne took the flask away. "I'll be right back. Don't go anywhere." It was a joke. Koscuisko seemed too deep in medicated drowsiness to notice.

This couldn't be a good time, but the question needed

asking. "What do you want me to do with the documents, sir?"

Koscuisko frowned again, lifting his head away from the padded headboard of the stasis-mover. "Oh. Bench specialist. Documents? Yes. Those."

He seemed to be lucid, just easily distracted. Jils repeated the question. "What am I do to with the documents, your Excellency?"

"I may need to remain at my post for some days, Specialist Ivers." He spoke slowly, but she could catch no sense that his mind wandered. Either it was an effort for him to speak, or else he wanted to be very sure of what he was saying. "I don't yet know. I think it may be best if you gave them to me. I will call for you, when I am ready."

Yes, but that meant that his relief of Writ would go unrecorded until then. "With your permission, sir." She wanted to satisfy herself that he knew what it was that he was doing. "You have for so long sought to set your Writ aside or, rather, regretted its exercise."

He nodded, with a considering expression on his face that she could not quite interpret. She pressed on, to try to see if he was truly listening. "Are you sure of what you do, sir? We don't know what may be happening. Without these documents, you remain subject to Fleet discipline. You know that."

Koscuisko's eyes tracked across the room from object to object; was he trying to focus? When he spoke, it was with perfect clarity, lucid and precise. She could not imagine that he was drugged and raving. There was too much implacable logic in what he was saying.

"Thank you for your care, Specialist Ivers. But here is the truth of it. It is not relief of Writ that frees me from the further commission of crimes in the name of the Judicial order. It is only my own determination which suffices for that. The Fleet and the Bench may do as they like with me, but I will be guided by my own heart. I cannot say decency. I'm unsure whether I have any left."

Stildyne was back with the Malcontent, Cousin Ferinc, and more rhyti. Stildyne gave her a sharp look, as though accusing her of tiring Koscuisko in his absence; but there was no help for it. She had needed to know.

Koscuisko had shaken himself free of the last of his cultural conditioning: he was a free man. That made him more dangerous than he had ever been.

"News for you, sir," Cousin Ferinc said, carefully, not raising his voice but fixing his attention very closely on Koscuisko's face. "From Cousin Stanoczk. About the *Ragnarok* en route to Taisheki Station. Are you awake, your Excellency?"

Koscuisko's eyes seemed about ready to roll back in his head. Frowning, Koscuisko focused with apparent effort. "Almost, Ferinc. Speak quickly. You may have to tell me again later."

Ferinc nodded. "Appeal to the Fleet Audit Appeals Authority on improper acquisition of evidence improperly read. There is no Bench warrant for these crew, sir, but there are hints that Taisheki is not in a receptive mood, nonetheless."

"Get the documents," Koscuisko said, to Chief Stildyne. Had he lost the braid? Or was it the last thing he wanted to say before he went down once more, as he clearly seemed about to do? "And remember. Four hours before. Pull the meds. I can't stand this."

Did that mean she had to wait till then to hear what Ferinc knew of what might be happening at Taisheki Station?

She had not been offered the use of the thula's communications. She didn't think she wanted it. The First Secretary needed to know about Noycannir, but the Combine could pass on that information. If she spoke to Verlaine he might give her instructions, and she might feel obliged to implement them. To seize the Record, by force if necessary, though all she could reasonably hope for on this trip would be to destroy it.

Koscuisko needed that Record. The *Ragnarok* itself might need that Record. It was better if she avoided the mischance that Verlaine might look to his own interest and direct her to actions which would support the rule of Law but suborn justice.

Garol Vogel had been there, years ago, at Port Charid. With his Langsariks. He had found a way to avoid an injustice, but it had cost him his lifelong submission to the rule of Law. He'd never been the same after

Port Charid, and that was almost five years ago. Now it was her turn.

"I'll sit for a while," Chief Stildyne said, which she knew perfectly well meant "Go away and leave me alone" in Stildyne. She was perfectly willing to. She needed to think.

There was more to this problem than Mergau Noycannir and a forged Record, and she had very little time for analysis left before the thula reached Taisheki Station and she would have to decide what to do.

From the Jurisdiction Fleet Ship Ragnarok *to Fleet Audit Appeals Authority, Taisheki Station, greeting. On behalf of the crew and Command of this ship the following appeal is transmitted.*

Jennet ap Rhiannon sat alone behind the desk in the Captain's office brooding over the printed text, analyzing it for the eighth or sixteenth time, wondering if she had said everything she'd wanted to. Wondering if her plea had been as convincing at Taisheki Station as she felt it to be from on board the *Ragnarok*.

A recent accident at Pesadie Training Command took the life of Acting Captain Cowil Brem. Although no Ragnarok resources were active in the area at the time of the accident, Pesadie Training Command's investigative focus has been on finding fault with the crew and craft that had just quit the area when the accident occurred.

It just didn't come out right. The words could not express her outrage; they didn't communicate her determination.

The preliminary assessment team posted by Pesadie Training Command took covert action to subvert ship's security and obtain information illegally and inappropriately. Fleet Admiral Sandri Brecinn's direct collusion in this cover-up was made evident by her resort to improperly obtained information as a basis to demand release of troops to stand the Question.

Nowhere in these legal terms and careful phrases could she hear the words that were in her heart: *I am responsible for these troops, these troops are blameless and not at fault. Once you start on troops it never ever stops at just the four or six or eight or twelve, and I will ram Pesadie Training Command with an explosive detonation charge before I will surrender one single soul to be used to cover up for her black marketing.* It wasn't there.

She couldn't say it, not in so many words; if her appeal was to succeed there had to be an out there, somewhere. She was in no position to back Taisheki into a corner and demand concessions. If the Appeals Authority would not listen to her appeal she didn't know what she was going to do.

Further evidence indicates the potential existence of systemic irregularities within the Pesadie Training Command injurious to the maintenance of the Judicial order.

The talk-alert's warning tone interrupted Jennet's brooding. Swallowing back a sigh of resignation, she toggled into braid. "Ap Rhiannon. Yes."

"Engineering bridge, your Excellency. Requesting the pleasure of your company. I've never seen anything like this."

Wheatfields. It was unusual enough for anyone to actually hear from Wheatfields; but this was even more unusual, because he sounded excited. She thought that was what he sounded. She wasn't sure she would be able to tell, not with Wheatfields.

One way or the other she needed to go see what he was calling about. He was off-braid already, but she didn't think it was a failure of military courtesy on his part. That would have been rude. When Wheatfields wanted to be rude he generally left one in no doubt at all about it.

She hurried down from her office to the Engineering bridge with all deliberate speed, paying attention to the expressions and the deportment of the people in the hallways, showing the rank. She was their Captain. She had gotten them all into a very great deal of trouble and they had gone with her willingly. She owed them all acknowledgment of that; and a successful outcome, of course. Unless they all elected to dive into Pesadie Training Command with her.

Ship's First Officer was standing in the doorway of the

observation deck when Jennet got there, waiting for her, his forehead creased in a worried frown but his face alive with what appeared to be good-humored excitement.

"Hurry on in, your Excellency," Mendez said. "You don't want to miss this. Any of it. Someone's tracking for intercept on vector. You'll never guess."

This was nonsensical. Nobody tracked for intercept on vector. There was too much vector, for one. And the speed differentials required to make any difference during vector transit were extreme, for another. Hurrying through the doorway as Mendez had encouraged her Jennet made for the railing and looked down into the engineering bridge, to see what the aft scanners were saying.

Mendez was right. There was an intercept blip. And it was moving faster than anything she had ever seen in her life. "Engineer," Jennet said. "What is that ship?"

Wheatfields looked up and over his shoulder at her from his post on the Engineering bridge below. "Do you like it?" Wheatfields asked, with a curious note of wistful lustfulness in his voice. "It's a Kospodar thula. Koscuisko's on board. Just say the word and I'll blow it up for you."

"Start at the starting place, please." To say "Wheatfields" would be rude, and "Serge" was out of the question. "Tell me what this is all about."

Wheatfields shook his head, as if in wonder. "Look at the spin vectors on that machine. I don't know what to tell you, your Excellency. We only noticed it coming at us an eight or two ago. It's not saying much. All it will tell us is that Koscuisko requests permission to come on board, and has two non-crew passengers."

"Strange," Jennet said. This was not good news: if it was Koscuisko, he logically had Security with him, and she had wanted those Security kept out of the way. "He wasn't due off leave for another two weeks at least, was he?"

Something chimed on the Engineering bridge, a transmission alert. Wheatfields nodded at one of his people, and the transmission came up on shared audio.

"Private courier ship, Aznir registry, Chief Medical Officer Andrej Ulexeievitch Koscuisko and party, two others. His Excellency wishes to rejoin his Command, and requires medical attention. Permission to come on board."

That "requires medical attention" sounded ominous. The *Ragnarok*'s maintenance atmosphere had been hulled over for vector transit; trying to pull a courier in was going to be tricky. "Engineer?" Jennet asked. "Can we rendezvous at all?"

The authentication codes were scrolling across the base of a status-screen to one side of the Engineering bridge. Voice-identity confirmed: Lek Kerenko, Security 5.1, Jurisdiction Fleet Ship *Ragnarok*.

Wheatfields shot her a look that was half serious and half mock outrage. "Do I have to, your Excellency? I want the ship. Not Koscuisko. Thula, this is Ship's Engineer, can you sustain position for entry with limited clearances?"

The containment field that held the *Ragnarok*'s atmosphere when the ship's underbelly was not hulled over could not sustain the speed at which the *Ragnarok* was traveling without potential damage. That was why they hulled the maintenance atmosphere over for vector transit in the first place. Wheatfields would want to minimize his exposure.

"With respect, your Excellency." Now that Jennet knew who was talking, she almost thought she recognized the voice. "This beast can do anything. Just try her."

Mendez stood at Jennet's side with his arms folded across his chest, frowning now in what appeared to be genuine concern. "Medical attention, Kerenko?" Mendez asked. There was a brief silence; then Security Chief Stildyne came into braid.

"Assassination attempt, sir. Neurotoxin, but he's got something he needs to read into the Record, and he was in too much of a hurry to listen to the doctors."

Koscuisko was accustomed to having his own way. Jennet felt a brief pang of concern in her belly: she hadn't precisely gotten along with Koscuisko before the accident; how were they to get along now? Because she could not afford to let him doubt that she was the captain of the *Ragnarok*.

"How bad is it, Chief?"

Content to let Mendez do the talking, Jennet watched the track of the thula as it gained on them, and listened. "He's pretty much drugged senseless, your Excellency. We'll want Infirmary to be standing by. They didn't want him traveling at all. He insisted."

"Good hostage," Wheatfields said suddenly, not looking up. "Koscuisko's an important man in his home system. We may need the leverage. I'll bring him on board, your Excellency."

She hadn't thought that far. But Wheatfields was right. She didn't have to worry about how she was to manage Koscuisko's adjustment to the changes that had occurred on the *Ragnarok* during his absence. He hadn't been here. He was not implicated or involved. He was a neutral third party—an innocent bystander. A bargaining chip.

"Very well." Let Koscuisko on board, even with the Security she had wanted him to shelter. Better Koscuisko should bring the Security back on board where she could keep a good hold of them than follow the *Ragnarok* to Taisheki Station and surrender his Security before he knew what a mistake he would be making. "Grant permission, Engineer. We'll alert Medical. Once we know what Koscuisko's condition is, we can talk."

Technically speaking it was the First Officer, not the Captain, who got to decide who was and who was not allowed to come on board. Wheatfields nodded. "As you wish, Captain. Thula. What's your name, anyway? Never mind. Sela, calculate a docking protocol. Kerenko. If it was anybody else driving, I wouldn't be doing this."

But they'd seen Kerenko's flying. They all knew that he was good. "Standing by for docking protocol, your Excellency, and thank you, sir." Still not even Kerenko could have that much experience piloting so exotic a ship—

It was the Engineer's lookout, Jennet reminded herself, firmly. "I'm going down to the maintenance atmosphere, First Officer." To be there when the ship docked. "Would you call Infirmary for us, please?"

An assassination attempt. By whom, and why, and what had they hoped to accomplish by murdering Koscuisko, or had it just been revenge? First things first. Let them get the thula into the maintenance atmosphere, and Koscuisko offloaded to Medical.

Time enough to press for all the details later.

When Andrej Koscuisko awoke he was in Infirmary on board of the Jurisdiction Fleet Ship *Ragnarok*, a circumstance both startling and disturbing. Startling because he had no memory of arriving; disturbing because he did not know where the *Ragnarok* was. "Mister Stildyne. What has happened?"

The drugs were clearing from his system; he felt clearheaded, if weak. He had never known a doctor for soft-tissue injury management like Narion. She knew what she was doing.

"Where to start, your Excellency?" Stildyne's response was reflective. "We caught up with the *Ragnarok* on vector. We've come off vector. The Second Judge has announced her platform. There's no encouragement from Taisheki Station on the *Ragnarok*'s appeal. You're going to live. I think that's the lot."

Whether he was going to live had not been at issue, so Stildyne was just padding his narrative. Or making sure that he had it all. "I need to place the Record into evidence, Chief, I've got to get up."

But Stildyne shook his head. "His Excellency may wish to reconsider. Fleet is not happy with Chilleau Judiciary. Specialist Ivers suggests we wait."

"She doesn't have the Record, does she? Chief? Brachi?"

"No, your Excellency." The smile on Stildyne's face to hear his first name was almost frightening. Because so much about Stildyne was. "Secured by order of the First Officer. Let me call First Officer, sir. He wants to talk to you."

Andrej didn't need to answer that. He closed his eyes; and when he opened them again, the room was full of people. Narion's soft-tissue specialty team, and him half naked on the inclined stasis-mover. First Officer. Stildyne. Specialist Ivers. Lieutenant ap Rhiannon, who'd started the entire mess by sending the wrong Security home with him.

Perhaps that was unfair, Andrej decided. Ap Rhian-

non hadn't had anything to do with Mergau Noycannir.
And if ap Rhiannon hadn't sent the wrong Security, they
wouldn't have been present at Chelatring Side to save
Andrej from Noycannir's plot by demonstrating that the
Record had been forged. So he owed her an apology.
And it would have to wait.

"Well, that's the excuse," First Officer was saying.
"Unsettled environment, you come to us if you want
Safes for those bond-involuntary troops. But I don't like
it, Specialist Ivers. No. We *aren't* going anywhere fast."

Blinking, Andrej waited patiently for his eyes to focus.
So they'd come off vector, but Taisheki had declined
to meet them with Safes, as would have been standard
operating procedure—an appeal was a Command action.
Bond-involuntaries weren't held accountable for it, but
the stresses of the situation could destroy them unless
they had the protection of the Safes.

"That statement of the Second Judge's does rather
threaten Fleet's power base, First Officer," Andrej
pointed out, very reasonably he thought. "I wouldn't
have thought Taisheki Station to be affected—"

Everybody turned to stare at him. What? Was he not
speaking Standard? What was the matter with everybody?

"Andrej," Mendez said. "Good to hear from you.
"How's the shoulder? Better?"

No, it felt much worse. That was the "better" part,
though, because it meant that Narion was pulling back on
the drugs. "I will get a report, First Officer, and let you
know. Specialist Ivers. Stildyne says you want to hold the
forged Record out of evidence. How can this be?"

Ivers looked down and to one side, carefully, as if
collecting her thoughts. "If you mean to endorse the
Second Judge's declaration. Consider. The forged Record is intimately connected with Mergau Noycannir,
and thus could discredit Chilleau Judiciary. With respect,
sir, now is exactly the wrong time to give Fleet any
weapons against the candidacy of the Second Judge, if
you agree with her declaration."

All right. Andrej supposed he could understand her
reasoning. He turned his attention to the bandaging that

the soft-tissue injury management team was doing; he'd never seen so much of his own flesh laid raw in his life.

Ivers spoke on, but was no longer speaking to him. "I don't understand why Taisheki Station would withhold Safes on these grounds, your Excellency. The Safes are there. They have only to send a courier. With your permission, I'd like to get to Taisheki Station and see if I can find out what's going on."

Who was she talking to? She didn't seem to be looking at Mendez. And Andrej himself was the only other Excellency in the room.

"Take the Captain's shallop. And those leftovers of Brecinn's, with you," ap Rhiannon said. "We keep the thula. Because Kerenko is driving it. And if Taisheki Station gets its hands on either, I'm not likely to get them back. But . . ."

Oh, all right. Yes. Ap Rhiannon was an Excellency by default. Acting Captain, and so forth. Andrej leaned his head back against the padded headboard of the stasis-mover and frowned, concentrating.

"Yes, your Excellency?" Ivers prompted.

"If I don't get satisfaction from Taisheki Station, Bench specialist, I can remove the *Ragnarok* to neutral territory and appeal to the Bench direct. And I will. I've come too far to let it all be for nothing."

What nonsense. The *Ragnarok* was a Fleet resource. There was no neutral territory for the *Ragnarok* in all of Jurisdiction space, if Taisheki Station should refuse the appeal. Ivers didn't bother to point this out, as though she was as aware of the patent absurdity of this claim as he was. "Yes, Captain, and we'll hope it doesn't come to that. Your Excellency."

Too many Excellencies, Andrej decided. It was making him dizzy. The only way he could tell that he was the "Excellency" she meant this time was the fact that she had turned her body back to face him. "Bench specialist."

"I need to report about Noycannir to Chilleau Judiciary, sir. The Malcontent will already have transmitted some information, but Verlaine will be waiting to hear from me. I must respectfully request that you refrain from putting the forged Record into evidence until we have time to strategize. To decide if here and now is when it should be done."

She was making sense. He was tired. Narion was probably not going to let him out of Infirmary very soon, and he dared not pull rank on his own staff without truly crucial overriding considerations. Mendez had secured the Record. What harm could there be?

"Leave also the documents that I for you countersigned, Specialist Ivers." If he didn't enter the forged Record into evidence before she logged relief of Writ, he could find himself barred from the Record, and unable to make the required statements. He couldn't afford the risk.

After a moment Ivers nodded. "Very well, your Excellency. Captain, I will go and find out what I can, and take those unwanted crew with me. General Rukota isn't returning, ma'am?"

Who was that? Rukota? General Rukota? He didn't know any Generals Rukota. What had been going on here while he'd been away?

"Nor do I blame him, Bench specialist. He's got damage-control issues of his own. Doctor Koscuisko. Welcome back. We'll get you a briefing once you've had a chance to recover a bit. You may wish to leave yourself but we can discuss it later."

What did ap Rhiannon know? This was his ship. His crew. He wasn't going anywhere. He'd just gone to a very great deal of trouble to get back here.

"You can be ambulatory inside of two days, your Excellency," Narion assured him, gravely. "Whoever parked you on the other side did a superlative job. But you still have strong painkillers in your system. Go ahead and sleep them out, sir. Everything's under control on this end and nothing's happening fast."

Now, that was a sensible suggestion. And with Ivers's agreement to hold processing of the documents that would cancel his clearance codes, he didn't have so much concern about the forged Record going missing before it could be logged.

This would all make sense when he woke up again, he was almost sure of it. "Make sure of the Record,

First Officer," Andrej said, and resigned himself to sleep once more.

"And I say that ap Rhiannon has conspired with a Clerk of Court from Chilleau Judiciary to trade in contraband munitions," Admiral Brecinn insisted. Jils kept her face clear of irritation; no one would believe that any emotion she displayed was genuine anyway. In the privacy of her own thoughts, she didn't know whether to rage or to laugh. She'd never met Sandri Brecinn; she certainly hadn't expected to find Brecinn here at Taisheki Station, rather than at Pesadie Training Command.

"The Fleet Admiral is who she is," Auditor Ormbach said, in a reasonable tone of voice. "We cannot simply discount her very serious accusations, no matter how extravagant they might seem. Work with us here, Bench specialist, please."

Brecinn was apparently feeling very sure of herself, basking in the deference being shown her by the Fleet's auditors. Jils knew that was likely to be an error of judgment on Brecinn's part. Fleet's auditors were in general not so quick to swallow a story—at least Jils hoped not.

"You've just come from the *Ragnarok*, Specialist Ivers," Brecinn pointed out, her tone at once unctuous and ingratiating. "What can you tell us that will shed light on the ship's truly inexplicable behavior?"

Brecinn's question was a challenge in good form. Jils thought about it. Brecinn had the advantage of prior persuasion on her side, having arrived here at Taisheki Station more than three days ago to make her case.

Her arrival in and of itself was suspect to Jils. Brecinn claimed that it was the critical nature of the *Ragnarok*'s crimes that had motivated her to leave her Command, but Jils suspected that upper Fleet echelons might well ask why she hadn't simply sent a courier. Or a priority transmit.

"I can tell the Bench specialist plenty," one of Brecinn's crew—a member of the preliminary assessment team that Jils had liberated from the *Ragnarok*—said. Her voice was venomous. "We've kept notes. I'm sorry about Rukota, Admiral, but he went over from the beginning. Noycannir and he must have been in collusion from the very start."

Noycannir. Yes. That was right. The Clerk of Court with whom ap Rhiannon was supposed to be conspiring was Dame Mergau Noycannir, from Chilleau Judiciary. So Brecinn hadn't heard. Verlaine had almost unquestionably been told by now. The Malcontent surely would have seen to that.

But since Brecinn didn't know it wasn't public knowledge yet, or even leaked out into the informal communications channels that existed side by side with official Fleet lines of transmissions. Not deeply enough for Brecinn to have heard, and if Jils had been Brecinn, she would have been listening very carefully to every tidbit of gossip that she'd been able to dig up on her way from Pesadie to Taisheki Station.

"Auditor, excuse the Pesadie team," Jils suggested. The fact that the news was clearly not out gave her all she needed to determine a strategy—only a temporary strategy—but it would serve to stabilize the situation here at the Fleet Audit Appeals Authority. "I have privileged information to impart."

She waited. Station Security validated the privacy fields; she spoke again, choosing her words carefully, trying not to enjoy herself more than she properly ought. "Dame Mergau Noycannir is the Clerk of Court you suspect of conspiracy with the *Ragnarok*, Admiral Brecinn?"

Brecinn was suspicious of the question, but she was trapped. There was no choice but to brazen this out now. "I do emphatically, Bench specialist." Oh. So polite. "And I can't help but suspect that she was involved in some plot or another with General Rukota. His presence at Pesadie Training Command might be taken as a little difficult to understand. A man with his connections can write his own posting-orders, after all."

Jils nodded. "Since this suggestion has been made, there is some information I need to share with you all. Noycannir has emphatically been implicated in a plot." Had unquestionably been plotting with somebody, and where had she got the Record to use for her forged evidence, if not from Pesadie Training Command? Jils didn't know. Stildyne hadn't let her examine the forged

Record, and she hadn't pressed the issue. It would all come out sooner or later: or not at all.

Brecinn seemed to know better than to let herself relax, even with this apparently encouraging information. She waited silently for Jils to continue; and the auditors—three of them—waited, too. It would be disobliging not to do so.

"But is unlikely to have been plotting with the *Ragnarok*. Because she has in fact attempted to assassinate its Chief Medical Officer. This behavior seems too contradictory for someone in collusion with the *Ragnarok*'s Command; Koscuisko was at home, out of the way. It just draws attention to Noycannir. Some other explanation must be sought." There was no need to mention the fact that Noycannir was dead.

Brecinn was not stupid enough to blurt out any self-incriminating denial of whatever Noycannir might have had to say about *her*; not yet. There would be time. And there would be the Protocols, when the time came, though Koscuisko was unlikely to be the man who would implement them. Ever again.

"So I don't need to tell you how delicate the situation is, Auditors. Dame Noycannir is clearly associated with Chilleau Judiciary. The Second Judge's platform attacks the entire system of Inquiry, and a Clerk of Court from Chilleau has tried to kill Andrej Koscuisko. I have to take immediate action."

Not the action that Brecinn might expect her to undertake. She needed to get to Chilleau, consult with Verlaine about the forged Record. Noycannir's crime could destroy the Second Judge's chances to be First Judge once and for all. And Verlaine had convinced her that he was sincere, which meant that Chilleau's bid for control of the Bench was the best hope for reform of the Judicial system she was likely to see in her lifetime—however much was left to her of that.

"What action, Bench specialist, if we may ask?" Senior Auditor Ormbach's voice was calm and politely curious, but Jils thought she could hear an undercurrent of amusement. Well. Brecinn had clearly felt confident of a sympathetic ear at Taisheki Station, and to a certain extent she had gotten it. But the Auditor was not turning off her own skeptical chaff detector, not even for Admiral Sandri Brecinn.

That heartened Jils. It meant that Taisheki Station might not be corrupt, though Brecinn seemed to be relying upon it to be. Jils didn't care for players in principle. Wasn't that ap Rhiannon's stance as well?

"I need to quarantine Admiral Brecinn and her team. This information is too potentially divisive to be leaked by mischance." Let alone on purpose, through a network of people who would take action to maximize their security and profit. "I will travel with the *Ragnarok* to Chilleau Judiciary to consult with Noycannir's superiors and determine what should be done. I'll want Safes. Bond-involuntary troops are Fleet resources, after all. It's our duty to safeguard them."

She didn't know how the *Ragnarok*'s Bonds were taking things. That was only part of the point. The larger part of the point was that a ship traveling under appeal put any assigned Bonds on Safe. Therefore she would put the *Ragnarok*'s Bonds on Safe: to confirm that the *Ragnarok* was traveling as a ship under appeal. A ship with a protected legal status. A very visible ship, one which could not be quietly shunted off to one side and consumed piece by piece, ship and crew.

"I understand," Admiral Brecinn said. Nobody had asked her. She did understand, Jils was sure of it; and was doing what she could to change her future. "You may rely on my discretion with absolute confidence, Bench specialist."

That wasn't going to be necessary.

"I agree to sanitary quarantine for Admiral Brecinn and her people," Auditor Ormbach said. "And to release the Safes, though I meant the *Ragnarok* to come here for them. But in light of your evidence, it is crucial that the ship not be permitted to remain in possession of a battle cannon. If their motivations are unworrisome, they should have no objection to surrendering the contraband item to be placed into Evidence."

This was unpleasantly unexpected, but not in the least remarkable. Unfortunately. "I have no personal knowledge of the existence of such a piece of contraband," Jils said, carefully. She had been told that the evidence

against Pesadie Training Command included a black-
market, main battle cannon, and its munitions load on
top of it. She had not actually seen the cannon, however.
"Consider your request, please, Auditor."

If the contraband that the Auditor demanded existed
only in Brecinn's imagination, the *Ragnarok* could only
prove that by submitting to an intrusive and time-
consuming search by Taisheki Station resources. Jils
couldn't wait. Nor could she afford to leave the *Ragnarok* vulnerable here, lest Koscuisko play his trump to
protect his ship.

And if the *Ragnarok* surrendered a contraband cannon, by the time it all came to explanations who knew
what the audit trail would look like?

"Questions have been raised as to the motivation and
loyalty of the *Ragnarok*'s chain of command, Specialist
Ivers, and an officer of the Court at Chilleau Judiciary
has by your report attempted to kill one of the *Ragnarok*'s officers. If the ship is armed, I cannot let it leave
here. I'm sorry. I see no alternative that would not be
grossly irresponsible."

Well, Auditor Ormbach was right. As long as there
was a main battle cannon unaccounted for, it would be
criminal negligence on Auditor Ormbach's part to permit a potentially compromised warship with an under-
standably aggrieved senior officer to leave the system.

Unless.

"Safes, Senior Auditor. I will take them with me as a
token of goodwill on your part, and convey your instructions to the *Ragnarok*'s Command and General Staff."
She'd get the Safes. She'd have Brecinn and Brecinn's
team sequestered under strict quarantine, not an uncomfortable imprisonment by any means, but bound to be
boring.

She had to get to Chilleau Judiciary, and the *Ragnarok* with her, so that she could get space between
Fleet and Jennet ap Rhiannon, so that the First Secretary could offer Koscuisko his personal assurances and
discuss mutual concerns. "As you say, Bench specialist,"
Auditor Ormbach agreed. "And we will in the mean
time initiate appropriate precautions."

And she had to hold the secret of the forged Record,

if she could, until after the Selection. It was not a very closely kept secret. Everyone who had been there in the great hall of Chelatring Side was in a position to know, but the Malcontent could do the damage control there. She had to trust the Malcontent for that. Bench specialists didn't like having to trust anything or anybody, but there was no help for that now.

After the Selection they could expose the fraudulent Record under Bench seal, and cancel any charges outstanding against those troops for whose sake Jennet ap Rhiannon had dared so much. She would log Koscuisko's documents then. He would be relieved of Writ. She would find a way to make it all come out right—once the Selection had been safely completed.

Stildyne helped Andrej up onto the upper tier in the little room, letting him down gently onto the slatted bench as Andrej grunted in reluctant discomfort. Andrej didn't think it was the wound in his shoulder. That was healing nicely now, from the inside out as desired; and the tissue itself was carefully protected by a therapeutic breathable membrane—one that would have to be exchanged soon, which was the only reason that Narion had allowed him into the sauna at all. And then only with strict conditions about heat and humidity.

"All right, sir?" Stildyne asked, with his hand at the back of Andrej's neck to keep his head from knocking up against the wall before Stildyne had had a chance to pad the point of contact with a folded towel. It was perhaps not absolutely necessary for Stildyne to be handling him so carefully, but Andrej couldn't begrudge it.

Stoshik had been right. He had wronged Stildyne. He was not going to make it right, either, because he couldn't imagine such a thing as that; but he could try to accept care more gracefully than he had in the past, with more self-awareness in his acceptance of courtesies that he had become dangerously close to taking for granted.

"Thank you, Brachi, it is fine." It wasn't the wound. It was his entire body. Strapped into a stasis-mover and scarcely conscious for all of that time, his arms ached and his back hurt, his neck was stiff, the muscles in his belly sore, his legs uncomfortable. They had done him

good service at Chelatring Side. But he had unquestionably annoyed them. "I am more travel sore than conva-
lescent. It is why I so particularly wanted a sauna."

Turning away without replying Stildyne crossed to the
other side of the room to settle himself on the lower
bench. It wasn't far across the room, since it was a sauna.
Stildyne's choice of the lower bench was the only way
Andrej could look Stildyne in the eye at that small distance, what with the difference of height between them.

At eye level, the impact of the rest of Stildyne's all
but naked body was manageable. Andrej had been taking saunas with Stildyne for years; he was accustomed
to the experience, but it was still a sometimes stressful
one. Stildyne's body was scarred as well as Stildyne's
face, and if the scars were not as disfiguring, they were
spread over a much larger canvas. Who was to say
whether the cumulative impact was more or less awful
accordingly?

"You'll have noticed that things are a little different on
board since we got back," Stildyne suggested. Andrej
closed his eyes and let his body drink in the grateful heat
of the sauna. He could feel his muscles relax. He had not
lied to Narion; it was simple therapy. The fact that he liked
sauna was a side benefit only, and the fact that sauna was
one of the few places on board the *Ragnarok* where a man
could be almost alone was also beside the point.

"Our Command Branch officers are out of their minds.
Yes. I had noticed." Lieutenant ap Rhiannon was a piece
of work if he'd ever seen one, and it was hard for him to
take her solemn assumption of her duties with a straight
face. Except that the other officers seemed to have no such
difficulty. Andrej hadn't decided yet whether they were
perhaps playing an elaborate practical joke on him. "I
think I like Command Branch better that way."

"Problem, though, Andrej." Stildyne's voice was grave
and considered, and Andrej thought his name sounded
very odd in Stildyne's mouth. Because it sounded just
like "Excellency" sounded, when Stildyne said it to him
rather than First Officer. "I've been talking to people.
If ap Rhiannon doesn't like what she hears when Specialist Ivers gets back from Taisheki Station, she's
leaving."

Andrej thought about this. Stildyne was right to be concerned, of course. Based on her actions since he had left, there seemed little doubt that the woman had become desperate. Did he not know what madwomen were capable of? Had he not the hole in his shoulder to prove it?

"I'm not sure what she might think she could accomplish by defying the entire Jurisdiction, Fleet and Bench alike." Wait, he couldn't say that. That was precisely what he meant to do. "I'm not about to leave my Infirmary at the mercy of a maniac. We have had quite enough of that already. Where the ship goes, I will go also."

He was in for the duration now. He could not in honor leave until the issue of the forged Record had been resolved to his satisfaction, if only by placing it into Evidence. As long as it was an undisclosed forgery, it threatened his people.

And yet Specialist Ivers had been right: if he valued the Second Judge's plans for a change in the system of Inquiry, he could not afford to place so destructive a weapon as the forged Record in the hands of Chilleau Judiciary's political enemies. So long as the Record lay undisclosed, he had to keep with it; and for so long as that, he could not have the relief of Writ completed.

"I'm glad to hear that. Sir. So will your people be."

The outer door into the changing room had opened. Andrej saw movement through the window in the door. Stildyne fell silent. Stildyne was up to something. After a moment, the inner door came open, and the First Officer came into the sauna. Andrej stared. He had never seen First Officer in a sauna.

He had never seen First Officer out of uniform that he could remember, and there was no rank on the towel that Mendez held in one hand. Stepping carefully past Stildyne's scarred knees Mendez took a position beside Stildyne, close to the back wall, and laid his towel across his lap.

"Good-greeting," Mendez said. "Warm enough for you? I don't know how you breathe in here, Andrej."

Andrej didn't know what to say. He was too surprised. He had grasped that Stildyne had a plot in motion; but he had to process the apparition of Ralph Mendez, third of three so named, in a sauna before he could begin to parse the meaning of it out.

"Just getting to the good part, First Officer," Stildyne said.

Mendez nodded. "What's he say, then, Brachi?"

"Means to stick it out. At least at first mention. But I haven't explained the problem to him yet."

Andrej caught his breath. "Speak to me," he said. "Explain. What problem? I do not tolerate to be ambushed, Brachi. Confess yourself at once, and with completeness."

Stildyne looked startled; Andrej considered that he had perhaps not yet quite readjusted to the Standard-speaking world. It was true that such language could be taken as referring to formal Inquiry, here—rather than a simple demand for an explanation.

"Easy as this, Andrej," Mendez said, but considerately, as if aware of how strange what he had to say would sound. "Unprecedented circumstances make new rules. And we're glad to have you back, we're used to you, your Infirmary missed you. But. There's two parts to it. Only half is that you want to stay. The other half is if we're going to let you."

What was this *we*? "I don't understand."

"Captain knows you haven't had much time to think things through. You've come on board wounded, for one. And of all the people here on *Ragnarok* you've got the most to lose. She isn't sure she means to let you."

Staggering. Andrej sat and concentrated on taking a deep breath, calming himself, thinking this thing through.

"I could tell you a thing that would convince you, Ralph." He could. He could explain that it had not been Garol Vogel who had murdered Captain Lowden in Burkhayden, and Mendez would realize that Andrej had nothing to lose by staying with the *Ragnarok*, that Andrej was in danger—real, if of unquantifiable likelihood—of being called to give accounting for that crime. "If I have to, I will. I came back to this ship because I am more indebted to its crew than my blood kin. To suggest I go away to secure my privileges insults me."

Someone else. The door was opening again. Wheat-fields, in the name of all Saints, and if there was a very great deal of Stildyne when he took off his clothing there was altogether too much of Wheatfields to be tolerated.

"I appreciate that, Andrej." First Officer took no special notice of Wheatfields, who sat down next to Andrej himself on the bench—well toward the wall, to minimize proximity. The lower bench, and he was still taller than Andrej was. It was a setup. He would have a word to say to Stildyne when this was all over. "But we need more of a commitment from you than that. We need your support. You have to believe that ap Rhiannon is your Captain, Andrej, or it isn't going to work. Serge. Explain."

Wheatfields had closed his eyes, his head tilted back to the ceiling. He made Andrej nervous, sitting so close. "It's still a dirty secret," Wheatfields said. There was something in his voice that Andrej could not understand—humor? "Or at least no one has taken official notice, yet. But it's true, that rumor of Admiral Brecinn's. We are mutinous. You'd better be sure of what you decide, Koscuisko, because once you commit to this there's no going back."

Didn't they think he knew?

"For this reason you should agree that I must be here," Andrej said. Considering whether he should perhaps be furious. "Because so long as I am here, it will be that much more difficult to notice. Have I come from my home for those days in a stasis-mover to have my motivation questioned? What do you wish for me to do?"

All right, he was furious. Yes. During the time that Andrej had been assigned to this ship, Wheatfields had told him many things about himself—his character, his sexuality, a wide range of issues relevant to his personal value and right to breathe the same air as decent souls.

But never had it been suggested that he'd run from threat and leave his people to face hazard alone. Not until now. In all of this time, not even Wheatfields had called him a coward. It was possibly the only thing that Wheatfields had not called him, once "noble and beneficent" was ruled off the list.

"You've got people at home as well, Andrej," First Officer pointed out. "You've got that boy. Your Cousin Ferinc says he's a beautiful little man, and that your wife is waiting for you to come back and warm her sheets; I've talked to him. Bonds are Bonds, Andrej. That child is your son. Are you suggesting you care more about troops than your own child?"

It was a dirty question. Had it been Wheatfields who had asked it, Andrej would have struck him. But First Officer was out of reach.

"He is a beautiful child. Much more than I deserve. And I would deserve such a wife and such a child even less if I could turn my back on the *Ragnarok*, just when I might be able to help save the ship simply by staying here. It has not been Marana who has kept me from the abyss all these years, First Officer. It has been Robert. Lek. Pyotr. Stildyne. All Saints forbid I should say Wheatfields, even."

Again with the movement in the anteroom. Again with the opening of the door. Andrej closed his eyes tightly in horror. There were only two other officers with rank to match or to exceed his own on board the *Ragnarok*. And Two scuttled when she walked. What would Two even look like, in a towel?

Jennet ap Rhiannon stepped up to the upper tier opposite Wheatfields, and met Andrej's horrified gaze with a level stare. She was not Dolgorukij; and her towel was in her lap. She could not know what it was to show her shoulders. And yet she was to be his commanding officer—

"Yes?" ap Rhiannon asked. She was crèche-bred, there was that. The habit of command was easier for her than it might have been for Seascape, for instance. If Andrej concentrated on being angry, on how sore his muscles were, he might be able to ignore her shoulders. Her bare shoulders. Holy Mother. This was beyond reason.

"I think he means it, your Excellency," First Officer replied. "Respectfully suggest you let him tell you."

Captain. Captain ap Rhiannon. Shoulders or no shoulders. Yes. That was the way to do it. "Your Excellency," Andrej said. "I had not realized that there might be a

question. This is my ship, and I am under so much obligation to its crew that I cannot explain. It's true that I
have better to look forward to once out of Service than
the most of us, but that makes me more difficult to kill,
either by accident or by Judicial mandate. I am the chief
medical officer on the *Ragnarok*. Respectfully request I
be permitted to perform as such."

Petitioning, and petitioning this little Lieutenant, of all
people. This little Lieutenant had gotten Mendez and
Wheatfields to accept her, though, and the rest of the
officers and crew as well. If he respected his own medical
staff, he could not disregard that judgment.

"Wheatfields wants Secured Medical for storage," ap
Rhiannon said. "Any problems?"

No. None whatever. Why, did she think he'd come
back to the *Ragnarok* for that? "I have no difficulty
in surrendering Secured Medical for any purpose, your
Excellency. To the contrary, rather." They'd have to find
some place to keep the Record. Or maybe they would
just leave it there. It would still be a properly secured
place, after all, whether used for storage or for torture.

"Very well. If First Officer agrees. Resume your duties, Doctor Koscuisko. It's good to have you back. And
I'm leaving now. It's too hot in here. No, don't get up."

He hadn't thought about it, but the others had. He
could tell that he had some adjusting to do. There was
silence in the sauna for some moments as the Lieutenant—as the Captain dressed. When the outer door of
the changing room opened and closed again, Wheatfields
stood up.

"Later," Wheatfields said, to the First Officer. "And
no, I don't think we should do staff here. Don't get any
ideas, Koscuisko. Nothing is changed, but a ship needs
its Chief Medical."

That was a welcome home, Andrej supposed. Wheatfields let another gust of cooler air into the sauna on his
way out; all of this traffic was annoying, not relaxing.
Mendez yawned, and leaned back against the wall.

"Well, I don't know, it wouldn't be so bad. If it were
dry heat. You're not off the hook for information, Andrej. If we need it, we still need it, and you'll still be
our best man for the job."

If this hadn't been so serious it would be utterly surreal. "And you'll have it if you need it, First Officer, but it'll come out of Infirmary. Or maybe your office. With the right drugs. And none of the other—complications."

Mendez was right. If it came to getting information he could not refuse. Would not refuse, because no one else on board knew as much as he did about the Controlled List and how to use it, and letting anybody else try would be inefficient. As well as unnecessarily unpleasant. And illegal.

"You'd better start showing up for staff, then. But get dressed first, Andrej. You can't go wandering around the corridors in a towel. What a notion."

On that note Mendez left; there was peace in the sauna at last, and the friendly ticking of the thermostat as the heat increased once more to proper levels. Andrej sighed.

"I had not anticipated a challenge, Chief," he said.

Stildyne seemed to consider this as Andrej relaxed with his eyes closed, drinking in the soothing heat of the sauna. "It's not a rational choice, Andrej. You can't blame them. If they'd seen your house at the Matredonat you might never have been able to convince them."

He had a child, Mendez had said, a wife as well. Both of them waiting. But so had others here, no less dear than his, perhaps more so for having better contact. When would he return? Or would he ever?

"To say that trust and affection are worth more than property and privilege would be too much of a cliché. Even the Valcovniye saga avoided such, and you will remember that there is every other cliché in the canon in the Valcovniye, Brachi. And I therefore will avoid it also."

But they both knew it was true. Stildyne did not challenge the sentiment of this observation, apparently content to let Andrej have the last word—as had indeed been Stildyne's habit, all these years.

Andrej let the tension in his body dissolve into the steam of the sauna, and set his mind at rest.

Chapter Fourteen

Mutiny in Form

Cousin Ferinc woke up when the threshold alert sounded; someone had crossed the security line at the entrance to the thula's loading ramp. He sat up in his bed, swinging his legs over the edge to put feet to floor. It was his sleep shift, but a cruiserkiller-class warship ran four shifts a day.

It was Security. No, it was Lek Kerenko, who was coming down the corridor and talking as he came. "Really very sorry, Cousin. Permission to come on board. Captain very especially requesting. Are you awake? Anywhere?"

Speaking Standard. This was in Jurisdiction space. Ferinc shrugged his shoulders hastily into his sturdy waffle-weave shirt and tied himself decently covered across the front. "In here, Lek, coming directly. There is something the matter?"

"Captain," Lek repeated, with a turn of his head and a lift of his chin back over his shoulder. "To be seeing you. With your permission, she doesn't understand, but the officer is there."

Something wasn't adding up. Ferinc followed Lek out and down the thula's ramp to the docking apron. Lek's Captain was there, and Chief Stildyne. The Captain of the *Ragnarok*. Officers assigned, by the shade of black they wore; Koscuisko himself. Security behind him.

The sight made Ferinc blanch, but he was Malcontent, he was not who he had been. Koscuisko made no sign of intending any threat. Koscuisko looked pale, and Stildyne stood very close behind him; it had not been very long since Koscuisko had been cleared to resume his uniform. Hours at most, if Ferinc remembered the gossip correctly. He bowed with careful precision, and as a Malcontent, not a warrant officer. "Your Excellency."

She would initiate the conversation. She had the rank, even if the rank was all she had. The other officers were older, taller, more experienced; but it was all she needed, in this instance.

"They've started to mine the exit vector," the Captain said. "Specialist Ivers is en route back to the ship, but it's clear that Taisheki Station doesn't mean for us to leave. Therefore likely that it's not in our best interest to stay."

All very interesting. "Yes, your Excellency?" Mining the exit vector. That was extreme. It was also defensive; an interesting sort of a signal to send. "And what service may my holy Patron extend to your command under this circumstance?"

"I want the thula," ap Rhiannon said, and pointed. In case there could be any question here about which thula exactly, Ferinc supposed. "I need it to clear the mine field. I'll want to mount the battle cannon. And therefore."

Security stepped up, as if on cue. They were all around him. They were far enough away to present no immediate threat, but he was surrounded. "Therefore, I must regretfully take your ship, with my sincere apologies, but I must have it. Cousin. You will surrender your navigation keys."

The Devil he would.

Koscuisko put out his hand, shaking his head; they hadn't told Koscuisko. Well. Several of the officers here looked a little less than completely put together. It had been someone else's sleep shift, too; ap Rhiannon had probably come as soon as she'd been told that Taisheki Station had started to mine the vector. As soon as the Intelligence Officer had woken her up to tell her that.

"Captain," Koscuisko said. "Your Excellency. With respect. It's not his ship, it's the Saint's. He can't surrender it. There must be a way around this. Because if I allow the Malcontent to be separated from his ship by force, I'm in much worse trouble with the Saint than any seven Benches could ever cause me."

Ap Rhiannon didn't know about Malcontents and it was obvious that she didn't care. "I'm sorry, your Excellency, but you also have no choice. I must have the speed and the carrying capacity. Serge thinks we can clear the mine field with the thula. Otherwise it's engaging artiplats with Wolnadis, and we'll lose them all. I'm not asking for your cooperation, Cousin Ferinc. I arrest you fairly and openly. You should suffer no adverse consequences from your superiors."

Koscuisko moved to grasp the Captain's arm and remonstrate with her. Stildyne put his hand to Koscuisko's shoulder; Koscuisko started back with such a look of surprise on his face that Ferinc could have laughed. Stildyne's expression had not changed.

This was fun. But it could not be allowed to drag on; Lek was starting to become uncomfortable, among other things. It would be self-indulgent of him to let misunderstandings multiply. Cousin Stanoczk expected better of him.

"I cannot surrender the ship, your Excellency, or transfer navigation keys. I have a sacred duty to my Patron. To fail in that would grieve my divine Patron, to whose affection I am more deeply indebted than I can explain." The Security around him shifted, just so he would remember that they were there. It would do them no good. He had his orders.

He explained. "I must faithfully carry out my orders to accompany the son of the Koscuisko prince to his ship of assignment, there to perform what tasks it should please him to nominate to me until such time as he should send us both back to Azanry—the ship and I— and forgive us for our errors." The Malcontent should have seen Noycannir coming. They should have known what she'd had in mind. It was the genuinely mad that were as dangerous as that, because their next moves could never be predicted with certainty.

Lek seemed to relax.

"The 'son of the Koscuisko prince'?" The tallest officer would be the Chigan Ship's Engineer, by repute. So the officer who was talking was the Ship's First. He might have been Ship's First some day, Ferinc thought; Stildyne would have been a Ship's First right now, if it hadn't been for Andrej Koscuisko. No. He never would have been Ship's First. He hadn't had the moral fiber for it. "That's you, Andrej. Isn't it?"

"At least for now," Koscuisko agreed a little sourly, his eyes fixed on Ferinc's face. He knew. But Ferinc had just been having a little bit of fun, that had been all. No harm to it, surely. "Ferinc, has my cousin Stanoczk truly granted me the use of this fine beast?"

"And me with it," Ferinc confirmed. Then he wished he hadn't expressed himself in quite that way, but Koscuisko didn't seem to notice. Koscuisko turned to his Captain, and bowed.

"I withdraw my objection, your Excellency. We may in fact fully exploit this thula. Cousin Ferinc will extend every possible assistance to ensure a successful mission, is that not so, Ferinc?"

"Yes, your Excellency," Ferinc answered, obediently, but hearing Marana's tone in Koscuisko's voice. Being very stern with her child Anton. It was a shame Koscuisko had not stayed at home, but Ferinc would not be sorry for a chance to see Marana perhaps again.

Ap Rhiannon looked from Ferinc to Koscuisko and back again; then shrugged her shoulders, as if dismissing the whole interchange as parochial in nature. "Very well, Doctor, Cousin Ferinc. Thank you. I have asked General Rukota to evaluate whether and how the main battle cannon can be installed in the thula's forward emplacement. If you will work with him, Cousin Ferinc. Will the ship support it?"

It had been built as a courier. But Fleet's couriers had been armed. "Specifications support main battle cannon and subsidiary stations. I will translate ship's comps for the General, your Excellency." Whoever he was. What was a General doing on a battleship? Generals were ground forces.

"Coordinate also then with my First Officer, Cousin Ferinc, on the ship's performance characteristics. We'll need to select a crew very carefully. The mine field will be almost fully deployed by the time we can get there, and we'll need the pathway clear before we can safely start a vector spin."

Or complete one successfully, to be more precise, but he took the point. "According to her Excellency's good pleasure," Ferinc said, bowing.

Koscuisko looked genuinely startled. Ferinc was a little startled to hear it from his own mouth under these circumstances himself. "Carry on," ap Rhiannon said. "With all deliberate speed. We don't have much time."

Turning, she walked away; Security went with her.

Koscuisko gave Ferinc a fish-eyed stare. "It is true, this dish you have invited to taste my Captain?" Koscuisko demanded. "Or another filthy Malcontent trick of some sort?"

"Blood-guilt, your Excellency, with regards to the incident at Chelatring Side. Truly. I wouldn't dare lie to you, sir."

Koscuisko was not convinced. "You should know better, Ferinc, but you are Malcontent and have no shame accordingly. And no sense of proportion. If you do not need me, First Officer, I go back to bed."

The officer Koscuisko had addressed nodded. "Leave us Kerenko, Andrej. We may want to talk to him. All right, Lek?"

Lek was under Bond. And yet Lek seemed to be dealing with this outrageously anomalous situation without much difficulty. Was it true what he had heard, that Koscuisko had liberated his bond-involuntaries through the shocking expedient of treating them like feeling souls?

"Very good, First Officer," Lek said, with a crisp salute. If Lek could fly the ship on a mine-clearing mission, it would help. Because Lek could really, really fly the thula. Ferinc could never have managed to locate the *Ragnarok* on vector transit on his own. Lek was good at this.

"Over to you, General," First Officer said, to the only other man left on the docking apron who had yet to speak. "General Dierryk Rukota, Koscuisko's Cousin Ferinc. Cousin Ferinc, General Dierryk Rukota. Gentlemen. Good-greeting, then. Andrej. Let's go get our naps in."

Stildyne would stay as well. Good, Ferinc could use

Stildyne. And all of the rest of the rank could just clear the docking apron and let them get to work.

"Kospodar thula," General Rukota said. He was a big man as Stildyne was big, but ugly in his own special way. Thin lips. Narrow eyes. Strong nose. "Take me through her, if you will, Cousin Ferinc. We've got to get her armed and deployed as soon as possible, if we've got a hope of breaking out."

Which did rather raise the issue of whether it was worth the effort to try. But it was their business. Not his. He just flew the ship—or navigated, with Lek on board—and followed his reconciler's orders. Or what his reconciler would have told him to do, if he'd been here.

"Starting at the forward emplacement, then, General Rukota." This would be fun. He'd never seen a mutiny in progress; wait till he got home, and told Stanoczk.

Jils Ivers stood before the Captain's Bar in the mess area where the *Ragnarok*'s officers held their staff meetings. There was a place for her at the table between the Captain and the First Officer, but she didn't feel like sitting down.

"Yes. They are mining the vector." There was no question about it; certainly no attempted subterfuge was any use. "I can't really dispute with Auditor Ormbach's point. I've convinced her that the *Ragnarok* has good reason to be antipathetic to Chilleau Judiciary. And if Brecinn's claims are correct the *Ragnarok* itself, as well as its Wolnadi fighters, is armed. Which makes the *Ragnarok* dangerous."

She didn't say "makes you dangerous." She didn't say "loose cannon." She didn't need to waste her breath. The *Ragnarok* had decided that it was in its best interest to leave the moment Taisheki Station had moved to ensure that it stayed. It was classic.

It was a disaster.

How could this ship have frozen so concretely in support of one acting crèche-bred Command Branch officer? It couldn't have. Ap Rhiannon had a lot going for her in the moral outrage department, that was clear, but for the *Ragnarok* to be functioning as well as it had been was a clear indication of genuine mutuality of goals. Ap

Rhiannon spoke for the *Ragnarok*, but she seemed perfectly aware that it was the crew who were in command of the ship.

"Engineer?" ap Rhiannon asked. "Your status, please."

Wheatfields straightened up in his chair, which brought his head that much closer to the ceiling. "Escape vector for Amberlin across Taisheki vector has been registered and read in, your Excellency. By your command."

Amberlin was uncontrolled space, well forward of the rule of Law. It was a notorious nest of vagabonds, derelicts, refugees, and rabble-rousers, with a thriving black market; Jils could understand the choice. If need should be the *Ragnarok* could survive there for an indeterminate period of time, taking what they needed as they found it—or would they prey on the stores of reasonable people for supplies, as they had done when they'd acquired the battle cannon?

Since activity in Amberlin was illegal by definition, they would have no necessary concerns about abusing the innocent. Staying out of the way of the powerful criminal fleets, now—that would be an interesting problem.

"We can be assured that Fleet will not pursue us to Amberlin." Ap Rhiannon could make that statement with such absolute conviction because so far Fleet itself had been unable to make an impression on the extralegal, ad-hoc governments that fielded their fleets in Amberlin space. "And we may have the opportunity to demonstrate our loyalty on a small scale where we can, while we pursue our appeal. First Officer. What if Taisheki Station should engage?"

The *Ragnarok* clearly meant to make no secret of its intentions; the speed with which the *Ragnarok* would be traveling would be enough of a signal. Taisheki might well field its small force of corvettes. How successfully could they resist? These were all their own people. Fleet.

Mendez glanced at the Engineer's blank, impassive face before responding. "The thula will be clearing the mine field, your Excellency. It can run interference for us. Fleet won't want to have to pay the Malcontent for the machine. They're expensive. It'll be tight, maneuvering the ship back up into the maintenance atmosphere on our way out, but using it will effectively control our exposure."

The Kospodar thula was as nimble as a Wolnadi, significantly superior for speed. With a main battle cannon for ginger, it could potentially hold off any Fleet pursuit short of a cruiserkiller-class warship like the *Ragnarok* itself.

"Very well, First Officer," ap Rhiannon said. "Do you have a crew on line?"

Interesting question, Jils thought. There was only one crew here on the *Ragnarok* that had any experience at all flying the thula: and one of them was under Bond. Under Safe, now, as First Officer had distributed those she had brought with her from Taisheki Station; but there were limits. The Safe only silenced the governor itself. It was fear of the governor that ruled a bond-involuntary; at least that was the theory.

This time Mendez's thoughtful gaze rested upon Chief Medical's aristocratic Aznir face for just that one moment before he spoke. Looked pale, Koscuisko did. Of course Koscuisko always looked pale, to her. "Elements of Security 5.1 for dedicated flight, your Excellency—and Lek Kerenko won't hear of being excluded. He flew her for three days, he says, he can fly her now."

"Safe or no Safe, First Officer," Jils said, just to remind them that she was here. "There's conditioning. It's not fair to the troop. Even if he is the best man on board for the job."

Ap Rhiannon frowned, tearing bits of rewrap off the lip of her bean-tea flask absentmindedly; Koscuisko spoke.

"It is true that he desires the thula, carnally." Koscuisko was clearly unwilling to hazard his people—but sensibly aware, not only that they were not his people to hazard, but also that the entire ship was equally at risk. "Also that they speak something close to the same language. If his officer of assignment were to be present, is it not possible that he could be clear to perform?"

His officer of assignment? Andrej Koscuisko? A medical officer, commanding a combat action?

The Engineer was shaking his head, apparently unimpressed. "You'd have to be there, Andrej, not just on the com, since they could jam the com. He's got to be completely convinced that he's in the clear with you, even on Safe. And what happens if he buckles in mid-flight?"

"But I mean to be there, if that is what it takes." Koscuisko challenged Wheatfields flatly, without the polite fiction of deferring to Command to soften his attack. "Lek and I have much more history together than just to be assigned each to the other on board of the *Ragnarok*. He and I also speak something close to the same language."

First Officer had put his head down into his hands, rubbing his forehead with a slow repetitive contemplative gesture. Wheatfields looked to ap Rhiannon, now; and after a moment—as if realizing his error, reminding himself that he was not in fact master in this room—Koscuisko did the same.

The personality interplay was fascinating.

Mere days on board, and Koscuisko was fitting himself in as though he'd never left. With occasional disconnects, yes, which would doubtless always be arising.

"If First Officer accepts your reasoning, Doctor, it shall be so," ap Rhiannon said. She could safely rely on Koscuisko's judgment; Jils knew that. Koscuisko would never have been as good as he was at what he did if he couldn't judge how far a person could be pushed, and with what stimulus, and under what kinds and degrees of pressure.

If Koscuisko said that Lek Kerenko could pilot the thula against the Fleet in overt action against the Bench authority, then Kerenko could do it. Ap Rhiannon's reservations appeared to have a slightly different focus— "If Fleet finds out you're on the ship, though, your Excellency, they're going to want to force you into Taisheki Station."

Which attempt would logically require the diversion of at least some of the corvettes Taisheki might send after them, leaving the *Ragnarok* with a clear run at the vector. But what if they were to lose their Ship's Surgeon?

"All the more motivation, your Excellency." Koscuisko's determination could not be shaken. "They would kill my Kerenko. They would take me hostage against my family and the Selection. She is a Kospodar thula, she belongs to the Malcontent. She will not betray us to Fleet."

Running his fingers up through his black-and-silver hair, Mendez blinked at ap Rhiannon with owlish eyes, green and genial. "Never argue with the medic, or the paymaster, or stores-and-receipts, your Excellency. So. Lek on the hot seat. Ferinc will have to stay here, of course, he hasn't declared war on Taisheki Station. Security 5.1 will take the rest of the flight tasks. They've had practice."

So they had. Practice under pressure, running hard from Azanry to Taisheki Station, intercepting the *Ragnarok* en route. Impressive flying.

"That weaponer has never fired a main battle cannon, First Officer," ap Rhiannon reminded him. Or at least seemed to remind him. Mendez nodded, lifting one finger of his knuckly right hand to mark his point.

"Avenham has, though, your Excellency. A few others, but she's got the most experience. Wheatfields and I have picked out a few more to man the guns we've borrowed from the Wolnadis. Close your ears, Bench specialist."

Too late. Jils sighed. "I'll be in my quarters," she decided, aloud. There was a Lieutenant's berth empty that she was using; they were keeping Rukota in another, and so far as Jils could tell he was feeling right at home. "Not noticing."

Ap Rhiannon nodded at her, so that she could take her leave and go without being rude. "I'll send for you when we're on vector, Bench specialist. You can contact Chilleau Judiciary at that time, if you wish."

Not before. That went without saying. Bowing, Jils turned and walked away, out of the room, and left the Captain and the crew of the Jurisdiction Fleet Ship *Ragnarok* to plot their mutiny in peace.

And now great *Ragnarok* stood steady—but too strong—for the Taisheki entry vector, and no one who had had any last-minute doubts could question her intentions any longer.

The mine field, the network of linked artillery stations that was to have denied the warship access to the vector, had yet to be completely fielded. Forward sensors clearly revealed the emplacement crews struggling with all of their might to throw the net at its full three-sixty orb around the near approach to the entry vector: but it would only take twelve, not more than sixteen, well-aimed shots to blow a hole in the unmanned portion of the fire wall and clear the *Ragnarok*'s route for the Taisheki vector, and Amberlin space.

Andrej Koscuisko stood in the thula's wheelhouse, listening to the confused babble of common-feeds coming in from four and five plaits at once. Emplacement crews, working at fever pitch. Two's comps talking to Engineering about the state of space ahead.

The gantry officer, talking Lek and Taller through their careful passage down past the lateral gap that had been left unhulled until the last so that the thula could go—and, of course, get back—before the final seal would be required preparatory to gaining the vector.

And, of course, the communication he was most interested in, the loudest strongest feed, Jennet ap Rhiannon versus Taisheki Station. "Fleet Receiving, Taisheki Station. This is acting Captain Jennet ap Rhiannon, Jurisdiction Fleet Ship *Ragnarok*, commanding."

The formal—lesser—rank sounded a little odd, to Andrej. It had been easier than he had expected to fall into the same habit that the other Ship's Primes had apparently developed, and take her for his Captain in deed as well as in word.

Stand by the thula, he heard the gantry officer say, *go for terce-tumble on mark. Two. Three. Four.*

"*Ragnarok*, this is Taisheki Station Receiving. Welcome to Taisheki Station, your Excellency. Please direct your craft through to docking facilities on transmit, estimated transit time three hours Standard."

There was a schematic displayed forward, beneath the primary spatial. Andrej could watch the thula make its move, sinking gently through the narrow gap remaining between the massive stalloy staves of the maintenance atmosphere's hull. It was a delicate business; he knew it from Taller's tension, Lek's concentration, and the calm steady voice of the gantry officer as she spoke. *Hold at five for now, we need to adjust. Good. Thula, make your drop.*

The thula cleared the *Ragnarok*'s maintenance hull and pivoted to align to the ship's axis. The gantry communication line went mute, to give the airspace over to the Engineer. On the public braid their Captain was not cooperating.

"Respectfully decline to enter Taisheki Station, Receiving Officer. We cannot comply with your request to submit to board and search, still less to surrender any troops assigned without presentation of a fully executed Bench warrant."

Detachment of heavy Security is on alert, Two's feed broke in. *Due to clear ready-state in two eighths, Standard. Estimated transit time to maneuver field, five eighths. These indications are on balance positive. So far.*

"Captain. Administrative procedures at Taisheki Station are at the discretion of the Fleet Audit Appeals Authority. Respectfully remind the *Ragnarok* that it has been administratively reassigned and directed to report."

Thula, take your targets, you know the grid. Field on command. The Engineer's voice was as calm as if he'd been discussing clearing a passage through a rock-cloud, rather than selectively attacking an orb of mechanized artillery platforms. At least Andrej hoped—knew they all hoped—that the platforms they were going to hit were mechanized. Because they were going to have to hit them one way or the other.

"Receiving Officer, an Appeal having been made in good form and formally accepted, the *Ragnarok* has been directed to Taisheki Station pending the initiation of an investigation. Recurrence of requirements previously protested indicates an investigation targeted against the *Ragnarok*, rather than of this ship's duly logged and registered Appeal."

The remote forward was beginning to pick up an on-screen trace. A set of eight blips, from the lower middle-right octant, beginning to pulse and brighten on the screen. Those heavy Security, Andrej supposed. And the thula was to engage them as well, if it came to that; or at least stand between them and the *Ragnarok*, if they could not clear in time.

"Willing to stand by to negotiate entry into Taisheki Station after dismantling of mine field currently emplaced," ap Rhiannon suggested helpfully.

If it came to engaging heavy Security, they would find out how intent Fleet was on preserving the thula—on preserving him—from destruction. Andrej was not unafraid: but all the same, Andrej knew for a fact that it was better to be here, in the thula, with his people, even if he had to die. Better than to be alive with Fleet, if *Ragnarok* should be destroyed, whether quickly in battle or more slowly through the deliberate predations of a Fleet Interrogations Group.

"Ragnarok." The voice of the Receiving Officer was beginning to show some signs of wear around the edges. "You are directed to proceed to docking facilities. Failure to comply with a direct lawful order is a violation of Fleet protocols and severely handicaps the investigation of your Appeal."

Security 5.1 was here, with Chief Stildyne on one of the weapons ports. Another weaponer had been borrowed from one of Wheatfields's teams; Wheatfields himself—Andrej noted, with a certain degree of detached amusement—seemed to be getting anxious about things, from the tone of his voice over braid.

Captain. Request vector initiate. With respect, we should start thinking about getting out of here.

But ap Rhiannon was cooperating with Wheatfields to approximately the same degree as she was with Taisheki Station—hardly at all. She didn't answer Wheatfields, not directly. She didn't need to. "Any order to place my Command at the mercy of arbitrary and unjustified Inquiries is not lawful. It will not be possible for us to comply with an illegitimate instruction. Please advise."

Target acquisition complete on fire-funnel, Taller was telling Engineering, over his board-plait. *Require clearances for sweep, at your command, confirm.*

Although the stress in the air was almost palpable Lek did not seem to be feeling any special pressure from his governor, at least not yet. Ap Rhiannon was being very clear: Taisheki Station's insistence that they enter was not lawful. The harder part for Lek would come later, when they had to defend themselves by taking offensive action.

And if he had been wrong about Lek's Safe and his personal authority, they were all as good as dead already, and the *Ragnarok* with them. At least in theory. Andrej was as certain as he had to be that they could do it, even with such a penalty for miscalculation staring him in the face from the grim shadows of the forward screens.

Taisheki Station had clearly reached the end of its patience. "As you wish, *Ragnarok*. Be advised that failure to comply with instructions will be interpreted as mutinous in intent and execution, and will be prosecuted to the fullest extent of the Law. You are directed—for the last time—to break speed and alter course for docking facilities, there to be boarded and secured pending a full Fleet inquiry."

That had cut it. Andrej scanned the back of Lek's shoulders, the tilt of his head, for any sign of conflict or of hesitation; and found none.

"Taisheki Station. You are out of order, Receiving Officer. We are unable in justice to comply with your demands. You leave us with no choice but to protect the integrity of this Command pending a full and fair investigation of our Appeal. Engineering. Your action."

Well, they were down to it, then, weren't they?

"Thank you, your Excellency." Now that ap Rhiannon had cut the braid to Taisheki Station, Wheatfields was coming over their line. "Thula, we need those artillery platforms taken out. We'll do what we can to hold the heavy Security off your tail, if need should be. Go for it."

"Confirm and comply," Lek answered, as cheerfully as if it were a leave-detail he was to move forward, and not a warship. "Thula away. Weaponers. Confirm assignment targets. Excellency, if you would strap in, sir."

It was almost the first indication that Lek even remembered that he was there. Andrej didn't want to take the single step back to his observer's station and strap in; he wanted to be as close to Lek as he could be, in

case there should begin to be a problem. But he had no
intention of arguing with Lek. He was far from his primary competencies—in command for legal purposes, but
by no means in charge.

The thula leaped away from the underbelly of the
Ragnarok, its transit showing on the forward screens as
a sudden shift in orders of magnitude as it made for the
artillery net. A good thing he was webbed in after all,
Andrej told himself. There was no motion to be sensed
on board the ship, no; but the rate of change on the
forward display was enough to make him dizzy.

Five eighths to come to speed, six eighths after that
to enter the artillery net's kill-zone. It would take *Ragnarok* nearly six times as long to follow, what with size
and rates of acceleration taken into account. That meant
nearly four eights, once all the eighths were totaled, for
the *Ragnarok* to transit the fields of fire, unless they
cleared a hole in the net.

Four eights . . . the sixteenth part of a shift, the sixty-
fourth part of a day. Too long, any way one looked at
it. Even with the thula's advantage of speed it seemed
too long to Andrej, because there were detail screens up
along the perimeter of the ship's main forwards, and
he could see the battery guns start to turn—taking aim
at them.

Wasn't it about time they shot at something?

A tone on Taller's board from the chief weaponer,
sounding clearly in the quiet of the wheelhouse. Taller
turned in his seat and looked back over his shoulder,
nodding in response to Andrej's questioning look. Oh.
Good. Time for his contribution, then.

Clearing his throat, Andrej toggled his braid to transmit. He'd rehearsed this, because it was critical that he
got it right, and they would have only this one chance.
The thula was gaining on an artillery platform at an
astounding rate: but there were so many of them out
there, and all turning slowly but surely to target the *Ragnarok* as she came—

"This is Andrej Ulexeievitch. Koscuisko." He was
thinking in Aznir, under pressure. There was no particular reason for Fleet to know who Andrej Ulexeievitch
was, let alone why he might bear listening to.

"I am in receipt of direct orders from my superior commanding officer to clear the transit lane for my parent ship. I have therefore issued orders in turn that the artillery platforms capable of impacting the transit lane be removed from operation. If there are any crew on any platforms—"

One of the side-screens went white as phosphorus; they had been fired upon, though not hit. It was nothing personal. The artillery platforms that comprised the mine field would have been given precoded instructions to fire automatically on whomever came within range without prior clearances. Andrej finished his assigned speech as smoothly as he could, surprised at his emotional reaction—anger. They were shooting at him. Were they, indeed?

"—within the defined transit lane you are cautioned to identify and evacuate. Firing will commence in three eighths. You have three eighths to identify and initiate evacuation. Koscuisko away, the thula."

The Malcontent's ship moved more quickly than the artillery batteries could efficiently track; the artiplats were designed to stop larger ships—and few ships as small as a Kospodar thula carried sufficient firepower to seriously endanger one of them. Would Fleet be expecting a threat from the thula? Taisheki Station surely knew from Admiral Brecinn that the *Ragnarok* had acquired a main battle cannon from Silboomie Station.

"Coming up on t-minus one, mark. Shani. Alport. Go."

The intership braid had cleared to all-ship access, now; Andrej could hear the weaponers exchange information. They needed to hear what was happening: because Taller and Lek were responsible for getting the thula to precisely where the weaponers needed it to be, and they could only spare the three weaponers to watch for rounds directed at the ship itself.

There was a flare, off to the side of the main screen. A voice Andrej didn't think he recognized. "Successful intercept, Chief. Confirm."

They were still within target overlap, the kill-zone. Surely almost clear by now, past the barrier that the overlapping fields of fire represented, through to the other side of the mine field, where only the closest artiplat would threaten the thula—because the ranges between them had been calculated carefully, each platform just less than twice the linear range of any one of them. Unfortunately the thula had to close, to kill. "Successful intercept, Alport, confirmed. Stildyne, mark on target."

One eighth left to the first platform, then. The first of sixteen. They had to take out sixteen of them to clear a space through the mine field that was big enough for a ship the size of the *Ragnarok* to traverse, and still be sufficiently removed from the remaining platforms that any residual rounds could be absorbed by the plasma sheath without damage to the hull.

"Mark on target, Chief, confirmed." Stildyne's voice, yes. It was a little odd, to Andrej, to hear Stildyne addressed without rank, and hear him return his own rank in address to the speaker. The chief weaponer for this mission was a junior weapons systems analyst from Engineering; but on a mission flight like this, ability took absolute precedence. Avenham was the best chief weaponer on board of the *Ragnarok*.

It was the same in his own area, Andrej reminded himself—he might have rank, and he unquestionably had the best qualifications for some surgeries, but that did not mean that he had any business controverting with Infectious Disease or Psychiatric. Quite the contrary.

Suddenly the braid from their parent plaited in again, an urgent message for Taller and Lek alike. "Thula, this is *Ragnarok*. We have an evacuation party on target six. Can you adjust?"

Target six. They had a preprogrammed kill-sequence laid in, and a set of alternates ready to load; all designed to prevent the intelligence that controlled the artiplats from predicting where the ship would strike next, and moving to target them accordingly. Andrej had no idea where "target six" actually came in their list of targets. Lek took a moment to find out; but when he answered, it was a relief.

"Convert to sequence nine. Weaponer Avenham. Resequence after target four, advise preferred response."

Advise him of what Avenham's preferred response was to be, Lek meant—whether he was going to want a different approach. These people understood the language they were speaking. It was only confusing to him because he had no place within the tight group dynamic of this crew, and couldn't share the most part of their communications.

"Lek, switch your flyby on proximate hit when we get to it. Shani, your kill, confirm. Preparing to discharge round."

The artillery platform grew gray and ominous on the forward screens. They were going to run dead into it at any moment—but the ship spun to one side, rather than colliding, and at the nearest possible approach, just before the thula broke its head-on course Andrej felt—rather than saw—the huge flare from the thula's forward gun, as Avenham fired.

Blooming like an astraffler in the side-panel screen the artillery platform blew up, sending bits of stalloy and debris in all directions.

"Piece of work, this cannon." Avenham's voice was appropriately respectful. "Next up on four, Lek? Stildyne. Pin it in the second laterals."

Now that they were through, now that they could run behind the mine field, it would be one round after another till the gap was cleared. Great *Ragnarok* labored to gain speed behind them, and they had less than the eighth part of a shift to clear the field before their ship would enter the kill-zone. The thula threw herself upon her target as if shot from a howitzer-piece; and Stildyne—on ship's-left laterals—hit the sequence perfectly. That was two, then.

Lek ran the ship at extreme tolerance, the consumption monitors cycling at an alarming rate. Silent and tense, Andrej watched the remote sensors, fixed as they were on *Ragnarok* well behind them—*Ragnarok*, standing for the vector, and the eager convoy of heavy Security from Taisheki Station straining after her.

Three and four; five, and the artiplat had the thula targeted a shade too narrowly for comfort, so that the energy wash blinded the screens for a long instant before the ship's auto-recovers picked up feed again.

Six and seven; eight, nine, and Lek played the thula's navigation like a man in a dream, his every gesture slow and deliberate—only at so fast a pace that he didn't seem to stop moving for an instant. He was working hard, and Taller beside him struggled to keep pace. Lek knew what he was doing; he didn't hesitate. And still the odds against which Lek had to fight to do his work were staggering, Safe or no Safe.

Ten platforms down. Only six to go. There was a voice in the forward cabinet, and it was neither Avenham's voice nor Lek's voice, Stildyne's, Lorbe's, anybody's. Andrej was confused, so focused on the target grid above the primary display that it took him a moment to realize who was talking.

"Thula. Evacuation party is reporting to host, damage to craft—translation injury. They're losing heat."

First Officer, that's who it was. The eleventh platform came up on the forward scan; Lek circled around it so that Alport could fire from the backside of his arc even as he was changing vectors for the next target. Was anybody paying attention to First Officer?

Or was Mendez talking to him? Plaiting into braid, Andrej reached for more information. "The evacuation party's craft suffering damage, First Officer. Losing heat. How bad is it?"

"The harriers are still four eighths behind us, Andrej, and we're not going to be able to afford to slow for tractor. If you can pull them on board. If not, well."

But they were running short of time, and Andrej didn't know for certain whether Mendez's braid had even fed into any plait but his. He was the last person on board of the thula who could hope to judge whether they were going to be able to pick up a damaged evacuation craft or not. "Thank you, First Officer. Thula away."

Twelve. It was a temptation to call the run off, and go for the evacuation party, and let the *Ragnarok* hazard the remaining guns. But it was unthinkable to try to stop now, unthinkable to hazard seven hundred lives to try for eight. No.

The evacuation craft had been damaged by debris; they had not fired on the evacuation craft—they were not responsible. The cold was not so bad a way to die. And the people in the evacuation party, they had all been willing that the *Ragnarok* should be forced into Taisheki Station, with a Fleet Interrogations Group all too probably in the wings. He had to keep his peace. To speak now would be to betray Lek. And not only Lek—but every soul on board of the *Ragnarok*.

Thirteen, and Lek shook the thula fiercely from side to side, running down the platform's line of fire as the guns tried to fix on them for long enough to get a target registration and shoot. One of the weaponers stopped a round midway between the platform and the ship, but the impact was too close—the thula lost her course for one terrible moment, and rolled against the shock like sea-wrack at flood.

Lek set the board to rights and closed on target. Stildyne fired the left-lateral battery and blew the platform into utter ruin. Only three to go. Those people on the artillery platform had surely expected to be well clear before the mine field was called into active play. For all Andrej knew, they weren't even Fleet resources but civilian contractors.

Fourteen. The thula heeled back on her own impulse-train and ran for the next target, eager for the kill, and the chief weaponer gave the word. "Go for it, Smath. Your hit. Good shot." It was fractions of an eighth left before the *Ragnarok* would come into range, and only one artiplat still threatened her. One last platform and *Ragnarok* was clear to breach the mine field; the ship already had the advantage of speed in the chase, because the pursuit ships were either too small to do the *Ragnarok*'s great black massy hull much harm or too big to gain sufficient speed to close.

One final platform, only one more, and it turned its primary guns toward them, blossoming into a cloud of dust and scrap and useless chunks of trash as the thula fixed and fired and killed. The *Ragnarok* was clear.

Steady, almost stately, the *Ragnarok* made full transit into what had been the kill-zone as the remaining stations fired on the ship in a vain attempt to reach beyond the range of their emplaced guns and put a stop to its deliberate progress.

"Nicely done, thula." First Officer, again, and Andrej unstrapped himself from the webbing in his secure-shell to go see that Lek was all right. "Well flown, Lek. Very nicely shot, weaponers all. Come on home, we've got a vector to catch, and the sooner we hull over the happier Wheatfields is going to be with all of us."

Andrej didn't like the confused sideways glance Taller was giving Lek, nor did he quite understand the fearful intensity of Lek's focus on his boards. The thula did not seem to be reorienting toward the *Ragnarok*, nor to face pursuit, scant eighths behind the ship.

"Mister Kerenko?"

The expression on Lek's face was one of utter concentration, not the anguished conflict of a governor going wrong. No conflict at all. Determination, rather, and— meeting Lek's dark sharp Sarvaw eyes—Andrej knew as surely as if he had been told exactly what was going on in Lek's mind.

"We can make it work, sir. Their only chance."

Yes. Plaiting into braid, Andrej keyed into the standard emergency strand. "This is Andrej Ulexeievitch Koscuisko. We have been given to understand that an evacuation craft is damaged. It is our intent to take this craft into cargo." Switching onto ship-strand, he continued. "Weaponer, if you would direct the tractor."

Three of the pursuit ships had veered off from their primary course, moving to intercept. That was their right, perhaps. The point that First Officer had made was that the pursuit ships could not reach the damaged evac craft in time: the thula could—so there was a chance.

Why should they risk their lives—and a death about whose full horror they suffered no illusions—for the lives of an artillery emplacement crew, just recently engaged in doing all they could to set the traps that would ensnare great *Ragnarok* and every soul on board?

"Yes, sir." Avenham's voice was clear, calm, neutral. Unquestioning. "Stildyne, Lorbe, on lateral forwards, mark. Alport, you and Shani and I, off-station, onto tractor."

Because they wouldn't have gotten into this desperate situation in the first place if they had been willing, as individuals, as a ship, to sacrifice anyone's life to their own survival, if they thought that there was any way around it.

It seemed to take forever to close on the evac craft, its external signals already warning of extreme stress tolerance, losing heat. Taller toggled into braid from his station, signaling urgently for a response, trying to see whether they were already too late. "Thula to evac craft. Prepare to tractor. Evac, are you there? Please. Respond."

No, only the mechanical code, in reply. The damaged ship no longer had enough power to maintain heat and transmit voice at the same time. Only the mechanical code, but that was hopeful, because someone had to be able to move, to initiate the transmit—*Extreme emergency situation exists. Failure of integrity imminent. Please expedite rescue effort. Eight souls in custody.*

"Evac craft on scan," Avenham said.

Lek did something to his console, and the thula shuddered like a wild animal cornered in a field trap, coming around. Three pursuit craft, on the second lateral, and it seemed to Andrej that they were making entirely too good a rate of acceleration for anybody's peace of mind.

"Tractor initiate. Very low reading off evac craft, your Excellency." Avenham's warning was predictable, but worrisome. It would be frustrating if they were to lose their lives—and still come too late for the evac craft. "Give us a little drop, Lek—good. Tractor is firm, gaining cargo bay now."

The tractor could not be rushed. If they damaged the thula's cargo bay, they wouldn't be able to pressurize, and then it wouldn't matter whether they had the evac craft or not. Did he imagine it—Andrej wondered—or could he hear the subtle sound of the closing of the cargo bay doors beneath the white noise in the wheelhouse?

"Chief." It was Stildyne, talking to Avenham. "Respectfully suggest we move this thula at the first possible opportunity—"

"Go for it."

Avenham's response was all the word Lek apparently needed. The thula shuddered and it seemed to groan, but the pursuit ships that Andrej could see on the second lateral screen disappeared, and when they reappeared on the tertiary dorsal scans they were appreciably smaller than they had been before.

They were going to need him down in the cargo bay. They all knew how to use emergency stasis suits to treat cold injury and blood-gas imbalance—it was one of the first and most important things anyone learned about exo-atmospheric travel. But he was the one who knew best how to set the respiration, whether circulation should be induced, and whether neural activity should be artificially suspended until they got their casualties to Infirmary on *Ragnarok*.

He needed to be there to stabilize, in case Wheatfields could not bring himself to release the thula from full implosion field without a thorough scan, especially in the middle of preparation for a vector transit. The chance that the evac craft's distress call had been just part of an elaborate trap was perhaps not very great, but it was there.

All of which meant that he had to leave Lek here alone, more or less alone, prey to the fury of his own governor. If the Safe should fail, and him not here to rescue his Lek—

Lek was steady, solid, almost relaxed. There was no conflict that Andrej could detect in his face, in his voice, in his manner as he made his moves and sent the thula straight and clean for *Ragnarok*. Andrej took him by the shoulders from behind as he sat, smiling at Lek's questioning look, at the basic blissful confidence that underlay his evident concentration.

There was no guarantee that they'd reach the *Ragnarok* in time to come on board for the vector transit. There were no guarantees that the people in the evac craft were still alive. Yet Andrej knew that Lek's choice had been the only honorable choice, and was glad to praise him for it.

"Thank you, Lek. Very well done, indeed. You will not need me?" Lek nodded almost absentmindedly and turned back to his boards, completely focused on his pilot's task. Taller gave Andrej a reassuring smile on Lek's behalf, and—satisfied—Andrej left the wheelhouse to get down to the cargo bay, and see what could be done for the people in the evac craft.

The officer's praise was only part and parcel of the joy Lek had in this fine thula; Koscuisko always praised their good performances, and Lek already knew that he'd done well. The officer's absence was not going to be a problem. There were reasons why Koscuisko had to leave the wheelhouse, and reasons why Lek had to concentrate all of his remaining energies on making their rendezvous with *Ragnarok*, because it would all be for nothing if he didn't get back to the *Ragnarok* in time.

"Let's see how much speed she has left in her," he suggested to Taller, easing the retards out to full liberty now that they were clear to run for home. "It'll be a little tight, maybe, but we can make it work. Pull off on reserve. Weaponer. Close ports."

The enemy still pursued, but they could not touch the thula's speed. "Closed, all ports, Lek." No weaponer was ever happy to have to put the guns away, but there was no argument. It was up to speed to save them, and not firepower. Borrowed firepower had blown a hole in the mine field and cleared a way for the *Ragnarok*; now speed was all they had to bring the ship, the crew, the officer back safely to their proper berths.

"We're starting to fling caramids," Taller warned; and the analysis of the drives was showing signs of stress— but there wasn't any help for it.

"We can afford it. Increase yield on quats. We only need another three eighths. Five eighths, max." Once they came level with the *Ragnarok* they could surrender motive power to the parent tractors, and divert all remaining power to turn the craft. It would be enough.

The massive black belly of great *Ragnarok* began to crown on ship's forward horizon. Checking his signatures, Lek frowned, but he wasn't worried yet. She had plenty of tolerance. Why shouldn't she? She was a Malcontent, after all, and a Malcontent stood in need of as much tolerance as a Sarvaw did, for mere survival. This ship and he had more in common than anyone could know—

They gained on *Ragnarok* in a great steady wave that

swept them ever forward. Well beneath the maintenance hull now, and the thula yielded gratefully to his instruction to ease up, stilling herself with perfect manners to find her place beneath the still-open slot and hold there motionless, precisely matched to *Ragnarok*'s exact speed and rate of acceleration.

Lek opened braid, watching the pursuit ships behind them, but not far enough behind. . . . "*Ragnarok*, the Malcontent's thula. We request transfer to ship-comp on primary drives."

Well, she wasn't the *Ragnarok*'s thula; Fleet couldn't afford her. And the Malcontent was going to want her back, Lek reminded himself sternly; but that inevitability had no power to grieve him, not just now. Not on the crest of the rush he was riding, the flying they'd done, the way she could move.

"Thula. This is *Ragnarok*." It was Ship's Engineer who came back in the braid; Lek couldn't quite decide what note it might be that he thought he heard in Wheatfields's voice. "Ready to acquire. On your mark."

Because the *Ragnarok* needed to take responsibility for holding the ship at speed, while the thula concentrated on the more delicate process of moving herself up into the host's waiting maintenance atmosphere. "We surrender primary, at mark four. Two. Three. Four."

Yes. Smooth as the cream from an Aznir dairy cow.

There were internal communications going back and forth around him, weaponers' status reports, Stildyne talking to Ship's First, Koscuisko calling for transport on emergency stasis. The crew of the evac craft were still alive, then. It was not outside the realm of possibility—in Koscuisko's characteristically cautious phrase—that they would be all right. That was good news, but nothing that he could afford to waste any attention on.

"Commence sequence, Taller," Lek warned; not that there was much Taller could do. He fired his laterals one by one, bringing the line up carefully to put a spin on the thula—east of forward heading, dead on meridian.

It was slow, and the pursuit ships were out there, but he couldn't afford to notice them any more than he could afford to listen to Koscuisko's voice over intraship braid. Too much nose, and the thula spun too far east, slipping away from the meridian line. He had to hold the meridian line. And he had to hold it now.

A touch at offside tailings, and she came true. "Request check for entry window, *Ragnarok*." She didn't stay perfectly aligned; she continued to slide ever so gently to one side or the other—the basic problem inherent in any reaction-correction process. He was tightening her orb moment by moment. He needed to be able to move the instant she was solid true and stayed there.

"Move that thula, Mister Lek. You're well within tolerance. Now, if you please."

Well within tolerance, his ass. He was dead solid perfect. And the *Ragnarok* knew it.

Lek hit his basal lifts, and the thula began to rise gentle and straight into the maintenance atmosphere of the *Ragnarok*. They had to bring it into the maintenance atmosphere if they were to hope to make a vector transit before the pursuit ships could reach them; but if the hull was damaged as they tried to berth, they wouldn't be making any vector transits at all.

Taller cut the ship's screens to real actual, and Lek watched the solid thickness of the maintenance hull seeming to sink as the thula rose, so close it was tempting to reach out from his chair and try to touch it as they passed. There wasn't much clearance—but they'd known that there wouldn't be.

They were clear of the hull, and rising toward the loading aprons overhead. Made it. He cut the thula's lifts; the ship rode on tractor, safe within the maintenance atmosphere.

On the ship's screens Lek could see a crew from Engineering—in full environmentals, and tethered, just in case—moving the final sections of the hull into place with disciplined urgency. The Ship's Engineer would be for vector transit, now. They couldn't have much time, so Lek was surprised to hear him coming over braid as the chief weaponer and Stildyne came forward into the thula's wheelhouse.

"Nicely done, Mister. Very pretty handling."

Of course. Hadn't he told them that he could do it? Still, it had been tight, and there had been that evac craft. Why it should have mattered that they pick up that crew, when it was the survival of the thula that had been at stake—or its freedom, which amounted to the same thing—Lek wasn't quite certain; but it had mattered.

That was all he could really keep in his mind, just now, because he was tired, and it was comfortable and familiar to have Chief Stildyne behind him, reminding him about things he had to do.

"Shut down and leave it for later, Lek. You've done all you could for now. And everything we asked you, too. Let's go, Mister."

Thula locked in traction, mover engaged to transit to maintenance apron. Medical was already offloading emergency stasis modules, eight of them. Eight. Were there supposed to be eight? The officer had told *Ragnarok* that they'd been on time. So eight was clearly the right number.

The officer was not following the stasis modules to Infirmary, though; he'd stopped on the receiving apron to have a word with the Captain, by the looks of it. It began to occur to Lek that there were a lot of people out on the receiving apron.

There was no arguing with the Chief; Lek rose stiffly from out of his place and went meekly before Stildyne out of the wheelhouse, through the ship, out to the mover, across to the landing apron. Tired out. Well, he'd been concentrating. It was a little unusual still, how tired he felt. First Officer was out there, too, now.

"Attention to pilot," First Officer called, loudly, in his direction. Lek was confused; he'd been the pilot, how was he to come to attention? Oh. It was the other people who were supposed to come to attention.

It wasn't "a lot of people" on the apron: it was a formation on the apron, and he was in front of it. He and Chief Stildyne, but Stildyne was behind him, and as Lek tried to figure out what was happening, Captain ap Rhiannon marched briskly front and center of the assembly with First Officer and Chief Medical, halting her officer-detachment right in front of his nose.

"Mister Kerenko."

She sounded very stern. Very serious. He hoped he wasn't in trouble. He was just a little confused. Bowing sharply, he acknowledged her address, in the best form he knew how.

"As it please the officer. Yes, your Excellency."

She wasn't his officer. The officer was his officer—but Chief Medical was subordinate to the Captain. Chief Medical was here, though, so it was bound to be all right.

"Based upon your expressed willingness and with the concurrence of Chief Medical, Ship's Engineer, and Ship's First Officer, you were entrusted with piloting this thula on a mission critical to the safe escape and possible survival of this ship. You accomplished your mission with exceptional skill, Mister Kerenko."

But he shouldn't have peeled off for the evacuation craft. He'd had no permission to deviate from assigned task. He hadn't even asked for a deviation.

"Yes, your Excellency." What else could he say? He knew he shouldn't have done it. He'd known at the time that he shouldn't be doing it. And he knew that under the same set of conditions he'd do it again, instructions or no instructions. What if the officer had told him to let the evacuation craft's crew die, and return to *Ragnarok*? What would he have done then?

"In addition to this essential mission, however, your ability to pilot your craft permitted the safe recovery of eight Fleet resources, living souls. This recovery was effected under extreme pressure, Mister Kerenko, and at considerable risk to the thula and everyone on it."

No one of which, Lek realized, had raised their voice in protest. No message from the *Ragnarok* had come, to bring him back into line. It was all right?

"For your demonstrated flight mastery in piloting the thula, and for your principle contribution to saving the lives of eight Fleet crew, you are to be commended in the second degree of performance. On behalf of Fleet, the Bench, and the *Ragnarok*, I thank you, Mister Kerenko."

He'd never earned a flight commendation in all his years under Bond. Such honors weren't usually issued to bond-involuntaries, no matter what their accomplishments; still less in public, in front of what looked like every Security troop assigned to *Ragnarok*—and some of Engineering, as well.

"The appropriate entries are to be made in your personnel records. That will be all."

He was supposed to salute again, now. The bow helped him wrestle with his startled pleasure, gave him time to get his face back into order. He wasn't expected to say anything. It was just as well. He was speechless.

"First Officer, dismiss."

Ship's First and Chief Medical bowed in unison, and ap Rhiannon left the maintenance apron. His officer came forward to embrace him, with evident emotion. "It was beautifully done," Koscuisko repeated. Koscuisko had been there. It must have been so, then. "Superlative performance, Lek. Stildyne. I have to go to duty, but it was well shot as well as well piloted. I am very proud of you all."

First Officer was about to say something; but the Engineer's voice came over all-ship, and overrode him. "All stations stand by for vector transit. Beginning spins in five eighths, mark. All stations stand by for vector transit."

Or, in other words, get off the apron, out of the maintenance atmosphere and to wherever you were supposed to be, right now. Lek's moment of glory was over—or at the least, postponed. He was just as glad of the distraction. He'd never had a moment of glory. He found he didn't have the first idea what to do with it.

Stildyne tapped him on the shoulder to get him moving, and Lek jogged after the rest of the crew to get to his post and await the vector transit.

Chapter Fifteen

The Devil and Deep Space

The thula outdistanced its hunters by a slim but adequate margin and gained the sanctuary shadow of the *Ragnarok*'s black hull. The main pursuit party was still vainly trying to come up to speed to catch the *Ragnarok*, but now that the thula had rejoined its foster parent—would the ship come about?

Admiral Brecinn blinked, and the thula was gone.

Staring at the great display station, frowning, feeling stupid, Brecinn tried to figure out what had happened. The thula had disappeared. The display was tracking *Ragnarok*, but the pursuit ships were on display as well, and there was no trail of debris and mangled metal that Brecinn could see in *Ragnarok*'s wake, no evidence of destruction. What had happened?

Senior Auditor Ormbach tapped the prediction module reporter at the front of the observer station with one well-groomed fingernail, and shook her head. "The Taisheki vector. As you predicted, Fleet Admiral. The corvettes are going to have to fall back. There isn't any sense trying to follow them from here."

Ragnarok had taken the thula on, that was what had happened. That explained the queer maneuver that the thula had performed, just prior to its disappearance— turning sidewise to the parent ship's heading, from what Brecinn had been able to gather from the target-detail screen. *Ragnarok* had taken the thula to itself. Now that

the thula was back on board, the *Ragnarok* would make
for the vector.

Brecinn felt a pang of loss and longing. That thula
was worth money. If only she could have found a way
to possess herself of it. "Bloodless engagement," another
of the auditors noted aloud, apparently just to make conversation. "That much to the good, at least. No lives
lost."

"That we know of," Brecinn reminded them all, a bit
sharply. "We don't know about that evacuation craft."

"Still, it's a Brief in the third order of magnitude at
most." Auditor Ormbach did not seem to be suffering
from any particular irritation at the *Ragnarok*'s escape.
"The most cause against the *Ragnarok* for that would
be destruction of Fleet resources with concommitant loss
of life, a disciplinary offense, but hardly a Judicial one.
And the crew may not be dead."

"They certainly would be if the thula hadn't gone back
for them—" one of the auditors started to point out.
The priority signal warning interrupted her before she
could finish her point, however.

*Chilleau Judiciary, Second Judge Sem Por Harr Presid-
ing. For Taisheki Station.* What could Chilleau Judiciary
want at Fleet Audit Appeals Authority?

Jils Ivers. She must have talked to Verlaine about
Noycannir. "Chilleau Judiciary, this is Taisheki Station,
Senior Auditor Ormbach. In the war and maneuvers
room, Fleet Admiral Sandri Brecinn accompanying as
an observer."

The signal stepped down from global transmit to the
observer station restrict, and Brecinn knew by the subtle
tingling at the nape of her neck that the privacy mutes
had been engaged. Verlaine didn't mind talking to Taisheki in her presence, then. That was encouraging.
Maybe she could salvage something from this after all.

"What is this news of the *Ragnarok*, Auditor?" First
Secretary Verlaine. Deep voice. Calm. Contemplative.
Concerned about something. Noycannir's treachery? Or
sensibly aware that he looked a great deal like an antag-
onist to Fleet, now that the Second Judge had issued
her program?

Auditor Ormbach watched the projections tile across

the alert-border of the far remote screens, apparently putting her thoughts together. The First Secretary was still the First Secretary. The Second Judge was still only the Second Judge, but she was the Second Judge all the same.

"*Ragnarok* has declined to enter Taisheki Station, citing as unacceptable requirements to submit to search; to surrender evidence; and to surrender crew, taken together as evidence of failure of intent to investigate its Appeal."

The pursuit ships had fallen too far away from the *Ragnarok* to do any good. As Brecinn watched the projections, the detail-insert came up with a plot projection, a vector transit line—tight, but they would be in a hurry. Either that, or the Engineer was showing off, since he could be certain that this particular vector transit was to be observed with keen interest.

"What is your current status?"

"The *Ragnarok* has started vector transit preparations for the Taisheki vector, having stated its determination to protect the integrity of ship and crew at some neutral location pending resolution of its Appeal. Possible destination, Amberlin."

"Auditor Ormbach." The First Secretary's voice paused, as though he was thinking carefully about what he was going to say next. "Andrej Koscuisko is in possession of very sensitive evidence that reflects negatively on this Judiciary. It is therefore of critical importance to the Second Judge that no punitive action be taken against the *Ragnarok* while its Appeal is pending. To do otherwise would present the appearance of reprisals contrary to the upholding of the rule of Law."

What was he talking about? What evidence?

Then Brecinn realized. He had to cover up Noycannir's crimes. He was soliciting the cooperation of the Fleet Audit Appeals Authority to help him, in return for implied benefit in the future; and Auditor Ormbach might decide to listen to him.

She wasn't about to let it go so easily. "First Secretary," Brecinn said suddenly. "Fleet Admiral Sandri Brecinn speaking. If I may, sir." And why shouldn't she? She had the rank. Not to speak of the influence.

"Fleet Admiral," Verlaine said, agreeably enough—Ivers clearly hadn't made the connection between Noycannir and Pesadie, at least not for Verlaine. "Please."

"Sir, while assigned to the Pesadie Training Command's administrative oversight, the *Ragnarok* left its area of assignment without leave, first for Silboomie Station and then for Taisheki. It has since explicitly rejected lawful and received instruction to surrender itself. There are strong indications of mutinous intent on the part of the acting Captain and an unknown number of her crew."

The majority of the *Ragnarok*'s crew actually, but there was no need to whistle against that reed. Verlaine might ask her how she knew, and she had no easy and appropriate reply.

Verlaine did not seem to understand the hints she was giving him, however. "The acting Captain is young and inexperienced with Command of equivalent complexity, Fleet Admiral. It would be a potentially tragic error on our part if we mistook a miscalculation under pressure for intent to commit so grievous a crime. I understand the officer is crèche-bred."

He couldn't mean to suggest that they interpret ap Rhiannon's insolence as a mere miscalculation under pressure, surely. Ormbach glanced at Brecinn with an amused expression on her face, but Brecinn kept her own countenance utterly expressionless. Ap Rhiannon knew exactly what she was doing; they all knew it. But when all was written and read in, it was to be the Audit Authority's careful and politically sensitive finding on the matter that was to become truth.

If Ormbach agreed that ap Rhiannon was just young and inexperienced, then Brecinn was going to have no choice but to play along—and look for a worthier and more responsive patron to support in the upcoming Selection. "We must of course take all such circumstances carefully under advisement," Brecinn said icily.

Ormbach continued, without acknowledging Brecinn's points; testing the limits of Verlaine's nerve, perhaps. "And still the *Ragnarok* has refused to enter Taisheki Station. Has blown a clearance through mine field, and is even now commencing its vector spin with a privately owned thula and an evacuation craft on board, as it happens. If the First Secretary would care to advise the next appropriate measure?"

Perfectly reasonable. Perfectly responsive to the existence of political pressures unrelated to the strict confines of the Audit Authority. She'd known that there were reasonable people at Taisheki Station, but she hadn't expected Ormbach to be quite so blatantly opportunistic, even so.

The *Ragnarok* was well into its vector spin. And it was clear that the First Secretary had made up his mind about something.

"Fleet does not have resources to spare chasing off to Amberlin after the *Ragnarok*. Senior Auditor, the Second Judge anticipates that Fleet Audit Appeals Authority will investigate the *Ragnarok*'s appeal in as full and fair a manner as may be possible, absent the ship and crew."

The on-screen tracks went blank, the scroll frozen at the last point of verified transmission. The *Ragnarok* had made the vector. There was no calling the ship back now; Verlaine was still talking, persuasively, calmly, cajolingly.

"I suggest a preliminary finding of mutiny in form. I believe we can all agree on the importance of preventing it from becoming mutiny in fact. If the *Ragnarok* will stay out of harm's reach until the Appeal has been completed, there is still good hope of proposing acceptable administrative disciplinary measures. We must not allow an error of such proportions to unbalance the Bench at the beginning of a Presidency, regardless of the outcome of the Selection."

Meaning that with so much work to do once the Selection was decided, they'd have no choice but to make an example of the *Ragnarok* if the ship continued to push its luck. Verlaine clearly didn't want it to come to that; but did he realize how angry Fleet was at the Second Judge?

"Mutiny in form." The mildest interpretation that could be put on it, and Ormbach rolled the words in her mouth with mild scorn. "As you direct, First Secretary, subject of course to Fleet endorsement." Because Tai-

sheki answered to the Fleet, not to the Bench. It was
not a bad idea, perhaps, to remind Verlaine of that.

"And in form only, Auditor, I assure you of that.
There are elements at play which cannot be revealed
prematurely. I ask you to excuse my silence. Fleet
Admiral."

Brecinn was surprised to be called out; Verlaine had
seemed to forget that she was there. "First Secretary,"
she replied, careful to give him no note of undue deference. Taisheki Station had just put Verlaine on notice.
He was going to have to solicit their cooperation.

"Go back to Pesadie, Fleet Admiral. You have no
business at Taisheki Station. Unless you have an Appeal
of your own? I am in possession of some interesting
information from one of my Clerks of Court, Dame Noycannir. Perhaps you would care to take advantage of the
coming break in training schedules to set your house in
order. For your replacement."

Ormbach looked at her, and almost sneered. Brecinn
felt her face go white with fury. "Thank you, First Secretary," she said, as calmly as she could. "You'll know
exactly how much of what Noycannir says to believe
soon enough. I only hope it doesn't cause the Second
Judge any embarrassment. But I appreciate the friendly
advice, and will leave immediately."

Go back to Pesadie, yes. Where she had lost the main
battle cannon with which she had been entrusted by reasonable people. Where she owed replacement in kind,
good munitions for bad, for inventory lost in an accident
that had been caused by the *Ragnarok*, a direct result
of the selfish arrogance of its Captain and crew.

Where she had in an unfortunate moment been gulled
into listening to—trusting!—a double agent for Chilleau
Judiciary, who had ingratiated herself only in order to
betray her to the First Secretary. Her mission to Taisheki Station had failed.

She *would* leave immediately. But she would be very
careful to avoid ever arriving, because the only things
that awaited her now at Pesadie were disgrace and humiliation and death.

*   *   *.

Andrej Koscuisko stood on the docking apron of the *Ragnarok*'s maintenance atmosphere looking up into the passenger bay of the Malcontent's thula, waiting for the time when it would be ready to close.

Technically speaking launch clearance was the Engineer's function, but First Officer had asked him to perform the formalities in this case on pretext of it being an Aznir ship. Andrej had his suspicions about that, though. He thought they—the Captain, Wheatfields, First Officer—were still waiting for him to change his mind and leave. He supposed he appreciated their attempts to make it as easy as possible for him to do so.

"I will keep the documents, yes, Bench specialist," he said. Jils Ivers stood beside him. The crew that they'd rescued from the evac craft were going aboard. One or two of them would help Cousin Ferinc pilot the thula from the interim Kazar vector back to Chilleau Judiciary, where Ivers had things to say to the First Secretary. "It is nothing personal."

She could hardly argue with him on that. They both knew that he couldn't surrender his Writ so long as the status of the *Ragnarok*'s Appeal was in process. Surrendering his Writ while remaining on board would make him unauthorized personnel, and generate an additional charge against the ship—that of allowing an unauthorized person to exercise command and control of the Infirmary, and failure to discharge persons no longer under orders.

"We can work it out, your Excellency. I'm sure of it." She was stubborn. He knew she hated leaving him here. "And when we do, Chilleau Judiciary is going to need your influence, sir, more I think than the First Secretary anticipated."

Because Fleet was much more angry about Verlaine's proposal than Verlaine had apparently expected. Verlaine had concentrated his attention on the humanitarian aspects, the legal aspects, the civil aspects of challenging the whole system of Inquiry. He had underestimated the degree to which Fleet would feel that its prerogatives were being taken away from it.

"All the more reason for a swift resolution to this

entire problem. A swift and bloodless resolution, Specialist Ivers. And he shall have my whole-hearted support, as expert witness."

Fleet was not particularly committed to the system of Inquiry in and of itself. As an institution that was at base military, Fleet cared little for the concept of dishonoring itself by torturing civilians. Information required for military purposes could be gotten very simply with the right drugs.

It was power, no more. What Verlaine proposed would significantly reduce the influence Fleet possessed in negotiation with the Bench for privileges, material, resources. Autonomy. It could be seen as a move to begin to draw Fleet more firmly under Bench control: and that was certainly how the Fleet appeared to be viewing the concept.

"You can come with me, your Excellency."

They had been over this before. "Thank you for all of your efforts on my behalf, Specialist Ivers, to the furtherance of the rule of Law. I am staying."

She held his eye for a long moment before she acknowledged her final defeat. "As you will, your Excellency. By your leave. And with my very sincere hope for a quick resolution."

And bloodless, Andrej added in his mind. But he didn't need to repeat it, not again. She knew.

Returning her salute with a respectful bow of his own—she was a Bench specialist, she wasn't required to salute anybody—Andrej watched her go up the ramp into the thula, with a moderate feeling of affectionate warmth in his heart for her. She had tried very hard. He liked her well enough. But she was a Bench specialist. Such people were dangerous to like, even on a professional level.

Now it only remained that he take leave of Ferinc, and probe to see what damages the Saint would assess for the use Andrej had made of his thula. It was all very well for Stoshik to claim that the Malcontent's efforts on Andrej's behalf were owed by its duty to the Autocrat, and that its loan of the thula was its apology for its failure to anticipate Noycannir's assassination attempt. That would be too easy all around. Things were never so straightforward where the Malcontent was concerned.

Andrej waited.

Cousin Ferinc had been waiting as well, watching, and came forward once Ivers was into the thula and out of sight. Ferinc had tied his braids together at the back of his neck, using the plaits to gather his long hair into a single fall; he looked more like Haster Girag with his hair back from his face, but Andrej had made up his mind to forgive Ferinc for having been that person. There was no sense in holding any grudges. And more for Ferinc to forgive Andrej than otherwise, really.

"You take the Bench specialist to Chilleau, then home?" Andrej asked, just to open the dialogue. "I hope that Anton will not be too much distressed that I do not come back. And yet it may be that he will not notice. If the Malcontent in mercy allows that you should remain his friend."

Ferinc shook his head. "Not so easy as that, your Excellency. He worships you like a saint under Canopy; it will cause him suffering. I'm sorry. But there's no way around it. I'll do what I can."

Ferinc was right. It would be too easy to pretend that having met his son and made re-contract with Marana, he could absent himself without explanation and for an unknown period of time to pursue his personal goals. There was no use in lying to himself. He was being cruel to his son, his own son, his beautiful child, a child who loved him.

"Be his friend still, Ferinc." He was an unnatural father, perhaps, to be unable to set his son's suffering above the lives of the crew of the *Ragnarok*. And if he was, Marana would tell him. There would be no use in hoping for a life with her, not if he betrayed her son to suffer for such a small thing as four or eight or seven hundred souls; or was he being unfair?

Marana. "And be a friend to my wife as well, if she will take solace. She will have much fault to find with my behavior, and rightly so, but I fear for her contest against my family. She will need powerful defenders. Will the Malcontent protect my wife, and my son Anton?"

"He is no longer your son, your Excellency," Ferinc pointed out, reasonably. "He is the inheriting son of the Koscuisko familial corporation. It is the Saint's natural business to look after his best interest. But since you ask. I will relay the request, your Excellency, to my ecclesiastical superior. Knowing that you know better than I do what it means to ask a favor from the Malcontent."

There was no help for it. The future was too much in question. He had made his son safe in the event of his own sudden death; and in so doing, had put Anton in need of a different sort of protection.

"Aside from that, Ferinc." Andrej paused for a moment to master his own irritation; it was no use losing one's patience with Malcontents. "And the Saint aside. You were only a man at one time. It may be that I wronged you once."

Cousin Ferinc shuddered and stepped back, apparently taken by surprise. It was another moment before he replied. "On balance," Ferinc said, "no, your Excellency. It was no more than Fleet itself would have done, had the crime been reported. Much less, perhaps. Fleet would not have so reduced me in spirit, I can admit that much, yes, sir."

If Andrej had reported the crime Ferinc would have lost rank and privilege, and gone to prison for some years. Andrej had spared him that, but not because he had meant to be pitiful. No. He had broken Haster Girag because he had believed Girag deserved to be broken into the dust, and because he knew that he was going to enjoy it. And so he had.

"My motives were vengeful." And he had been drunk, in those days, on the absolute power at his command, his absolute privilege to execute it, the absolute atrocity that Fleet and the rule of Law permitted him. Required of him. "All else apart, that was a sin. I have savaged you. To elect the Malcontent is a desperate thing, Ferinc. I am to blame for it. If I were to ask you for the peace of the Saint, could you from your heart grant it, and forgive me?"

"For my own part?" Ferinc asked, as if in wonder. Yes, it was an extreme sort of a thing to ask. Andrej could recognize the selfish unreason of his demand.

"And not what my reconciler has demanded? If you could not have let me see Anton. But you did. And therefore."

Coming closer to him, standing between Andrej and the ramp into the thula, Ferinc put his hand to the back of Andrej's neck; a very precise signal, for Dolgorukij, and one that Ferinc had obviously learned. "The peace of the Malcontent I give you," Cousin Ferinc said, and kissed him. Very seriously.

Breaking off suddenly, though, to straighten up, leaving Andrej to wonder—

"But not where Chief Stildyne can see me," Cousin Ferinc explained. "Might cause all sorts of misunderstandings. With all my heart, your Excellency, peace between us, and I'm out of here."

There was the sound of Stildyne feet behind Andrej on the docking apron as Cousin Ferinc ducked his head and disappeared into the thula.

The loading ramp began to close.

"You'll want to wash your neck, sir," Stildyne said, and his voice was deeply disapproving. "Maybe rinse your mouth. Malcontents. Filthy people. Or so at least they tell me."

Watching the thula prepare to take flight, listening to Stildyne, Andrej's mind went back to the night he'd had dinner with his family at Chelatring Side, before Mergau Noycannir had arrived to attack him. Stildyne had disappeared. Stoshik also. The Gallery; and on the following day—

"One never knows what such depraved souls will get up to. No. You are quite right. Let us by all means go, Brachi."

Anton would be loved and cared for until his father could come home again. Marana perhaps also, and though there was less comfort in that idea than the first it was still good to know that he had not abandoned her entirely without resources.

And when the *Ragnarok* and its crew were safe he could go home and bow down at her feet and beg for her forgiveness, as well. When the ship was safe.

Until then he could not abandon the people to whom he owed so great a debt, on board the *Ragnarok*.

Epilogue

Jils Ivers came direct from the common transport docks at Chilleau Judiciary up through the maintenance corridors, past the Security checkpoints, and onto the grounds that held the Chambers offices. It was early in the morning. Verlaine would be in his office already, she was sure of it. She didn't bother to signal ahead. Security would let Verlaine know when she crossed the checkpoint. He would know that she was coming.

It was much busier in Chambers than it had been the last time she'd come through these gates, across the park, into the administration building. More than forty days from span to span, but the Second Judge had announced her program and her intentions now. The bid was active; the stakes much higher.

Verlaine was probably living in his office. She knew he had a foldaway in a closet, and kept a supply of clean linen there. The morning shift had yet to come into the offices; there were just Security there, and the janitors finishing their nightly cleaning tasks.

It was quiet. Jils relished the peace, knowing how short a period it would last. She could catch Verlaine at the start of the day. If she was lucky she would not find him at the end of a long sleepless night, still less the end of several sleepless nights run together. If she was lucky.

The door into the First Secretary's central office complex was propped open, for the cleaners. There were no lights on except for the dim lamps in Verlaine's office itself, diffusing out into the quiet office area through a gap in the not-quite-completely closed door.

She didn't hear anything. Had Verlaine fallen asleep? Gone out to the canteen, perhaps, to ask for breakfast, taking an excuse to get away from his office while it was still early enough in the day that he could?

She knocked at the door to announce herself. "Specialist Ivers, First Secretary, may I come in?" But there was no response. So he was out. She pushed the door open and stepped into the room, meaning to sit and marshal her thoughts as she waited for him to return to his desk.

She hadn't taken four steps into the room before she realized that it wasn't going to be necessary to wait, after all. Verlaine was there. He was seated behind his desk, his head laid down across the documents that he had been reviewing. One arm had slid forward across the desk's surface, as though he had been turning a page when he had slumped forward. Blood all over. On the desk. Pooled on the floor. Dead.

She stopped and stilled herself and listened, sniffing the air. Blood had ceased to drip. And the room was cold. There were no signs that she could see of violence or forced entry. How had this happened?

She didn't think she needed to ask why he had been killed.

"Security alert," she said, to catch the attention of the room's monitors. "Complete quarantine in effect, all transport, immediately. Forensics team to the First Secretary's office. No transmission secured or unsecured. Confirm."

It took a moment, as the communications protocols alerted attendants, attendants the officers, officers the Security forces. Interpreting the orders and the physical location, cross-referencing with Jils Ivers's voice-ident, realizing what the problem was.

"Confirmed."

She waited. It would take some time for the quarantine to be properly implemented from the outside in. She could expect to see forensics within moments; that gave her moments alone still to think.

Verlaine who had been Noycannir's patron, who had

obtained relief of Writ for Andrej Koscuisko, Verlaine whose administration was potentially compromised by a forged Record, whose announced program challenged the entrenched power of the whole system of Inquiry— Sindha Verlaine was dead.

She had no hope of enlisting his support in constructing a solution to the problem of the Jurisdiction Fleet Ship *Ragnarok*. The *Ragnarok* would have to be left to its own devices, now, until the death of the First Secretary could be investigated, until the Selection could be carried out and confirmed.

The Second Judge had had a strong position for First Judge. But now Verlaine was dead, and with him the strength of the Second Judge's administration as well as the suspected source of her radical plans. Now everything was cast into confusion.

The political stability of the Bench was all that stood between the rule of Law and chaos, failure of infrastructure, anarchy and barbarism. One misstep now and all of Jurisdiction could fall into dissention and disorder and the unimaginable horror of civil war.

The *Ragnarok*'s Appeal would have to wait.